## Donald Thomas and The Murder Room

››› This title is part of The Murder Room, our series dedicated to making available out-of-print or hard-to-find titles by classic crime writers.

Crime fiction has always held up a mirror to society. The Victorians were fascinated by sensational murder and the emerging science of detection; now we are obsessed with the forensic detail of violent death. And no other genre has so captivated and enthralled readers.

Vast troves of classic crime writing have for a long time been unavailable to all but the most dedicated frequenters of second-hand bookshops. The advent of digital publishing means that we are now able to bring you the backlists of a huge range of titles by classic and contemporary crime writers, some of which have been out of print for decades.

From the genteel amateur private eyes of the Golden Age and the femmes fatales of pulp fiction, to the morally ambiguous hard-boiled detectives of mid twentieth-century America and their descendants who walk our twenty-first century streets, The Murder Room has it all. ›››

**The Murder Room**
**Where Criminal Minds Meet**

**themurderroom.com**

**Donald Thomas (1926–)**

Donald Thomas was born in Somerset and educated at Queen's College, Taunton, and Balliol College, Oxford. He holds a personal chair in Cardiff University. His numerous crime novels include two collections of Sherlock Holmes stories and the hugely popular historical detective series featuring Sergeant Verity of Scotland Yard, written under the pen name Francis Selwyn, as well as gritty police procedurals written under the name of Richard Dacre. He is also the author of seven biographies and a number of other non-fiction works, and won the Gregory Prize for his poems, *Points of Contact*. He lives in Bath with his wife.

*By Donald Thomas*

Mad Hatter Summer: A Lewis Carroll Nightmare
The Ripper's Apprentice
Jekyll, Alias Hyde
The Arrest of Scotland Yard
Dancing in the Dark
Red Flowers for Lady Blue
The Blindfold Game
The Day the Sun Rose Twice

*As Francis Selwyn*
Sergeant Verity and the Cracksman
Sergeant Verity and the Hangman's Child
Sergeant Verity Presents His Compliments
Sergeant Verity and the Blood Royal
Sergeant Verity and the Imperial Diamond
Sergeant Verity and the Swell Mob

*As Richard Dacre*
The Blood Runs Hot
Scream Blue Murder
Money with Menaces

# Sherlock Holmes and the Running Noose

Donald Thomas

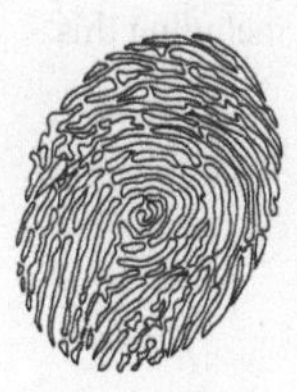

An Orion book



This edition published by
The Orion Publishing Group Ltd
Orion House
5 Upper St Martin's Lane
London WC2H 9EA

An Hachette UK company
A CIP catalogue record for this book is available from the British Library

ISBN 978 1 4719 0454 7

All characters and events in this publication are fictitious and any resemblance to real people, living or dead, is purely coincidental.



www.orionbooks.co.uk

For Linda

Illa quae libros amat, a libris quoque amatur

Fragment *De Popina Candelarum*

For the stroke of eight is the stroke of Fate
That makes a man accursed,
And Fate will use a running noose
For the best man and the worst

Oscar Wilde, The Ballad of Reading Gaol

# Contents

# The Two 'Failures' of Sherlock Holmes

*A Fragment of Biography by John H. Watson MD*

It is an acknowledged truth that Sherlock Holmes loathed with his whole bohemian soul the reputation of being a 'schoolbook hero'. This thought must have occupied me unconsciously one evening, while I was thinking of how I should introduce the cases which follow. Nothing seemed to suit my purpose. Then, as I sat there, I heard in my mind that familiar voice.

'Watson! If you are an honest man, you will record this also and set it against my successes!'

Well, I am no believer in ghosts! Still, this set me wondering where I had heard those words before. A moment later, I had it. More than thirty years had passed since Sherlock Holmes stood by the sunlit windows of Regent Street, shaking his head and uttering these very thoughts. We had been left, like a pair of fools, watching our quarry vanish from sight in a hansom cab with no means of pursuit. It was the first skirmish in a dark narrative of family misfortune, given to the world as *The Hound of the Baskervilles*.

In the next few weeks, as the world knows, we faced the beast with the blazing fangs in the lee of the rain-swept Dartmoor rocks. We tracked John Stapleton of

Merripit House to his slow death in the foul ooze of the Grimpen Mire. Yet that sunny moment in Regent Street was recalled by Holmes when he knew better than any man how close the end of his own life must be.

'If you are an honest man, Watson, you will set these records against my successes!'

He was sitting on the plain wooden stairs that led up to the Baker Street lumber-room, holding out to me several folded legal documents and a notebook. On the cover of the book, in ink now tarnished by damp, he had written simply, 'A Tabular Analysis of Hyoscin as a Homicidal Poison.'

Long before this, he had tried retirement and soon wearied of it. The simple life of bee-keeping on the Sussex downs was not for him. Having protested so much that he longed for rural solitude, he returned to Baker Street and took on his old rooms again. The excitement of life as a 'consulting detective' was as necessary to him as the vice of cocaine and a good deal less injurious. When his hands were idle, the drug mania laid claim to him. I never knew him to have the least need of narcotics when his mind was occupied.

The records of many unpublished adventures lay in the lumber-room, to which he would retire each day after lunch and remain until the winter afternoon darkened. The tin box, which formerly reposed among the bric-à-brac of his bedroom, had been carried up to this attic level on the orders of Mrs Clatworthy, his resident nurse. This good woman vowed repeatedly that she would not be 'answerable' if her patient's bedroom were not put into better order.

But where the box went, Holmes followed at every opportunity. It contained a mass of papers, most tied in bundles with red ribbon and each representing a case long concluded. Some dated from a time before I had first met him. Others dealt with matters 'for which the world is not yet ready', to use the familiar phrase by which he forbad publication. Two or three recorded his 'failures'.

One afternoon, he had retired to make a survey of these records. I went up at five o'clock to help him down to the sitting-room again, as the October light faded. He was sitting on the stairs, which declining strength obliged him to use as both chair and desk. His head was bowed over a black-letter legal parchment from one of the bundles, on which he had written in his own hand, 'The Case of the Naked Bicyclists.' He handed it to me without a word, so that I might replace it in the box and turn the key. While I did so, he made his way slowly but unaided down to our rooms.

I took the document he had handed me and gathered up a number of other papers whose red tapes he had not even bothered to tie again. Here and there I noticed some familiar copperplate script. It was usually the hand of a legal clerk, more often than not Mr Bowker, from the chambers of Sir Edward Marshall Hall. That 'Great Defender' had performed almost as many wonders in the court-room as Holmes the 'Great Detective' accomplished outside it, many of them when the two men worked in harness.

Among the writing on the briefs, I caught sight of *R v. Crippen and Le Neve*, then *Oscar Fingal O'Flahertie Wills Wilde, Esq. v. John Sholto Douglas, Marquess of Queensberry*, and *R v. Oscar Slater.* More perfunctorily, in Holmes's own writing upon the back of a legal brief, was 'The Yarmouth Beach Murder.'

Some of these names recalled his most difficult clients. Yet no other man would have regarded his efforts as a failure. I recall the summer of 1910 when, on the recommendation of Edward Marshall Hall, Dr Crippen's attorney called upon Holmes in the preparation of that famous murder defence.

All the world knew that Hawley Harvey Crippen had poisoned his faithless and violent wife, burying her dismembered body under the cellar floor of their house at 39 Hilldrop Crescent, Kentish Town. 'Belle Elmore', as Cora Crippen called herself on the music-hall stage, might have been a bullying slattern, but the little doctor surely put the rope round his own neck by his conduct after her death. He fled to America on the cargo liner SS *Montrose*, taking his demure young mistress Ethel Le Neve, whom he disguised to little effect by dressing her as a boy. Even before their arrival in Quebec, the Hilldrop Crescent cellar had revealed its macabre secret to Scotland Yard. The fugitives were pursued by wireless telegraph and fast passenger liner. Inspector Dew came aboard the *Montrose* off Quebec, disguised as the pilot, and arrested the two fugitives before they could leave the ship.

The drama of the chase turned the trial into the most celebrated criminal case for fifty years past. Mention the words 'cold-blooded murderer' and the world thinks at once of 'Dr Crippen'. How different was the truth!

Holmes was retained as the greatest 'criminal expert' on the rarer and more recent types of poison. He begged that Crippen would confess the truth, by admitting that Ethel Le Neve was present in the house and, indeed, in his bed, when the hyoscin was administered to Cora Crippen. The properties of this hypnotic drug, which derived from the deadly nightshade plant, were then not commonly known. However, it was used by physicians in a small dose as a sleeping draught or to treat delirium tremens.

In pursuit of the truth, Holmes shut himself away in the chemical laboratory of St Bartholomew's Hospital. While the rest of the world took its August holidays, he worked among shelves of bottles, benches and retorts, test-tubes and Bunsen burners. By several gruesome and malodorous experiments, he first proved that some of the hyoscin in Mrs Crippen's body was of animal origin and had been produced naturally by the decomposition of her corpse. Then he established beyond any question that a fatal dose in a woman of her size and weight would be between .25 and .5 of a grain. The amount found in Mrs Crippen's body was .29 of a grain. It was a very narrow margin of suspicion. Take away the amount produced naturally by the decomposition of her body, and there was no sufficient proof that Dr Crippen had administered even the minimum fatal dose to a woman so well-built, let alone that he had intended to kill her. The case against him was reduced from proof to mere speculation.

I truly thought that Holmes had saved Dr Crippen. If only the doctor would admit the fact that he had smuggled Ethel Le Neve into the house on that fateful night, his life was as good as saved. Hyoscin, in its anaesthetic dose, abolishes the memory of events, so that one who is rendered unconscious by it comes round with no memory of having been unconscious. Was this not the weapon of the adulterer rather than the murderer? Strychnine or aconitine were a killer's weapons. Was it not plain, Holmes argued, that Crippen merely intended to use a non-fatal dose of hyoscin to render his wife unconscious while Ethel Le Neve was on the premises and in his bed? In the event, the dose had proved lethal by a very narrow margin of miscalculation. Surely a man who hoped to kill his victim would have administered a far larger dose to make sure of the result.

The work that Holmes had done in the chemical laboratory certainly appeared to disprove any motive or intent to murder. Logic, too, seemed to rebut the case for the Crown. One look at Miss Le Neve was enough to convince those who saw her that she was too timid to be Lady Macbeth or Queen Clytemnestra. Poisoning is a planned murder, not one committed in the heat of the moment. If Dr Crippen were the cold precise killer that the prosecution alleged, would he risk his neck while there was a witness like Miss Le Neve in the house, when he might as easily have done the deed in secret? He would certainly have been far better without his young mistress as an accomplice, for Ethel Le Neve could not have held out for two minutes under a police interrogation.

Holmes insisted to Dr Crippen's attorney that a first-rate defender like Marshall Hall would persuade a jury to find the accused man guilty only of manslaughter. Indeed, it might be no worse than a conviction and a short prison sentence for the lesser offence of administering poison so as to endanger life.

Would that it had been so! What peals of victory would have rung through the halls of the Central Criminal Court and the pages of the morning papers! Sherlock Holmes, the Great Detective, would be trumpeted as the saviour of Dr Crippen, the most notorious defendant in a trial for murder! Yet the fruit of triumph turned to ashes of 'failure' almost at once.

I could scarcely believe my ears when I heard that Dr Crippen would have none of it! Why the devil not? The answer was simple. He loved Ethel Le Neve more than his own soul. Nothing would persuade him to admit that she was anywhere near the house at the time of Cora Crippen's death. When he heard of the suggestion that her presence was to be put in evidence, he refused to let his solicitor brief Marshall Hall to defend him.

That solicitor, Arthur Newton, and Sherlock Holmes argued with Dr Crippen in vain. They assured him that the door of his prison cell would open to set him free, if only he would admit that Ethel Le Neve was in the house on the night of his wife's death. The stubborn fellow shook his head. Suppose, for reasons that even Marshall Hall could not foresee and despite all that the great advocate could do, the jury took against him? The defence would fail. The verdict would be murder and, far worse, his young mistress would be an accomplice. Ethel Le Neve would be hanged as surely as he.

There was never such a 'disappointment' for Sherlock Holmes. Crippen loved this young woman so tenderly that he was determined to shield her to the last with his own life. He would have nothing said in his own defence that might imperil her. A lesser defender than Marshall Hall was found for him and the services of Sherlock Holmes were dispensed with.

Dr Crippen went to the gallows and Miss Le Neve was saved. Among the Crippen papers in the tin box is a letter to Holmes, the prison ink darkened and the paper a little yellowed. It was written by the condemned man on the night before his execution. 'In this farewell letter, written as I face eternity. I say that Ethel Le Neve has loved me as few women love men, and that her innocence of any crime, save that of yielding to the dictates of the heart, is absolute . . .'

Holmes could never read that letter without a moistening of the eye and a certain gruffness in the throat. Not Eloisa and Abelard, nor Tristan and Yseult, let alone a mere Romeo and Juliet, could hold a candle to Hawley Harvey Crippen and Ethel Le Neve. To my friend, Dr Crippen was ever afterwards 'a gallant little gentleman'. Holmes insisted on making the terrible journey to Pentonville to see the condemned man, late on the last night. He told me that the only time the poor fellow's courage failed was when they brought him a final telegram from the young woman. His request, that two of her letters and her photograph should be buried with him by the prison wall, was granted. He died declaring his innocence of any intention to murder his wife, something which Holmes never doubted. Wrongly hanged he may have been, but he had his reward when Ethel Le Neve was acquitted of any part in the crime.

Few people ever knew how closely Holmes was involved in some of the most sensational cases of the day. He was triumphant again and again but success did not always come his way. He worked with Marshall Hall on the so-called 'Yarmouth Beach Murder' of 1900, when Herbert Bennett was convicted and hanged for the murder of his wife, despite the solid evidence of an alibi witness. When I asked my friend, on his return from court, as to the outcome of the case, he said dryly, 'I fear, Watson, that British juries have not yet attained that pitch of intelligence when they will give preference to my theories over Inspector Lestrade's evidence.'

How hard it was in some cases to distinguish success from failure! In the ordeal of Oscar Slater, who was first condemned to death and then reprieved to life imprisonment, Sherlock Holmes thought he had failed where, in truth, he succeeded. Upon the evidence he gathered, showing that Slater could not be the murderer of Miss Gilchrist in a shabby Glasgow tenement, a campaign was built which set the innocent man free after eighteen years in prison. It is much to be regretted that the intransigence of the authorities delayed this act of justice until it was too late for Holmes to savour the victory.

All the same, those cases in which he was unable to secure a verdict for his client were few indeed. More often than not, as in the tragedy of Dr Crippen, they were investigations where the client turned away from the advice that had been offered. There was never a more memorable and obdurate example of this than the late Mr Oscar Wilde, who visited our Baker Street rooms on a windy afternoon in February 1895.

It must be said that the self-admiring paradoxes and the egregious vanity of the playwright were anathema to Sherlock Holmes. They were two men, each accustomed to being the centre of attention, and therefore ill-suited to one another's company. I do not think, however, that the pathological inclinations of Mr Wilde much perturbed my friend. Holmes had been well-acquainted with the work of Professor Krafft-Ebing since its first appearance in German nine years earlier. Indeed, he was to contribute three cases to later studies by Dr Havelock Ellis, as well as making available to him findings based on his own privately published monograph, 'The Mechanism of Emotional Deviation'.

In the first weeks of 1895, Oscar Wilde was enjoying a theatrical fame that can scarcely have been equalled in modern times. *The Importance of Being Earnest* opened at the St James's Theatre to enthusiastic audiences and universal praise. *An Ideal Husband* was still running at the Haymarket Theatre a little distance away. I had, myself, been to the opening night of the earlier play and had returned full of its praises. Holmes was engaged in calculating the errant weights of base coinage at his 'chemical table' in the corner of the room. He made no response until I said, in the hope of interesting him, that I had never experienced such a torrent of epigrams as in the first act of the *Ideal Husband*.

He did not look up from his nicely-balanced miniature scales, but said quietly, 'A torrent of epigrams, indeed! I daresay you would do well to remember, Watson, that everything which shares the properties of a torrent necessarily has in common with it that it is shallow at the source and wide at the mouth.'

Argument, like discussion, was futile on such occasions. However, when the second play opened, the subject of Mr Wilde came up between us again. It was plain that Holmes's antipathy towards the author was as sharp as ever. In this case, the unfortunate truth was that both Holmes and a younger contemporary, the historian Sir George Young, recognized the origins of many of the witticisms and paradoxes in the famous plays. They were not Oscar Wilde's own, but had been purloined by him from the clever sayings of the author's fellow undergraduates at Oxford a decade before.

I was thunderstruck by this. However, everyone had heard that an entire act had been cut from *The Importance of Being Earnest* to match the more usual length of a West End theatrical performance. Holmes was informed by his brother Mycroft that this superfluous act was full of these stolen gems. Among them was a deathbed pleasantry by Dr Benjamin Jowett, the great Master of Balliol, who had been a controversial debater in theological wars of faith and doubt many years before. To a young female friend, who questioned him on his present belief, the old man replied with a kindly smile, 'Ah! You must always believe in God, my dear. No matter *what* the clergy tell you!' When Mycroft Holmes and his fellow members of the Diogenes Club heard of this proposed larceny in the mouth of the stage-character of Dr Chasuble, they threatened to fill the first night of Mr Wilde's play and cry 'Cheat!' every time a stolen paradox was uttered. For whatever reason, the superfluous act was cut from the performance and the immediate cause of offence removed.

The borrowing of other men's epigrams was not the worst scandal attending Mr Wilde. Among the glitter of theatrical success, only a few people had yet heard of a certain friendship contracted by the playwright with the Marquess of Queensberry's son, Lord Alfred Douglas, while the young man was an Oxford undergraduate. The father's resentment at this infatuation grew beyond all restraint. Mr Wilde's world of aesthetes and green carnations filled him with honest disgust and made him suspect something far worse.

Even I had heard nothing of this until Holmes himself was approached by the greatest criminal solicitor of the day, Sir George Lewis. Mr Wilde had gone to him, alleging defamation by Lord Queensberry, whom the world still knew best for his formulation of the Queensberry Rules in boxing. However, Sir George found himself in a fix, being both a friend of Mr Wilde's and yet already retained as legal adviser to the marquess. He resolved this conflict by withdrawing from the case completely but he could not act, in good faith, as an informal adviser to Mr Wilde. He urged the play wright, before taking any other course of action, to consult Sherlock Holmes.

Before Mr Wilde's visit, we had received from Sir George Lewis an outline of the events in the case. Lord Queensberry had left his misspelt and often misquoted card with the porter at the Albemarle Club, to which Mr Wilde belonged. He had written five words upon the back of it. 'To Oscar Wilde, posing somdomite.' If Mr Wilde was to be believed, this was by no means the first insult of its kind he had received from Lord Queensberry but the public nature of it made it by far the most serious. Having been unable to retain Sir George Lewis, the author had gone to another and more pugnacious lawyer, Mr Charles Humphreys. Humphreys at once recommended prosecuting the marquess for a criminal libel.

As we awaited our client, Holmes showed little of his usual relish for the fight. It was not, I think, that he found the nature of the case distasteful, given his unconcealed fascination with human waywardness. It was rather the prospect of Mr Wilde's habitual self-appreciation that grated upon Sherlock Holmes.

When our visitor came through the sitting-room doorway, he gave the impression of a clumsy and ponderous man, with something of the gait of an agricultural labourer, despite his verbal adroitness. There was heaviness in his body, his head, and in the features of his face. Surprisingly, he exuded an air of weariness in his conversation. To meet the famous aesthete in the flesh, however, was still to catch something of the pose of the photographic studio. The whole world had seen photographs of Mr Wilde, at theatres and in booksellers' windows, taken in the years of his fame. He stood before us now with that familiar expression, jaded and unsmiling, indeed with the mouth pressed tighter than seemed natural.

He ignored the chair that Holmes had indicated and sat awkwardly in another, directly facing the great detective with the late winter sky at his back.

'I throw myself upon your mercy, Mr Holmes,' he said with a half-wave of his hand, 'Sir George Lewis is unable to take me on. To hear a lawyer turn away one's money undermines one's confidence in the entire natural order of the universe.'

Holmes accepted this pleasantry without a movement. His features might have been carved in ivory.

'I am acquainted with the circumstances, sir,' he said coolly. 'Pray continue.'

Mr Wilde was more than a little shaken by such unaccustomed abruptness. His face seemed a little more tired and flabby.

'Very well, Mr Holmes. I must decide by tomorrow whether I am to bring an action against Lord

Queensberry for a criminal libel. Mr Humphreys is for proceeding with it. Sir George Lewis, I think, would not.'

'I daresay Sir George is the wiser,' Holmes said quietly. 'Do go on.'

'Eddie Carson . . .' the unfortunate author began, 'I am told that Sir Edward Carson QC is to be briefed in any defence.'

'A foeman worthy of your steel, Mr Wilde. I take it that you are prepared to face cross-examination by him over this matter?'

'I am sure you know, Mr Holmes, that we were undergraduates together at Trinity College, Dublin. He will no doubt carry out his duty with all the added bitterness of an old friend who has since been neglected.'

Holmes received this witticism in arctic silence, then he said, 'That was not precisely what I asked, sir. Play games like that with Sir Edward Carson and he will cut you in pieces.'

Mr Wilde was brought up short. He stumbled on – there is no other phrase for it. However, he still talked in his other-worldly terms.

'Games? An artist, Mr Holmes, is one who plays sublime games with immortal words. I cannot deny that an artist in the eyes of artisans appears, therefore, as a figure of affectation. Lord Queensberry's crime is to confuse the affectation of genius with a perversion of the soul's beauty.'

Holmes touched his fingertips together before his chin. His words, when they came, were so softly-spoken that I scarcely heard them but they struck with the speed and accuracy of a whiplash.

'I beg, Mr Wilde, that you will make no such error! By the law of the land, Lord Queensberry's crime is either a criminal libel – or there is no crime. As to the rest, whether a man appears affected may be a question of opinion. Whether he is perverted in his actions is a matter of fact. In this, the burden of proof will lie upon you as the prosecutor. If that burden is too great . . .'

Our visitor had recovered himself sufficiently to interrupt.

'My reputation, Mr Holmes, has been trampled in the gutter! That is indisputable. Does any other fact matter, beside the damage done publicly to my reputation by these foul accusations?'

'For the purposes of this case, Mr Wilde, you may take it from me that it matters.'

'Very well,' said our visitor sulkily, 'let us suppose that the distinction between the affected and the perverse may be in issue. Yet the difference lies only in the eye of the beholder.'

'You would do well to remember, sir,' said Holmes brutally, 'that under the Criminal Law Amendment Act of 1885, the difference between affectation and perversion is the thickness of a prison wall.'

I was never so uncomfortable in my life as during the next thirty minutes of these exchanges. At last Mr Wilde could bear it no longer.

'Mr Holmes, I have listened to your sermonizing for the past half-hour and I have to say I am none the wiser.'

'I daresay not,' Holmes muttered, 'but much better informed, I trust.'

'And that is all you can do for me?'

It was almost like a child's cry.

'Not quite,' said Holmes. 'You say you are an innocent man. Then I will give you my advice without charge. Take that absurd visiting card of Lord Queensberry's and tear it into fragments. Then, if you are an innocent man, continue to behave innocently and you will have nothing to fear. It is as simple as that, Mr Wilde. The action you propose to bring against Lord Queensberry will publish this libel across the world, whether you are innocent or not. Whatever the outcome, the wise world will think that there is no smoke without fire.'

'This is abominable! I would stop at nothing to make my protest!'

'Methinks . . .' said Holmes. And through all our minds ran the rest of that famous line from *Hamlet. The lady doth protest too much, methinks.* The colour rose from the base of Mr Wilde's soft neck until he blushed the colour of a beetroot.

'I will take no more of your time.' In anger or embarrassment, he stumbled over the words again.

'Tear up that card!' said Holmes, rising from his chair.

'I shall be the judge, Mr Holmes, of what is to be done in this case!'

'I doubt that you will,' Holmes said grimly, 'I doubt that very much.'

On this note of mutual antipathy, they parted. Little as I sympathized with Oscar Wilde the man, I was shocked by my friend's dealing with him.

'How could you, Holmes?' I said angrily when the street door had closed. 'You gave the poor fellow no chance!'

He was standing at the window now, staring down into the street as he watched the waiting hansom drive away with a light rattle of harness.

'Because I would save him from destruction, little as I care for him.'

'He will be destroyed if the message on that card is the gossip of London and he takes no action!'

Holmes shook his head.

'No. Gossip may merely harm him. He will be destroyed only if he goes into court.'

'How?'

'The evidence will destroy him.'

'How can you say that? Neither of us has seen the evidence on either side!'

'We have both seen the evidence in this case. I was the only one to realize it.'

This shook me, for I did not understand how it could be so.

'You have seen it?'

'And so have you, if you had cared to observe it! Did you not take note, Watson, how he ignored my invitation and sat in another chair?'

'What the devil has sitting in a chair to do with it? Perhaps he was more comfortable.'

'Did you not notice that he was careful to sit with his back to the light, so that we should not see his face so clearly?'

'What has that to do with the case? We had seen his face already when he came through the door. The tone of his voice would have told us the rest.'

'He dare not go into court and confront a jury. No matter what the cause of the offence.'

'I cannot see it, Holmes.'

'He did not intend that you should. But the jury will see it. The judge will see it. Sir Edward Carson will see it. My dear Watson, if that man goes to court he is doomed. As soon as he opens his mouth, his case is lost. Small wonder that his lips are so tight in all his photographs!' His voice became softer.

'Perhaps, my dear fellow, you were not at an angle to see his teeth.'

'His teeth? He is not being libelled for his teeth!'

'He might as well be. Those teeth, Watson, are all in place and healthy in appearance, somewhat protuberant – but uniformly black! Did you not notice, when he stood in the doorway, the habit of putting a hand near his mouth when he spoke?'

I stared at him, for it was something I now recollected but had thought nothing of at the time.

'Does that mean nothing to you, Watson, as a medical man?'

'Mercury? That he has been treated for syphilis?'

'Precisely,' Holmes turned back from the window. 'A man is treated by mercury in that manner for one reason and one alone. Mercury and blackened teeth, the subject of cruel jokes and private gossip. At the trial, he must stand in the witness-box of the Central Criminal Court with the light full upon him. When he opens his mouth to give evidence, he will advertise to every man on the jury that he, the champion against slander and indecency, is in the grip of a most loathsome disease, contracted in a very familiar manner. If he hung a card about his neck, he could make it no plainer to the world. What chance will he have of a verdict then?'

It was many months later that I was to hear from

Sir George Lewis how the famous playwright had contracted this disease from a woman of the streets, as the result of undergraduate folly while at Magdalen. I now guessed why, when the Prince of Wales and the leaders of society applauded and called for the author at the end of the first night of *An Ideal Husband*, Mr Wilde had prudently absented himself.

'He must not do it,' Holmes persisted, 'but nothing I could say would stop him. Little as I care for Mr Wilde, I should not like to be in court when Sir Edward Carson begins to cross-examine a fellow so vain and, worse still, when he begins to interrogate those young gentlemen who dote upon their master. Believe me, I would not wish on any man the destruction that our client is hell-bent to bring upon himself.'

I was still more astonished by this.

'Then he is still our client?'

Holmes shrugged.

'The matter is at his discretion.'

But we never heard from Mr Wilde again.

I shall let the words of that afternoon's encounter fade from my mind. I fold the stiff law-stationery of *Oscar Fingal O'Flahertie Wills Wilde, Esq. v. John Sholto Douglas, Marquess of Queensberry*, and lay it in the tin trunk.

As I sit in my chair and recall that familiar room in Baker Street, I see the chemical corner with its acid-stained, deal-topped table. There upon a shelf stands the formidable row of scrap-books and volumes of reference, which so many of our adversaries would have been glad to burn. The diagrams, the violin-case, and the pipe-rack, the Persian slipper which contained his tobacco – all these take shape in the imagination. As for Sherlock Holmes, I imagine him most often at the breakfast table, having risen late as was his custom. The silver-plated coffee-pot stands before him. *The Times* or *Morning Post* lies beside his plate. Sometimes his profile is like a bird of prey as he scans the columns and says sourly, without looking up, 'If the press is to be believed, Watson, London has singularly little of interest to offer the criminal expert at the present time. I wonder whether our friends in the underworld have become a good deal less active of late – or a good deal more clever.'

This impatience was usually short-lived. Sometimes, even before the remains of his mid-morning breakfast had been cleared away, a clang of the bell or a stentorian knocking on the well-hammered Baker Street door would be followed by the appearance of Mrs Hudson with a card upon her salver. Or else Holmes would lean back in his chair at the end of his meal and hand me the newspaper, where his finger had dented a paragraph, saying simply, 'Read that.'

On such occasions, as the newspaper was put down or the visitor's tread was heard upon the stairs, he would chuckle and say quietly, 'I believe, after all, that this morning may present us with infinite possibilities.'

How familiar these memories are and how often were we confronted by infinite possibilities! Yet the earliest bundle of papers that comes to my hand dates from several years before my friendship with Sherlock Holmes began. Looking at it now, who would think that it threatened to rock the state and government of Great Britain, to bring down law and order in utter ruin? It is inscribed with the laconic title that Holmes himself gave it: 'The Case of the Racing Certainty'.

# The Case of the Racing Certainty

## I

This remarkable case in the career of Sherlock Holmes was concluded four years before the summer day when I first met him in the chemical laboratory of Barts. From time to time during the period of our friendship, as we sat over the fire in Baker Street on a winter evening, he would lug from his room the familiar tin-box and hand me a bundle of documents, tied in red tape. In one of these I first encountered the case of the *Gloria Scott*, in another the mystery of the Musgrave Ritual, published long ago in *The Memoirs of Sherlock Holmes*.

One evening, I learnt of a bizarre adventure, dated several years before our first meeting in 1881. We were talking of Inspector Lestrade and I remarked that I had never been quite clear how he and Holmes became acquainted. My friend withdrew and brought me one of the familiar bundles. With an eye to life's absurdities, he had inscribed upon it, 'The Case of the Racing Certainty'.

By the time of our first meeting, Holmes had been 'a consulting detective' for some years. He was trusted in matters of great delicacy and had been called upon by Scotland Yard, notably by Lestrade, when that officer had 'got himself into a fog over a forgery case'. Odd though it now seems, I had never yet heard the details of this investigation.

When Holmes handed me two papers from the bundle, chuckling as he did so, I saw at first no connection with Lestrade. My friend had untied a mass of documents, including counsel's brief for the Crown, marked *Regina v. Benson and Kurr 1877*. How that prosecution affected our colleague at Scotland Yard, the reader will presently see. Meantime, as a storyteller's narrative is preferable to a mere report, I tell the tale as I heard it from Holmes that night but with no apology for interpreting the nuances of the drama.

The first sheet which he had given me was a page from a newspaper devoted to horse-racing. It was *The Sport*, dated 31 August 1876. Still chuckling, he watched me read an article devoted to the misfortunes of Major Hugh Montgomery, evidently a man of honour, and a hero to whom the nation owed debts of gratitude upon many a field of battle, from Inkerman to the Abyssinian campaign.

Major Montgomery was that legend among racing men, a gambler who has never lost a bet – or nearly so. *The Sport* outlined his career, naming many winners he had backed. I am no racing-man, but even I had heard of most. Alas, this gallant officer had now fallen victim to a conspiracy among the bookmakers of England, who had ganged together to refuse his bets.

The editor of *The Sport* rounded upon these 'vultures', as he called them, whose sole object was to take a man's money when he lost and to refuse payment when he won. Knowing little of the turf, I should not have realized the extent of Major Montgomery's tragedy but for the newspaper's account. My first thought was that he could surely continue his success by giving the name of each horse to a friend who would place the money for him. Alas, this proved to be impossible. As *The Sport* reminded its readers, betting must take place on the race-course, where the Jockey Club is supreme. By its rules, no person may bet for another. This had become a necessary regulation, after the Gaming Act of 1845 had made gambling losses irrecoverable at law. The article ended with another blast on the major's behalf against the 'vultures' of the profession.

The second sheet was a still more curious production. It was a letter from 'The Society for Insuring Against Losses on the Turf'. It was written in French and this particular copy had been sent by Major Montgomery, the apparent founder of the philanthropic body, to the Comtesse de Goncourt living near Paris, at St Cloud. He drew her attention to the article in *The Sport* and explained that neither the Jockey Club nor the Gaming Act could prevent bets being placed for him by those living beyond the jurisdiction of the English courts. However, the Act required that money from abroad must be placed only with a 'sworn bookmaker' in England. I had heard of 'sworn brokers' on the Stock Exchange and supposed these others were something of the same kind.

Major Montgomery's letter went on to explain how he had at first demurred at trusting large sums of his money to strangers. However, he had approached the Franco-English Society of Publicity to ask if they could recommend men and women of proven integrity in France who might assist him. The name of the Comtesse de Goncourt had received the society's warmest endorsement.

The fact that Holmes found the business so amusing made me uneasy. Yet I could not see how those who assisted Major Montgomery could be losers. At regular intervals, he would send them a cheque, drawn on the Royal Bank of London in the Strand, and the name of the horse to be backed. They would forward the cheque and the horse's name to the 'sworn bookmaker' in England. If the horse won, as it always seemed to do, Major Montgomery would send his new friend ten per cent of the proceeds. If the animal failed, the major would bear the cost. The Comtesse de Goncourt felt, as I had done, that she could not lose. On the contrary, she stood to gain a substantial sum for very little effort.

Holmes assured me that Major Montgomery sent his first cheque, the bet was placed, and Madame de Goncourt received news that the horse had won. A cheque for her share of the winnings followed. So did another cheque to be 'invested' and the name of a horse for the next race.

At that time, Sherlock Holmes still had 'consulting rooms' a little to the south of Westminster Bridge. They were convenient for the laboratory of St Thomas's Hospital, to which he had grace-and-favour access. I have written of his origins among the English squirearchy. The indulgence shown him by the hospital governors stemmed from a bequest made by one of these kinsmen. To the handsome but decayed terraces and tree-lined vistas of this neighbourhood Holmes returned each evening from his labours among test-tubes and Bunsen burners.

He came home on a fine but windy autumn evening in 1876 to find that a visitor had been waiting for half an hour in his landlady's ground-floor parlour. Holmes described his guest as a well-dressed 'pocket Hercules', dark haired, and with a face to which nature had given the pugnacious lines of a fairground bruiser. As soon as Mr William Abrahams opened his mouth, however, he was no show-ground boxer. In a voice that was gentle yet inflexible he apologized, as they entered the upstairs sitting-room, for calling upon the 'consulting detective' without notice. Holmes waved the courtesy aside.

'It is I, Mr Abrahams, who should apologize for keeping you so long. I confess I have been a little pressed today. However, had your problem not been so confidential as to require my anonymity, I should willingly have come over to your Temple chambers and saved you a crossing on the penny steamer. Now, I fear, you have missed your train home and it may be well past dinner time before you arrive in Chelsea. Ladies are sometimes impatient on these occasions, so I daresay it as well that you are not a married man.'

Mr Abrahams stared at him, the lined face more deeply incised with suspicion.

'Surely we are perfect strangers, Mr Holmes? How can you, to whom I had not spoken until this minute, talk of my chambers in the Temple, or my travelling habits, or my house in Chelsea, or the fact that I am not married?'

Holmes smiled and motioned his guest to a chair.

'Pray sit down, Mr Abrahams. It has been a dry day

and yet there are fresh water-marks upon your shoes. Though you carry a hat, your hair, if I may say so, is a little ruffled. Where does a man ruffle his hair most easily on a blustery day? Why, on the river, crossing by steamer from the far bank. Where does water lie to wet the shoes so conveniently as on the decking of the piers at the ebb – and notoriously upon the Temple Stairs? That you are a lawyer is suggested by your manner. It is confirmed for me by a small blot of sealing-wax on your right cuff and the seal upon your waistcoat-chain. A man who seals documents for himself is something more confidential than a mere trader. You might be a banker, of course. Yet the banks have already been closed for some hours. The courts frequently rise later, so that the time of your arrival suggests to me a busy lawyer.'

Mr Abrahams relaxed, smiled, and nodded his head in acknowledgement.

'As for your mode of travel,' Holmes went on, 'like many men of affairs, you have a habit of concealing the return half of your ticket in the lining of your hat-band, causing a slight deformity of the silk which is visible to the trained eye. The Temple station would take you as far as Chelsea. You might, of course, travel a shorter distance on that line but a man whose time is as valuable as yours would more probably take a cab for a short journey. As for being a bachelor, I observe that you wear a gold signet ring and one other. I have found, when a man wears rings and is married, a gold wedding-band appears on the fourth finger of his left hand. In your case it does not. I daresay, however, that I am quite wrong in every particular.'

Mr Abrahams laughed, like a child delighted by a Christmas conjurer.

'You are correct in every detail, Mr Holmes. What you have said persuades me that you are the man whose help I need. Expense is no object, sir, for there is a good deal of money at stake. You might call it a fortune. I represent the interests of the Comtesse de Goncourt in England and would like your opinion on these documents.'

So saying, he handed my friend the two sheets of paper which I was to read so many years later. While Holmes perused them, the lawyer walked over to the bookshelves and learnt from their contents something of the man whose advice he sought. No one boasted so oddly-assorted a library as Sherlock Holmes. You would look in vain for volumes that were in half the families of England. But if you sought industries peculiar to a small town in Bohemia, or unique chemical constituents of Sumatran or Virginian tobacco leaf, or the alienist's account of morbid psychology, or the methods by which a Ming is to be distinguished from a skilful imitation, you had only to reach out a hand for the answer. In far more cases, however, Sherlock Holmes carried all those answers in his head.

'Dear me,' he said presently, laying down the papers. 'How far, Mr Abrahams, has this merry little swindle progressed?'

The lawyer swung round from his study of the bookcase.

'You are sure it is a swindle?'

Holmes gave him the glance of the cold practical thinker.

'Major Montgomery boasts that he is able to insure

against losses on the turf, a proposition which I take the liberty of doubting. Of course, the terms of his offer suggest no more than a tawdry race-course deceit. Yet I am much mistaken if this does not disguise a plot of quite remarkable scope and ingenuity.'

Mr Abrahams sat down again.

'I had hoped you would tell me that you had heard of Major Hugh Montgomery.'

'I have not,' said Holmes coolly, 'nor I imagine has anyone else, for the very good reason that Major Hugh Montgomery does not exist. I ask, again, how far this lamentable matter has proceeded.'

William Abrahams drew out another sheet of paper, which he consulted but did not hand over.

'I knew nothing of it, Mr Holmes, until a communication from Madame de Goncourt today. I went to call on the major at once. There was no news of him at the accommodation address he gives in City Road. Several weeks ago, however, Madame de Goncourt replied to him and offered to place his bets. She received by express a cheque, the names of three horses, and the address of a sworn bookmaker, Archer & Co., in Northumberland Street, Charing Cross. She forwarded these papers and in due course received a wire from Major Montgomery informing her that all three horses had won. Some days later came a cheque for herself and another to back two more horses.'

'But you have not gone to the police? Nor has the lady?'

'So far, Mr Holmes, we have no evidence that this man - swindler though he be - has swindled anyone. Must we wait until that happens? Impossible!'

'But, Mr Abrahams, if that is all, why come to me?

Madame de Goncourt places the money and the major continues to pay her when his horses win. What more is there?'

The lines of Mr Abrahams's face tightened, as if with embarrassment. He was silent for a moment while cabs and carriages rattled through the autumn dusk from Westminster Bridge to St George's Circus.

'Madame has been much taken with the major's obvious skill and evident honesty. Why else should *The Sport* have come to his aid? In short, she has begged him to let her add a wager of her own.'

'Ah,' said Holmes. 'This grows warmer! And so soon! What then?'

'The major wired her and swore he could not take the responsibility, if he were to fail her. She wired him back and insisted. He relented at last but begged her to bet only upon those horses of which he could be absolutely certain – while urging her to place whatever she could raise upon those.'

'And she has done so?'

Mr Abrahams looked at him mournfully.

'It is worse, Mr Holmes. She did it twice last week and won both times. A cheque came to her for her winnings. Then Major Montgomery wired her in great haste. He advised her to back two sure things, as he called them, Saucebox and Minerva at Brighton, with all the money she could raise or borrow. He swore they were the surest racing certainties of his career. He had confided this only to his most loyal friends, for fear of shortening the odds. Such a chance, he added, comes only once in a lifetime. She has done as he advised and waits the result. I have had only an hour or two to act upon my information. As you say, there is nothing as yet for the police. By the time there is, we shall be too late. So I have come to you. I confess my first instinct was to go straight to the sworn bookmaker and see if the money might be retrieved.'

'On no account must you do that,' said Holmes sharply. 'If this is the plot that I suspect, you would alert the conspirators before it matures.'

He stared at the lawyer for a moment longer and then said, 'It is better that Madame de Goncourt should learn wisdom late than never. Her money is probably lost already, from what you tell me, but you may rely upon my doing all I can.'

Mr Abrahams looked very straight at him.

'And what will you do, Mr Sherlock Holmes? I should like to know.'

Holmes stood up, plainly indicating to him that the time had come to leave.

'It is better that you should know nothing, sir. It is also better that you should say nothing. Indeed, it is better that your visit here should be regarded for the next few hours as something that has never taken place.'

His visitor also stood – and looked decidedly uneasy.

'I do not understand, Mr Holmes.'

'I did not intend that you should. You, Mr Abrahams, are a professional man. You are not only amenable to the criminal law but to the Law Society, who may discipline or expel you for something much less than a crime. I, on the other hand, am answerable only to myself. Have no fear, I shall communicate with you at the earliest opportunity. Let us pray that we may yet save this lady from her most ruinous folly.'

## II

An hour of the windy evening passed, while Mr Abrahams distanced himself from what was to come. Sherlock Holmes charged his pipe with strong black tobacco, lay back in the comfortable old-fashioned chair, which was his parents' sole legacy to him, and stretched his long thin legs towards the fire. From time to time, he began a slow chuckle at the preposterous 'Society For Insuring Against Losses on the Turf' and the gullibility of its victims. Firmly in his mind, however, was the address of 'Archer & Co., Sworn Bookmakers', of 8 Northumberland Street, Charing Cross.

At half-past seven precisely, he buttoned himself into a long grey travelling cloak and close-fitting cloth cap. Turning towards Lambeth, he strode into a clout of icy air, then north into a razoring wind, where the river slapped against the steamboat pier and the wharves. The bell was ringing as he hurried through the toll-gate, paid his penny, and jumped aboard the paddle-boat a second before the plank was withdrawn. The pilot stood at the helm, the cable was cast off, and the paddle wash frothed against wooden piles. A few minutes later he was at Hungerford Stairs.

The broad boulevard of Northumberland Avenue lay lamplit but deserted. To one side, the dark lane of Northumberland Street led to the Strand, many of its old and shabby houses used for still darker purposes. The narrow front of number eight consisted of a house door with an uncurtained sash-window to one side. Of 'Archer & Co., Sworn Bookmakers', there was no sign.

Yet, as Holmes had intimated to Mr Abrahams, the

address to which money was sent must be the hub of the conspiracy. There was enough street-light to see through the sash-window that the office was a mere shell of an unfurnished slum house, a narrow stairway at the rear leading to the upper levels. A number of envelopes strewn on the floor behind the door was evidence of uncollected post. Yet since so many cheques might still be in transit, it seemed probable that the birds of prey had not yet flown.

At one end of the street, cabs and buses flashed by in the lamplight of the Strand. Along Northumberland Street, every window was dark and the narrow thoroughfare appeared deserted. Holmes required only a means of entry, for the lock on the house-door was one that would open easily from inside to let him out again. He touched his hand to the peak of his immaculate travelling cap, as if to straighten it, and drew a slim file from the lining of its brim. A casual inspection would detect only a wire frame that kept the cap-brim rigid. Now, however, this fine steel entered the division between two halves of a sash-window in an unlit side-lane and eased back the catch. In a moment more, he had crossed the sill, dropped down in the darkened room, and locked the window behind him. With the natural caution of the professional burglar, he put the house-door on the latch to ensure an immediate means of escape.

In the room lit by reflection of the street-lamps, he picked up from the door-mat eight letters addressed to 'Archer & Co'. Seven had been through the post. Two of the stamps were French. The last envelope was addressed in pencil and delivered by hand. A trained observer would notice the slight movement of

Holmes's fastidious nostrils. He breathed the air of each envelope in turn, as if searching for the boudoir fragrance of a billet-doux. He placed seven on the window sill and retained the eighth, with its pencilled address.

Slipping a hand into his cloak he drew out a small enamelled pocket-knife, chose a tiny blade and, with the delicacy of a surgeon excising a growth, eased open the envelope down an inch of its side, so that the top would remain intact. He drew from it a single folded sheet of paper. This he held to the light, and saw an advertisement. It displayed a tin of cleaning-powder and a row of sparkling dinnerware on a side-board, proclaiming the brilliance of Oakley's Silver Polish. It was Holmes's habit not to finish with any specimen of paper until he had looked for a water-mark. He therefore examined the envelope and slipped the advertisement into his pocket.

The office of Archer & Co. had been almost stripped, like premises at the end of a lease or upon a bank-ruptcy. In one rear corner there remained a cheap plywood desk, on which he saw only a dried-out ink-bottle and a cardboard blotter. The drawers yielded nothing but a small quantity of envelopes and a few sheets of paper with the firm's letter-heading. Like the envelope he had opened, those in the desk bore an identical 'Windsor Superfine' mark.

He tore one sheet of headed paper in half and inserted the blank lower half in the opened envelope. Then he returned to the desk, stooping over it with his long aquiline profile in silhouette. His fingers ran over the cardboard blotter with as much sensitivity as they ever touched the strings of his beloved violin.

Presently he took a twist of paper from his cigarette-case and struck a match. Holding the match to one side, he sprinkled a little graphite powder from the twist of paper and smoothed it on the blotter at one end. Shaking out the spent match, he struck another and saw, pale in the dark graphite, 'Archer & Co., Most Immediate and Confidential'. Crossing back to the window, he picked up the pencilled envelope, and returned to the desk. Seeing that the handwriting on the envelope was identical to the imprint on the blotter, he slid the envelope out of sight beneath the cardboard square.

A second or two later, a chill at the nape of his neck caused the skin to contract and the hair to rise minutely. Only then did he hear a creak of the floor-boards in the room behind him. In Sherlock Holmes, that uncanny sense which knows a sigh of timber or the movement of a rat in the wainscot from a human footfall, was supernaturally developed. He looked up at the door to the street and saw a shadow blocking the crack of light at its base. With his hypersensitive sense of danger and his acute perception, he could have sworn that no one had seen him as he entered the building. In any case, they would surely have made their move against him at once. Therefore, the alarm had been given by those who chanced to see the flare of a match in a darkened building - or perhaps heard his movements through the adjoining wall - and had now trapped him.

He afterwards claimed that in the few seconds of liberty remaining, he was struck by a lightning-bolt of inspiration, beside which the finest moments of the great poets appeared mundane. With scarcely time to reason, he took his pencil from his pocket and wrote by instinct in block capitals upon the blotting paper. MOST URGENT. MEET ME UNDER THE ARCHES CHARING CROSS STATION OPPOSITE THE KING WILLIAM IN VILLIERS STREET TOMORROW - TUESDAY 3 PM SHARP.

Then two of his assailants were through the unlatched doorway from the street. The older man with mutton-chop whiskers and a drinker's face was followed by a wiry bulldog of a young fellow with a lean body and grim features.

As he drew himself up to meet them, a third man ran into him from behind, knocking him against the desk. Holmes, though no lover of sport or exercise for itself, had been trained in his youth as boxer, swordsman and single-stick player. In a movement that a circus artist might have envied, he went forward in a tight roll across the desk, with such force that the man on his back was thrown over his head and landed sprawling on the bare boards. Holmes followed in a gymnast's fall and sprang up to face his two remaining antagonists. As he did so, he wondered if murder lay behind the humorists of the Society for Insuring Against Losses on the Turf. These men had the look of race-course roughs and he quite thought, as he said afterwards, that such desperadoes meant to have him at the bottom of the river in a few minutes more.

In that bare room, by reflected lamplight from the street, the confused and brutal struggle could have only one outcome. He was seized from behind again by his first attacker. The two men in front closed on him. Had they been the ruffians he imagined, Sherlock Holmes would have fought his last fight.

To his astonishment, his arms were wrenched behind

his back and his wrists were circled by steel. He heard a click of handcuffs. A freckled giant with ginger hair said in a Scots brogue, 'So y'would, would you, my dandy?'

A bullseye lantern illuminated the scene as the shutter was drawn back and the older man in the loose-fitting flannel suit said, 'I am Inspector Clarke, Metropolitan Police. Now, my fine fellow, we'll have some account of who you are and why you might be on these premises.'

Holmes contrived to be unruffled.

'I am here to inquire after Major Montgomery, on behalf of the Comtesse de Goncourt, not to be set upon like this by footpads. You can see for yourself that the door is unlocked. Montgomery had presumably gone out for a few minutes, so I came in to wait for him. He owes me money.'

As he spoke, he knew that he staked everything on his belief that they had not seen him come in but had been attracted by the intermittent light of the matches. His explanation that Major Montgomery owed him money must do for the present.

As they studied him by the lantern and heard him speak, they became a little less sure of themselves. Sherlock Holmes was more dangerous to civil order than a regiment of Fagins or Artful Dodgers, but he did not look it. Clarke stepped up and stared him hard in the face.

'Your name, if you please.'

'By all means,' said Holmes equably, 'William Sherlock Scott Holmes, of Westminster Road, South-East.'

The contempt of a police functionary for the born gentleman was plain in Clarke's face.

'Very well, Mr William Sherlock Scott Holmes, I think it best if Sergeant Lestrade and I were to escort you a little way down the street to the rear gate of Scotland Yard. We shall have a talk about this story of yours. See if you feel quite as frisky then! What have you to say to that? Eh?'

'I think it an entirely admirable suggestion,' said Holmes politely, as they still scrutinized him by the light of the bullseye lamp. 'Indeed, I should have insisted upon that, had you not proposed it yourself.'

Inspector Clarke was unmoved by this suavity. He gave a light snort of contempt.

'I daresay you may find it less admirable when you are charged as being found on enclosed premises with intent.'

Sergeant Meiklejohn was left to secure the premises. As Holmes walked in handcuffs the short distance towards the river, between Clarke and Lestrade, he said cheerfully, 'With intent to commit a felony, to give the phrase its full value, Mr Clarke.'

'As a burglar,' Clarke said indifferently.

'Oh, I think not a burglar. Not when the night is still so young. I have always understood that the crime of burglary begins at one minute past nine, when housebreaking ends. Not before.'

'Housebreaking, then,' said Clarke abruptly.

'But I think it cannot be housebreaking where nothing is broken. Can it? You found the door on the latch, why should not I? A civil action might lie for trespass, of course, if Major Montgomery can be found. I expect he was just called away for a moment.'

This continuing chaff rattled Inspector Clarke, as

Holmes intended it should. They came to a halt in the street and the inspector turned upon his captive.

'In a moment, while we are among ourselves, I may teach you to learn better than to come the letter of the law with me, Mr William whatever-it-was Holmes.'

'William Sherlock Scott,' said Holmes pleasantly. 'But it is not I who will come the letter of the law with you, Mr Clarke. The law itself will do that. Upon the bookstalls you will find, newly-published, Mr Justice Stephen's admirable compendium, *A Digest of the English Criminal Law*. You would find it a rewarding and, if I may say so without offence, an instructive volume.'

Clarke aimed a vigorous clout of his open hand at the side of Holmes's face. But where the face had been half a second before, there was only space. Disconcerted by the speed of his victim's response, the inspector swore at him, and walked on.

Lestrade later confessed that he was appalled by the incident. Though George Clarke boasted of giving many a felon a 'fat lip' for less insolence than this, he had seldom exhibited such an abrupt loss of self-control. Lestrade dreaded being a witness to an assault on a man of Holmes's calibre. He must either deny the truth or live as a traitor to his colleagues for having told it. Perhaps Holmes sensed this, for he kept silent. However, as they approached the rear of Scotland Yard, he said, 'When we arrive, Mr Clarke, perhaps you would present my compliments to Superintendent Williamson of the Detective Police. Pray inform him that I should like an interview at his earliest convenience. He will know who I am.'

Clarke's fists tightened as he walked but he said

nothing more. The two detectives brought their prisoner to the charge-room and stood him before the desk-sergeant, among the drunkards and pickpockets called to answer before the night-court of the Westminster magistrates. Clarke withdrew to confer with the night-inspector. When his name was called, Holmes stepped up with a quick nervous smile to hear the decision in his case. The sergeant looked at his sheet.

'Police bail of ten guineas in your own recognizances to appear here three days from today.'

'I shall appear,' said Holmes quietly, 'you need have no fear of that.'

Then he dangled his handcuffs for the sergeant's attention.

'Perhaps you would care to have these back. I trust I shall have no further use for them.'

'Who took those off?'

'I did,' said Holmes amiably. 'There is no trick to it, I assure you. Merely art.'

## III

Sherlock Holmes was not in general an admirer of the press, whose practitioners he was apt to describe in the good old phrase as 'lice upon the locks of literature'. He was fond of remarking that newspapers exist 'to promote the interests of those of whom one has never heard before and of whom, in all probability, one will never hear again. Of whom, I may add, one is vexed to have heard at all.'

In this condemnation of the daily press, however,

he made an exception of the criminal news and the agony column. 'The latter is particularly instructive.'

He had just finished this column next morning at the end of a leisurely breakfast, following his late return the night before, when there was a knock at his door. His landlady announced Mr Abrahams. Holmes had already set aside thoughts of the chemical laboratory that day and admitted to a lifting of the spirits at the sound of the lawyer's name. William Abrahams came bustling upstairs in the landlady's wake, his face drawn in lines of vindictive satisfaction. Without ceremony, he threw down his hat and burst out, 'Well, sir, she has done it! Such utter stupidity never was! By God, Mr Holmes, I have had a fool or two as a client but this beats them all!'

Holmes raised his eyebrows inquiringly and gestured his visitor to a chair.

'May I take it that Madame de Goncourt has had another little flutter?'

Mr Abrahams looked a shade grimmer.

'Give or take a few centimes, she has placed the equivalent of five thousand pounds with Archer & Co., upon those two horses of Major Montgomery's. God knows how many other idiots have done the same!'

Holmes pushed the silver cigarette-box towards his guest.

'I take it that these unfortunate animals lost their races – or not?'

It seemed to the lawyer that his detective quite failed to understand him.

'They neither won nor lost, sir. They did not exist. I cannot find that Saucebox or Minerva ever ran at Brighton. Nor did the races take place in which they were said to be entered. As for the cheques, it appears, there never was a Royal Bank of London, whose spurious notes were used to pay the victims their first winnings. Then, as I ascertained this morning, there has never been anything known to English jurisprudence as a sworn bookmaker. It was a swindle, start to finish, as anyone less foolish and rapacious than my client would have seen.'

In his agitation, he crossed to the window and stared over the cold wastes of the Westminster Road. Then he turned round.

'Mr Holmes! These criminals not only forged cheques for a non-existent bank, they fabricated a page from a well-known racing newspaper. Therefore they have a printing press. A press that may even print bank stationery! This is larceny on the grand scale. What might they do next?'

Holmes brushed a fleck of cigarette ash from his waistcoat.

'As to that, Mr Abrahams, I believe I know precisely what they will do next. I know when and I know where. Almost to the minute.'

This quite took the wind out of the lawyer's sails.

'How can you possibly know that?'

Holmes tried to calm him.

'Let us return for the moment, if you please, to Archer & Co.'

In his agitation to deliver the news from Paris, William Abrahams had so far given Holmes no chance to describe the events of the previous night. When he heard them, the lawyer turned quite pale.

'Arrested for housebreaking? You might go to prison for fourteen years!'

Holmes tossed his cigarette into the fire.

'I think not,' he looked up at Mr Abrahams. 'I am not charged with any offence so far but released on bail for lack of motivation or a witness. I am a little curious as to the speed with which Mr Clarke and the night inspector sent me on my way, but we may return to that matter in a while. As for the evidence against me, I should imagine the police will find witnesses of Major Montgomery's calibre remarkably shy. I went to the firm's premises in a legitimate response to his advertisement as a tipster. I found my way open, I broke nothing. The police can hardly prosecute if Major Montgomery declines to appear. As Madame de Goncourt now knows, the major is only a name, a ghost. While I am disposed to allow that spectres may sometimes trouble our sleep, I recall none materializing in the witness-box of the Central Criminal Court.'

He took Oakley's 'Silver Polish' advertisement from the table.

'When I was brought to the charge-room last night, my pockets were turned out and a most shoddy search carried out. My little pocket-knife was remarked upon but it was so clean and slight that it could not be evidence against me. This advertisement, quite the most important clue in the case, was ignored. Such, I fear, is the blinkered mentality of Scotland Yard.'

Mr Abrahams looked up at him.

'Oakley's! Why the devil should they concern themselves with an advertisement for silver polish?' A tic of ill-temper teased the lawyer's mouth as he handed the paper back. Holmes smiled.

'It lay with the post, just inside the door, where it would attract no particular attention. It was addressed in pencil and appeared to be delivered by hand.'

'Is that so unusual with tradesmen's circulars?'

'I observed the blotter on Messrs Archer's desk,' Holmes said evenly. 'The softness of blotting paper takes a remarkably good impression. The mere finger-tips of a criminal expert may trace the more forcible indentations. A skilful application of graphite will highlight anything of that kind. Of course, my practice excludes the matrimonial tragedies of the divorce court. However, I can assure you that pencil impressions have dissolved many a happy marriage.'

'And what are we to conclude?' Mr Abrahams sat stiff-necked and sceptical.

'That someone came with an urgent and secret message to Northumberland Street. The person to whom he wished to speak was not there. I daresay no one was there. However, the visitor had been able to enter the office – believe me, it is not difficult. The circular in his pocket was already prepared for such a situation. But it must reach the right person. What then? He put it in an envelope and addressed it in pencil. He slipped it among the letters on the floor. It would attract no notice from anyone, except the man who expected it. Even a policeman would drop it in the dustbin.'

'I daresay,' Mr Abrahams began impatiently but Holmes held up his hand.

'The visitor was plainly agitated, however. His pencil indentation went through both sides of the envelope, through the folded sheet of the circular, and deep into the blotting-paper. Haste is also evident to the trained eye. I noted the breaking of a pencil point on the first down-stroke of "Northumberland".'

'All for a silver-polish advertisement?'

Holmes chuckled.

'For the message it may carry. A prearranged code depending on certain letters from Messrs Oakley's well-known slogans is too fanciful. No, sir. As I picked up the letters, I sensed an odour from this envelope. There are certain chemical and aromatic scents which the criminal expert should be able to identify. Household bleach or ammonia is among the most common. It is also one of the most significant, being the most easily perfected form of invisible writing.'

'Then you have read a secret message?'

Holmes shook his head.

'I was tempted. However, I require a witness to testify as to what I do.'

'As a policeman might have done last night.'

'Not a policeman, I think. If you will draw closer, I will hold this paper before the fire. As the vulgar saying has it, if some phantom script does not manifest itself in a minute or two, I shall be quite prepared to eat my hat.'

The two men watched. For a moment they saw only the glow of flames playing behind the printed pattern of silver vessels. Then a brownish edge appeared on the blank margin at the foot of the paper, as though it might scorch and burn. Pale marks on the tawny patches began to take the form of letters. In a moment more they ran round the margins of the circular like figures on a frieze.

*Dear Bill, – Important news. Tell the young ones to keep themselves quiet and be ready to scamper. I must see you as early as possible. Bring this note with you under any circumstances. I fancy the brief is out for some of you. If not, it soon will be. So you must keep a sharp look-out.*

'There you have it,' said Holmes softly.

In that moment, Mr Abrahams's attitude towards him underwent a total conversion. He saw that Sherlock Holmes was the one man in the world who might even now save his client. Yet he still nagged at the difficulties.

'If their man opens the envelope you have left and finds blank paper, will he not expect trouble?'

Holmes frowned a little.

'The reverse, I think. If the man who sent this message opens the envelope, he may assume that my blank paper means his message has been received. He will be reassured. The other man will perhaps suppose it to be a signal or warning. There will be confusion for a while, rather than suspicion, which I confess suits my purpose admirably.'

Though better-disposed towards Holmes, the lines of anxiety in the lawyer's drawn face remained deeply incised.

'At the best, Mr Holmes, I fear this may be a goose-chase that will take months to conclude. It may lead us all over Europe.'

Holmes affected genuine astonishment.

'I should be sorry if that were so, Mr Abrahams. I had proposed to bring the entire investigation to its conclusion by the end of the week – or next week at the very latest. As for distance, I shall be surprised if our inquiry takes us more than five miles from where we are now sitting. However, there is no time to lose. It is imperative that I should immediately interview the commander of the Scotland Yard detective police, Superintendent Williamson. It must be done this morning.'

Mr Abrahams looked at him in dismay.

'Impossible! You would be fortunate to see him a week from now. If you follow the political news . . .'

'I do not,' said Holmes hastily.

'If you did, you would see that he is appearing morning and afternoon just now before a parliamentary select committee on criminal law reform.'

'Is he indeed?' Holmes walked across the room and took his cape from its cupboard. 'That is where my elder brother Mycroft will prove of the greatest assistance to us. He is the government's inter-departmental adviser and was instrumental in setting up that very committee, to which he told me the other evening that he now acts as secretary. I do not generally take a great interest in such bodies but where criminal law is concerned I allow an exception. Mycroft Holmes, as you perhaps know, is also a founder of the Diogenes Club in Pall Mall. Almost all its members belong to that little circle of government in Whitehall. Brother Mycroft knows everyone who is anyone in that celebrated thoroughfare. Prime Ministers may come and go but he goes on for ever. By a happy chance, he was the seconder when Frederick Adolphus Williamson – who, by the way, is known as "Dolly" to his friends – was proposed for membership of the Diogenes.'

'You astonish me,' said Mr Abrahams, smiling for the first time that morning.

Holmes finished the last button of his cape and looked up.

'I had not intended to surprise you. However, I believe you will find that Lord Llandaff, as chairman of the select committee, will find it inconvenient to sit between eleven o'clock and lunch today. He does not yet know that, but I promise you it will be so after I have communicated with Mycroft. As for Mr Williamson, he will find himself a captive with time upon his hands in the Palace of Westminster. The company of a fellow member of the Diogenes Club will be some consolation to him. I daresay, he will quite welcome a little chat.'

## IV

A few moments before noon, Sherlock Holmes followed the footsteps of a uniformed flunky down a corridor that was tiled in blue, yellow and brown diamonds. Officials in red livery with buckle-shoes hurried by, playing-card figures overtaken by time. The gothic doors, embellished by fretwork or gilding, were labelled as 'Motions' or 'Questions', 'Court Postmaster' or 'Table Office'. Fan vaulting spread high above him. In bright murals, King James threw the Great Seal in the Thames, and King William found it again.

The flunky opened a door and stood back, as Holmes entered a long room looking upon the river. Foundries, glass-houses, and printing-works on the Surrey shore poured their feathery smoke into a cold sky. An oak table ran the length of the room, set with upright chairs carved in Tudor style and padded with red leather. By a grey marble fireplace stood two men, one of whom was recognizable as the brother of Sherlock Holmes, despite differences of size and shape.

Mycroft Holmes was the elder by seven years, a big lethargic man, his heavy face lined by the same incisive lines as his younger brother's. His unwieldy frame supported a massive intelligence in the great brow and in penetrating steel-grey eyes. He extended a large flat hand, which those meeting him for the first time were apt to think of as the flipper of a seal. He turned to his companion, a stocky nervous figure, a dwarf beside Mycroft.

Frederick Adolphus Williamson was a broad-faced man with mutton-chop whiskers and a gentle manner. The son of a Hammersmith constable, he had risen by self-education and diligence to exercise an uneasy command over the Detective Police of Scotland Yard.

The three men sat down at one end of the long table, still littered with papers from the joint select committee.

'Archer & Co.,' said Mycroft to his brother, 'Northumberland Street. We are ahead of you there, Sherlock. Would you not say so, Dolly?'

'An international affair,' Williamson replied with a quick smile of apology, 'Scotland Yard and the French police at the Sûreté.'

The keen profile of Sherlock Holmes showed the least suggestion of hostility.

'You speak of forged newspapers and fraudulent investments?'

'Just so,' said Williamson, sweetness itself.

'I should guess, Sherlock,' mused Mycroft Holmes, 'that, grateful as we are to you for noticing the matter on our behalf, we shall soon have the City of Paris Loan swindle well in hand.'

'Guessing is a shocking habit!' Sherlock Holmes said sharply. 'It is destructive to the logical faculty . . .'

Mycroft broke in with a mocking apology.

'You see, Dolly? My brother could keep a red-hot coal in his mouth more easily than a clever remark. The City of Paris . . .'

'I am not here about the City of Paris,' said Sherlock Holmes quietly. 'My concern is with a Society for Insuring Against Losses on the Turf, and its creator, Major Hugh Montgomery.'

Mycroft and the superintendent looked at one another. It was plain that they had never heard of Major Montgomery.

'Not the City of Paris Loan?' Mycroft inquired. 'Perhaps, Sherlock, we must take you into our confidence a little.' He raised his eyebrows at Superintendent Williamson who looked down at his hands, then gave a quick nod.

'The City of Paris Loan,' Mycroft went on slowly, 'is advertised as a means to finance the rebuilding of ancient sewers in that city. It promises to eliminate death by cholera and similar contagions. It is said to be backed by guarantees from the French government, who will pay fifteen per cent a year to stockholders with return of capital in full after five years. English and French private investors have been solicited and are almost begging the promoters to take their money. As well as the company's brochures, these investors have received copies of the most enthusiastic pages from the French papers. *Figaro, Le Monde,* and the Paris financial press describe it as the investment of a lifetime. Small wonder that there has been such a race among English clients to invest while the loan-stock remains on sale.'

He glanced at the superintendent who sat, as Sherlock Holmes later described it to me, like a man hunched under the knell of doom.

'May I tell my brother the rest?' asked Mycroft Holmes.

Williamson hesitated, then nodded but without looking up.

'I think it may be necessary.' Mycroft Holmes turned to Sherlock again. 'What I tell you must not be repeated outside this room. I must have your most solemn word that you will not disclose the matter to another soul until it has been brought into public view.'

Sherlock Holmes assented by a certain petulant quirk of the mouth at the thought that his brother should have stooped to demand his solemn word in such a manner. Then Mycroft Holmes continued.

'The City of Paris Loan and the turf fraud of which you speak, but of which I had never heard until just now, are only the latest of their kind. A series of these crimes has occurred during the past three or four years, though they have been kept from the public and the press. Presently you will understand why. Sometimes the villains are Gardner & Co. in Edinburgh, then they are the Paris Discretionary, next we have Colletso and the Egyptian Loan, then comes George Washington Morton and the New York Discretionary Investment Society. They grow like summer flowers, are cut down, and appear again next day. There is no end to them.'

'And the perpetrators?' Sherlock Holmes inquired sceptically. 'Are they so fleet of foot?'

'In every case so far, it seems they have been trapped, only for the arresting officers to find the premises empty and the criminals gone.'

'It is often the case,' said Sherlock Holmes with a philosophical yawn. 'Can it really be for no more than this that I am sworn to secrecy?'

Mycroft shook his head.

'You are sworn to secrecy for this.'

He drew out an envelope containing a photographic print. Sherlock Holmes took it, fingered a magnifying-glass from his breast pocket and studied it. The print showed three fragments of half-burnt paper, photographed when they were almost too brittle to touch and in the moment before they would crumble to ash. There was little to be seen except the words 'Gardner & . . .' on one fragment, '19 January' on another, and 'wanted in connection . . .' on the third.

'And this,' said Mycroft Holmes, as he handed his brother a second print.

Sherlock Holmes wasted little time on the second specimen. There was a crest of the City of Edinburgh Constabulary, a day and a month. The words 'drawn on the Clydesdale Bank', appeared faintly and 'to be detained for questioning' very plainly.

'Dear me,' he said quietly to Mycroft, 'this is rather as I had supposed. Will you tell me where these interesting scraps were found?'

'They are all that remains of several sheets of paper, which the man – or men – who disposed of them thought had been entirely destroyed. The fragments were found on separate days, so we may never know how many more acts of this kind were not even suspected. Each of these fragments was picked out from the back of an office dog-grate, which stands clear of the wall a little. In both cases, someone had overpitched the grate by placing so much coal on the papers that it preserved them in part rather than destroying them completely. These scraps were found unburnt at the rear of the ash-cans. For that we must be grateful to someone whom I will merely call an honest servant.'

'Indeed,' said Sherlock Holmes casually. 'And am I to be told where this grate – or grates – may be located?'

Mycroft glanced at the superintendent but received no response. He turned to his brother again, watching the face of Sherlock Holmes with the calculation of a falcon.

'In the offices of the Detective Police at Scotland Yard. One in the Sergeants' Office and one in the Inspectors' Room. The date of the discovery in both cases is that upon the messages. Their receipt was not entered in the office day-book and they must have been destroyed soon after their arrival by whoever opened them. Therefore, it seems a moral certainty that these most urgent messages from another police force, requesting the immediate detention of suspects or known criminals by the Metropolitan Police, were being systematically burnt upon the office fires by men of the Detective Division. The fact that one was found in the Sergeants' Office and the other in the Inspectors' Room indicates the extent of the conspiracy.'

While Mycroft Holmes made this careful explanation, Superintendent Williamson appeared to be suffering death by a thousand cuts.

'A matter of some gravity,' said Sherlock Holmes, calmly indifferent to moral considerations. 'If my advice is sought, I would first of all observe that a common mistake on these occasions is to search high and low for the traitors within. On the contrary, one should begin by deciding which men among them all may be shown to be honest beyond doubt.'

Williamson looked up at him.

'You will be relieved to know, Mr Holmes, that we have proceeded on those very lines. Of twenty officers in the Detective Division, I believe without hesitation that a great majority are innocent. Inspector Tobias Gregsen, for all his faults, is no traitor. I would stake my life on that. Sergeant Lestrade is most certainly innocent. Apart from his moral qualities, he was not in the division at the time of these felonies and so had no possible connection with any conspiracy.'

'Indeed,' said Holmes airily, 'I have met Sergeant Lestrade and may say from personal knowledge that what you believe of him seems to me true.'

The superintendent was startled but also gratified.

'Tell me, Mr Williamson,' said Holmes presently, 'would you lend Mr Lestrade to me for a few days? A week perhaps?'

'Lend him to you?' Mycroft Holmes burst in like thunder. 'In heaven's name why, Sherlock? To what end?'

'The reason,' said his brother in the same off-hand manner, 'is that I have only one pair of hands and cannot be in two places at once. The end? So that the conspiracy which threatens my client through the action of a gang of swindlers, and that other conspiracy which threatens to bring down Scotland Yard in ruins, and then the Paris swindle, may all be a thing of the past by this time next week.'

The suggestion roused the superintendent.

'I do not see what purpose it would serve. Besides, it would be materially irregular, Mr Holmes! Entirely without precedent!'

But, on reflection, Mycroft Holmes now moved to the side of his brother.

'Hardly more irregular or without precedent, Dolly, than to have Scotland Yard in ruins and to see anarchy upon our streets. If Lestrade's leave of absence for a week or so may avert that, I believe I can settle any questions that the Home Secretary or the Prime Minister may care to put to me.'

The two brothers were seldom so united in their views and purposes. When they were, I truly believe that no power on earth could stand against them.

## V

Sergeant Lestrade's secondment was to begin that evening. Meantime, Holmes went alone to Villiers Street in the afternoon, lightly disguised by snow-white hair and whiskers, shoulders stooped like an older man, so that his posture and movements took two or three inches off his height. When he told me the story of the Racing Certainty, he chuckled over that message, written in block capitals the night before on the blotter of Archer & Co., a moment before he was seized. It seemed to him one of the neatest things he had ever done. MOST URGENT. MEET ME UNDER THE ARCHES CHARING CROSS STATION OPPOSITE THE KING WILLIAM IN VILLIERS STREET TOMORROW – TUESDAY – 3PM SHARP.

Who would read it? And who would the reader believe the author to be? It was ten minutes to three when he took a table in the window of the saloon bar of the King William, from where he might survey that narrow street running down to the river. On the far side, station arches supported the booking-hall and the platforms, where the South-Eastern Railway runs out across Hungerford Bridge. Below the station, Villiers Street with its little shops was like a busy canyon in perpetual shadow.

The crowds that flowed between the Strand and the Embankment would have daunted any man who lacked the trained eye of Sherlock Holmes. He had practised his art until, if you had filled Trafalgar Square with as many people as it would hold, he could pick out a single face in an eagle's sweep.

A few minutes before the hour, a man appeared at the top of the street. This was a burly fellow dressed in a dog's-tooth check suit that belonged to the enclosure at Epsom or Newmarket, a sporting fashion-plate from the *Winning Post* or the *Pink 'Un*. Holmes did not suppose for one moment that this uncouth figure was the likeness of Major Montgomery. The tout waited for a moment, looking down the street, and then said something over his shoulder to another man who was still out of view round the corner. Then his companion appeared, a dapper dark-haired man of slight build in a frock-coat, grey trousers, spats, and lemon-yellow waistcoat. This ill-assorted pair began to walk slowly down Villiers Street towards the arches.

The racing-man had a rolling gait, like a sailor ashore, the other walked with the precise steps of a dancing-master. Sherlock Holmes uttered to himself that quiet chuckle which usually boded ill to someone. He recognized his quarry.

The two strollers were looking at a man who was walking carefully towards them from the Embankment. Holmes watched this tall figure with ginger hair and pale freckled face. He heard in his mind the words spoken behind him the previous evening, as he was seized in the offices of 'Archer & Co'.

'So y'would, would you, my fine dandy!'

Sergeant Meiklejohn walked slowly towards the other two men. He came to a halt before them. The dapper dancing-master engaged him in conversation, while the heavily-built tout scanned the street as if to see whether they were observed. At this distance, watching them through the interstices of the moving crowd, it would be impossible to gather much of their exchanges. Yet Holmes saw all that he needed from the expressions on their faces. He knew that Meiklejohn and the natty dresser were each asking whether the other had left a message in pencil on the blotter, an urgent appeal which brought them together now. And now each was shaking his head to deny it. Presently they were asking one another how it came to be there. They were looking about them as they spoke, trying to do so unobtrusively, waking too late to the trap that had been laid for them. Then something else was being discussed. Holmes guessed that it was the blank half-sheet of paper found by one man in the envelope where the other man had left a different message.

They were taking leave of one another now, carefully but quickly. Holmes stood up behind the barroom window, watching through the crowds, intending to follow the dapper little man and the race-course tout. Meiklejohn was nothing to him now. As he stepped into the street, however, he glanced down towards the river and saw a fourth man, Inspector George Clarke. Whether Clarke had been in company with Meiklejohn it was impossible to say. He was nowhere near Meiklejohn, as he handed a copper to the newsboy, took his paper, and walked slowly down to the Embankment and Scotland Yard.

The two men whom Holmes had in sight used every familiar tactic to shake off an unseen pursuer. They stopped, walked back, then turned and walked on again, to see if this would make their shadow reveal himself. Holmes outflanked them, watching from the eminence of the stairs to the railway platforms. They could not be sure there was anyone on their trail at that moment but, for safety's sake, they now split up and went in opposite directions. Holmes had expected this and had decided long before that the dapper fellow was the one he would track. By now, however, Holmes bore less resemblance to the man who had tracked his quarry from the King William. His coat was reversed to show the shabbiest gabardine waterproof and his natty cap had undergone a transformation into a working-man's 'cheese-cutter'. He wore heavy spectacles whose lenses had the thickness of a counting-house clerk's with failing sight. Most of all, however, it was the metamorphosis of the upright carriage of Sherlock Holmes into a pathetic round-shouldered drudge which concealed him most effectively.

At first, the game was played out in Charing Cross Station. For twenty minutes, there was a curious hide-and-seek as the dancing-master performed a pattern of turns and diversions to shake off any possible pursuer, leading the way round the busy platforms, over the footbridge, down to the washroom, through the booking-hall where he purchased a ticket and walked at once past the barrier on to a platform. Holmes watched, sure that a man who intended catching a train would not have bothered to lead him such a dance beforehand. He was proved wrong as the quarry opened a carriage door of the first train to pull in.

Now it was the turn of Sherlock Holmes to stride across the booking-hall and take a ticket for Dover. With a moment to spare, he passed the ticket-barrier and entered the last carriage. The train rumbled slowly across the iron span of the long river bridge and pulled in at Waterloo. There was a slamming of doors and then a pause. By use of a pocket-mirror, Holmes surveyed the length of the train without showing his head outside the carriage. The whistle blew. At the last moment, a door at the far end flew open and the dapper man sprang out. Holmes leapt for the concealment of a laden luggage-trolley before the other could finish closing the carriage door and turn to look at him.

Cat and mouse began their game again, the cat never quite seen by the mouse but scented none the less. For a moment, Holmes lost his man yet knew the way he must have gone. Striding up the covered stairs of the footbridge, two at a time, he reached the top and to his surprise found the crossway empty above the tracks below. There had surely been time only for his prey to reach the first stairs down to the next platform. Holmes sprinted and then descended cautiously, alarmed to find the platform also empty. On the far side of the next railway track, however, a train was pulling out on the return to Waterloo. The dapper man was waving to him from behind the window of the first carriage.

Another hunter might have lost the game in that half-hour. For Holmes, so much had been won. His quarry had striven with ill-concealed desperation to shake off his tracker. Most important to him was the determination of the quarry to return to Charing Cross. Why such resolve? What bound him to that railway station? Was there a train to be caught to another destination in London – or England? No, for every train that leaves Charing Cross goes to Waterloo. Was there a confederate to be met? No, because the half hour when that might have happened was now gone. What else? Why must he return, as if to his home? Because it was his home! What place could be more useful to a man who links the City of Paris Loan and insures against losses on the English turf in Northumberland Street? Where was closer to the phantom Royal Bank of London in the Strand – even to Scotland Yard?

Like a grand excrescence in the mind of Sherlock Holmes blossomed the Parisian opera-house splendour of the Charing Cross Hotel.

Twenty minutes later, his appearance restored to dignity and with a newspaper in his hand, Sherlock Holmes was reflected by a gilt-columned mirror between pillars of raspberry-coloured marble. In a moment more the reflection was gone and he sat patiently near the door of the writing-room, behind the wide concealing pages of the *Morning Post*. Yet his eyes never left the mirrors. Almost an hour passed, before he caught a momentary reflection of a man tipping his hat to an elderly woman in black velvet, as she walked forward with the aid of a stick. There was no mistaking the trim, chivalrous figure in his suit of cream linen, the moustache neat and the eyebrows trim. If he had been holding a cane just then, he might have swung it with the air of a boulevardier.

From behind a pillar, Holmes caught the murmurs at the reception-desk.

'The Marquis Montmorency . . .'

' "Poodle" Benson, as I live and breathe,' said Holmes softly, for his own benefit.

## VI

'They tell me, Lestrade, that you are an honest man.'

'I hope that I may prove so, Mr Holmes,' said the Scotland Yard officer without a flicker of resentment.

'Quite. To prove the truth of that hope is the reason for your presence. You are also said to be an intelligent and resourceful detective officer. Too many of your colleagues are apt to give the alarm everywhere and discover nothing.'

'That must be for others to judge, sir,' Lestrade said guardedly.

'You may depend upon it that they will.'

Such were the first words spoken directly between Holmes and the future Inspector Lestrade of the Special Branch and the Criminal Investigation Department, as the two men occupied a cab in the forecourt of the Charing Cross Hotel that evening. It was dark and a light drizzle was falling through the mist. Wet cobbles caught the lamplight in wavering pools. Through this gloom, the profile of Lestrade's face appeared still leaner and grimmer. Holmes was wearing his cloak and ear-flapped travelling-cap, a leather bag beside him, labelled for the night-ferry via Folkestone and Boulogne.

He turned a little in his seat to look directly at the policeman.

'Your orders for the next few days are quite clear in your mind?'

'What Mr Williamson and Mr Mycroft Holmes told me at the Home Office is plain, sir. I am to carry out your instructions, provided they are not manifestly illegal. If I have doubts in the matter, I am to communicate with Mr Williamson through Mr Mycroft Holmes at the Home Office department.'

'I could almost wish,' said Holmes piously, 'that it had been possible to leave my brother out of this business. I suppose, however, that would not have done.'

'As to that,' Lestrade said enigmatically, 'it would not be for me to say.'

'Very well, then these are your orders and the reasons for them. For as long as I am allowed to give you instructions, you will be employed at the reception-desk of the Charing Cross Hotel, or in whatever other employment is most prudent.'

'As a clerk, sir?' There was no mistaking Lestrade's alarm. 'I know not the first thing about hotel clerking, Mr Holmes!'

'You are supposed to be there on approval in whatever capacity is necessary. You will not be required to work alone and there is only one person, in a very senior position and entirely trustworthy, who knows your true identity.'

'And that is all I am to do, sir?'

Holmes made an effort at infinite patience.

'You will earn your wages, Lestrade. At this moment, a most dangerous criminal conspiracy embraces both Paris and London. Therefore, one of us must be here and the other in Paris. I shall go to Paris tonight, being familiar with the language, the city, and the officials whose assistance may be necessary to us. I shall probably be away for a few days. What needs to be done here is merely work-a-day but it must be done none the less.'

In the reflected oil-light, Lestrade looked apprehensive.

'Done by me?'

'Of course. The Charing Cross Hotel, estimable in many ways, is convenient for international criminals, standing as it does at the heart of London yet so close to the route to Paris and the Channel ports. I have just spent two hours at the Home Office. My brother has information of a new conspiracy against James Lester Valence, a most powerful man in Australian commerce. That is all we know at present. He is by no means the first victim of these scoundrels but stands head and shoulders above the rest. Valence made and lost a fortune in the gold-fields, then made another from building railroads in New South Wales and Queensland. He was in London six weeks ago, staying at this very hotel to which he is about to return. I cannot protect him for the moment, therefore you must. You will report every day to the Home Department and will receive your instructions there. Do not attempt to communicate with me in any other way. Do not go anywhere near Scotland Yard. As for Valence, he has been touring in Europe, and is due here in a day or two. I understand he is soon to be married. Whatever villainy is plotted against him, the Charing Cross Hotel appears to be the scene of it. Such is the extent of my information.'

'Does that information include a photograph of him?' Lestrade asked hopefully.

'I have not seen one. However, you could scarcely mistake him. The description I have from my brother is of a man taller than you or I, as well as a good deal more bulky. He wears a black and somewhat bristling beard. His face, such as one may see of it, is marked by the outdoor life of sun and wind. When going out, he carries as a matter of habit a black ebony stick with a silver band, embossed with a small griffin and the initials "J. L. V." '

'And his voice?' the detective asked quietly. 'Appearance is one thing, Mr Holmes, but the voice gives a man away.'

Holmes looked at him, as if he had not thought of this but approved of Lestrade's quick-wittedness.

'As to his voice, I fear we know nothing. None of us has ever heard it.'

The Scotland Yard man was not to be beaten to the post by his temporary employer. He reached for his bag.

'Then I shall bid you good evening and a pleasant journey, Mr Holmes. There may be much to be done in the next few days and I should like to make a start.

I am to go to the desk and ask for the manager, I presume?'

'Just so,' said Holmes, staring acutely through the gloom at his new accomplice. 'You will hear from me, through my brother, either tomorrow or the day after.'

The policeman opened the door and stepped out into the drizzle. In such circumstances, Lestrade set out upon his first adventure in partnership with Sherlock Holmes.

## VII

Two mornings later, from behind the polished mahogany of the reception-desk, Lestrade first set eyes upon James Lester Valence, crossing the hall between pillars of raspberry marble. It was impossible not to recognize the unkempt giant whose outlines had been described by Mycroft Holmes to Lestrade.

Sherlock Holmes had also been correct in his description of Valence as a burly bearded figure who had lived much of his life in the roughest terrain. He seemed more like the habitué of a farmers' inn than of a grand hotel. Yet beneath this exterior there was evident gentleness and simplicity. The hard-handed gold-prospector and railroad-builder behaved like a mere child among the ways and wonders of European cities.

Two things in particular drew Lestrade's attention to this new arrival. In the first place, Valence was an inveterate smoker of strong cigarettes. So far as he occupied the public rooms of the hotel, he was always to be found in the genial, tobacco-stained dimness of the smoking-room, with its darkened oil-portraits of famous sportsmen, its subdued lighting, brass lamps and table-furniture, card-tables and red plush. A second matter of interest was the arrival by every morning and evening post of a lightly perfumed envelope on pink stationery, addressed to Valence in a neat female hand. A small and discreet coronet was printed in blue on the flap of the envelope. From this Lestrade concluded that whatever trap was laid for the Australian, a woman might be the bait.

Two other pieces of correspondence, identifiable by a printed sender's address on their envelopes, appeared to be grateful acknowledgements to Valence by the Distressed Gentlefolks Aid Society. When he reported all this information to Mycroft Holmes, Lestrade was greeted by an outstretched telegram. He caught the words 'Holmes, Hotel Crillon, Place de la Concorde', and then the message. KINDLY TELEGRAPH ALL PECULIARITIES OF ANTIPODEAN SUBJECT'S LEFT THUMB AND ANY APPARENT CHANGE OF SAME AT MORNING OR EVENING.

Lestrade confessed to me, years later, that nothing in his dealings with Holmes had ever baffled him so much. How could Valence's left thumb have any relevance to the case? What changes could occur in its abnormalities during the course of the day?

Happily for the detective officer, the manager was able to leave him pretty much at liberty. There was no means by which he could answer Holmes's query, except by closely observing Valence throughout the day. The Australian's attachment to the smoking-room and the card-table made this easier than it might have been. Lestrade became a supernumerary smoking-room attendant.

However diffident Valence had been in the outer world of London society, he came into his own among the familiarities of the card-table, which was occupied by hardier souls day and night. To one bluff racing-man and that linen-suited aristocrat, the Marquis Montmorency, who seemed to be his habitual neighbours, Valence remarked that poker was his game but that during his travels he had improved his hand at baccarat.

The conviviality of the game, rather than the hock and seltzer which accompanied it, loosened the tongue of this diffident giant. He spoke of a sweetheart in England. Indeed, he went so far as to draw out his notecase and produce a photograph of a young woman whose every feature confirmed her breeding. Compliments and polite congratulations were breathed in his direction from all corners of the table.

So far, the vigilance of the Scotland Yard man revealed no immediate sign of abnormality in Valence's left thumb, nor any change as the hours passed. However, on the second evening, as he was emptying and polishing the glass bowls that had contained cigarette and cigar ash, he heard Valence speak of marriage and the diamond necklace which was to be his gift to his beloved upon their betrothal. He had ordered it from a Bond Street jeweller before departing on his tour of Europe. Now he had returned to collect and present the finished article. The racing-man inquired politely where the necklace was being made.

'Regniers in Bond Street,' said the Australian modestly.

The Marquis Montmorency looked astonished.

'I am delighted to know it, sir, for Henri Regnier himself is related to me by marriage, through my cousin, Antoine Mellerio of the rue de la Paix. A small world, to be sure! I congratulate you on your choice of craftsman. You know, I imagine, that it is possible in the trade to arrange a little discount for oneself or one's friends. Perhaps you have already done so.'

The bearded giant looked abashed.

'A discount? No, Marquis. It never crossed my mind to suggest such a thing.'

Montmorency looked down at the cards in his hand and shook his head.

'That is much to be regretted. The reduction is not so great, of course. Ten per cent. Perhaps less. But on so large a sum . . .'

He left the rest unsaid. Lestrade was now obliged to move out of earshot. He saw only that, during the rest of the evening, Valence pulled ahead of the others and at the end of the game was almost thirty pounds to the good. A little after midnight, as they pushed their chairs back and rose to go their separate ways, the dapper marquis twinkled at his companion.

'I would not for the world, sir, presume upon so short an acquaintance. However, if you would permit me to put in a word, I will see if my cousin might not arrange a discount, even at this late stage of the purchase. Between ourselves, you understand. If you will trust me with the details, I will see what can be done tomorrow. It is usual to agree these things at the beginning of a transaction but a man in your situation, who would be so valued a customer for the future, surely deserves a degree of *ex post facto* consideration.'

Valence plainly had no idea what the term meant and appeared troubled by embarrassment at such unexpected kindness. Yet he could scarcely refuse so generous an offer, made out of pure friendship.

The next morning brought another of the perfumed envelopes, which Lestrade was certain must come to Valence from the intended recipient of the diamond necklace. The Australian spent most of that day in his room. In the mild warmth of late afternoon, however, he went out alone with nothing to indicate where his destination might be. Almost as soon as Valence had entered a cab, Lestrade noticed the racing-man and the Marquis Montmorency going up the stairs together in something of a hurry. To the mind of a detective, they appeared an ill-matched pair. Following at a distance, Lestrade saw the two men take separate directions at the first landing. The racing-man retired to his room, his companion followed the corridor where Valence slept.

Lestrade was clear as to what was about to happen. Montmorency had by now had ample opportunity to acquire a copy of the key to Valence's room. The means might be easy enough in a hotel of this size. He or his racing friend had only to ask for Valence's room number, take the key, then return it a few minutes later, apologizing or complaining that it was the wrong one and did not fit his door. Such errors, in all honesty, were not frequent but nor were they uncommon. In this case, a wax impression of the key would soon be taken.

By the time that Lestrade turned the corner of the landing, the corridor ahead of him was empty. There had been no time for Montmorency to reach the far end, unless he had done it at a sprint. Therefore, he was in one of the rooms. The detective reached Valence's door, knelt down, and squinted through the keyhole. He saw only a segment of the sitting-room but it was enough to show him the marquis patiently going through the contents of Valence's ash-bowl, examining the cigarette-butts, holding them up and considering each in turn. Presently he put the ash-bowl down and swung round to the door. Lestrade moved quickly but without a sound. There was just time to reach the end of the corridor and disappear from view.

However, from where he stood, the Scotland Yard man was able to hear the door of Valence's room opening very slowly, as if the dapper little aristocrat looked cautiously in either direction, slipped out, and closed the door very softly behind him.

To enter Valence's room for no other reason than to inspect the remains of the cigarettes he had smoked, ignoring money and valuables, was surely the maddest thing in a mad business. Or so it seemed to Lestrade.

## VIII

A further day passed and Lestrade had yet been unable to observe the essential peculiarities of Valence's left thumb. It was a thumb that pressed upon the paste-board cards with as firm a hold as any man's round the card-table, nor did it appear to change as the day progressed. Perhaps the change was a certain twitching that sometimes occurred as the evening wore on. Lestrade felt that he certainly noticed something of the sort. Upon his next visit to the Home Department, Mycroft Holmes silently handed him another telegram.

> MATTERS IN FRANCE COMING TO A HEAD STOP. KINDLY ATTEND TO PREVIOUS INSTRUCTIONS IN MINUTEST DETAIL STOP. ESSENTIAL YOU CONTINUE TO DO SO STOP. HOLMES HOTEL CRILLON.

In the course of his smoking-room duties that evening, the Scotland Yard man caught another scrap of conversation. Montmorency, the smiling gamester, said to Valence, as they drew their chairs in round the table, 'I must tell you that it is all arranged, my dear fellow. Twelve per cent is to be the discount on your purchase. I tried for fifteen on your behalf, but twelve was the best I could manage. Still, it is preferable to nothing, is it not?'

The black-bearded giant, in his good-natured simplicity, seemed so overcome by such a selfless action that for a moment he appeared tongue-tied.

'Twelve!' he said at last. 'But that is far more than I had expected! Five, I had thought; perhaps ten at the extreme. What can I have done to merit such consideration from you? It is more than I can guess.'

'In that case, my dear Valence, you need only guess that you are a good sportsman and a most agreeable companion,' beamed the dapper little lord. 'Besides, these jewellers always stick the price on at first, thinking they will be beaten down in negotiation. In that case, old fellow, it is only justice to knock 'em down a bit. They quite expect it, you know. And then, what is this world, if we cannot do one another a good turn from time to time?'

'What, indeed, sir?'

'However, if you will permit me,' the dapper nobleman went on, 'I believe it would be best if I were to collect the necklace myself and bring it to you. Though the matter is arranged with my cousin, I shall be better acquainted with the shopman than you would be. If I deal with him, you may be sure that your discount will not wash off, as they say!'

At this there was something, less than suspicion but more than doubt, which flickered briefly in the Australian's eyes.

'Then you would wish me to give you the cash or a cheque, so that you might take it to Regnier's?'

He did not so much as hint at a natural misgiving that this man he had known only as a card-player might run off with his money, though the suspicion ran through the minds of everyone else present. As if to confound them by sheer good-nature, the slightly-built Montmorency lay back in his chair and fairly rolled about with laughter, like a pleased child, at such a suggestion.

'I should not dream of it!' he giggled at last. 'No, my dear Valence. I will pay for the necklace with my cheque, it is better that way and will absolutely secure the reduction in price. My cousin would not go back on his word to me, of all people! When I return to the hotel with the necklace, you may reimuburse me for a sum twelve per cent less than you thought the cost would be. Is that fair?'

The bulky Australian was in a confusion of gratitude and remorse for having suspected the other man's good faith.

'It is more than fair, sir. It is generosity on a grand

scale. May I ask how you would like the money to be repaid?'

The marquis looked a little sheepish.

'As it is most convenient to you. I confess, however, that having written a cheque for such an amount, I should not at all object to being reimbursed in cash. Specie may be paid into the bank so much more easily and quickly. After all this, I should not care to hear that the cheque I had written had been returned by my bank for lack of funds!'

There was general laughter round the table at the absurdity of such a proposition.

'All the same,' Valence said, as if now eager to make amends for his suspicion, 'why should I not give you a cheque or money in the first place to take to Regnier's?'

The Marquis Montmorency beamed and spread out his hands.

'You shall not pay a cent, sir, until the necklace is in your hands. I insist upon that. Besides, suppose I should be waylaid by footpads between here and Bond Street?'

There was great hilarity at the notion of such an old-fashioned robbery in the streets of the modern West End.

'I do not know,' said Valence softy, 'I never dreamed when I came to Europe that I would receive so much friendship on all sides.'

Despite the strictest instructions in the latest telegram from Holmes, Lestrade abandoned his surveillance that afternoon, as Valence withdrew to his room. Instead, the Scotland Yard man shadowed the Marquis Montmorency. In his fawn hat, cream linen suit and lemon waistcoat, patent-leather shoes and spats, a rose in his buttonhole, the slim figure of the nobleman was not hard to track. He did not take a cab but walked quickly past the clubs of Pall Mall, up the broad elegance of St James's Street, across Piccadilly, and so into Bond Street.

Outside Regnier's, with its old-fashioned shopfront and gilt mouldings, Montmorency paused to watch a man taking the jewels on their velvet display-cushions from the window, in preparation for the shop to close. Before the metal grille was put across the window, however, the marquis had slipped inside. Lestrade could see him talking to the frock-coated shopman. After a few minutes, the customer came out and made his way back to Charing Cross.

Whatever suspicions Lestrade might have had about the purchase were put to rest by Montmorency's insistence that he would take no money until he handed over the necklace. Nor could it be doubted that he behaved with perfect openness and honesty to Valence in reporting the afternoon's visit. That evening, as they sat down to cards in the dark-walled smoking-room, Lestrade heard him say to the Australian, 'I paid a call on Regnier this afternoon. There will be no difficulty at all in the transaction. If you choose, of course, you may just write a little note, authorizing me to collect and pay for the item on your behalf. As for your discount, however, it is as safe as if it were in your pocket at this moment.'

Perhaps this was as well. They played baccarat that evening and, by the end of it, Valence was quite twenty pounds down. However, he had won as much on other occasions and could scarcely begrudge such a sum to his benefactors. Lestrade could not, in all conscience, see any trickery in the game. He was familiar with the most common ruse at baccarat whereby, under cover of his sleeve, a man might slip an extra counter over the line, or not, to adjust his stake according to the fall of the cards. There was not the least sign of that.

Indeed, Lestrade thought, he would have believed entirely in the good faith of the Marquis Montmorency, had it not been for the curious business of the nobleman entering his friend's room to inspect the stubs of his cigarettes in so furtive a manner.

On the following day, Mycroft Holmes, behind his wide desk, the green spaces of St James's Park filling the window behind him, showed a magisterial indifference to Lestrade's report.

'One is apt to think that men who play cards for greed and are fleeced deserve it,' he observed at one moment. 'As for the matter of the necklace, I opine that it is a service being performed so that Mr Valence will feel obliged to remain at the card-table in a game where the others take money off him. After all, they have him as a companion now whether he likes it or no, do they not? I daresay my brother would take a different view of the matter. For a third time, by the way, he asks after Mr Valence's left thumb.'

'It is a thumb,' Lestrade said bluntly, 'that is all it is.'

Mycroft Holmes heaved his untidy bulk from the chair and shook his large head, like a dog coming from water.

'No, it is not all. If my brother occupies himself about it to this extent, you may be sure that it is not all. However, I can make no more of it. Nor can I answer your question about the ends of the cigarettes. There is a war breaking out between the Khedive of

Egypt and Abyssinia, into which we may all be drawn. Turkey threatens to make trouble between ourselves, the Russians, and the German Empire by carrying out massacres in Bulgaria. It would be expedient if you and my brother should realize that I have more to occupy myself with than left thumbs and cigarette ends. Good day to you.'

However, the suspicion that Valence was being held at the card-table and fleeced by a specious promise of discount on a necklace was wired to Sherlock Holmes. The reply came almost at once.

REQUIRE FACTS NOT CONJECTURES STOP. CEASE
OBSERVATION OF LEFT THUMB OF VALENCE STOP.
HOLMES HOTEL CRILLON.

## IX

Valence's losses were little enough at the card-table on the next day. Indeed, for much of the game he was ahead. The day following that, he lost moderately. If he took this disappointment philosophically, it was because his friend Montmorency was able to inform him that the diamond necklace would be ready next day and might be collected in the afternoon. Valence assured the amiable nobleman that he would make arrangements to reimburse him for the cost immediately.

Lestrade gathered enough of these exchanges to know that the purchase was almost complete. Next day, towards the end of the afternoon, Valence retired as usual to his room and the card-table was deserted.

Montmorency approached the polished mahogany sweep of the reception-desk in the hotel's marble foyer. Lestrade heard him ask that his bill should be made up in readiness for his departure on the following morning. Then the dapper marquis walked out into the Strand and called a cab from the station rank.

Try as he might, Lestrade could still see nothing worse than a hint of sharp practice at the card-table. Even this was more than balanced by Montmorency's act of generosity. As for the racing-man in the dog's-tooth check, he was scarcely a proper companion for a marquis. However, as Lestrade remarked to me years afterwards, the association seemed no more questionable than that of the celebrated Marquess of Queensberry and his kind with the riff-raff of the sporting world and the smoking-room. The detective officer had half made up his mind to follow this benevolent marquis, out of curiosity, when a bell on the panel rang and he was summoned by name to Mr Valence's room.

According to the account given in the papers of Sherlock Holmes, events now followed with great rapidity. The Marquis Montmorency kept his promise to the last detail. He ordered the cab to wait for him in Bond Street, outside Regnier's shop, while he went in and greeted the jeweller with unfeigned geniality. He then wrote his cheque, took the necklace, and returned to the Charing Cross Hotel. There, in company with his friend the racing-man, he asked at the reception-desk whether it might be convenient to call upon Mr Valence, who was expecting him. The clerk inquired and replied that it would be most convenient but that

Mr Valence would be grateful for a delay of ten minutes while he finished dressing for dinner.

When this interval was over, the two men were shown up to Mr Valence's room by a page-boy. The lad knocked and was summoned by a voice from within. The Marquis Montmorency and his friend entered, surprised to find that Valence was not alone. Beside him stood the wiry grim-faced figure of the smoking-room attendant, whom the card-players had laughed at behind his back as the hotel's drunken butler. Most disconcertingly, for the marquis and his friend, James Lester Valence, gold prospector and railroad-builder, had lost his Australian voice. He had acquired a more precise and rather clipped English accent.

'Lock the door, if you please, Lestrade,' he said crisply.

The cadaverous butler obeyed, stepping round the other two men to do so.

'One cannot be too careful in dealings of such value, after all,' Valence observed for the benefit of Montmorency and his friend.

This seemed to reassure them a little.

'You have the necklace?' Valence asked, raising his eyebrows at Montmorency.

The dapper little nobleman drew a leather case from his pocket and handed it to the Australian.

'Eighteen hundred pounds, sir.'

Valence nodded as he opened the case and drew up from its velvet a ripple of glass fire that hung and swayed from his fingers.

'Admirable,' he said softly, 'wholly admirable. Shall we say – not eighteen hundred pounds, of course – perhaps eighteen pounds?'

The racing-man seemed about to start forward at Valence but Montmorency laid a hand on his friend's arm and smiled at the Australian's pleasantry.

'I can promise you, Mr Valence, that I have a receipt from Messrs Regnier in my pocket for eighteen hundred pounds.'

'I do not doubt it,' said Valence politely. 'Nor do I doubt that somewhere else you have a receipt for eighteen pounds - or whatever the price may be - for a set of imitation glass, made up as a replica of the true necklace. True diamonds do not sparkle in the light as these do, they glow in twilight and obscurity.'

Montmorency stared at him.

'Then I have been as much deceived as you, sir.'

'I do not doubt it, though not deceived in quite the way that you imagine.'

'I should like a word with that fellow Regnier!'

'You shall have one, never fear. Mr Regnier, if you please!'

The door leading to the bathroom opened and the jeweller appeared.

'I regret that you were kept waiting downstairs, sir,' said Holmes to Montmorency, 'but it was necessary that Mr Regnier should be one of our company. Be so kind, Mr Regnier, to repeat to these two gentlemen what you have already told Lestrade and I.'

The jeweller cleared his throat and began.

'A little while ago I was visited by you, Mr Holmes . . .'

'Holmes?'

The Australian, with a slight wince of discomfort, peeled aside the bristling black beard to reveal that familiar aquiline profile.

'Though I have had some little theatrical success in my youth, even playing the role of Horatio on the London stage with the Sasanoff Company,' he remarked wryly, 'I have never mastered the art of drawing off a beard without pain.'

Next he raised from his head the unkempt pate of dark hair and laid it aside.

'Now, Mr Benson,' he said, 'forgive me but I cannot continue to call you the Marquis Montmorency without some feeling of mirth. Nor would Major Montgomery serve you as a title any longer. Let us resume the narrative. I beg your pardon, Mr Regnier.'

The jeweller began again.

'I was visited by Mr Holmes who informed me that a plot by professional swindlers was in preparation against himself, masquerading as a wealthy Australian gentleman. With the knowledge of the authorities, I gave my consent to assist in frustrating this. A few days later, I was visited by a man who gave his name as the Marquis Montmorency and who I now know to be Mr Harry Benson. He explained that he wished to buy a very fine diamond necklace which I then had in stock. Mr Holmes had already spoken to me of this article. Mr Benson, as the Marquis Montmorency, said he would pay for this necklace with a cheque. However, he would leave both the necklace and the cheque with me until such time as the latter had been cleared and the funds were in my account. How could I have any objection to that arrangement?'

'How, indeed?' Holmes murmured.

'However, gentlemen, the Marquis Montmorency also wished to have a good imitation set made, so that his wife might generally keep the original necklace at her bank and have the imitation at home for less formal occasions. It is not an uncommon request and the imitation, being mere glass and paste, was easily done. This afternoon, as agreed, the Marquis Montmorency came with his cheque. He left the diamond necklace as a pledge for the cheque's clearance and took away the imitation. Naturally I wrote him two receipts, one for each article.'

There was a moment of total silence.

'And so,' said Holmes at last, 'Mr Benson brings us the imitation necklace with a receipt for the genuine one. In respect of this, Mr Valence, as he believed me to be, would pay him eighteen hundred pounds in cash. A vast sum of money for an imitation that is worth next to nothing. In due course, Mr Regnier would discover that the cheque had not the value of the paper it was written on. However, he would still have his diamond necklace and would not be much worse off. It was Mr Valence who was the target of the conspirators.'

The dapper little man's eyes flashed with anger.

'No, sir! It is I who am the victim and you who are the conspirator! You are a prime mover of the plot!'

'I baited the trap,' said Holmes modestly, 'and the bait was taken.'

But Harry Benson had now recovered his self-command.

'I do not think, Mr Holmes, that such a case of trickery or entrapment would stand a moment's examination in court, once your chicanery was revealed. You might very well find yourself in prison.'

Holmes wiped the Australian climate from his cheeks with a handkerchief.

'You may well be right,' he said cheerfully. 'Indeed,

I have always rather suspected that I should find myself in prison one day. Yet I think in this case that the forgery – the cheque signed to Mr Regnier as the Marquis Montmorency – would be more than enough evidence to put the boot on the other foot, as the saying has it. As it happens, I am little concerned for that. My client is the Comtesse de Goncourt, or to be more accurate Mr William Abrahams. My object has been to flush out those who sought to cheat that lady of many thousands of pounds. When you stand your trial, Mr Benson, it will not be for the necklace swindle but for a grander design represented by Archer & Co. of Northumberland Street and the City of Paris Loan, perpetrated from the rue Réamur. In the world of the racing certainty, a single forged cheque passed to Mr Regnier will come in a very poor third.'

Billy Kurr, the racing-man, had so far watched these proceedings with a dumb incredulity. Now he reached into his pocket and drew from it a small but efficient-looking revolver. Benson swung round to Lestrade.

'Give me the key to this door!'

Lestrade's features were set more like a bulldog than ever.

'Put that gun down!' he snapped at Kurr.

'Give Mr Benson the key, Lestrade,' Holmes said calmly.

'I shall do no such thing.'

'By the authority of Superintendent Williamson, you are under my orders until this matter is concluded. The lives of all those in this room are in my keeping. Now, give him the key!'

There was such rage in the face of the Scotland Yard man that Holmes thought he would still refuse, or else make some move to wrest the revolver from Kurr's grip. However, the fight seemed to go out of Lestrade and he tamely handed the key to Benson. The 'Marquis Montmorency' unlocked the door, ushered his companion through it, then locked it securely on the outside.

Lestrade rattled the handle of the door unavailingly.

'I owe you an apology,' Holmes said equably. 'However, it was necessary that you should think me in Paris. Brother Mycroft connived in getting the telegrams relayed. Had you known of my Australian masquerade, I feared your behaviour might have betrayed it.'

'And the thumb?' Lestrade asked gruffly.

'Ah, yes, the thumb. I am glad you paid such attention. By keeping your eye upon it, I could be sure that you were seldom too far off to miss the conversation of Benson and his companions. Had I merely asked you to eavesdrop, I fear you might once again have given the game away.'

Lestrade made no reply to this but returned to his rattling of the door-handle.

'Something must be done, Mr Holmes! They're getting away!'

Holmes had stepped out of the specially-built shoes which had increased his height by two full inches and was now divesting himself of the padding which had given such bulk to James Lester Valence. In the course of this transformation, he spared the Scotland Yard man a glance.

'Of course they are getting away! Have you grasped nothing, sergeant? In captivity, Benson and Kurr would be of no use to us. The diamond necklace is no more than a necessary bauble in my scheme. Even the Turf swindle and the Paris Loan are little enough. Let us allow Harry Benson a little freedom and he will lead us to the heart of the conspiracy.'

## X

As they walked out of the hotel entrance, Sherlock Holmes tightened his collar against a cold street-wind that had come with the darkness of the spring day.

'Poor Regnier,' he said wistfully, 'I believe he thought we should never have been released from our room. And now, if you please, Lestrade, we must look lively and take a cab to Canonbury. From there we shall send a telegram to Scotland Yard, while there is still time.'

Lestrade stopped and turned to him.

'But we could walk to Scotland Yard from here, Mr Holmes, quicker than any telegram might get there. Five minutes would be more than enough.'

'So it would, Lestrade, and that is precisely why we shall not do it. A telegram describing the day's developments, sent to the duty-officer of the Detective Division from Canonbury, will serve the purpose far better. I have taken the precaution of obtaining a copy of the duty roster from Mr Williamson, so that I may know who the recipient will be.'

As the wind fluttered the gas-lamps, the two men were driven from the elegance of the Strand, through the streets of Clerkenwell, past the smoky brickwork of St Pancras and out to the more spacious suburb of

Canonbury. Lestrade's apprehension appeared to deepen as they passed Holloway and Highbury.

'You know,' said Holmes conversationally, 'I am a little surprised that someone as sharp as Benson did not sniff me out. I thought from time to time that he half-suspected something.'

'He was in your room yesterday afternoon, sir, going through the cigarette-ends. That I can tell you.'

'Was he, by Jove?' said Holmes approvingly. 'I should certainly have done the same in his place. With such a beard as I was sporting, a man who smoked a cigarette down to the very end would singe his whiskers, if not set fire to himself. He knew that I did not try to do so in company. Had he found that the butts in my room were smoked to the limit, he would have known for a certainty that the beard was false. You see? It was as well that I allowed for that.'

Sherlock Holmes was unknown to the Canonbury police-station in 'N' Division. However, one or two of the officers were acquainted with Lestrade and this paved the way for the request that Holmes was about to make. When he heard that request, as Lestrade told me long afterwards, he came closer than ever to a 'turn-up' with Holmes. 'For two pins, Dr Watson, I should have refused point-blank to have anything more to do with this madcap business.' The detective officer had lost almost all confidence in his temporary employer. Even the unmasking of Harry Benson had led only to the trickster's escape.

At length, on Holmes's insistence, Lestrade asked for a telegraph message to be wired urgently to Scotland Yard. When the form was provided, Holmes wrote upon it in bold pencilled capitals.

HENRY BENSON, ALIAS MONTGOMERY, ALIAS THE MARQUIS MONTMORENCY, NOW IN CUSTODY HERE STOP. AWAITING INSTRUCTIONS STOP.

Then he addressed it carefully to the duty-officer of the Detective Division, and marked it 'Most Immediate'.

Lestrade stared at the message. In a shadowy corner of the Islington police-station charge-room, there was a muttered exchange.

'But he's not in custody, Mr Holmes! You know he isn't!'

'Nor ever will be, Lestrade, so long as you continue to obstruct my investigation.'

'But what's the use?'

'It has many uses,' said Holmes, in the same muttering tone, 'one of them being to save your career and possibly to keep you out of prison.'

At this point, Lestrade concluded that his mentor had gone off his head or that, in any case, argument was useless. The wire was sent. Twenty minutes later, the reply rattled out. Holmes read it and showed it to his companion.

FIND THAT BENSON IS NOT THE MAN WE WANT STOP. RELEASE FROM CUSTODY STOP = CARTER, INSPECTOR, SCOTLAND YARD.

Lestrade looked up with a terrible realization dawning in his dark eyes.

'Carter? I have never heard of any Inspector Carter!'

'No,' said Holmes grimly, 'nor has anyone else. However, I would scarcely expect our correspondent to put his own name to this. I had intended to leave the arrest of Benson and Kurr until tomorrow but you may be sure that before this wire was sent to us another was despatched to them, advising them to get out of the country at once.'

'You know where they are?'

Holmes paused, then he said, 'They are not unfamiliar to me. Unless I am greatly mistaken, they are in a house owned by Kurr at Canonbury, packing their traps. To say that there is not a moment to lose is generally an exaggeration. On the present occasion it is correct. Gather all the men you can from this division and we shall do this thing by dark. They cannot expect us yet.'

Twenty minutes later a dozen helmeted officers followed Holmes and Lestrade through the darkened avenues of Canonbury.

'How could you know where to find him?' Lestrade asked uneasily.

'Benson has a villa on the Isle of Wight. They would scarcely have gone there at this time of night. Billy Kurr is a bookmaker and the owner of two racehorses. The names of the animals and their proprietor are to be found in the breeders guide. Ah, yes! The Laurels, if I am not mistaken.'

They were standing at the gateway of a house set back at the end of a long drive. Through the fir trees and the laurel shrubberies, Holmes could make out a long veranda with two doors and several windows opening on to it. There were lights on behind two of the three windows, though the curtains were drawn. With Lestrade and two of the senior men from Canonbury, he went on ahead. They walked on the wet grass to one side of the drive to silence their footsteps. It was not difficult to keep the thick laurel bushes between themselves and the windows. Yet the wind was so strong that evening and its gusts moved the branches so erratically that it was hard to tell whether anyone was concealed ahead of them.

Where the drive curved to the left, towards the portico of the house, Lestrade was suddenly blinded by a magnesium brilliance. He could hear his antagonist but it was impossible to see him through the glare. Holmes had stopped, his hand shielding his eyes. The flare illuminated him like a stage spotlight. At that moment there was a crash that made his ears ring. The bullet made a sharp crack as it chipped a stone wall.

Lestrade and the two men from 'N' Division threw themselves flat. Holmes remained upright, without the least movement, like a predator about to spring. Lestrade assured me that he could swear our friend's pulse did not change nor did that steely resolve falter as a second bullet flew past him.

Holmes, however, paid no less a tribute to the Scotland Yard man. Lestrade was on his feet again. He scarcely raised his voice, yet his words rapped across that damp shrubbery as plain and ominous as the bullets.

'Don't be a fool, Billy Kurr! This means murder!'

There was no sound nor movement.

'You haven't got enough bullets in that gun for us all, Billy! One of us will catch you if the others don't. And if it comes to that, you'll hang long and hard!'

There was a long minute of silence. Lestrade spoke again, as if someone had just given him news.

'Give it up, Billy! The others have taken Benson! You can't do it on your own!'

A man walked towards them slowly from the light. Billy Kurr stopped and looked at Lestrade. Then he looked at Sherlock Holmes, who said not a word, and then at the other men barring the driveway. Lestrade, lean and grim, was the hero of the hour.

'It's no good, Billy. The game's over.'

Kurr, in the same dog's-tooth check and gripping the revolver that he had held on them in the hotel-room, stretched out his hand and surrendered the weapon to Lestrade.

The other men came into the glare of the lamp.

'You haven't got Benson,' said Kurr sadly. 'You couldn't have. He's still in the house.'

Sherlock Holmes nodded to Lestrade. He walked forward with long easy strides, pushing open a veranda door to claim the fugitive.

## XI

The scandal that broke in the wake of these arrests filled every newspaper in October 1877, when a third of the Detective Division of Scotland Yard stood in the dock of the Central Criminal Court. Both Sergeant Meiklejohn and Inspector Clarke, the second-in-command of the division, were among them.

Benson and Kurr had already gone to prison for a string of frauds so long that there is scarcely room to recite them here. As Mycroft Holmes had told his brother, the Society for Insuring Against Losses on the Turf and the City of Paris Loan were only the two latest in a series stretching back for many years. No sooner were the criminals in custody, however, than Harry

Benson offered the authorities what he called 'Flower Show Information'.

Believing that his Scotland Yard officers, whom he had bribed and entertained so lavishly over the years, had deserted and deceived him, Benson gave his gaolers the full story of systematic corruption within the Detective Division. In Edinburgh and other cities he had practised the boldest and most widespread swindles, knowing that he had only to run back to London to be safe. From police forces throughout the land, even from the Continent, had come letters and wires to Scotland Yard, naming Harry Benson and Billy Kurr as the wanted men. One after another these messages were destroyed by officers so steeped in corruption that to turn back was more perilous than to continue. Detectives and criminals alike stood in fear of their crimes being brought to justice.

Holmes took little pleasure in witnessing the tragedy of such men as Clarke and Meiklejohn. Yet the consequence was that he now established himself as a confidant of Superintendent Williamson and the senior echelons of the Metropolitan Police. Inspector Lestrade, in his new rank, was vindicated as an honest and able officer, despite the occasional strictures passed upon him by Sherlock Holmes. Indeed, though the old structure of the Detective Police was abolished and a new Criminal Investigation Department set up, Lestrade was first to be a senior inspector in the newly-created Special Branch, whose activities were naturally of great interest to Sherlock Holmes.

I have always thought that the arrest of Benson and Kurr, as well as the cleansing of 'Williamson's Augean Stables', to use Holmes's term for it, was the culmination of my friend's early career. Within a fortnight of being called upon, his skill had put an end to the most dangerous series of frauds and rooted out corruption at the heart of Scotland Yard. In dealing with the swindlers, his keen mind had seen where the weakest point of his antagonists lay. He knew that a sharper like Benson would never be able to resist a 'mug' like James Lester Valence. Taking the jeweller Regnier into his confidence, Holmes had laid his snare with a skill that few confidence men could have rivalled. He assured me he knew, before he started, that 'Poodle' Benson had performed a similar trick on a wealthy American in Paris. The chance to repeat it in London would therefore be irresistible. My friend would tell his story, chuckle, and then say, 'I don't mind confessing to you, Watson, I have always had an idea that I would have made a highly efficient criminal.'

For that reason alone, he was a match for Harry Benson and Billy Kurr. Perhaps, in describing his triumph over them at the Charing Cross Hotel, he might better have called his adventure, 'The Case of the Biter Bit'.

# The Case of the Naked Bicyclists

## I

It was very seldom that I felt a sense of oppression during the tenancy of our Baker Street rooms. However, the visit of Mr William Coote, Solicitor to the National Vigilance Association, scarcely promised to be a light-hearted affair.

Holmes and I had met Mr Coote several years previously in the matter of a forged will. During that transaction, the lawyer elicited that Holmes had been a friend and admirer of the late Sir Richard Burton, renowned as an explorer, anthropologist and translator of *The Arabian Nights*. Mr Coote had heard that Lady Burton intended to dispose of a manuscript of her husband's, Sir Richard's translation of *The Perfumed Garden*, a somewhat racy classic of Arabian love-literature. Mr Coote expressed great interest in purchasing this rarity.

We assumed that Coote intended to publish this work in a learned edition or perhaps to offer the autograph to the British Museum. What was our horror on hearing that the relic had been bought so that he and his confounded vigilance association might commit it to the flames! The burning of any book, let alone this monument to a friend's labours, was an abomination to Sherlock Holmes.

It had therefore taken some persuasion before my friend would consent to receive Mr Coote in his consulting-rooms. Had it not been for the inertia of the criminal classes in the warm summer weather, and the tedium consequent upon this, Holmes would scarcely have bothered to listen to Coote's submission. As it was, he promised 'to hear what the wretched fellow has to say'. I quite expected him to grant Coote an audience merely for the pleasure of telling him to go to the devil. Indeed, I believe that had been his intention. As for Miss Pierce, the client who accompanied her legal adviser to Baker Street, she was described as the tenant of a grim, remotely-situated house near Saffron Walden, and a warm supporter of the Vigilance Association.

It is seldom that two people look so absurd, side by side, as this couple appeared. Mr Coote, with his ample watch-chained waistcoat, large head, mournful moustache, and a soulful superiority in his brown eyes, brought to my mind Mr Chadband in *Bleak House*: 'A large, greasy, self-satisfied man, of no particular denomination'. Whether the lawyer's baritone voice sounded unctuous or melodious must be a matter of taste.

Miss Pierce was a starveling sparrow paired with a glossy crow. She was a lady of middle years, slight and frail, the type who is destined to outlive us all. She wore a grey old-fashioned bonnet, trimmed with mauve and white silk flowers, a specimen of headgear whose very fit was tight and mean. Her features were strict and almost motionless. Such movement as there was came principally from the glint of her spectacle-lenses in gold-wire frames.

After Holmes had waved them to their chairs, Mr Coote presented his client's complaint. Miss Pierce said little, except that she had a curious habit of echoing softly what she considered the most important word in the lawyer's previous sentence, lest Holmes should miss it. Sometimes she gave sound to the word. Where the utterance was repugnant, her pursed lips formed the syllables with significant emphasis but no voice. Mr Coote cleared his throat deeply and significantly, as if to launch into an aria beside a piano and a fern.

'Miss Pierce, as I indicated in my letter Mr Holmes, has been much troubled in past weeks – months I might say – by the indelicate conduct of her neighbour.'

'Indelicate,' mouthed Miss Pierce in her slight, bird-like tone, 'yes.'

'My client is a maiden lady, living alone, but for the company of a single servant-woman.'

'Servant,' Miss Pierce murmured, with an eye to the niceties of social class.

'My client's residence lies in a remote part of Essex, separated by a field and a rivulet from the adjoining property of Coldhams Farm. It is six-and-a-half miles from Saffron Walden, eight-and-a-half from Bishop's Stortford. From the railway at Audley End, it is four miles, twelve hundred and twenty-seven yards.'

I guessed that these meticulous measurements would prove a useful means for Mr Coote to run up a tidy little bill at Miss Pierce's expense.

'I find it curious,' said Holmes quietly, 'that such care has been taken over these distances and none at all as to that between your client and the house at Coldhams Farm.'

Mr Coote gave a faint but satisfied smile.

'Mr Holmes, we should require permission to go upon Captain Dougal's land. My client would rather not make such a request.'

'Rather not,' echoed Miss Pierce nervously.

'Very well,' Holmes shrugged, as if it did not much matter, since he might give Coote his marching orders at any minute. 'Pray continue if you wish to.'

'Captain Dougal,' said the lawyer, frowning at such levity, 'is the proprietor of Coldhams Farm, scarcely more than a small-holding. The offence alleged is one of the most blatant indecency.'

'Blatant!' Miss Pierce mouthed the word silently but with a significant nod.

'I venture to think,' said Coote in a silkier Chadband voice, 'that it may in all probability be a case of devil-worship.'

At this point, Holmes ceased lounging and sat up.

'Pray do continue, Mr Coote.'

'Dougal is a man of bad character and evil reputation with young women. In the three years he has lived at the farm, no less than four paternity summonses have been served upon him on behalf of young women of the labouring class.'

'Summonses!' Miss Pierce gave a satisfied nod at the memory of seeing justice done.

'Female servants have come and gone. Respectable girls are soon fetched away by their families. Those of no character remain until they depart to childbed. It is common knowledge that while there were two sisters in his employ, he had his way with one of them in the very presence of the other.'

Miss Pierce looked quickly at the three of us, finding no word that could be decently echoed.

'Forgive me,' said Holmes with the faintest hint of malice, 'I take it that your client does not seek a post as servant in Captain Dougal's household. Nor is she of the labouring class. I daresay that Captain Dougal is as you paint him. However, there is surely nothing in law that even such a man as he may not live on land adjoining Miss Pierce's.'

'It is a matter of the bicyclists in the field, Mr Holmes, if it is not indeed something worse,' Mr Coote said abruptly.

Miss Pierce looked at us significantly. Holmes stared at Mr Coote.

'I see – or, rather I do not see. What bicyclists in which field?'

The solicitor assumed the expression of a man weighted with grief.

'This scoundrel, Dougal, leads a life of unrepentant viciousness and unexampled impiety. In such a remote part of the county, it is not difficult for a rascal of a little wealth and plausible manner to entice the ruder and more rustic young women into his repellent practices. I concede that what he does in his own house is something difficult to control. What he does in the open air, in the public view, is quite another matter. I speak of Captain Dougal and a dozen of the village girls, as they perform their lewd ceremonies in the field adjacent to Miss Pierce's land.'

Miss Pierce gave us a flash of her spectacles.

'Like Satan at a witches' coven,' Mr Coote continued,

'this man spends his nights training these female clod-hoppers as a team of naked bicyclists!'

'Naked!' Miss Pierce's lips formed the word sound-lessly but with great vigour.

Holmes and I avoided one another's eyes, though I confess I was reduced to the expedient of vigorous nose-blowing.

'Dear me,' said Holmes at length, addressing Mr Coote and avoiding Miss Pierce, as seemed to be her wish. 'Then you already have the remedy at hand, my dear sir. The rural constabulary, though slow in acting upon information received, may generally be relied upon in the long run. There are laws of public nuis-ance, are there not? There are statutes to punish in-decent display.'

'Exactly!'

'Then surely, my dear sir, you have your answer.'

Mr Coote shook his head.

'No, Mr Holmes. You misunderstand me. If Miss Pierce were to lay an information in that way, she must be drawn into the centre of the scandal, for these particular activities in the field affect only her. Pub-licity could scarcely be avoided. Suppose that it should be, as I suppose, some form of diabolism! Greatly though I sympathize with my client . . .'

Miss Pierce nodded emphatically.

' . . . it would scarcely do for the name of a legal adviser to the National Vigilance Association to be quoted in such a context. There are not wanting those who would mock, Mr Holmes!'

There was a silence while Miss Pierce looked round at us all and waited.

'Am I to take it,' said Holmes slowly, 'that you

propose my name as the centrepiece of this bicycling scandal?'

Mr Coote had the grace to look a little embarrassed. 'You are known as a detective, Mr Holmes. Your name has been associated with murder, robbery, blackmail, adultery, espionage. It would do you no harm and, I say without doubt, you would put a stop to these insults easily enough.'

'Indeed!'

'Chivalry will remind you, Mr Holmes, how much a lady of gentle ways like Miss Pierce would suffer. The local esteem in which she is held would be compromised by association with such proceedings. Of course, if you will not take the case, you will not. I urge it as a matter of respect for gentility, sir.'

Miss Pierce performed a brief cat-like and confidential closing of the eyes.

Sherlock Holmes reached for his pipe. Miss Pierce uttered a quick cough-like sound of alarm. He withdrew his hand.

'Tell me, Mr Coote. What precisely takes place in the field at night?'

'As I understand it, Mr Holmes, these women are entirely naked. They disport themselves in gross rituals, forming a circle about the evil one, if I may so term him. Captain Dougal stands at the centre and commands their depravities.'

'I do not quite follow you. How does he command them?'

'I believe he shouts at them,' said Mr Coote self-consciously. 'He tells them what to do.'

'And what do they do?'

'I understand that they perform lewd acrobatic

postures upon bicycles,' said Mr Coote, a little angry at this continued cross-questioning.

'Postures,' Miss Pierce confirmed.

'Dear me,' Holmes said, as if the outrage were beyond anything he had supposed, 'and what costume does Captain Dougal wear?'

'None,' said Mr Coote snappishly. 'He stands there quite naked!'

'Quite!' said Miss Pierce, sharp in her turn.

'In a state of gross and rude excitement,' added Coote portentously.

After twenty minutes more of this sort of thing, Mr Coote and Miss Pierce took their departure. Sherlock Holmes had yet to commit himself but assured them that he would give their request, that he should make an immediate visit to the neighbourhood of Coldhams Farm, his most careful consideration. As soon as they had gone, I turned to my friend in some indignation.

'I call that the most infernal cheek! To come with such a story, when they had only to go to the police-station at Saffron Walden! Do they suppose we have nothing better to do with our time than follow a goose-chase of this kind?'

Holmes was lounging in the old-fashioned chair, filling his pipe in earnest.

'You are quite right, my dear fellow. It is absurd, is it not? That is half its attraction. It verges upon the pathological. Indeed, there is an item in the works of the great German baron upon *equus eroticus*. Unless I am much mistaken, Watson, there lurks in that bleak fenland a criminality of which Mr Coote and Miss Pierce have never dreamt. I doubt if there could be better use of our time than a visit to this bucolic Lothario and his bumpkins.'

I feared there would be something like this, as soon as I heard a suggestion of devil-worship.

'I don't see it,' I said impatiently.

He chuckled.

'I daresay not, my dear old Watson. We will reflect, and then discuss it again this evening. For the moment, let us just take the precaution of consulting Bradshaw upon the trains between Liverpool Street and Bishop's Stortford. In this instance, I believe the Cambridge line will prove the most convenient.'

## II

After so much scoffing at the absurdity of Miss Pierce's complaint, I do not think that in all my life I was so occupied as in the next few weeks. Two days later, Holmes and I stepped from the train at Bishop's Stortford to be met by Henry Pilgrim's pony and trap, commandeered as a cab in this flat desolate country. We drove through summer fenland for several miles, the hedges white with hawthorn blossom, at first following the railway line where it ran northwards to Cambridge. Then our driver veered briskly into a lane, which soon forked into a smaller lane, then into a track that was scarcely a lane at all.

Ahead of us I glimpsed, through a screen of trees, the outline of a modest farmhouse with a steep dark roof, diamond-patterned by tiles of a lighter red. There was a yard in front of the door. A narrow water-filled moat appeared to surround the property, with a screen of dark firs and stunted apple-trees that made a gloomy enclosure even on a sunny afternoon. I supposed that this must be Miss Pierce's residence but our driver pointed his whip as we clattered past and said confidentially, 'Captain Dougal, Coldhams Farm.'

I suppose a further half-mile passed before we turned into a by-way of trim hedges and clipped verges, ending at our client's porch.

'It seems a good distance between the properties for her to see from one to the other, with the light failing,' I said to Holmes sceptically.

He glanced round.

'I daresay it does. If you will observe the lie of the land, however, the field surrounding Coldhams Farm comes out almost as far as this.'

So much for our arrival. As I feared, the grim outer landscape of fens and drainage ditches was a pinprick compared to the comfortless domestic economy of Miss Pierce. Supper was a spartan celebration of boiled cod and hard peas, which I should prefer to forget and could not eat. When I murmured a complaint to Holmes, he merely said, 'Since the mental faculties become refined and sharpened by starvation, I suppose one should not object to such a bill of fare. It has often crossed my mind, Watson, to remind you that what the digestion gains from the blood supply is lost to the brain.'

It was then almost ten o'clock and we were led by Miss Pierce and Mr Coote to a room at the attic level. From this vantage, we were to keep observation that evening, and all night if need be.

'Forgive me,' said Holmes, as he passed to a round-arched landing window at the level of the main bedrooms, 'surely one's view of Captain Dougal's field is blocked at this height by the lime tree and the beech?'

Mr Coote looked as if he were dealing with a simpleton.

'Of course it is, Mr Holmes. It is from the top floor that one sees the performances of Captain Dougal and his harlots.'

Holmes and I glanced at one another but made no reply. We followed our guides up a narrower set of bare wooden stairs to a box-room at the level of the attics. A single camp-bed with three army 'biscuits' as a mattress was the sole concession to sleep. At this level, it was true, a window looked directly across the field to the little moat and the dark stifling fir trees of Coldhams Farm, almost half a mile away. In the foreground a waning half-moon glimmered on reedy pools and patches of mud in the intervening pasture. Black trees stood low on a vast horizon and the dim figures of cattle were visible here and there.

I do not know how long we waited, with the intense silence of that landscape weighing upon us. I thought of Baker Street and how we should now be taking a glass of something warm in the company of Inspector Lestrade and hearing news of Scotland Yard. At length Mr Coote said, 'See for yourself!'

I looked at the field before me but saw only the grey outlines of cattle. Even Holmes, as he narrowed his keen eyes, looked puzzled.

'I see nothing,' I said gruffly.

'Of course you do not!' said Miss Pierce angrily. 'Not here! Over there! Take these! And stand up there!'

With that she handed me a pair of binoculars whose variable lenses included a pair for night vision. They were such glasses as would only be used by a serving officer on campaign – or a troublesome crone determined to spy on the world after dark. She also indicated a stout wooden shoe-box, necessary to increase her own diminutive height as observer but scarcely for us.

What Holmes and I saw – through a glass most darkly – was a foggy impression of Dougal and his rustic wenches two or three hundred yards away. There was an occasional call or cry and a fleeting drift of laughter. What I saw might have been libidinous, had it not been so absurd and indistinct. Half a dozen clod-hopping young females were riding bicycles with a little difficulty over the fenland turf.

At this distance, it seemed that each young equestrienne had been chosen for her ample or muscular form, each pair of haunches more than overlapping the saddle while strapping legs strove to drive the pedals. From time to time, one or other of these rustic valkyries would attempt to perform some mildly acrobatic feat in response to the command of her ringmaster, and several fell off. Since the turf was soft, I suppose it was little hardship.

At the centre of this ensemble stood a tall and portly man with dark hair and an abundant beard. He was completely naked and, unless my eyes deceived me in such obscurity, both his face and his loins suggested a state of priapic frenzy.

Though I am conscious that I may already have described too fully a scene which would better remain veiled, some account of it is necessary to an understanding of what followed. Our hosts retired, leaving Holmes and I to perform the rest of this ridiculous sentry-go. From our observation, it was supposed that we were to present a complaint against Dougal – in our own names, so that the modest cheeks of Miss Pierce or Mr Coote should not be brought to the blush. What fools they were making of us!

As soon as we were alone together I swore to Holmes that I should return to London the next morning. If necessary, I would go alone. My friend was convulsed with laughter, struggling not to allow his eruptions of mirth to be heard all over the house.

'That woman cannot see so far as her own end of the field but by climbing up a window in the attic,' I said furiously. 'Even then she can make nothing out except with military binoculars. Do not tell me, Holmes, that her maiden modesty is insulted! She has done everything to ensure that she may not miss a single lewdness! I daresay the whisper of her conduct has got round the neighbourhood, so we are now brought in to save her reputation.'

For reasons which I could not have anticipated, however, we did not go back to London the next day. At breakfast, while the servant was replenishing the coffee-pot, I remarked to Holmes that the case against Dougal was a fuss about nothing. I did this in the hope that Miss Pierce, who was in the adjoining parlour with Mr Coote, might hear me – or that if she did not hear herself, the honest servant would repeat my words to her. The servant, a round-faced aproned body, put down the pot and said, 'Never mind those young trollops on the bicycles, sir. You ask him where that poor gentle soul Miss Holland went to. She's gone a year or two now and never been seen nor heard from since.'

The change in Sherlock Holmes was characteristic.

His back straightened, his features were as still as carved ivory while he listened to her. Then he said softly, 'Tell me about Miss Holland, if you will.'

The woman looked towards the parlour, where lurked Miss Pierce and the lawyer.

'I can't tell you more, sir. All I say is that such a refined and gentle lady as she was, she went unaccountably away without a word and never came back. Not a word of warning. As if she'd been swept off the face of the earth.'

'Will you not, at least, tell me who she was?'

Now there was no mistaking a mixture of triumph and contempt in the servant's face.

'Mrs Dougal, she liked to call herself, until the real Mrs Dougal come and put a stop to it all.'

'Then it is scarcely surprising that she should vanish, is it?' I suggested.

But the woman would say no more, beyond murmuring significantly that she knew the value of her place and the cost of an action for slander with which Captain Dougal had threatened others. Miss Pierce, when asked about Miss Holland, professed to know nothing about the dealings of the captain with any of his women.

'Such creatures come and go at Coldhams week by week! How should anybody know which is which? Mrs Dougal? They'd all be Mrs Dougals, if they had their way. As it is, there's half a dozen that must have borne his children but don't bear his name.'

Breakfast had been little more than bread and gruel, accompanied by coffee whose odour was chiefly of dandelions and chicory. Nothing would persuade me to spend another day under Miss Pierce's roof. I had gone to pack my overnight things. Holmes announced his intention of taking his morning pipe out of doors, smoking being forbidden on Miss Pierce's premises.

I finished my preparations and waited. A full hour passed as I stood at the window of that uncarpeted and unpainted box-room, staring morosely across the fenland that glimmered in the morning sun. The dark trees screened Captain Dougal's property and his rustic harem from the world. There are those who, in the smoking-rooms of their clubs, might chaff one another about the captain's midnight romps with country lasses. To such vulgar souls, the promiscuous intercourse of Dougal and his bicyclists seems no more shocking than the couplings of bull and cow. Perhaps it was my mood that morning, or perhaps it was the flat and unfrequented countryside before me, that made Coldhams Farm appear at that moment one of the darkest and most sinister retreats upon this earth.

It was quite an hour and half before I heard Holmes climbing the attic stairs. He threw open the door, looking extraordinarily pleased with himself.

'I think we shall move on,' he said cheerfully.

'Do you mean to return to London?'

He sat down on the only chair, an abandoned relic of the dining-room, and began to refill his tobacco-pouch.

'Not quite, Watson. However, I have found a far more agreeable lodging from which we may continue our observation.'

'Why continue it? Have we not seen everything there is to see?'

He frowned and put away the pouch.

'I should have thought so until this morning. Yet

something in my bones forbids me to abandon this investigation just yet.'

'Miss Holland?'

'Precisely.'

'But what have we to do with Miss Holland?'

'Possibly nothing, Watson. Ladies may vanish and never be heard of again in the place where they were. That is quite true. The naked cyclists are exciting only to a sterile soul like Miss Pierce and a pompous buffoon like Mr Coote. Put it all together, however, add the gloomy spirit of Coldhams Farm, and I should never rest quite easily if I returned to London today.'

'Then you feel it?' I asked eagerly. 'The sinister air that the place has, so remote, so enclosed, like something out of . . .'

'A gothic romance?' he suggested with a laugh.

'But where shall we find rooms? We must be miles from anywhere.'

'It is arranged. Moat Farm takes in paying guests. I am to be Professor Holmes, holder of a chair of entomology at Cambridge, here for a few days' holiday, and you – well, naturally, my dear fellow – you are Dr Watson.'

'Where is Moat Farm?'

'Very close. We passed it yesterday.'

For a moment I was puzzled and then a doubt clouded my mind.

'You don't mean . . .'

'Moat Farm,' said Holmes simply, 'is the name that Captain Dougal gave to Coldhams when he purchased it.'

## III

'Impossible!'

'Hear what I have to say,' Holmes suggested soothingly. 'Dougal is not the particular villain that Coote and Miss Pierce have painted, though he seems to have arrogated the rank of captain to himself. In many respects, he is thought to have led a blameless, even estimable, life. He is spoken of at Quendon, in the Hare and Hounds, as a very decent fellow.'

'He did not seem so last night!'

'You have never seen the man. Can you swear that the creature was Dougal? Perhaps, if it was he, there is still a better side to the man. Even you, Watson, can scarcely believe that those bicycling antics amount to devil worship! That is all Coote's nonsense.'

'A better side to him?'

Holmes stood up and crossed to the window.

'What would you say as an army man, Watson, to a fellow who had served for twenty-two years in the Royal Engineers, earned a pension for it, and was described on his discharge sheet as being of excellent character?'

'How have you seen his discharge sheet? Or how do you know what is said about him in a public house?'

'I spoke to the landlord, with whom I fell in during my stroll. As for the discharge sheet, Dougal himself showed it to me.' Holmes turned from the window. 'He takes in paying guests, has rooms vacant, and produces his army record to seal the bargain.'

Despite my misgivings over Coldhams Farm, I relented a little towards its owner.

'I have still half a mind to go back to London this morning.'

Holmes sighed.

'One more thing, before you do. On my little walk, I spoke to two other folk who happened to pass me. They do not seem to like Captain Dougal much. For that matter, nor are they much smitten with Miss Pierce. One of them, however, also recalled Miss Holland and the abrupt manner of her departure from Dougal's household. If my informant is correct, there was talk of foul play at the time and the matter was investigated by the local police. They were convinced that there was nothing sinister in Miss Holland's departure.'

I moved towards my leather bag.

'Then it is high time we were on our way.'

Holmes touched his finger to his lips.

'One moment, friend Watson. Do I assume that you now regard a rustic police force as the last word upon a lady's disappearance?'

'Unless there is evidence to the contrary in this case.'

'There is a further puzzle in this, more suited to the alienist than to a police officer. I am told that Miss Camille Holland was a genteel spinster, quite fifty, older than Captain Dougal. In religion, she adhered to the quaint London sect of the Catholic Apostolic Church in Gordon Square. A devout lady of some means, her family consisting of two nephews with whom she rarely communicated.'

'Scarcely surprising, then, that no one knows where she went.'

'One moment more. There was, it seems, another side to Miss Holland. She was quite fifty. Yet her hair was coloured and styled, her face was improved, in such a way that she looked some ten years younger. She strove also, they say, to wear the trousers. Our fading spinster relished equally the roles of vamp and martinet. Aphrodite and a dash of Juno.'

'My dear Holmes, this is nothing. A woman of some maturity may surely try to make herself look less than her age. As for the martinet, women who are uncertain with men, or lack experience, sometimes take refuge in a maternal authority. Miss Holland's type is not at all uncommon. I see no puzzle.'

'The puzzle,' said he, 'is what such a ladylike, refined, devout creature was doing in the arms of a reprobate like Dougal.'

'Perhaps she was not in his arms.'

'Why, then, did she bother to present herself as Mrs Dougal to everyone in the neighbourhood?'

I shrugged and gave it up.

'Unfortunately, Holmes, you and I have reason to know that refined, ladylike creatures are not infrequently drawn to reprobates and ruffians rather than to men of their own kind. I can tell you no more than that.'

He stared from the window at the wide sky and the vast fenland horizon.

'It is true,' he conceded, 'that the most abandoned female lusts often thrive more vigorously in the schoolhouse or the rectory than in any den of thieves. How curious, however, if she should be buried somewhere out there.'

'If it is so, and if we stay under that fellow's roof, we may soon be buried out there ourselves. We have already missed the best morning train from Bishop's

Stortford. At this rate, we shall miss the 1.30 from Cambridge to Liverpool Street as well.'

But even as I spoke, I knew that Holmes would not leave matters as they were. I knew also that I could not return to London without him.

## IV

Closer acquaintance with Dougal and Coldhams Farm did not reconcile me to either. He was a large man with an abundant head of hair, a brown pointed beard somewhat streaked with grey, brows high and slanting. His eyes were almost Mongolian in shape and had a cruelly humorous look. I fear he laughed at the world rather than with it. Despite Holmes's suggestion, he was at once identifiable as the figure standing among naked bicyclists the previous night.

No doubt this owner of the farm, with a little money in hand, would be thought a good fellow in the public house where he stood drinks to the locals. At home, two lumbering young servants, Sally and Agnes, attended the captain and his guests. I cannot say that I witnessed improprieties between the young women and their employer, yet the glances between them were more eloquent than spoken assignations or invitations. The nocturnal orgy in the field was not repeated during our stay. Even Dougal was not blatant enough to amuse himself a few yards from the windows of his guests. I supposed that he took his bicycling troupe elsewhere for the duration of our visit.

I concede at once that the food and accommodation proved in every way superior to Miss Pierce's joyless fare. Captain Dougal ate separately but our table was plentifully supplied with well-cooked dishes and local ale.

'Professor' Holmes of Cambridge was also masquerading as an amateur lepidopterist. Therefore, next morning, we set out for Bishop's Stortford to procure a butterfly-net, a chloroform bottle, and a specimen case. Holmes then took the precaution of despatching a telegram to Lestrade at Scotland Yard. I caught only the last line. REPLY CARE OF MARDEN, ESSEX CONSTABULARY, SAFFRON WALDEN STOP. LETTER FOLLOWS STOP.

That afternoon, Holmes went off, conspicuously alone, in tweed-suit and gaiters, deer-stalker, magnifying-glass in hand, butterfly net upon his shoulder. His satchel contained the killing-bottle and specimen case. The hedges were bright with white flowers in May sun, the little rivers well-watered.

I made a survey of our quarters. Moat Farm, as Dougal called it, was surrounded by twenty feet of lawn. Beyond that, the entire plot was cut off by the moat, several feet wide and well-filled. A single footbridge crossed the water to the farm-yard, with its cowshed and an annexe for the pony-trap. Beyond a screen of trees lay a pond and barn, then the open stretches of flat pasture stretched to the very horizon.

Next morning, with sandwiches and a flask, we started together in our search for Purple Emperors and Marbled Whites. Once out of sight of the farm, Holmes took a field-path that led to the village of Quendon. A few minutes more and we had negotiated the hire of a horse and trap. By eleven, we faced Inspector Marden at the table of the interview room in Saffron Walden police-station. Marden was a tall cadaverous man with a look of gloom that might have graced a professional pall-bearer. Yet he was a decent enough fellow, who spoke quietly and made his arguments with care. Before he had finished, I was sure we must pack our bags and go home, for all the good we should do here.

'I don't see it, Mr Holmes,' he said cautiously, 'Miss Holland left Captain Dougal, as all his ladies seem to do sooner or later. There was talk at the time, there always is. Inquiries were made and they proved entirely to our satisfaction. We made them discreetly, of course. I don't suppose he or she knew of them.'

'But not so discreetly made as ours may be,' Holmes said quickly, 'for we are under the man's roof.'

'So you may be, sir. A police force, however, is not to engage upon espionage. Nor, if you take my advice, will you.'

'Where did she go?'

'I understand she left Captain Dougal to travel abroad with another man. She was to join him on a yacht, I was told. Just before she left, Miss Holland bought new clothes accordingly. The captain had no reason to get rid of her, for as long as she was with him, her money was there.'

'Did he have much need of it?'

Marden pulled a face.

'I can't see he did, Mr Holmes. He owns the farm outright, or did when we made inquiries. Since then, he always seems well-breeched, as they say.'

'And what of her money now?'

'She does not draw directly at the bank, but then she never did. The last we heard, Miss Holland was drawing by cheque so that it went to wherever she might be or to whomever had to be paid. When necessary, she would write for a new cheque-book. Her family bankers are the National Provincial in Piccadilly. Her stockbrokers are Messrs Hart of Old Broad Street in the City of London. She dealt with them both long after she left here. Mr Hensler, her broker, and Mr Ashwin, the senior accountant of the National Provincial, both swore that the signatures on her cheques and letters match the specimen signature she gave at the bank a little before she left here. We asked advice from our handwriting experts. They confirm it.'

'These signatures . . .'

'Ah, yes, Mr Holmes. Your reputation goes before you.'

Marden managed a dry smile as he opened a drawer and shook several photographs from an envelope. They were exact confidential copies, taken from the files for our benefit. I could see plainly the specimen in the book and the signatures on the cheques. 'Camille C. Holland'. There was a further photograph of a demure woman, slightly-built and pretty, her fine hair elegantly-coiffeured.

'Golden-haired,' I said at a guess, feeling sure it was so.

'So she was, Dr Watson, and may be still.'

Holmes studied the prints through his glass for several minutes. Then he looked up.

'It pains me to say so, Mr Marden, but there can be no doubt that the hand which wrote the signatures upon the cheques is also that which provided the specimen in the book.'

'There you have it, sir,' said the inspector philosophically. 'If that is her signature, then she was certainly still alive a little while ago, two years and more after the rumours began.'

Holmes nodded. He put away his glass and picked up his hat.

'You are a busy man, inspector, and we will take up no more of your time. I shall communicate with Lestrade directly.'

As Marden led us to the police-station entrance I felt a mixture of regret for my friend's disappointment and relief that we might see our comfortable quarters in Baker Street that evening. As we stood with the inspector upon the steps, Holmes said casually, 'Tell me, did your informants recall any other event about the time Miss Holland attended the bank to sign the specimen book?'

Marden looked blank for a moment, then he nodded.

'There was one matter, though of little relevance. Just before this, her younger nephew's little girl had died. Miss Holland was much affected by the child's death and wrote very kindly to her nephew. However, Mr Holland recalled that his aunt did not attend the funeral. Perhaps she feared questions about her removal to Quendon, or suspicions that she had taken a lover. I fear that will not help you much, Mr Holmes.'

'I daresay not,' he remarked cheerfully. On walking back to the waiting horse and trap, I noticed with misgiving that his step was far jauntier than upon our arrival. When we were out of earshot of Inspector Marden, he turned to me.

'She is out there, Watson!' he said softly, 'I thought so once – and now I know it!'

# V

How he could know anything of the sort from Inspector Marden's answers was quite beyond me. Holmes, as usual, preserved an infuriating silence upon the matter, which was usually the prelude to some startling discovery. That afternoon, he set off alone again with his net and satchel. As he passed the wicket gate of the bridge across the little moat and strode towards the sunlight of the pale green fens, he had altered nothing in his dress or physical appearance. Yet, suddenly, he was every inch the professor from Cambridge, as if he could never have been anything else.

He returned half an hour before dinner. There was not a butterfly to be seen in his killing-bottle, for he abominated the destruction of such beautiful creatures. Instead, there reposed the remains of a most unpromising insect which appeared to be a cross between a daddy-longlegs and a dark brown moth. I am no expert on the vast insect population of the English fields and had not, so far as I was aware, ever noticed this one in my travels. Holmes said nothing further and I was not disposed to inquire. When I went to rouse him from his room, as the gong sounded downstairs, I found him with the creature lying on a square of white paper, his pipe in his mouth and his magnifying-glass closely applied to the remains. From time to time, he would jot a note and then resume his scrutiny.

Jaded by the collapse of our adventure, I retired after dinner with a copy of the *Lancet* and an article upon Richet's discovery of abnormal sensitivities to the anti-diphtheria serum, a matter of possible interest in my own practice. A little after ten o'clock, I was aware of voices below me, a burst of dull-witted laughter, a gate closing, and then silence. Absorbed in my journal, I paid no attention. A moment later there was a thundering on my door. Before I could reply, Holmes had thrown it open.

'Get up, Watson! Quickly, man! We must make the most of every minute.'

'To what end?'

'To search the house, of course! We are alone here for the moment, unless Miss Holland – or rather some other woman of his – should be a prisoner or a corpse within these walls. He has gone out with those two young women, his servants. I swear that they and the others are up to their games again, no doubt at a more discreet distance during our tenancy. I believe we may count on an hour at least before his return.'

With the greatest reluctance I heaved myself out of bed and followed him. It seemed a further waste of our time. Each room was just what it appeared to be. The dining-room, the parlour, the kitchen, the master's bedroom, the servants' attics, even the cellar. Not a door was locked or bolted to prevent our progress. This was scarcely the lair of a secretive and hunted man. To be sure, we did not know what furniture had belonged in the first place to Dougal, Miss Holland, or any of his other mistresses. The same was true of women's clothes which hung in one of the wardrobes of the spare room. Though some were of a size to fit the petite figure of Camille Holland, as she had been described to us, others would have done justice to the ample forms of his servant-girls.

'The clothes will tell us little,' Holmes said impatiently, 'but there is something here that will hang him more surely. I know there is.'

As he spoke he was opening, inspecting, closing again, a series of round hat-boxes at an upper level of the mahogany tall-boy.

'We shall have to give up presently,' I said anxiously, 'he will be back.'

Just then he gave a cry of triumph. In his hand was a bottle of liquid, which might have been the very colour of Miss Dougal's artificially-golden hair.

'What of it?' I said furiously. 'If she left that behind it still proves nothing.'

He looked at me pityingly and produced from the hat-box a pad of golden hair, a tortoise-shell comb and a wire hair-frame upon which the hair and comb would have been worn. He placed the pad upon the frame, added the comb and we saw again the back of Camille Holland's head as it had appeared in Inspector Marden's photograph.

'She left them behind,' I said hopefully. 'What can it signify? She had no need of them. To whom else would they be of any use?'

He paused and said, 'To the woman who visited the National Provincial Bank in Piccadilly, when the form with a specimen of her hand was signed in Miss Holland's name.'

'They had seen her before. They would recognize an imposture. Ashwin at the bank knew who she was. A pad of hair would be no disguise.'

Holmes sat down on the bed.

'I was certain of it, as soon as Marden described the death of her nephew's child.'

'What the devil has that to do with it?'

'If I did not know you better, my dear fellow, I should believe that the country air had addled your brains. Think, man! What does a woman do when there is a bereavement in her family?'

'She attends the funeral and makes herself useful, but Miss Holland did neither.'

'Quite so. What else?'

'She goes into mourning.'

'In what form?'

'I daresay black crape, weeds anyhow, mourning jewellery, a veil . . .'

As soon as I said it, the whole thing was clear.

'Exactly!' He sprang from the bed and paced about the room. 'Miss Holland in mourning garb attended the bank that she and her family have used for a generation, though she seldom visited it. Her little niece was dead, a fact which the very newspapers might confirm and Mr Edmund Holland would, in any case, be obliged to refer to at some point. Mr Ashwin knew this lady by her dainty form, the golden hair-pad supported by the wire frame and the familiar comb. The veil was not too heavy to prevent her features being dimly discerned but enough to make them somewhat indistinct. Her voice was quiet in her grief and a little thickened, perhaps, by tears. With a proper sense of delicacy, Ashwin left her to sign the form in her own time.'

'If it was so.'

'If it was? My dear fellow, you heard Marden say that the child's death was the only other event remembered at the time of the visit to the bank! I am concerned at what may not be remembered. Was this other Camille Holland able to write in a passable imitation of the true signature? It would not have to be of the finest quality. Convinced of her identity and seeing her shaken by grief, even Mr Ashwin was convinced. Or was there a sympathetic female companion or male escort who formed the actual signature? Was Dougal himself somewhere at hand? Whatever the answer, when the work was done the form was inserted in the file of papers for her account and became her signature so far as the bank was concerned.'

He stared at the open hat-box, closed it, and replaced it on its shelf in the tall-boy. Then he turned to me again.

'That child's death was a gift from the gods for him – or rather from the devil. The only true part that the devil has had to play in all his schemes! How easy it must have been! At any other time, the imposture would have been plain. But the bank's knowledge of the child's death and the evidence of their own eyes that showed them the woman in mourning was a perfect coincidence.'

'If she was murdered by him . . .'

'She is out there, Watson, lying in this dark night, somewhere beneath the dank fenland, while Dougal and his naked trollops caper upon their bicycles above her.'

'I was about to ask whether you had concluded that she was murdered before or after the visit to the bank.'

'As to that, my friend, I have an open mind. After the visit, I expect.'

I was relieved to find him a little less dogmatic and this made me bolder.

'More to the point,' I said, 'if she is out there as you

say, how are you to find her body in mile upon mile of fenland stretching from here to Cambridge, supposing that by this time there is anything left to find?'

He smiled.

'I should not allow that to disturb your rest, Watson. I have an extremely clear idea of how this investigation will end. I believe I know where she is.'

Then we had a day of Holmes at his worst. He would do nothing but lounge in a basket chair in Captain Dougal's conservatory, reading the papers and then purloining my copy of the *Lancet*, which I had scarcely begun. This continued all day. Next morning, while we were at breakfast, a boy in a blue uniform came running over the bridge and handed an envelope to Captain Dougal. Dougal brought the telegram to Holmes at the breakfast table. He made no pretence of courtesy, standing by the table as my friend read it. Holmes put it in his pocket.

'Dear me,' he said in a tone of mild apology, 'I believe I shall have to start back in a day or two. I had quite forgotten that there is a common-room meeting on Tuesday, at which we must elect a new Senior Tutor.'

Captain Dougal gave a smile that revealed, rather than hid, his contempt for such a milksop as this.

## VI

As soon as Dougal was out of the room, the academic gentleness dropped like a mask from the face of Sherlock Holmes.

'We must make our move, Watson, before that fellow twigs what we are up to.'

'Why should he?'

'If I knew the answer to that, old fellow, it would not concern me. Wait here.'

I saw him go out, across the bridge and into the first field. He stood by the hedge at a point where a rabbit had made its burrow, or more sinisterly, where an animal of some sort had dug. After a careful inspection, he came back.

'I think that we must abandon the niceties of butterfly-hunting, go straight to Saffron Walden, wire Lestrade, and summon the assistance of the local police force. No, my friend, let us postpone explanations until we have Marden in our company. Once is enough.'

It was not Inspector Marden but his colleague Eli Bower who confronted us, a man who plainly loathed Holmes and his kind as much as Holmes distrusted him. Ten years later, Bower was to secure the conviction and execution of John Williams in the Hooded Man murder, which my friend always swore was a grave miscarriage of justice. We confronted this squat burly figure across the table where we had first met Marden.

'For a start, Mr Holmes,' said Bower sternly, 'I don't need your assistance in this matter. I have men enough to carry out any investigation and . . .'

'Yet you have failed to do so!'

The inspector's colour deepened.

'Who says I have not done so?'

'This little fellow says so.' Holmes took the jar from his satchel, spread a sheet of notepaper on the table, and shook on to it the remains of the insect he had been studying.

'What the devil might that be?'

'The species is a phorid fly,' said Holmes deliberately, as if addressing a backward student. 'The identification is confirmed by this telegram from Dr Cardew of the Natural History Museum, the leading man on the subject.'

'I have a police-station to run, Mr Holmes! What should I care for flies or museums?'

'Very little I should say, and very little about running a police-station either, it seems. Perhaps it will assist you if I add that the insect is more commonly known as the coffin-fly. This fragment to one side is the pupae sheath of a second specimen. In other words they are still breeding at the site.'

The mention of coffins brought Bower up short. He looked at the remains on the notepaper with a twist of revulsion in his mouth but also with a new respect.

'Where did it come from?'

'Coldhams Farm,' said Holmes casually. 'Please listen, Bower, to what I have to say. The coffin-fly begins its disagreeable work at the time of burial. Some three years are required for it, or rather its maggots, to devour a corpse. When that is done, the colony dies in its turn. Whoever or whatever is buried at Coldhams Farm cannot, therefore, have been dead more than three years. Dougal has been in residence some four years. Death and burial therefore took place within the time of his occupancy. Do I make myself plain?'

Bower, so confident a few minutes earlier, was now like a trapped animal.

'How did you get that thing?'

'It came to me,' said Holmes equably. 'A fox, a dog perhaps, had been digging by the shed in the farm-yard. I confess I had been looking for such activity in and around the property. I noted a dozen sites, for the most part in the surrounding pasture, where the earth had been disturbed, had settled a little, and had then been subject to feral digging. A phorid fly would only get above ground if the excavation had been shallow with a means of egress. Whatever – or whoever – lies there, is not far down. Do I continue to make it clear to you?'

Inspector Bower did not growl his defiance, but looked as if he would like to.

'I understand, Mr Holmes, that Inspector Marden has already explained to you that there is ample evidence of Miss Holland being alive and unharmed.'

Holmes looked at him coldly. Then he looked at his watch and said, 'Miss Holland is dead. As dead as you and I will one day be.'

Before Bower could reply, there was a knock and a constable handed the inspector a telegram. I contrived to see at its foot the words, LESTRADE, SCOTLAND YARD. The capitulation of Eli Bower was now complete and unconditional, though scarcely graceful. He sighed.

'Very well. What would you have me do?'

'Gather every man you can and whatever equipment is available to you. Begin to search at once, starting under the shed where the pony-trap is kept.'

'That cannot be done without a warrant!'

'Then I suggest you lose as little time as possible in getting one.'

Before the afternoon was over, a justice's warrant had been obtained. Two serge-clad constables in gum-boots, assisted by a labourer, had cleared a shallow trench along one side of the shed. While Bower watched, his sergeant stood guard at the wicket gate of the bridge. A little after six, the digging stopped. A constable lifted an object, from which clay fell in scattered lumps. Despite the coating of earth, there was not the least doubt that this was a human skull.

The four diggers, the sergeant, Holmes and I gathered round.

'Fetch Dougal!' said Bower to his sergeant. The proprietor of Coldhams Farm was 'Captain' no longer. The sergeant and one of the constables crossed the little bridge and entered the house. There was a pause, during which I had a dreadful suspicion that Dougal might have taken his own life, that he might even now be dangling from a rafter in anticipation of the hangman's work. Then the face of the sergeant appeared at a bedroom window.

'He must have got a plank over the moat on the far side, sir,' he called to Brewer. 'He's done a bunk!'

Brewer's face went dark as thunder. Holmes turned to him.

'I congratulate you, inspector. I confess I had underestimated your reading of the man.'

'What?'

'You are too modest,' Holmes said, his face as straight as a poker. 'You might have put him under guard and got nothing from him. But you knew that a guilty man, given the chance, would bolt from such a terrifying revelation as this. You let him go, confident in your own ability to find him again easily enough. There are few officers, in my experience, who might play the game with such subtlety.'

Bower stared at him, uncertain whether Holmes was

skinning him in fine strips or paying him a true compliment. He made no reply but shouted at the men to resume work, for there were more than two hours of daylight left. But those two hours revealed nothing more, nor did the whole of the next day. The site by the shed was exhausted without any further discovery. Worse still, I was obliged to tell Bower that this skull was too large to belong to a petite woman, five feet and two inches in height. Worse than that, for the inquiry he was pursuing, it was the skull of a man. Worst of all, I was more confident than not that its owner had died many years before Dougal's arrival at the farm.

'Which scarcely matters,' said Holmes indifferently, 'for if Miss Holland were not here somewhere, Dougal would surely not have bolted as he did.'

## VII

Next day, Dougal's description was wired to every police force in the land, while Bower and his men searched what was now called Moat Farm. Every inch of the house was tapped and measured without result. Holmes and I found quarters ten miles away in Cambridge, at the University Arms. At Quendon, the diggers had taken over the farm-house, cooking and even sleeping there. The lawn was soon a trench fortification with Bower's constables working up to their waist in fenland slime. At the end of three days they had found nothing.

The moat seemed, to our earth-bound inspector, too good a chance to miss. In his mind he created a story of an argument or fight between Dougal and the little woman, as he called her. The brute killed her, by a blow of his fist or the thrust of his thumbs on her windpipe, and flung her body into this narrow moat.

'Very good,' said Holmes coolly. 'A little strange, however, that the body never came to the surface during decomposition.'

We watched them drain the moat and saw the constables digging away the filthy black mud of its bed. Bower was standing beside us as Holmes took a heavy stone with a sharp edge. Shouting to the diggers to stand clear, he tossed it down and heard it land with a thud in the bottom of the moat. It splashed the mud a little but remained in full view.

'If a stone of that weight will not sink below the bottom of the moat,' he said reflectively, 'you may be sure a human body did not. What remained of the skeleton, now that your digging has removed the sludge, would be lying in our view at this moment. It is not. Therefore, I suggest, Miss Holland was not thrown into the moat, either alive or dead.'

Bower glared at him. I think the word is not too strong.

'And do you care to suggest, Mr Holmes, where we should look instead?'

Holmes affected not to notice the anger. In his most friendly manner he said, 'I observe a line of young trees on the far side of the yard. You see? They run from the moat to the pond. I should guess they were planted two or three years ago. The level of the earth along that line stands somewhat higher than the yard. That is often the case when digging, or rather filling-in, has occurred. Something lay along that line. It was dug up, or at least filled in, about three years ago and trees were planted. You may find that of interest.'

There was a steely triumph in Bower's narrow eyes.

'We found it of such interest, Mr Holmes, that we inquired about it two days ago. There was a drainage ditch from the farm-yard to the pond. Dougal had it filled in and trees planted upon it. It was done at a time when Miss Holland was still alive and they were living amicably together here for weeks afterwards.'

'Dear me,' said Holmes, unruffled by the disappointment. 'Then it would hardly seem to warrant digging.'

'My very thought, Mr Holmes.'

Holmes turned to the inspector with eyes that seemed to look straight through him.

'And perhaps it was Captain Dougal's very thought, as he chose the place to dispose of the body of the woman whom he had just foully murdered.'

Bower was a little rattled by this but not defeated.

'Now,' said Holmes politely, 'we will take ourselves off. We shall return by train to Cambridge for the night and be with you again tomorrow.'

Bower did not look best pleased at this promise of our return. However, we had made ourselves comfortable at the University Arms and turned out on that fine evening to stroll along King's Parade in the late May sunshine. As we did so, a tradesman of some kind passed us, tipped his hat and said, 'A very good evening to you, Professor Holmes, sir.'

I scarcely liked the sound of this, but my companion gave a slight self-conscious smile and would say nothing.

We returned next morning to watch the progress of the digging by the line of trees. At one end, where the topsoil was removed, the drainage ditch had been filled in by blackthorn cuttings. This loose-packed layer was cleared by two men with pitch-forks, the surrounding earth being sodden with sewage and liquid manure from the yard. Then there came a shout from one of the diggers. He held up his fork, from one of whose prongs dangled a piece of old cloth.

We gathered round that spot, knowing yet dreading what might be underneath the blackthorn. I heard the fork strike something solid. The labourer stooped and drew out a small boot from the muddy soil. From where I stood, I saw inside the boot the delicate bones of a human foot. The work went on more cautiously. Soon we were looking down at a shape, little more than the half-clad skeleton of a woman, face-downwards with her head turned slightly to one side. On one side, where the body rested against the mud, almost everything had been destroyed. On the nearer side, the corpse had been sheltered from the mud by the cuttings of the bushes, its state of preservation much better. By the end of the afternoon, the poor woman's remains lay upon a trestle-table in the greenhouse. A wire hair-frame was found in the muddy grave, the twin of that found by Holmes in the hat-box. From that moment, 'Captain' Dougal's number was up.

We returned to Baker Street the next day. That evening, we received our usual visit from Lestrade. After the horrors of Moat Farm, as Coldhams was now universally called, it was a relief to be among homely surroundings and friendly faces. Lestrade settled himself, took a long pull at his glass, and said, 'Well, gentlemen, I suppose you have had something of an adventure. But how you persuaded that cuss Eli Bower to start digging, when his face was set against it, I do not know. He is the most stubborn and dogged fellow, as a rule.'

'I was able to show him where he might find a skull,' said Holmes innocently. 'After that, the rest followed.'

'So that was it! Well, you may put that skull from your mind. It has been examined by the pathologist and is far too old to have anything to do with Dougal. Dr Watson was right about that.'

'And what of Dougal?'

Lestrade's face assumed an expression of humorous self-importance.

'That is my news. This afternoon, Detective-Inspector Henry Cox of the City of London police was duty officer at the Bank of England. He was called discreetly to the office of the bank secretary at the request of the clerk. It seems that Mr Sydney Domville, of Upper Terrace, Bournemouth, had presented fourteen ten-pound notes to be changed for gold sovereigns. There were irregularities in nine of these notes, for they could not be traced as issued to Mr Domville. They had, however, been issued through the Birkbeck Bank account of Samuel Dougal.'

'Ah,' said Holmes, closing his eyes in contemplation, 'so that was it.'

'On being challenged, the suspect Domville admitted he was Dougal. Mr Cox then escorted him to the detective office at the bank. At the door, Dougal suddenly turned and ran, clear of the bank, and fled towards Cheapside. Cox caught him at Frederick's Place and they fell to the ground together. Padghorn, a uniformed constable, saw them. He recognized Mr Cox and handcuffed Dougal. You may be thankful, gentlemen, that you have not been briefed to defend Dougal, for there was never a clearer case against any man.'

'I do not defend the guilty,' said Holmes gently, 'merely the innocent.'

When Lestrade had gone, there still was one piece of unfinished business.

'Tell me, Holmes. What is all this mystery about Professor Holmes of Cambridge? Why did that fellow call out to you on King's Parade?'

Holmes drew at his pipe and said, 'I daresay he was mistaken.'

'I think he was not! He called you Professor Holmes! After our talk with Marden, you were not to be seen for several hours after lunch. There was ample time to take the Cambridge train from Audley End and return with what you called a coffin-fly. It was more likely a common hedge-moth. It is the only time when you were out of my sight long enough to go to Cambridge alone.'

'Your deduction is entirely admirable,' said he.

'Why did you go? What for?'

'Hold hard a moment, Watson,' he said with a laugh, 'I do not say I was there!'

'It was for something that would fit into your satchel. My God, it was that skull! You went to the university anatomy suppliers, as medical students do to buy a skeleton. You bought that skull! You buried it by the cart-shed, so that Marden or Bower must dig! You knew they would find it and would dig up the entire place! That coffin-fly was a harmless insect, vouched for by a telegram sent to yourself from Cambridge the next morning! There is no Dr Cardew!'

'Such a welter of deductions, my dear chap . . .' His eyes shone with laughter.

'Suppose Miss Holland had still been alive – had driven into the farm-yard in the middle of Bower's digging?'

'She could drive nowhere, Watson. She was lying dead at the bottom of the drainage ditch, if you recall.'

'But you could not have known – so you fabricated evidence to make them dig!'

'Forgive me, my dear fellow, I have known she was dead since the moment that Marden mentioned the tragedy of her nephew's child.'

'Yet the rest of what I say is true?'

He laughed again.

'My old friend, you really must allow justice to the accused, which accords to every man the right to silence.'

'You mean that what I do not know, I cannot tell!'

'That is certainly true, in any event.'

For a moment we were silent. Then I put my last question.

'There is one flaw in your hypothesis. Where is the woman whom you claim impersonated Camille Holland at the National Provincial Bank?'

He shrugged.

'That is no flaw. I simply do not know. Alive – or dead. Perhaps not far away. Search your mind, Watson, for a demure petite of Miss Holland's type.'

'I cannot say we have cast eyes on one.'

'Oh, come,' he said, 'surely we have done that, even if it be not she.'

I did not follow this at first. Then it dawned upon me what he meant.

'Miss Pierce? The very idea of her and Dougal is outlandish.'

'So was that of Miss Holland. The conquest of devout spinsters, no longer young, seems to have been something of a profession with Captain Dougal.'

'She would hardly ask us to take action against him, if that were the case.'

'As I recall, it was to avoid publicity that she came to us and not to the police.'

'Absurd,' I said, thinking as I did so that perhaps it was nothing of the kind.

Holmes sighed and knocked out his pipe.

'Hell hath no fury like a woman scorned, Watson,' he said, standing up and yawning. 'Especially if she who has forfeited her virtue for love be a subscriber to the National Vigilance Association.'

# The Case of the Sporting Major

## I

The intuitive faculty of Sherlock Holmes was generally beyond my power to comprehend, let alone to emulate. From time to time, however, I matched him in his anticipation of regular events. One of these was the impending arrival of a certain eminent guest, whose visits had long been familiar to us. On such occasions, Mrs Hudson's nervous housemaid would open the door to make her announcement with the air of a twittering cage-bird. Or Billy the page-boy would appear with eyes bright at the excitement of an adventure to come. Even our impassive and long-suffering landlady would utter the six resonant syllables in a tone of superior awe.

'Sir Edward Marshall Hall!'

Before us stood that splendid figure, an athlete and philosopher of noble brow with a fine sweep of hair. Small wonder if Lord Birkenhead remarked that no man could possibly have been as wonderful as Marshall Hall appeared. His presence and voice were such as Sir Henry Irving and the great actors of the day would have given a fortune to possess.

Yet Marshall Hall had a nobler fame. He was the

Great Defender in the criminal courts, equipped with sharp intelligence and eloquent address. Times without number, he saved from the gallows those whom public opinion had already condemned. He opened the gates of life for a score of men and women, in defending the humble prostitute Marie Hermann, Edward Lawrence the brewer, Robert Wood the Camden Town artist, Thomas Greenwood reviled as a poisoner, and then among his greater triumphs came the Green Bicycle case, the Derham shooting, and the acquittal of Madame Fahmy who had killed her unnatural husband.

One fine September morning in the last years of the late Queen's reign, Marshall Hall sat upon the sofa of our Baker Street lodgings, his eyes bright, his fingers drumming upon the padded arm of the furniture. That whole being was alive with a characteristic energy which wants to be up and doing – a perfect mirror of Sherlock Holmes! It might seem at first that their only common pleasure was in chaff and banter. Beneath this, however, lay an adamantine resolve to see justice done and innocence set free.

On this particular morning, Marshall Hall wore the black velvet jacket of those more casual days when he was not engaged to appear in court or chambers.

'Whatever your business, Sir Edward,' said Holmes airily, 'I am pleased that you first had leisure to sit and listen to your wife playing the Chopin Polonaise in A Flat Major, upon a Schiedmayer concert grand-piano. I regret that the tone of the instrument was not all that it might have been. I should recommend you to consult Messrs Chappell in New Bond Street, should you require advice in the matter.'

Another visitor might be dumbfounded that Holmes should know the very piece of music that Sir Edward had heard half an hour before, who had played it to him, the precise make of the instrument, and what had been discussed. Sir Edward merely threw back his head and laughed at his friend's cleverness.

'My dear Holmes, you will plainly not be content until you have explained your brilliance. Put us poor mortals out of our misery!'

Holmes shrugged, disclaiming any gift except common sense.

'I observe your jacket. Nature has designed velvet fabric as a means of collecting evidence. Upon your right sleeve, a little above the cuff, you have picked up a fleck of cream-coloured felt, somewhat worn. If one looks closely, the cream has a red inlay of a different texture along its edge. I grant the red is scarcely perceptible, but it is there. Such a combination of fabrics comes from one source only in my experience. It has been acquired from a damper of the string on a grand-piano. The precise key is close to the middle C. That particular red inlay is characteristic of the instruments made by Schiedmayer of Stuttgart, which I have several times tried in Augener's showroom. It occurs solely on the damper, where the felt is softer than the hammer and more inclined to fray. The great use made by so accomplished a pianist as Lady Hall must require the re-felting of hammers and dampers alike. The more commonly-used the key, the greater the wear, hence in the region of middle C. How easy it would have been for your sleeve to brush the mechanism as you were closing the piano-lid for Lady Hall. The fact that the lid was closed so early in the day hints – does it not? – at some dissatisfaction with the state of the instrument. Hence your discussion.'

'Is that all?' asked Marshall Hall tauntingly.

'Not quite. That discussion was plainly interrupted, in turn, by the arrival of a message which brought you here at once. A letter, I believe. I should say your advice has been sought urgently in a case to come before the Scottish courts. The north of England would be possible but, on the whole, I think Scotland. It would have been too early in the day for so complex a telegram as the facts of such a case require. Therefore I plump for a letter by the second post. Yesterday's post from Manchester, York, or the English counties would be delivered first thing. So we must look further afield. I observe that the Scottish courts are already sitting, the English assizes are not. It remains to decide what matter might have been referred to your particular accomplishments. I have seen in the *Morning Post* some reference to the dramatic arrest in Glasgow of a certain Major Alfred Monson in connection with the shooting dead of a fellow officer during a hunting-party. That has a ring of probability to it. I daresay I am quite wrong.'

Sir Edward laughed again.

'You are quite right Holmes, and you know it, otherwise you would not have dared the deduction. And, indeed, Lady Hall's practice-piece this morning was the Chopin Polonaise.'

'I thought as much,' Holmes said reassuringly. 'Its rhythm is exceptionally well-defined. When a man fingers his impatience on the arm of a sofa, he is very likely to imitate unawares the last melody he has heard. But enough of these games. Precisely what has occurred in this case to bring you here at a time when you might otherwise have been in chambers?'

The laughter went from the fine eyes of Marshall Hall.

'The evidence against Major Monson, gentlemen, is indeed of murder and the case is as black as it could be. My friend Mr Comrie Thomson holds a watching brief. It was impossible that I should do so. I have other commitments and am neither a member of the Scottish bar nor sufficiently conversant with Scottish criminal law. To speak frankly, on the evidence available to me, the major's situation appears hopeless.'

'Excellent!' said Holmes with relish. 'Do, pray, continue.'

'Alfred Monson is a middle-aged, down-at-heel retired major who tutors young officers to pass War Office examinations and so advance their careers. The pupils that he chooses are men with quite a little money. They live with Monson, his wife, children, and nursemaid. They are coached for these War Office tests and in every case appear to have been systematically plundered. His latest dupe was one Lieutenant Cecil Hamborough. Hamborough's father soon guessed the major's intentions. He resented the influence of the Monsons and sought to end the association. Unfortunately, young Hamborough would not see sense. He appeared blind to reason, even though he was bled white by Monson and a criminal scoundrel known variously as Edward Scott, Edward Davis, and Edward Sweeney.'

'The disgraced bookmaker from Pimlico, who two years ago lost his licence for fraud!' cried Holmes, as if recognizing an old friend.

'Precisely. Monson and Scott worked hand-in-glove with a so-called money-lender, Captain Beresford Tottenham, lately and briefly of the 10th Prince of Wales Hussars. Hamborough's money was obtained by IOUs combined with an extortionate rate of interest. The last of his funds was used to rent Ardlamont House near the Kyles of Bute, where he, the Monsons, and Scott would spend the summer and the August shooting season. After they had drained the poor young devil, I daresay they meant to be rid of him one way or another.'

'What a story to put to a jury!' Holmes said thoughtfully.

'That is by no means the worst of it.' Marshall Hall inspected and removed the fluff on his velvet sleeve. 'Some time after their arrival at Ardlamont there was a boating accident in which young Hamborough was nearly drowned. Next morning he was shot dead, apparently by accident, while out hunting rabbits with Monson and Scott, *alias* Davis, *alias* Sweeney.'

Holmes reached for a pencil and made two or three notes on his shirt-cuff as Marshall Hall continued.

'Both men swore that Lieutenant Hamborough was walking alone and must have stumbled in the woods, jarring his short-barrelled 20-bore, which had gone off and shot him through the head. The local doctor, never having seen such a thing before, accepted the story and signed a death certificate. Scott then left Ardlamont, that same afternoon, and has not been seen since. It appears, however, that he cannot have fired the shot. Perhaps he feared that the publicity sur rounding Hamborough's death would result in prosecution for certain past offences of fraud and embezzlement, if he waited for the police. Young Hamborough was interred a few days later in the family vault on the Isle of Wight. Now I must tell you what the world does not yet know.'

'Pray do so.' Holmes reached a spill to the fire to light his pipe.

'On the day of Hamborough's funeral, two life insurance companies alerted the Procurator Fiscal to a demand by Major Monson for £30,000. Cecil Hamborough's life had been insured in this sum, which he had assigned and made payable to the Monsons in the event of his death. A third company had declined a further proposal for £50,000. Monson had been the intermediary on each occasion, attempting to secure an interest of £80,000 all told, in the event of the young man's death.'

'Making Hamborough worth a good deal more dead than alive,' said Holmes softly.

'Quite. The day after the policies for £30,000 came into effect was the one upon which Monson took Hamborough out into Ardlamont Bay in a rowing-boat, from which the bung had been secretly removed. Nothing was seen amiss at first but water poured in under the boards from the moment the boat was pushed into the sea. The young fellow was nearly drowned. The very next morning he was shot dead in Ardlamont woods, while the three men were hunting rabbits.'

'I fear,' said Holmes, waving aside a cloud of tobacco smoke, 'that no one could accuse Mr Thomson's client of subtlety.'

Marshall Hall shook his head.

'As a result of the reports from the insurance offices, the body was exhumed. There was no blackening round the head-wound, just behind the right ear. Therefore the shot could not have come from less than three feet. By the spread of shot, it was probably thirty feet away. We know from other witnesses that only Monson was that far away at the time. Since the investigation was renewed and the major arrested, Scott has fled and will no doubt be outlawed when Monson is charged.'

Holmes was now jotting a few scattered notes on a sheet of paper.

'After the boating-accident, Hamborough made no accusation?'

'None. However, Monson is arrested on suspicion, for that incident as well as the shooting.'

'And what would you have me do?'

'Prove the major's innocence,' said Marshall Hall simply, 'for that is what it will mean, no matter what the law says about a presumption in favour of the defendant. The facts are deadly and the prejudice at his fraudulent way of life will go deep in any panel of jurors.'

'His position does seem quite hopeless, from all that you have been told?'

'As much so as any I have ever known.'

'Good,' said Holmes briskly. 'Then I shall certainly take the case. I confess that Watson and I had made no plans to go to Scotland just now. However, such a very incriminating set of circumstances really is too good to overlook.'

'Could you go at once?'

My friend looked a little doubtful.

'There is Kreisler at the Wigmore Hall this evening and I must have time to put matters in order for our absence. The criminal fraternity is apt to become overexcited when I am out of town, and Scotland Yard feels lonely. Will you give me a day's grace and allow us to take the North-Western Railway tomorrow?'

There was no mistaking the relief in the lawyer's face.

'That would be splendid. Monson is certain to be formally charged with murder and brought before the sheriff's court. The Procurator Fiscal works more slowly and thoroughly than the English police. Charges will be brought soon but hardly before Wednesday.'

'Capital,' said Holmes quietly, making a final note. 'Then we shall take the North-Western Railway express from Euston, tomorrow morning at ten.'

## II

Our first visit in Glasgow on the Wednesday morning was not to Ardlamont House but to the sheriff's court, in whose basement lay a concrete and white-tiled corridor of police-cells. We had been met by Mr Comrie Thomson at the Central Station on the previous evening with the news that Major Monson was now formally charged with the attempted murder of Cecil Hamborough in respect of the boating incident on 9 August and with actual murder for the Ardlamont shooting on 10 August. Of Scott, *alias* Davis, *alias* Sweeney, there was still no sign

On that Wednesday morning, we met Mr Thomson in front of the grim pillared façade of the High Court Buildings. From there it was a very little distance to the court where Monson was to appear at a formal committal hearing. As we made our way, Mr Thomson said mournfully, 'I cannot say that it looks hopeful, gentlemen. There are now two more witnesses who were in the schoolhouse on the edge of the Ardlamont wood and another who was working on the road to one side. They saw the three men enter the wood, well apart, Monson on the right, Hamborough in the middle, Scott on the left. They all agree that only two shots were fired after that. Unfortunately none of the guns was examined at the time, Dr Macmillan having certified death from accidental shooting. However, the first shot came from the direction of Major Monson, who was behind Hamborough and Scott and to their right. The second was either the accidental discharge of Hamborough's gun, a second shot by Monson, or a shot by Scott. We cannot be sure.'

'What of the ranges?'

Mr Thomson shook his head.

'The spread of the pellet-holes in the trees where the body lay, and the width of the wound behind the young man's ear, suggest that only Monson can have been far enough away to have fired the fatal shot. Had Scott been as far as thirty feet to the rear, he would have been seen from the road that passes the schoolhouse where one of the witnesses was working. He was not seen. I am informed privately on the best authority that if Hamborough had shot himself at a range of even three feet, it would have blown his head clean off.'

'Then we must pay a little more attention to Edward Scott,' said Holmes thoughtfully.

Thomson shook his head.

'Scott was not only too close to fire the fatal shot, Mr Holmes, he was on the wrong side of Hamborough.

Hamborough was hit in the right side of the head, where only Major Monson fired.'

'Well, well,' said Holmes philosophically, 'then it does not look good for Major Monson.'

'It looks bad, Mr Holmes. And then there is the insurance on the young man's life . . .'

'So there is,' Holmes said brightly. 'Let us see what our client has to say for himself when the case comes on.'

During these preliminary proceedings, we had what proved to be our first and last view of Major Monson as he stood in the dock of the panelled court-room. When the accused was 'put up', he appeared above the rail of the dock as a stout, unprepossessing man in his late thirties with a clipped ginger moustache and hair to match. His watery eyes and stocky build made him appear somewhat older than he was. I had seen his type often during my army service, the adjutant who passes his life at the depot, shuffling papers, then takes his pension at forty and lives the rest of his life at Cheltenham or Harrogate as the gallant swordsman of a middle-aged spinster's dream. From time to time, during the interval before the proceedings began, a nervous ferret-like smile broke cover from Monson's ginger moustache as he recognized someone he knew.

Before the matter went further, there was some discussion between the sheriff and Mr John Blair who was Monson's agent, or solicitor as he would have been in England. This revealed the unsurprising fact that the major was an undischarged bankrupt and must rely upon a poor prisoner's defence to pay his costs, which had already begun to mount up. This financing of the case occupied several minutes of discussion.

'I understand, Major Monson, that you have been an undischarged bankrupt for the past two years?' inquired the sheriff.

'That is so,' said the rheumy-eyed trickster.

'You and your wife employed a maid, a nanny for your children, and were able to afford a summer at Ardlamont House. How was that?'

'It was all Mrs Monson's money, sir.' The major's eyes watered harder, as if he might weep for pity.

There followed a recital by the prosecution of the preliminary case against the accused. Such evidence was damning enough in itself but Monson made it a good deal worse by his frightened interjections. The sheriff, either wanting to be fair to him or perhaps to let him damn himself, allowed him too much latitude. When Mr Cowan, for the Solicitor-General, remarked that the major had insured Cecil Hamborough's life for £30,000, the watery eyes cleared a little as if there was still some fight in him.

'There is no law against that, sir! The boy had broken with his father. This was the only means by which Lieutenant Hamborough could repay board, lodging and tuition, if he should not live to get his military position, don't you see?'

'Board and lodging at £30,000?' Mr Cowan asked the question of everyone who heard it. 'And, indeed, he did not live to get his position, did he?'

Mr Thomson looked down at the floor and Sherlock Holmes at the ceiling. The major's face was a grimace of pure terror, as if Mr Cowan had been the hangman entering his cell on the last fateful morning.

Presently, in his recital of the evidence for the sheriff's benefit, Mr Cowan came to the events in the woods and the firing of the shot that killed Cecil Hamborough. Monson, unable to endure the allegations of his guilt, blurted out, 'It was a pure accident, sir! The boy stumbled and shot himself, knocking the gun so that it went off.'

He laid himself open to Mr Cowan's retort, directed to the sheriff.

'Forgive me, your honour, but I do not recall any man managing to shoot himself from a distance of three feet – let alone thirty! Even at three feet, your honour, the wound would have been scorched and the skin impregnated with burnt powder.'

'Not with smokeless amberite cartridges, d'you see, your honour?' cried the major hopefully. 'Cecil Hamborough was carrying the 12-bore shotgun with the amberite cartridges. I was the one who had the short-barrelled 20-bore with gunpowder.'

Mr Cowan glanced at his notes.

'Your honour, Major Monson has told the police that he was carrying the 12-bore with the amberite.'

'They have it wrong!' What a cry of pain it was from the doomed man! 'To be sure I was carrying the 12-bore when we set out. As we were about to enter the wood, Hamborough asked to borrow it. We exchanged guns. I said so when they first questioned me at Ardlamont.'

Mr Cowan paused and consulted a uniformed inspector sitting at the bench behind him. Then he turned to the sheriff again.

'Your honour, this evidence about the exchange of guns has been heard for the first time in this court-room at this moment. Nothing was said to the police by Major Monson about it, either at Ardlamont or in custody. Nor is it mentioned in the written witness-statement by the accused man.'

'I thought they had put it in! I did not write the statement myself, only signed it!'

The sight of such a wretch as this, a congenital liar and trickster, struggling forlornly like a summer-fly in the web of evidence which his prosecutors spun about him, was terrifying. It did not end there but the damage that Monson had already done to his own case seemed mortal.

Outside, with Mr Comrie Thomson, I said, 'The poor devil has put the noose round his own neck!'

The barrister, in his quiet Scots voice, added, 'I had hoped, Mr Holmes, that your arrival would give some hope. As it is, I fear your journey may have been to no purpose.'

'Mr Thomson, I have promised Sir Edward Marshall Hall that I will take the case. I have not the slightest intention of abandoning it in the light of what we have heard this morning. All the same, if you have no objection, I shall not interview the client. It would irritate me to be lied to by such a novice in deceit as Major Monson. Indeed, I am bound to say that it would irritate me to be in the same room with Major Monson.'

'Then you will continue with the investigation? You think there is a chance in a million that he might be innocent?'

'Innocent? Dear me!' Holmes looked about him as if he feared that he had caused offence unawares. 'Major Monson is a reprobate and a liar, to be sure. Facts, however, are not liars. If the facts of the case are as I believe them to be, I have little doubt that I shall prove him to be innocent. Indeed, I had almost made up my mind to that effect before leaving Baker Street.'

Comrie Thomson reddened a little at this.

'I do not think I understand you, Mr Holmes.'

'Perhaps not,' said Holmes suavely, 'but in the morning Watson and I are to become seekers after truth at Ardlamont. Thanks to your good offices we shall have the company of Mr David Stewart of the Procurator Fiscal's office. In the meantime, Mr Thomson, I should be obliged if you could find it convenient not to go to your chambers tomorrow.'

The attorney stared at him.

'But there is work to be done, Mr Holmes! Now, of all times!'

'Even so, you would oblige me by doing it elsewhere. Let that be settled. And now let us return to the comforts of the Argyle Hotel, where we may forget our client and his misfortunes over an agreeable glass or two. Malt whisky with water from the Highland springs, I think, followed by lunch.'

## III

Next morning we set out by the paddle-steamer *Duchess of Montrose* for Ardlamont Bay. After two hours, we cleared the river and turned north in a freshening breeze towards the Kyles of Bute. With the tide racing against the bow and the wind in our faces, we stood on deck and watched the tree-lined bay approach. Ardlamont House is accessible only by water, unless one makes a considerable detour from Kames. It stands in a wooded bay, where we were met at the little pier by David Stewart, the Deputy Fiscal at Inveraray. Mr Stewart's reputation went before him, a quietly-spoken and courteous man, who had proved deadly to Major Monson in his interrogation.

Ardlamont is a tall white house of recent design, built for solid comforts. Around it lies a considerable estate of pasture and woodland, including a disused school building let to holidaymakers in the season. We paid a brief visit to the house, where the gun-cases and leather chairs in the hall, the shooting-jackets and waterproofs hanging by the hat-stand, the doors to the billiard-room and smoking-room, left little doubt as to its clientele. Since the 'tragedy' a few weeks before, however, not a shot had been fired on the surrounding estate. In point of law, Major Monson had paid the rent, albeit with Hamborough's money, and was still the tenant.

With Mr Stewart, we then walked back towards the main gates, so that we might follow the route taken by Cecil Hamborough and his two companions on the morning of the young man's death. The carriage-drive at the gates is only a short distance from the tideline of the bay. After a hundred yards or so, we passed the stone and brick building which had once housed the village school. The main woodland lay ahead of us, bordering the carriage-drive.

'From the windows of the schoolhouse back there,' said Stewart softly, 'two witnesses saw Major Monson, Lieutenant Hamborough, and Mr Scott. The men had told the butler at the house that they were going rabbit-shooting. It was too early in the month for game birds and, in any case, you can see that the terrain is quite unsuited to that. The three men were carrying shotguns when they reached this point, though the witnesses at the window of the schoolhouse cannot identify which guns were carried by which men. The three of them walked down the main driveway for some distance. A hundred yards or so from where we stand, they found the easiest place to straddle the fence and enter the woodland. They walked at a diagonal into the woods, Lieutenant Hamborough still in the middle, Major Monson to the right, Scott to the left. They walked at this angle and Scott was therefore most easily seen by the witnesses through a thinner screen of trees. The men were spaced out, of course, but the most important evidence from the two witnesses in the schoolhouse shows that Scott and Hamborough were ahead, with Major Monson lagging somewhat in the rear on the right flank. If you please, we will take that way.'

We followed Mr Stewart into this unkempt woodland, among beeches, limes, and rowan, where high birch trees along the paths formed a vaulting that almost obscured the sky. The white house of Ardlamont with its tall sash windows and terrace was now completely hidden. There had been a contested legacy and a protracted sale of the estate, I believe, during which the copses and spinneys had been left to run riot. All the same, these shadowy bridle-paths and alleys, with their carpeting of dark leaf mould which silenced one's footsteps, were a paradise to the hunter with dog or gun. The way was dry underfoot. Though it had rained before the day of the tragedy, it had not done so since and the ground was firm enough now.

The path was so overgrown in some places that it was scarcely any path at all. Tall bracken brushed the legs of our trousers at either side. At length we came out into what might be called a clearing. Across a further expanse of bracken the trees dwindled to a thinner screen of branches. To one side was a 'sunken fence', where the land fell to a lower wood on our left. This fence took the form of a stone retaining-wall at the level of our feet, holding back the earth from the lower woodland, so that we seemed to walk through the bracken upon a terrace. A hundred feet or so beyond this, the trees opened out on our right and there was a view of the house again. Such was the scene of the 'Ardlamont Tragedy', as the newspapers had called it.

Stewart approached the further screen of trees. I noticed that a beech, a rowan, and a lime tree bore circular yellow dye-marks on their trunks, some no more than three feet from the ground and others as high as eight feet. Our guide turned to us.

'Lieutenant Hamborough's body was found just here. Edward Scott told Monson and the doctor that he had seen the young man lying at the foot of the sunken wall and had lifted him up to the higher ground. It may be so, or it may not. There is no independent witness. When the body was seen by others, it was lying at the higher level on its back, the head six feet from the rowan tree and thirteen feet from the beech. The yellow dye-marks painted by our officers on the beech and rowan trunks show clearly the spread of shot as it hit the trees. There had been no shooting in this plantation for two or three weeks before Lieutenant Hamborough was killed. Therefore, where an earlier shot had hit the trees, the pellet-wounds had already healed over. The pellet holes you see marked were new, from the shot that killed Mr Hamborough.'

'And what is the spread?' Holmes asked casually.

'The spread of the shot is about five feet, as you may see from the trunk of the beech. Its trajectory can be traced back. It is a matter of geometrical calculation. By that calculation, the gun was most probably fired some thirty feet behind him and about five feet above the ground. A man who fires five feet above the ground is not shooting at rabbits, Mr Holmes! Nor does one sportsman fire a shotgun thirty feet immediately behind another without knowing that death or grievous injury is likely to result. A defence of accident at thirty feet can scarcely be sustained. Major Monson would surely have heard Lieutenant Hamborough's movements, even if he could not see him. And yet he fired, as the witnesses heard. In Scottish law as in English, Mr Holmes, a man is presumed to intend the natural and probable consequences of his acts.'

'I understand that the major maintains that he did not fire in any such a direction or at such a height,' Holmes said firmly.

Mr Stewart looked at him and shrugged.

'Unfortunately for Major Monson, Scott was seen on the far side of the wood by the third witness, too close to Hamborough to have fired a shot which spread as far as this. He was also on the wrong side of the deceased to have inflicted a wound to the right of the head.'

Holmes seemed not to be listening to him. The keen grey eyes were scanning the trunk of the beech tree, at a higher level.

'Allow me one moment, Mr Stewart.'

He took off his jacket and handed it to me. Then he gave a short jump upwards. His bony hands gripped a lower bough of the beech like a steel clamp. He swung his feet up and caught the branch between them. A moment more and he was astride it, examining the pale grey trunk at a height of ten or twelve feet above the ground. Out came his trusty pocket-knife from his trousers pocket and he attacked a tiny scab on the bark. Presently he called down.

'I fear, Mr Stewart, that your men overlooked a most interesting piece of evidence. I daresay when they found pellets as high as eight feet above the ground, they felt that they had done enough to show that only Monson could have fired the shot. That was remiss of them. I notice that there are three holes at quite twelve feet, not yet healed over, and that a shotgun pellet is still embedded in one of them. You shall see it for yourself in a moment.'

Stewart stared up, as Holmes swung himself down and dropped to the ground.

'Surely, Mr Holmes, all you have done is to turn suspicion against your client into certainty!'

'I have turned it into a matter of evidence, Mr Stewart! The spread of shot is plainly greater than you had measured. It was a capital error that once your men had gone high enough to establish that Hamborough could not have shot himself, they stopped. Given the true spread, the gun that fired the pellets would be quite sixty feet away, would it not? You may calculate it for yourself in due course but you may take it from me that the calibration is correct. Now, sir! What man, seeking to kill another, would choose a range of sixty feet with a shotgun? Would he not be far more likely to wound than to kill?'

The Deputy Fiscal was courteous but unmoved. 'Theories will not alter facts, Mr Holmes.'

'So my friend Lestrade is always telling me. However, I myself deal in facts and only then do I offer theories.'

Before the argument could continue, I was aware of a threshing in the undergrowth and saw the face of the Ardlamont butler, crimson with exertion.

'Mr Stewart, sir. There is a boy at the house with an express telegram, requiring an immediate reply. I should be obliged if you would come at once.'

There was time for only the briefest apology from the Deputy Fiscal before he hurried off in the wake of the butler. Holmes watched him go with an air of satisfaction, tempered by concern.

'A very decent young fellow, Watson. I regret that I had to deceive him.'

'Over the spread of shot?'

He looked at me in despair.

'Of course not! In the matter of the telegram, however, it was a simple matter to send a wire from the purser's office of the railway company's steamer. They undertook to despatch it by way of the piermaster at the next port of call. There are no such facilities at Ardlamont Bay, of course. However, I verified that it would go from Kames Pier half an hour later.'

'You sent Stewart a telegram to be delivered here?'

He looked still more concerned at my obtuseness.

'I sent a wire in the name of Mr Comrie Thomson, requesting an immediate comment on the information that Major Monson is to be released today for lack of evidence against him. I do not think our young friend will ignore that.'

'One day, Holmes,' I said feebly, 'you will go too far!'

'I have always thought that very likely. Meantime, I imagine that poor Mr Stewart is at this moment endeavouring to communicate an incomprehensible message to Inveraray and to get an equally incomprehensible reply in answer from Mr Thomson who, unfortunately, is away from his chambers today at my request. I think we may count on having the woods of Ardlamont to ourselves for at least the next forty-five minutes.'

## IV

Holmes put his pocket-knife away and pulled on his jacket.

'Let us go back to first principles. If Hamborough had shot himself with the short-barrelled 20-bore loaded with plain gunpowder, the wound would have been blackened. It was not. If he had shot himself by dropping the 12-bore loaded with amberite, he would have blown his head off. He did not. He was therefore shot by either Monson or Scott. But we are told that Scott was too close for his gun to have spread the shot as widely as the pellet-marks upon the beech tree indicate.'

'I cannot believe that Marshall Hall will thank you, Holmes,' I said curtly. 'As Stewart remarked just now, all you have done is to prove that our client did indeed shoot Hamborough, though perhaps at a range of sixty feet. It is the only conclusion to which your precious facts point.'

Holmes turned to me, his eyebrows raised in surprise.

'They do nothing of the kind!'

'I understood you to demonstrate that the spread of shot was consistent only with a range of sixty feet.'

His aquiline features assumed a weariness born of long patience as he sighed and looked about him.

'My dear Watson, I have demonstrated that the spread of shot so high up the tree-trunks was inconsistent with a range of thirty feet! So it is. But no one could have fired that shot from sixty feet. Consider the situation. Imagine how the pellets would fan out and lose velocity over sixty feet. The spread of shot might cover an area of ten by ten – say a hundred square feet. There might be no more than four or five individual pellets in the area of the victim's head. No murderer could be certain of accomplishing his object in such circumstances.'

'Then Monson shot Hamborough accidentally at a distance of sixty feet.'

'Quite impossible,' said Holmes sharply. 'As a medical man, even as an intelligent observer, one thing must strike you above all. If Hamborough had been killed with a shotgun at sixty feet, the shot would have spread so wide that his head would have been pockmarked by individual pellets. In the report of the post-mortem, there was a single central wound and no pock-marking whatever. You may therefore be quite sure that he was not shot at sixty feet . . .'

'Nor at thirty?'

'Correct. Let us waste no more time on the

impetuous theorizing of the Deputy Fiscal. Come, now. There are two paths running back to the carriage-drive. Monson must have approached the scene of the tragedy along one of them. We will search both, as well as the areas immediately to their right and left. I should think fifty feet back along each path would be sufficient.'

'Sufficient for what?'

'To look for a message left by Major Monson at the time of the shooting. To find a few torn scraps of paper.'

Why should the suspect write a message, before or after he fired? Had I not been accustomed to his unpredictable methods, I should have thought Holmes had taken leave of his senses.

'If Monson left a message, why would he – or someone else – then tear it up?'

Holmes ignored this.

'The fragments may be crumpled up very small and possibly singed but, let us hope, not all of them will have been entirely destroyed.'

If my friend was to be believed, Monson had composed a message in the middle of a shooting-party, then torn it up and burnt it. There was no time to argue over this, when the Deputy Fiscal might return at any moment. For ten minutes or so we searched without success for scraps of paper. There was none of any kind. With Holmes on my right, we again followed the two western footpaths, by one of which Monson must surely have made his way through the tangled briars and bracken of the wood.

'All the witnesses agree that it had been raining and that the major was wearing tweeds, not waterproofs,' Holmes said impatiently. 'Monson would therefore have followed the paths rather than stood up to his waist in wet heather.'

'In which case the ink would long ago have run on the paper and any message become indecipherable.'

'I think not. If it is here, and I have no doubt that it is, the message will remain perfectly clear.'

We extended our search further back until we were almost in sight of the fence and the carriage-drive again. Then we turned and made our way towards the scene of the shooting once more, heads down, seeking. We had patrolled up and down a dozen times and were about forty feet from the pellet-marked rowan and beech when I saw, at the edge of his path, what might have been a small white flower head. Before I could direct his attention to it, Sherlock Holmes's long arm reached down and snatched it up. With an unaccustomed carelessness, it seemed to me, he opened the scrap out, crumpled it again, and dropped it into his pocket. I was close enough to see that it was blank on both sides, though a little stained by wet.

A moment later, he darted down again and retrieved two more fragments, neither of them larger when opened than a *carte-de-visite*. If he had found a fragment of a message, my friend certainly kept it to himself. So far as I could see, however, this paper was also unmarked.

'Capital!' he said to himself, so quietly that I could scarcely hear him. Then he turned. 'Now let us walk back to where Hamborough's body was lying when Major Monson first saw it.'

As we reached the place, he took a twig and planted it into the earth to mark a spot that was both six feet from the rowan tree and thirteen feet from the beech.

'Here is where his head lay. The post-mortem gives his height as five feet eleven inches. Here, then, were his feet. The impact of such compacted shot as the post-mortem wound suggests would knock him down almost where he stood. We may allow a little distance but not much.'

'A fatally wounded man may stagger some distance before he falls.'

He sighed.

'A hunter will gallop several yards with a broken back before dropping dead, Watson, but not with such a discharge of shot in its equine brain! Moreover, the rain had stopped, the ground was examined at once and no blood was found except where the head lay.'

'But surely he fell over the sunken wall when he was hit. Scott found him lying down there and lifted him up to this level, out of the bracken. It was the most natural thing to do.'

'Cast your mind back to your military service at the battle of Maiwand,' Holmes said gently. 'Recall how much blood would flow from a wound like this in the man's dying moments, flowing on to the clothes of the injured man and thus on to those of anyone who tried to lift him. The evidence is that Edward Scott vanished from Ardlamont that afternoon in the very tweeds that he was wearing in the morning. No drop of blood appeared on them.'

'If he took the very greatest care . . .'

Holmes inclined his head.

'In that case let us admit that the weight of a man like Hamborough falling upon the bracken below would break it down hard where he landed, for several feet in each direction. I will give you five pounds,

Watson, for every broken stalk of bracken that you can find at the foot of this wall. See for yourself.'

He jumped down and I followed him. A man who had fallen from the upper level would certainly have landed within six feet of the sunken wall. At no point below the spot where Scott claimed to have lifted the body was the bracken disturbed. It had plainly grown for months as we saw it now.

'Why should Scott murder him?' I asked.

'For the same reason as Monson might have done. They had squeezed the poor young fellow of everything that they could get while he was alive. There remained only his far greater value to them when he was dead.'

'They planned the murder together?'

'That is possible but I do not think it likely. Neither would trust the other that far.'

While we talked, Holmes was examining a rough footpath, below the sunken wall, trodden through the lower bracken during the spring and summer months. It was no more than ten inches wide on bare soil. Towards the wall, there were a dozen prints of walking-shoes, preserved in compacted earth by the dry weather. They had therefore been made during or just after the last rainfall.

'The very morning of the hunting-party!' Holmes said softly. 'But look! Along here there is the full print of the man's shoes as he walks towards the sunken wall. Then, where the last half-dozen impressions end at this bramble bush, the print is only of the soles of the shoes with no sign of the heels.'

'It was Scott!' I said at once. 'Running the last few paces when he saw the body fall.'

Holmes uttered a dry, humourless laugh.

'No doubt it was Scott! Look at this. One may calculate a man's approximate height by the length of his stride. In this instance, I should judge from the footprints that our sportsman was of less than medium height, say five feet eight inches, the figure given for Scott in the police records. However, when a man runs, his stride lengthens, which is not at all the case here. The stride remains identical, though only the soles of the shoes are imprinted. Be so good as to stand on the higher ground, on the spot where we assume that Lieutenant Hamborough's feet might be once he lay dead.'

I scrambled up to the higher level and did as he asked. Holmes raised his walking-stick as if it were a gun, aiming over the top of the bramble bush towards my head.

'Though it will prove nothing in itself, Watson, my line of sight from here, at a range of fifteen feet or so, runs squarely to the level of your eyebrows. A little high, I grant you. The post-mortem on Hamborough confirms him as being one inch taller than you. Scott is quite four inches less than I am. Those last few prints are not of a man running but of a man standing on his toes, in order to raise his aim at a target situated where your head is at present. Were I to fire from here, I assure you the line would continue beyond your head to the beech tree, to the very centre of the pellet holes in the vertical spread of shot.'

'Stewart could not have missed such evidence!'

'Stewart missed it because his mind was overcome by the theory that the gun had been fired thirty feet behind. His minions found a sufficient spread of shot to make Monson the only suspect. Then they looked no higher. It seems that the incompetence of the Procurator Fiscal's office is quite a match for Scotland Yard. The yellow dye-marks are proof of that. Unfortunately, they could not test the true range by measuring also the horizontal spread, for there are no trees within five feet on either side to catch the pellets. Nor, it seems, had they any conception of a shot that was fired upwards, rather than on the level.'

It was clear that he was right, as he always seemed to be. However, one objection remained.

'The fatal wound was behind the right ear, whereas you or Scott would have been on the young man's left.'

He chuckled, as if moving a chess-piece to checkmate.

'As to that, Watson, you will see the answer written on the lime tree behind you.'

Instinctively, I turned to look. Before I had finished the movement, I knew that Holmes had just shot me through the right side of the head at no more than fifteen feet. He was correct. The vertical spread of the rising shot against the beech tree would make it seem a far greater range, as if fired from a spot where only Major Monson had been standing.

'Then your case is proved!'

He shook his head.

'I wish it were. Unfortunately, it is very far from proved. We have evidence that may convince the firearms experts but the pathologists will hold out against us. So long as the fatal wound is consistent only with a range of thirty feet, no amount of speculation with your head and my walking-stick will save Major Monson's neck.'

## V

Our sitting-room window in the Argyle Hotel looked out towards the length of the Trongate. Tall shops with sash windows on their upper floors stretched away like cliffs beyond the signs advertising the waxwork display and Percy's Boot Bargains. It was Saturday evening, when the courts and alleys behind the streets poured out their population into the commercial arteries of the city. The pavements with their ornate lamps were too narrow to contain the crowds, who spread out into the streets among brewers drays and open-topped horse-buses.

To and fro across this view passed the tall spare figure of Sherlock Holmes, pacing the room with controlled energy, his hands clasped behind his back. As he measured the carpet to and fro, he listened to the case against Major Monson outlined by David Stewart from the sofa, where the Deputy Fiscal sat with Dr Henry Littlejohn. This Edinburgh police surgeon was principal medical adviser to the prosecution. At length, Holmes stopped and straightened up, taller and gaunter than ever.

'I compliment you, Mr Stewart, on the care and diligence which you and Dr Littlejohn have lavished upon the investigation. However, I have invited you both here this evening to suggest that you should waste no further time upon it.'

'You are beyond me, Mr Holmes,' said Stewart quietly.

'I should not be surprised. For the moment, however, I tender my advice that you should drop the prosecution of Major Monson forthwith. You have not the slightest chance of winning a verdict in court.'

Mr Stewart opened his mouth and then closed it again. Dr Littlejohn looked like a man who has accidentally swallowed a peppermint humbug whole. The Deputy Fiscal recovered his wits.

'With great respect, Mr Holmes, there have been few cases in my experience where the chance of a conviction was greater. Certainly there have been none in which the accused has lied so consistently and so ineptly as Major Monson.'

'Just so,' said Holmes quickly. 'Then you would hang him for being a liar?'

Mr Stewart hesitated.

'He will hang himself, Mr Holmes. Sir, you have a reputation for ingenuity, far beyond London or Glasgow. However, since your request to me yesterday morning, your theory that Lieutenant Hamborough was shot from below the sunken wall by Scott has been examined and rejected.'

Holmes seemed not the least put out.

'May I ask why?'

Dr Littlejohn intervened.

'Such a wide wound, Mr Holmes, some three inches by two at its extreme dimensions, could not have been inflicted on the deceased at so short a range as fifteen feet, for one thing.'

'And for another?'

'Two shots only were heard by the witnesses. They are all in agreement. Major Monson admits firing the first shot. It is quite possible that he fired both of them. However, if Scott fired the second shot, we come back once again to the fact that he did so from too close a range to kill Lieutenant Hamborough by that wound.'

'Moreover,' added Stewart, 'had Scott fired at a range of thirty feet or more to cause such a wound, he must have been much further back down the path. He would have been visible to the witnesses when he fired.'

Holmes paused. Then he swept all this aside.

'I see. May we take it as common ground that Major Monson was lying when he changed his story about the guns to suit the absence of blackening on the skin?'

'Indeed we may!' Mr Stewart was astonished and a little wary at the zeal with which Holmes tightened the noose round his client.

'Good. First he tells us he was carrying the 12-bore loaded with smokeless amberite cartridges. We believe him. Later, when he discovers that this is the only ammunition with which Hamborough could have accidentally shot himself, the major changes guns – or rather stories – and is carrying the short-barrelled 20-bore with gunpowder? We think that is a lie?'

'Correct.'

'Excellent. You see? We are in agreement already! Very well, then Monson was carrying the 12-bore with amberite cartridges, as he said at first.'

'Certainly. Lieutenant Hamborough had the 20-bore whose powder would have blackened his skin at such a range. It did not. Therefore he did not shoot himself by accident.'

'Precisely!'

A great weight seemed to be lifted from Holmes by this general consent that his client was an unprincipled liar. His next observation did little to reassure me.

'I think, Mr Stewart, that we are very near to the end of this case.'

Neither David Stewart nor Dr Littlejohn looked as if he thought so.

'One thing, however,' Holmes swung round to the Deputy Fiscal, a long forefinger raised. 'As adviser to Mr Comrie Thomson, I have requested sight of the packet of amberite cartridges from which we agree that Major Monson was loading his gun on that fatal morning. I should like to see them.'

The packet which Mr Stewart now took from his attaché case was almost empty, containing no more than three or four shotgun cartridges. They were of the most ordinary kind. He handed the packet to Sherlock Holmes, who studied the contents with narrowed eyes.

'Have these cartridges been examined?'

Stewart's answer was abrupt, as if he suspected Holmes of playing some game with him. Had he known Holmes better, the Deputy Fiscal would have had no doubt of his earnestness.

'You may see for yourself, Mr Holmes, that there is nothing to examine. The unused cartridges have been seen and noted for the court as exhibit 241, item 9, in the list of evidence appended to the charge of murder. They scarcely warrant further examination. They were never used, not even loaded in the gun, and played no part in the crime.'

'How very remiss,' said Holmes coolly, sitting down at a small walnut table in the window and taking out his magnifying-glass. 'I fear I must tell you that they played the decisive part in this crime. By such blunders as yours, sir, are innocent men and women hanged.'

Mr Stewart and Dr Littlejohn looked at one another.

Holmes put down his magnifying-glass. His eyes flashed and he turned upon his two visitors.

'As I suspected!'

Before anyone could stop him tampering with the evidence, he had opened his neat ivory-handled pocket-knife and was deftly slitting the hardened cardboard of a cartridge case down its length.

'Mr Holmes! I must beg you will desist!'

The Deputy Fiscal was on his feet, crossing the room to rescue this 'exhibit' from the depredations of the sharp little blade. Holmes waved him away. In any event, the damage was now done.

Dr Littlejohn and I got up and joined them. Holmes had spread open the cartridge case like a frog on a dissecting board. There was the percussion cap at the base to detonate the powder when the hammer of the gun struck the pin. The lower half of the cardboard casing was filled with yellow amberite powder. Above that, the interior of the cartridge was divided by a felt wad.

Between this division and a second wad at the top of the cartridge was a space which should have been filled with several hundred lead pellets. Instead, this upper cavity was packed by tightly compressed pellets of paper. Confined as they were by the cardboard tube, they appeared smaller and harder than the paper 'flower heads' which we had found in the woodland at Ardlamont. Yet a single glance at the paper and the fragments was enough to confirm that they were of the same origin. Before Mr Stewart recovered his presence of mind, Holmes had slit open a second cartridge with the same result.

'What is the commonest way of rendering a cartridge

blank and harmless?' he said, as if speaking to himself. 'To slit its upper half open neatly and substitute some innocuous substance for the lead pellets. Paper pellets are an excellent replacement. Almost all of them are burnt up in the discharge of the gun. A few are merely dispersed, though many of those are touched by flame.'

As he spoke, he took from his pocket the two scraps of paper picked up at Ardlamont. To be sure they were blank. However, in opening them out he showed that one was singed a light brown down its edge. Such was the 'message' which Major Monson had unwittingly left.

'Monson fired nothing more lethal than paper,' Holmes said quietly to Stewart, 'Scott saw to that. As Monson said at first, he took the 12-bore and the cartridges on entering the woods. To be sure, had he opened a further packet of cartridges he would have fired live ammunition. What remained in the first packet was intended to suffice him until after the death of Lieutenant Hamborough. During that time, provided he used no more than five cartridges, he was no danger to man nor beast. We know from the witnesses that he cannot have fired more than twice.'

'Then he cannot have killed Hamborough?'

'He cannot,' said Holmes gently, 'but the poor perjured wretch thinks he did, for he believed that he was firing live ammunition and that he alone had the range to cause a dreadful accident! Worse still, after the boating accident and the insurance of Hamborough's life for his own advantage, he thought quite reasonably that not a single juryman in the country would believe in his innocence! As for Scott, his trick would never have been discovered. Monson fired – but did not guess what he fired! If Hamborough's death had continued to be accepted as an accident, as it was by Dr Macmillan, the remaining few cartridges in the packet would have been used up by some other sportsman and Scott's secret would have been safe for ever.'

'But Scott cannot have inflicted such a wound at so short a range,' said the Deputy Fiscal, sitting down again. 'There is no altering that.'

Holmes turned to Dr Littlejohn.

'On what day was Hamborough killed?'

'I understand it was 10 August.'

'The day upon which Dr Macmillan certified accidental death? The poor boy was then taken to Ventnor on the Isle of Wight. He was buried there on 17 August, a week to the day after his death. Correct?'

Dr Littlejohn nodded but said nothing.

'After which,' Holmes continued, 'his body lay in the family vault. For how long?'

'The exhumation was carried out on 4 September and the post-mortem followed.'

'Did it indeed?' Holmes turned to the window and glanced down at the crowds in the Trongate. Then he looked round. 'In your experience as a police surgeon, Dr Littlejohn, how many of the bodies examined by you in cases of suspicious death have been exhumed?'

The bald bespectacled surgeon stared back at him.

'Not many as a percentage but quite a few in total.'

'From what causes?'

'Almost always where there is a suspicion of poison. Also I have known two or three who have died from violent blows and where there has been a question raised later of *mens rea*, deliberate harm.'

'I see.' Holmes turned to the window again. 'What is

your experience of cases where the deceased has died of gunshot wounds?'

Dr Littlejohn shrugged.

'I have known two cases of homicidal shooting and quite a number of accidental shootings in the hunting season.'

'In how many of those cases was the deceased interred and exhumed before post-mortem examination?'

Dr Littlejohn stared at him, this time without speaking.

'There was not one,' said Holmes at last, 'was there, doctor?'

David Stewart had been fidgeting upon the sofa.

'What can that matter, Mr Holmes? Dr Littlejohn is expert and vastly experienced in the examination of gunshot wounds.'

Holmes bowed his head a little, as if to acknowledge this.

'Indeed he is. Perhaps he is less experienced, however, in the effects upon gunshot wounds of decomposition, a warm summer month later and after a few weeks of interment.'

'There was no decomposition to speak of!' said Littlejohn indignantly.

'Permit me,' Holmes turned to the table, from which he took a sheet of paper. 'Your post-mortem report, Dr Littlejohn. May I read you a word or two? "*The features were swollen . . . Decomposition was making progress . . . The hair, owing to advancing decomposition, was easily detached . . .*"'

'There is nothing in that!' said the Deputy Fiscal, now plainly rattled.

'Is there not, Mr Stewart? Are you familiar with the work of Professor Matthew Hay, who acts as police-surgeon for the City of Aberdeen?'

'I have met him several times.'

'Are you familiar, specifically, with his work on gun-shot injuries?'

'His work?'

'His published work.'

'I cannot say that I am.'

'Would it surprise you to know that three weeks after death the progress of decomposition would make any measurement of the surface extent of an original shotgun wound almost impossible?'

The gaze of Sherlock Holmes now pinned his young victim like a moth to a specimen board. He went on without respite.

'The post-mortem report by Dr Littlejohn gives the maximum extent of the wound as varying from two to three inches, which in itself is consistent with a shot fired at a range of fifteen feet. Now, gentlemen, either there was decomposition or there was not. If there was, no accurate measurement of the wound can be given. If there was not, then the measurement is accurate and Hamborough was shot from fifteen feet. He was certainly not shot by Major Monson with paper pellets! In either event, I fear that your case against the defendant is blown to smithereens.'

Stewart stared at him with that mixture of exasperation and incomprehension characteristic of so many adversaries of Sherlock Holmes. The young man seemed to be listening to the door of a trap as it closed behind him. He then made the same mistake as so many of his predecessors, seeing a promise of salvation and leaping at it.

'Why should Scott do Monson's work for him? It was Monson who would benefit directly from the insurance, not Scott.'

Holmes walked across and laid a hand sympathetically on the young man's shoulder.

'He did it for the money, Mr Stewart. He meant to be rich for life. There was no way to do that so long as Hamborough lived, once his funds were exhausted. Scott and Monson were partners in fleecing the poor fellow but until he was dead, they had nothing more. Fortunately for Scott, Dr Macmillan knew little of gunshot wounds and gave the young man a death certificate. Scott then withdrew from the scene to attend to his own affairs. His undoubted intention was that Monson should believe that he himself had killed Hamborough accidentally. If the coast had remained clear, Scott could have returned to claim from Monson the "debts" his young friend Hamborough owed him. I do not doubt that Hamborough's signature, forged where necessary, would appear on far more IOUs than he ever wrote to Mr Beresford Tottenham, the moneylender. Such claims on the young man's estate, on the insurance money of £30,000, were more than enough to make Scott's fortune. The shooting would remain an accident, as Dr Macmillan thought it was. Naturally, when Scott read the reports of Monson's arrest, he preferred not to show his face.'

'Monson would surely refuse to pay him,' said Mr Stewart hopefully.

Holmes shook his head.

'Scott, *alias* Davis, *alias* Sweeney is no stranger to

blackmail. Least of all when he might threaten to fabricate evidence of murder against his partner. Monson, the poor swindling booby, already believes that he shot Hamborough by accident. It would only need Scott to whisper in his ear a promise of going to the authorities with a story of having seen Monson creep up on the young man and take deliberate aim. For good measure, he might swear to having seen Monson take the bung out of the rowing-boat the night before. Scott himself, of course, was the perpetrator of that curtain-raiser.'

There was an uncomfortable silence, until Holmes added quietly, 'You, Mr Stewart, would have hanged Monson even on the evidence you have now! Think how much easier your task would have been had Scott offered you such evidence as I have just suggested. Do you still doubt that Monson would give Scott half of the £30,000 to shut his mouth? I promise you he would give him all to save his neck from the rope!'

The Deputy Fiscal got slowly to his feet.

'I will report what you have told me.'

'Please do so,' said Holmes graciously, 'and when you do, pray inform the Procurator with my compliments that Professor Matthew Hay, Police-Surgeon of Aberdeen, has already agreed to give evidence for the defence in any trial of Major Monson.'

It is a matter of history that Professor Hay did so and that the charges against Alfred John Monson were found 'not proven' by the jury at the High Court of Justiciary in Edinburgh. Holmes and I heard no more of the major, except that he sued Madame Tussaud's Waxworks for placing an effigy of him in the Chamber of Horrors. Edward Scott, or Edward Sweeney as he was born, remained at large. I was putting together the papers in the case, so that they might be deposited in the tin trunk, when something struck me in one of the depositions.

'Is it not curious, Holmes, that having hired a place like Ardlamont for the summer, Scott absented himself so much at night? He seems to have risen late, gone to Glasgow by the afternoon steamer and returned late, except on Sundays when he dined with the Monsons at Ardlamont. On Wednesday and Saturday, he went still earlier, to be in the city by two in the afternoon. It is all here in the butler's statement. I suppose the fellow was probably taking street-girls to some low-class hotel.'

Holmes listened with eyes closed and fingertips pressed tight together. Then he opened his eyes and said, 'But scarcely on Wednesday and Saturday afternoons with such regularity.'

He closed his eyes again and appeared to have gone to sleep. Then he sat up abruptly.

'It is his profession! Of course! Not an admirable one but, such as it is, I suppose it is his *métier*. What professional man is occupied every evening but Sunday – and upon Wednesday and Saturday afternoons?'

'I have no idea at this moment.'

'Dear me,' he said with a yawn, 'did you never, in your wild youth, Watson, attend a music-hall? It is available every evening with matinées on Wednesday and Saturday. I daresay you might have found Mr Scott on the stage of the Glasgow Empire.'

'That is quite absurd!'

'So it is. However, if I had a guinea for every occasion

on which what is absurd has proved to be true, I should be a good deal richer than I am.'

We did not discuss the matter further. A long time later, a letter came to Holmes from David Stewart, the Deputy Fiscal. Edward Scott had been seen briefly, working as the assistant to a music-hall magician. Then he had vanished for good. In the course of the stage performance, there was some 'trick-shooting', when the blindfold magician shot the segments from an orange on his assistant's head – or something of the kind. The trick is one of the oldest in the world. The fruit, or whatever the target be, is carefully dismembered beforehand. The pieces are plucked from it by a concealed thread in the moment when the audience blinks at the firing of the shot and the scene is veiled by smoke. One of the chores of the brave but humble assistant is to ensure that the cartridges in the pistol of the magician have been rendered blank.

'I assure you,' said Holmes, stretching out his long legs towards the winter fire, 'Scott is probably quite safe, even if he should be found again. To prosecute him now would be difficult in any event. Moreover, if they could not get a verdict against Monson, they will hardly get one against Scott. Mr Stewart and his colleagues must admit publicly the falsity of all their evidence in the previous case and the fact that I was right in every particular. I do not somehow think that they will swallow so bitter a pill.'

It is a matter of history that they never did.

# The Case of the Hygienic Husband

## I

On a rainy morning of early autumn, in the last days of peace before the Great War, Sherlock Holmes leant back in his chair, the remains of his breakfast still littering the table. He began to open his correspondence. As I took up the *Times* report on the Serbian crisis, there was an exclamation from my friend. I put aside the paper and saw his face writhing with inward merriment, his eyes shining, as if he was restraining a convulsive attack of laughter.

He read out to me from a sheet of notepaper in his hand.

> *'Sir – In answer to your question regarding my parentage, etc. My mother was a bus-horse, my father a cab-driver, my sister a rough-rider over the arctic regions. My brothers were all gallant sailors on a steam-roller. This is the only information I can give to those who are not entitled to ask such questions – contained in the letter I received on the 15th inst. Your despised son-in-law G. Smith.'*

'Who the devil, Holmes, is G. Smith and to whom is this nonsense addressed?'

He looked at two more sheets of paper and shook his head.

'I have no notion, my dear fellow. At least, it can scarcely be addressed to us. Curiously, however, there seems to be no covering letter. I have no doubt that we shall discover something more before the day is over. One moment. Here is a second from the author of the first!'

He held up this sheet of paper and read it out.

> '*Sir – I do not know your next move, but take my advice and be careful. Yours etc., G. Smith.* Now that, Watson, sounds more businesslike. And here is a third, dated like the others within the past ten days. *Sir – I have all the copies of the letters, &c., my wife and self has sent to you and yours, also all letters &c., we have received relating to same and family affairs which I intend to keep for the purpose of justice. G. Smith.* Whoever Mr Smith may be he shows, does he not, an engaging innocence of the conventions of grammar and syntax?'

'But why have these things been sent to us with no explanation?'

'I believe we shall have an answer to that soon enough.'

Without another word, he knocked out his pipe and stretched upon the sofa with his violin and a score of Scriabin's tone poem *Prometheus*. Holmes had lately conceived an unfortunate enthusiasm for the 'new music' of Stravinsky and Scriabin. Such cacophony may do well enough in a concert hall, but in one's domestic quarters it is insupportable. The score of *Pro-*

*metheus* he professed to find interesting because the composer claimed that he had allowed religion, occultism, and even the properties of light to dictate the unmelodious music. A better reason for destroying such tosh would be hard to find!

As Holmes predicted, however, there was a happy interruption half an hour later from the clang of the bell at the street-door. Mrs Hudson came upstairs alone.

'A gentleman,' she said, rather archly as I thought. 'He has no appointment but believes Mr Holmes may be in possession of some papers belonging to him. The gentleman is here to collect them.'

Holmes seemed not the least put out as he laid down his violin and bow.

'By all means show him up, Mrs Hudson. He shall have our undivided attention.'

While we awaited this visitor, Holmes recited phrases from the letters as if they had been a schoolboy's lesson.

'My mother was a bus-horse, my father a cab-driver, my sister a rough-rider across the arctic regions. This promises rather well, Watson. I am inclined to think . . .'

What he was inclined to think remained unspoken. At that moment, the door of the sitting-room opened. We confronted a tall pleasant-looking man, a little more than fifty years old. His face was high-nosed and pale, his clothes of a dark clerical cut with a pearl-grey cravat.

'Pray come in, sir, and be seated,' Holmes said genially, 'I am Sherlock Holmes and this is my associate Dr Watson. I imagine, however, that you already know that.'

The tall pale man made a little bow in each direction and said awkwardly, 'The truth is, Mr Holmes, I had heard of neither of you until two days ago. My wife and I lead a quiet and, until recently, a contented life. Even the newspapers have little claim on my attention.'

'No matter,' said Holmes, guiding him to a chair, 'I fear I did not have the pleasure of gathering your name from the letters you kindly forwarded.'

Our visitor looked at him quickly, as if he did not expect Holmes to connect him so easily with the curious correspondence.

'It was not my intention to deceive you,' he said guardedly as we sat down.

Holmes gave him another quick but reassuring smile.

'My dear sir, there was no deceit. What is a name at this stage? It is enough for me that you are plainly a devout man held in high regard. A Methodist local preacher, I fancy, living in Buckinghamshire. Your daughter has made an injudicious marriage to Mr Smith, a scoundrel. On Tuesday afternoon, two days ago, I rather think you went to Oxford to consult Mr Henry Howes, of Howes and Woodhall, solicitors in St Michael Street. On his advice, you sent me copies of three letters from Mr Smith, demanding sums unpaid by you from a promissory note given him a month or two ago. This was understood to be payment for removing himself and leaving your daughter alone. Unfortunately nothing was put in writing to that effect. The result is that he has married your daughter since then and now proposes to enforce payment of the money. This morning, on the advice of Mr Howes, you came up by train and have just walked here from Marylebone station.'

Like so many clients, our visitor stared as if he suspected witchcraft.

'I could almost believe, sir, that you have spied upon me!'

Holmes set him at his ease.

'I have done nothing but exercise a little common sense. The cut and clerical pattern of your suit, like the label in your overcoat, comes from Harris and Rogerson of Victoria Street, close to the Methodist Central Hall, well-known as tailors to the clergy of that denomination. You do not wear a clerical collar but you have the manner and address of a public speaker. This leads me to suppose you are a local preacher in your circuit. You did not come by cab, for we should have heard it draw up, therefore you have walked a relatively short distance or your shoes and trouser-cuffs would be wetter. Marylebone is our closest terminus. Your coat and umbrella have kept you dry for the most part. I merely note that your lower right trouser-leg is marked by rain, while the left is not. After many years of residence, I recognize that as the sign of a man who has walked from Marylebone station in the prevailing wind rather than from the Metropolitan line at Baker Street. The time of your arrival suggests you have come by the line that runs to Buckinghamshire. So early in the day, you could scarcely have come from a greater distance.'

Our visitor shifted uneasily.

'Then Mr Howes has not betrayed my confidence?'

Holmes shook his head.

'I observe that the postage stamp on your envelope was cancelled in Oxford at 6a.m. yesterday. You yourself would hardly be in Oxford at such an early hour, of course. At least, you would not go all the way to the sorting office to post a letter at that time, when you might just as well have sent it from any post-box during the rest of the day. The envelope was, therefore, placed in the box on Tuesday night, after the day's final collection, at about 10p.m. If you were in Oxford prior to posting these most important documents, then it is reasonable to suppose that you went to seek advice and that you spent some hours considering whether to follow it.'

'That is the case precisely,' said our visitor, somewhat relieved.

'Indeed,' said Holmes comfortingly. 'As for the recommendation, I am acquainted with Warden Spooner of New College, Strachan Davidson the Master of Balliol, and several senior members of the School of Natural Science at the University. However, they are not men to be approached in such a matter as this. On the other hand, I was once able to render a small service to Mr Howes. He is the most likely person in that city to have mentioned my name to you. The fact that he did not forward the papers himself also suggests to me that you spent some hours pondering the matter. At length, you decided to post them without a covering letter, so that you still did not commit yourself by name. You then returned home by the last train. Aylesbury or Tring on the 10.45 from Oxford, I should guess. I daresay I am quite wrong.'

'Tring was the station, but my home is not there,' said our visitor quietly. 'You are wrong only in that,

Mr Holmes, for I live at Aston Clinton, several miles away. I could not have believed in such powers of deduction if I had not witnessed them for myself.'

'I assure you,' Holmes said gently, 'it is not difficult to construct a series of inferences, each dependent upon its predecessor and simple in itself. If one merely knocks out the central inferences and presents only a starting-point and conclusion, it has a startling effect. But it is simple enough, for all that.'

'My name,' said the tall pale man, 'is William Maxse. My daughter Constance is a handsome young woman with a little money. She trained as a nurse for three years at Southsea and has held some excellent positions.'

'Until she met Mr Smith?'

'Precisely,' Mr Maxse's colour rose. 'Unfortunately there is more to it than that. I have a dear friend and colleague at our chapel, Charles Burnham, whose daughter Alice trained with mine. Both girls came from Wesleyan families in the same town. When they went away to Portsmouth, the chapel at Southsea, as well as the hospital, became a centre of their lives. The scoundrel of whom I speak attended the Southsea chapel.'

'Allow me,' said Holmes, who was taking a few notes. 'How long ago did this matter begin?'

'Two years ago, Smith courted and married Alice Burnham, to her parents' great distress. No sooner was the wedding over than he began to demand what he called the money due as a marriage settlement. He did so in the most abusive terms, almost word for word such as you have seen in his address to me.'

'And was the money paid?'

'It was paid, Mr Holmes, for poor Burnham feared

that any legal action would destroy his child's reputation.'

'How most unfortunate. Pray continue with your narrative.'

'It almost makes me weep to do so,' said Mr Maxse quietly. 'After Smith and Miss Burnham had been married a little while, Alice Burnham died in a swimming accident of some kind at Blackpool, where they were on holiday. Smith returned to Southsea and appeared once again in the chapel, distraught at his loss. He swore that he could no longer bear the memories which the town evoked and so he went to live elsewhere. I heard this much from Charles Burnham himself and supposed we had heard the last of the wretch.'

'One seldom hears the last of such men,' said Holmes thoughtfully. 'When was it that Smith reappeared?'

'Two years later he returned to Southsea. I think it is not too much to say that he laid siege to my Constance's heart when they met again in chapel. He corrupted my girl's affections, Mr Holmes. I warned her in vain against him. She wrote back swearing that he was the most loving and Christian-like man.'

Holmes muttered something which I did not catch. Mr Maxse continued.

'The result of my warnings was to turn poor Connie against me. I heard nothing for a week or two and prayed that this meant a separation between them. Alas, it did not. I swear it was Smith who persuaded my girl that it was best to marry him first and tell her mother and I afterwards. So it happened. I knew nothing of their register-office wedding until a week later, when the demands for money began. No bride-cake, no photograph, no loving words from my darling. I ask you, sir, if I may legitimately refuse payment to him and if you can bring my Constance back to me?'

Holmes let his chin rest on his chest, showing his bird-of-prey profile.

'Unless there is money already settled on her in the event of her marriage, he has no such claim on you. As to her return, it is she who must will it.'

'Then let the money go, Mr Holmes! How may I bring my child back and – God forgive me – see this devil destroyed?'

Holmes crossed to the window, and in a characteristic pause looked down into the street for a moment before replying. Then he turned round.

'You may depend upon me to do whatever I can. But you must understand that the law will support your son-in-law as a husband in almost every respect.'

'I care nothing for money!' cried the poor man in his despair.

'Just so. Mr Smith counts on that. I must repeat, however, as to bringing a daughter home, there is little a father can do that will not drive a bride deeper into the arms of such a . . .'

'Such a reptile! I saw it in him the first and last time our paths crossed.'

'Quite. Now your daughter must see it, for herself. When she does so, your time will come. Until then, right remains on your side. The law, unfortunately, is on his.'

Mr Maxse had twisted in his chair to face Holmes squarely, his face flushed with anger.

'Then you can do nothing for me?'

Holmes walked back and sat down just opposite him.

'I did not say so, Mr Maxse. The law can do nothing, as matters stand. I, however, am not the law.'

I never saw such gratitude sparkle in the eyes of a client. Before Mr Maxse left us, Holmes was no less to him than a knight in arms. When we were alone, my friend lit his pipe in silence and sat lost in thought until I interrupted him at last.

'They have been married two weeks already. It is presumably too late for an annulment and certainly too early for a divorce. How is such a case to be won?'

He put down his pipe.

'It astonishes me, Watson, that you have gathered so little. As a medical man, you surely see that Smith is no common scoundrel. He steps full-grown from Dr Albert Moll's admirable treatise on criminal psychopathology.'

I saw nothing of the kind but it seemed neither the time nor place to say so.

'The wedding-photograph,' Holmes said thoughtfully. 'Why was the newly-married Mrs Smith forbidden to send a copy to her parents? Was it not the most natural thing for her to do?'

'Perhaps no photograph was taken.'

'Where there is a wedding,' he said sourly, 'there is a photograph, usually of questionable artistry.'

'You think Smith did not want his wife's parents to see a likeness of him?'

'Come, Watson! They had seen him in the flesh. No. Friend Smith is concerned that no one else should see his wedding picture. What crime might that photograph reveal to a person who saw it by chance and identified him?'

'Bigamy? A wedding under other circumstances can scarcely constitute a crime where the bride is of age.'

He looked at me, as if I might be his despair.

'This illiterate boor exercises such power over two intelligent and capable young women that they, at his command, cast off their parents and all their love for them. Who, short of a hypnotist or Dr Mesmer in person, could accomplish such a feat twice with two such loving daughters – and who knows with how many more? If Mr Smith proves to be a mere bigamist, Watson, I shall regard him as a sad disappointment.'

## II

For several days, following Mr Maxse's visit, Holmes abandoned Monsieur Scriabin's tone-poem. Nothing would do but he must lounge about the sitting-room with his violin, singing the phrases of Mr Smith's absurd letters to tunes that took his fancy. I recall, painfully, 'The Keel-Row', tortured on the fiddle-strings until it fitted, 'My mother was a bus-horse, my father a cab-driver, my sister a rough-rider across the arctic regions.'

So far as his case was concerned, he appeared to have forgotten it.

It was several mornings later when I chanced to see an official envelope among the letters awaiting his attention. As he lifted the one above it, the form of address on the lower one was revealed: 'Miss Phoebe Golightly, 221b Baker Street, London W.' I stared at him as he read its predecessor, until at last he looked up, as if suddenly aware of my attention. I pointed at the envelope.

'What the devil is that, Holmes?'

He glanced at it with complete unconcern, then stared back at me.

'It is I, Watson. I am Miss Phoebe Golightly, by courtesy of the typewriter, which is impartial in matters of handwriting and sex. I am a youthful spinster who attended a wedding on Saturday week at the Portsmouth Register Office. Indeed, I was a bridesmaid to my cousin. In the excitement which, for reasons that baffle me, follows these ceremonies, I gave a shawl to be held by the photographer's assistant while the pictures were taken. The jollity of the occasion was such that I was half-way to the reception before realizing that I had left the garment behind. I feel sure that some register official would know the firms of Portsmouth photographers likely to be present that afternoon.'

I watched him open the letter and scowl at it. Then his face brightened.

'And here we are. Mr Collins of Wellington Street, Southsea, or, perhaps the larger business of Whitfield and Buller of Stanhope Road, Portsmouth. You will observe from the letters sent to Mr Maxse that the Smiths are lodging at an address in Kimberley Road, East Southsea. The probability must be that Mr Collins of Wellington Street was their man.'

'If a photograph was taken.'

'If it was not, Watson, we must pursue another course. I think, however, Mr Smith would not be so foolish as show his true meanness so early to his bride.'

That afternoon, a further fabrication devised by Holmes in the name of Mr Maxse, solicited a copy of his daughter's wedding-photograph. Before the week was out, a stout envelope brought back this full-plate print. The photograph showed too plainly the meanness of the occasion, whose ceremony had been attended only by the bride and groom. The witnesses, who stood either side of the couple, were plainly a pair of register officials. Constance Maxse appeared a well-built and rather plump young woman with dark hair and an air of resolve. She did not seem in the least like a wayward daughter but a figure of somewhat matronly decorum.

Far more interesting to Holmes was the image of the bridegroom. His was a strong broad-boned face in which the nose and chin were sharp rather than regular. He had a full dark moustache, which an Italian waiter might have affected, but wore it as if to conceal a line of cruelty in his mouth. The eyes looked hard and straight under low and frowning brows. They shone with a dreadful clarity and a merciless sanity. His brown hair was worn short and neat, so that the high points of the ears appeared prominently. There was no flabbiness in the face, the skin being tight over the bones and still shining from the razor, yet the neck was one of the thickest in proportion that I have ever seen.

'Ah!' said Holmes at once. 'What would the great Lombroso not have given for the skull of such an hereditary degenerate! Look at the features, Watson! The eyes stare down at you, just as a man regards a beetle in the moment before he crushes it with his boot! The power of those cheek-bones! The strength of that neck! Mr Maxse told us he knew the man for what he was. I doubt if the poor fellow guessed the half of it!'

We studied the portrait in silence for several minutes. Then Holmes said coolly, 'I do believe the strength of that neck may cause some little inconvenience to Messrs Pierpoint and Ellis in the exercise of their gruesome trade. For, Watson, if ever I saw a man born to be hanged, this is he.'

Sherlock Holmes had, to a remarkable degree, the power of detaching his mind at will. He was also exceedingly reluctant on occasions to communicate his plans or his thoughts to any other person. During the next few days I once again concluded that he had given up any active interest in the case for the time being and was now waiting for the sinister bridegroom to make his first mistake. This impression became all the stronger when he told me that his second cousin, Lieutenant-Commander Holmes-Derringer of the admiral's staff at Scapa Flow, had invited him to attend the live-firing tests of the new Whitehead torpedo in the vicinity of that remote island anchorage. For three days at least he would be absent from London. I hoped most fervently that I should not be the subject of Mr Maxse's reproaches during this period.

I was about to say as much, shortly before he left, when I saw that I was already too late. I had been out and had just come back as far as Mrs Hudson's open street door, about to go upstairs, when a neatly-rigged and capped naval officer, his light-brown hair and beard well-trimmed, came cantering down with a brown binocular-case in his hand. He called out to Holmes who was evidently already in the cab that waited in the street, 'Sit tight, old boy! I've got them for you!' Then, as if noticing me for the first time in the shadows, he snapped, 'Morning to you!'

The sharp air of command was such that I very nearly saluted him. So much for Lieutenant-Commander Holmes-Derringer. As I watched, he tossed the overlooked binoculars into the hansom, swung himself aboard as if it might be a battle-cruiser's whaler, and the cab clattered north towards the Euston Road.

In order not to incur the reproaches of Mr Maxse, I decided that I would withdraw to my club for the greater part of the next day or two, leaving Baker Street after breakfast. I should then come home when I judged that the last train from Marylebone to the counties had left.

It was on the second day that I entered the sitting-room, at 11 p.m. or thereabouts, and found a wire waiting for me.

> IMPERATIVE YOU SEEK SMITH IN WESTON-SUPER-MARE AT ONCE STOP.
> WILL JOIN YOU ON RETURN FROM SCOTLAND STOP.
> FURTHER INSTRUCTIONS AWAIT YOU TELEGRAPH OFFICE, TEMPLE MEADS STATION, BRISTOL STOP.
> = HOLMES, C/O ADMIRALTY INTELLIGENCE STOP.

I put down the scrap of paper with the feeling of a man commanded to make bricks without straw. With no further information than this, how was I to find Smith, or anyone else, among the resident population and teeming summer holidaymakers of a seaside town that was utterly unfamiliar to me? What further instructions of any value could Holmes possibly send me from his present isolation in the Orkney Islands? I certainly had no means of contacting him. I could scarcely wire a message to him through Lieutenant-Commander Holmes-Derringer in the middle of the night and, in any case, I had no time to wait for a reply next day.

I slept uneasily with the phrases of that telegraph running and twisting like railway tracks, crossing and parting, in my brain. Once I woke sharply from a dream with the face of Mr Smith in his wedding-photograph shimmering like a gargoyle in the darkness. By next morning I decided that there was nothing for it but to do as I was told.

## III

By the evening of the next day, the express that had brought me from Paddington was pulling into the long curve of the railway platform at Bristol, the hills of the city rising high above the river on either side. At the telegraph office, to my dismay, there was no wire from Holmes. Perhaps by now he was on the high seas in a cruiser or a destroyer and was forbidden such communication, for German intelligence was keenly aware of our development of submarine warfare. However, on further investigation there was a telephone message for me, which the clerk had scribbled down without bothering to put the name of the sender. I stared at the pencilled letters.

*Dr Watson to proceed to Grand Atlantic Hotel,*
*Weston, and await instructions.*

As evening sunlight mellowed over the flat coastal fields of north Somerset, I accomplished the last part of my journey and found myself in a fine modern hotel like a French château. There was a view of sands and donkey-carriages, two islands in the foreground, the hills of Wales beyond, and a wide expanse of grey sea stretching to the Atlantic. I had ample time to stare at this prospect from my window, for neither the usual telegraph service nor the next morning's post brought me any instructions. It was a Saturday and the town full of trippers. That afternoon, weary of my confinement, I took my stick and crossed the beach lawns with the object of taking a stroll along the broad two-mile stretch of promenade above the sands, where the sea breeze brought a healthy tingle to the cheeks.

Unfortunately, this broad paving had lately been given over to the American plague of roller-skating. Men and even women of the lower orders rumbled or sped past one, weaving in and out among the respectable pedestrians, endangering the lives and limbs of their betters. The audacity of these pests to society was beyond belief. There was one jaunty fellow, in a tweed jacket, gaiters, and cap, who fancied himself something of a virtuoso. He wove among the walkers, deliberately caught the rear of my hat-brim with his hand and tipped it forward over my eyes. This was an insolent devil with a bushy moustache that failed to conceal the high-coloured cheeks and broken capillaries of the inveterate beer-drinker. I shouted after him but he took not the least notice.

Somehow, though I did not see him do it, he must have circled back. The next thing I knew was a sharp tap behind me and my brim settled over my eyes once more. As I pulled up the hat, he had the damnable effrontery to turn and laugh at me, idling on his skates just beyond the reach of my stick.

'Do that once more,' I shouted, 'I will summon a policeman and give you in charge!'

'Oh dear!' he chuckled merrily. 'I beg you will do no such thing, Watson! I have just established a most cordial working relationship with Inspector Gerrish of the Somerset Constabulary, who is no less than Lestrade's cousin. I cannot but feel that my arrest might cast a cloud upon it.'

To say that this knocked the breath from me would be an understatement. Of course I asked him what the devil he was doing here, when all the world thought he was at Scapa Flow. Indeed, I demanded an explanation as to what all this nonsense about Weston-super-Mare signified.

'My poor Watson,' he said jovially, as he sat on a bench, unlacing his skates before we returned to the hotel, 'I did not dare let you into the secret earlier, for fear you might give the game away. It was imperative that I should be thought to be well out of circulation by Mr Maxse, his daughter, her husband and the whole world. It is true, of course, that I was not at Scapa Flow, but Portsmouth is no less famous in our naval history.'

'Portsmouth!' In the room he had taken at the hotel, which was only a few doors from my own, I watched him peel off the moustache and rub the rouge and gum from his cheeks with surgical spirit. 'You have been down there after this fellow Smith?'

'It was not difficult,' he said more seriously. 'It is clear that he thinks himself quite safe from all but Mr Maxse. However, I confess that even I had not imagined the extent of his depravity. I followed him between Portsmouth and Southsea for a day and a half, to little avail. But then, to my surprise, he suddenly made for the harbour station with a Gladstone bag in his hand. He took the train as far as Bristol, decamped, and boarded the tram to Clifton. Thence he returned with a young woman whose name I gathered from a question or two to an errand boy is Miss Pegler, though known sometimes as Mrs Smith. They are here at the moment, staying as man and wife. What story he has told to his poor bride of a fortnight ago, heaven only knows.'

'There may be enough for a divorce petition when the time comes,' I said darkly.

'Oh, no, Watson. I should be greatly disappointed if this led merely to divorce. Besides, this practice of ours does not stoop to concern itself with what the papers call matrimonial cases. On that, I am inflexible.'

'Where is he now?'

Holmes shrugged.

'I have lost him,' he said, as if it were not of the least consequence.

'Then what are we to do?'

Lights were beginning to twinkle like strings of pearls in the mauve dusk, strung between the lamp-standards along the shoreline. Above the rush of the returning tide, the music of a band drifted inland from the theatre pavilion of the Grand Pier.

'We shall take a walk,' he said jauntily. 'Just so far as the sea-front photographer's kiosk. Mr Jackson, of Jackson's Faces, has become quite a holiday friend of mine.'

Any visitor to the seaside is aware of that other promenade pestilence, the man who pushes his camera at your face, 'snaps' you, hands you a ticket, and enjoys the privilege of sticking your likeness on his billboard until you pay to have it removed. Jackson's Faces possessed a kiosk by the causeway of the muddy harbour, flanked by those boards on which prints of the photographs taken in the last day or two were pinned.

'Allow me to present Mr Smith,' said Holmes quietly.

My companion was indicating the somewhat wrinkled photographs pinned on the board. He did not need to tell me which he had in mind, for it was a most extraordinary picture. It showed an incongruous couple walking arm-in-arm along the very stretch of promenade where we now stood, the lights glinting in the harbour tide. The woman wore her hair loose with an expression of simpering stupidity. The man was absurdly-dressed for a seaside visit in a top hat, stiff wing-collar and bow-tie, a frock-coat and waistcoat with gold chain. Such was the holiday masquerade of a would-be 'man of property'. To anyone who had seen the recent wedding-photograph, however, there was no mistaking the bold stride and the contemptuous eyes above the abundant moustache, a frightening moral indifference to pain or distress.

Such were Mr Smith and Miss Pegler.

'I rather fancy, Watson, that there is enough in that photograph to send our man to penal servitude for seven years to begin with, under section 57 of the Offences Against the Person Act.'

'I have no idea . . .'

'Bigamy. Do you not see the ring on the fourth finger of the lady's left hand?'

'That means nothing. It is for show.'

'I think not,' he said softly, 'I think he may be married to this lady, validly or not. If validly, then the marriage to Miss Maxse is bigamous. He wants that young lady's money, or her family's money, and mere seduction will not do. Whatever else Mr Smith may lack, he seems accomplished as a professional swindler of the female sex. One moment.'

He turned into the entrance of the kiosk, from which came the harsh chemical odours of bleach and ammonia. The bald proprietor in his neat suit stood behind the counter.

'Mr Jackson, allow me to introduce my colleague, Dr Watson. Pray tell him what you told me this afternoon about the man in that photograph.'

Mr Jackson's eyes brightened behind his wire-framed spectacles.

'I can't say, gentlemen, that I remember every name that goes with every face. We get too many. But I have a natural recollection of many. That's how I was first called "Faces."'

'Most interesting,' said Holmes impatiently, 'and this one?'

'I'd good reason to remember him, though it was a year or two ago. I took his likeness then, just here by Knightstone harbour, and put it on the board. He never wanted it. However, we keep them there a few days. Just before it was to be took down, a lady came in. Mrs Tuckett that has a boarding house in Upper Church Road above Glentworth Cove. "That man," she says, "him in the photograph. He left the day before yesterday and bilked me of three weeks money."'

'Had she been to the police?'

'Where's the use?' Mr Jackson became philosophical. 'Police won't do nothing. They'll tell you it's a civil matter and you can sue him if you like. If you can find him, they mean!'

'And his name?'

'Williams,' Mr Jackson emphasized the name as if to impress on us the reliability of his memory. 'Him and his wife.'

'And you remembered him and his name all this time?' I asked, I fear with a touch of scepticism.

Mr Jackson looked at me as if I were an imbecile.

'He came back,' he explained slowly. 'That's how I remembered him. His wife came back first, going to stay with Mrs Tuckett again, paying the arrears and offering apologies, saying how her husband had deserted her the year before. She had some money of her own now from her father's estate, he having been a bank manager, and so she paid the debt. A week or two later, as Mrs Tuckett told me, Mrs Williams went out to buy her some flowers. She came back quite shocked, but pleased, saying that she'd just met Mr Williams her husband, that she hadn't seen for a year. There he was, standing by the bandstand near Glentworth Cove, alone and looking out to sea.'

'A curious coincidence,' said Holmes blandly.

'Coincidence?' Mr Jackson tightened his mouth. 'Cold-blooded and deliberate, if you ask me. According to Mrs Tuckett, they were reconciled. First thing Williams did then was to take his wife down to Mr Littlington, of Bakers the Solicitors, in Waterloo Street, and make her sign everything of her father's over to him.'

'Ah, yes,' said Holmes, as if approving of such prudence on the part of Smith, *alias* Williams. 'That is just as it should be.'

Mr Jackson looked at him sharply but my companion smiled and bowed himself out of the kiosk.

'I fear, Watson, that Constance Maxse is by no means Mr Smith's first bigamous bride. I should give a good deal to know how many there are altogether.'

As we walked past the pier and heard the music of the band drifting in towards the shore, I said, 'What can it matter? He will go to penal servitude for seven years, if he goes for a day.'

Holmes frowned at me.

'I should like something better than that for Mr Smith. He is an artist to whom a mere seven years would be an insult. A true artist in crime, Watson, plays the game with nothing less than his feet on two boards, the pit beneath him and the noose round his neck. *Qualis artifex pereo*, as the Emperor Nero remarked wisely at the last. The execution shed is a far nobler exit for such men than a mere convict cell.'

## IV

Our return to Baker Street from the coast of the Bristol Channel coincided with another of those periods of lethargy that overtook Holmes without apparent warning. Since the beginning of the investigation I feared that he might be suffering from a psychic ailment of some kind. He seemed, from time to time, to lose interest in a case that was far from concluded. Much of the day he leaned back in his chair, in gloomy speculation. When Lestrade came to see us of an evening to impart the criminal news of London, he now found Holmes leaning languidly against the mantelpiece, scarcely endeavouring to conceal his yawns.

This lasted for about five days after our return, during which he said not a word to our Scotland Yard friend of the inquiry which we had in hand. It was the morning post on the sixth day that put an end to his indolence. I was aware that from time to time an envelope embossed with the crest of Somerset House appeared among my friend's correspondence. He had been indebted on several occasions to Dr L'Estrange, the archivist of that estimable institution where all births, marriages, and deaths are recorded. On this occasion, Holmes appeared from his bedroom well after ten o'clock and, showing none of his usual disdain for correspondence before breakfast, snatched at the Somerset House envelope. In a single cut, he slit it open with the silver and ruby-handled paperknife that had been a token of gratitude from a prime minister of France, Georges Clemenceau, following the resolution of the Dreyfus espionage scandal and the vindication of an innocent man.

He read the enclosed letter with a chuckle.

'Dear me, Watson! We have underestimated Mr Smith!'

I could see that there was a second sheet of paper attached to the letter. He looked up, his eyes shining with merriment.

'This, my dear fellow, is the marriage certificate of George Joseph Smith!'

'To Miss Burnham – or possibly to Miss Constance Maxse?'

He shook his head.

'Better than any of those. This records his marriage, under his own name in 1908, at Bristol, to Edith Mabel Pegler. We should have done that lady a grave injustice in assuming an irregular relationship between them. She is described here as a housekeeper, no doubt to her bridegroom. George Joseph Smith appears as thirty-three years old, a bachelor and general dealer, son of George Smith deceased, described as a figure artist.'

'Then the man is a bigamist! Thank God, there is an end of the matter.'

He looked at me and shook his head.

'My dear Watson, your capacity for bourgeois moral calculation never ceases to amaze me. If Smith is a mere bigamist, then Miss Maxse may be set free and our interest ends. I venture to think that will not be so. However, let us count up. Our general dealer marries Miss Pegler in 1908. Two years later, he marries a woman, yet unknown to us, as Henry Williams. A year later he marries Alice Burnham, now deceased. A few weeks ago, he becomes a bridegroom for the fourth time that we know of. How many times he may have walked down the aisle with other brides is yet to be revealed.'

With that, he began to open the rest of his correspondence, glancing briefly at each letter and tossing it aside.

'Can it be for money?' I asked sceptically. 'How many of these women had much to give him?'

'In the case of Alice Burnham and Constance Maxse, I have no doubt that their families might be blackmailed or bullied into parting with a handsome sum in exchange for Smith allowing himself to be divorced at the first possible moment. Better still, think what he might demand by revealing that a union was yet unconsummated and that a complete annulment might be possible. You see? We can be sure of something like that in two cases. What the financial position of the *soi-disante* Mrs Williams may have been, we have yet to discover. It is certain, from the details already sent me by the Clerk of Probate, Admiralty and Divorce, that no divorce action between Smith and the former Miss Pegler was listed before 1910 or even 1912. As you acutely observe, that makes him guilty of bigamy, a subject we will now put to rest.'

'Put to rest?' I got up from my chair and watched him dismember a kipper. 'But, for God's sake, Holmes, we have a duty to free our client's daughter from the clutches of the man!'

He put down his fork and looked at me.

'Our first duty, Watson, is to use our best efforts to ensure that our client sees his daughter alive again. As matters stand, I should not count upon it.'

I stared at him, not understanding, until he retrieved and handed me a second letter. This was from Mr Maxse. He had endeavoured to contact his daughter, only to be told by the Southsea landlady that Mr Smith had been away for a week – as our visit to Weston-super-Mare already informed us. On his return, the couple had moved from Southsea and were now thought to be somewhere in the Midlands.

'He is on the loose with that poor girl!' I said in dismay, as I put down Mr Maxse's letter. 'Surely, then, the time has come to alert Lestrade? A warrant may be put out for the man, if only for bigamy.'

Holmes stared ahead of him, at the August sky framed by the window.

'I think not, Watson. We will not yet involve Lestrade, if you please. Once our suspicions reach Scotland Yard, they become public property. There is no discretion in that organization. They could not keep a secret if their lives depended on it. Moreover, bigamy is not a crime actively pursued by our police force. They prefer the comfortable method of waiting for the criminal to make an error. In any case, if my suspicions are correct, I fear that any bigamy warrant for Smith might also prove to be the death-warrant of Constance Maxse.'

With this flourish of Hoxton melodrama he dropped the subject and would not be provoked into taking it up again. Nothing was said of it to Lestrade on his visit that evening. Next morning, a further embossed envelope arrived from Somerset House. It contained a copy of the marriage certificate of Henry Williams and Bessie Mundy, dated at Weymouth on 26 August 1910. This was accompanied by a further certificate, recording that Bessie Williams, *née* Mundy, had died of 'misadventure' at Herne Bay on 13 July 1912 and that an inquest had been held.

'A coroner's jury,' I said cheerfully. 'Well, I must say, that rather puts Mr Smith in the clear, so far as everything but bigamy may be concerned.'

Holmes fixed me with an expressionless stare that was far worse, in its way, than any glowering or glaring.

'I doubt that,' he snapped, 'I doubt that very much indeed.'

So it was that on the following afternoon we landed by a steamer that had brought us from Tower Pier to

Herne Bay, and were taken by cab to our rooms at the Royal Hotel.

## V

Next morning, in a shabby brick-and-tile police office, we sat opposite the rubicund and self-confident figure of Constable John Kitchingham, Coroner's Officer in the case of Miss Bessie Mundy, as the bigamously-married wife of 'Henry Williams' was still known in law. Constable Kitchingham showed an ill-placed self-confidence.

'I'm afraid we aren't Scotland Yard, Mr Holmes, not down here. Nor we aren't Baker Street neither, with respect, and don't need to be.' As he talked, he shuffled through a few papers, looking at them and not at us. 'We know what people are round here, all the same, and that's a good deal. This town, Mr Holmes, has a good name, and we depend upon that for the summer trade.'

Had this bumpkin been looking at us he might have seen the beginnings of cold anger in Sherlock Holmes, usually evident only to those who knew him well, and avoided the consequences before it was too late. Kitchingham opened another folder and read resonantly from a paper.

'Mr Henry Williams took a yearly tenancy of a house at 80 High Street, Herne Bay, on 20 May 1912. He lived there with his wife, Bessie, on affectionate terms for some weeks. On 8 July, he says, they made mutual wills.' Seeing the suspicion in Holmes's eyes, Kitchingham added hastily, 'That had to be done. A new marriage or divorce invalidates an existing will.'

'A fact of which I am aware,' Holmes said bleakly. 'Pray continue.'

Constable Kitchingham continued.

'The premises were shabby and had been derelict for long periods. It seems Mr Williams was vexed there was no bath for his wife. On the day after the making of the wills, an enamelled bath was ordered from Mr Hill, ironmonger of the same street. 'Owever, the rooms had never been brought "up to date", so there was no means of plumbing the bath. It was delivered without taps or pipes, standing by the bathroom window to be filled and emptied by hand. This was done by carrying up hot water in a bucket from a copper in the downstairs kitchen.'

A horse and trap rattled over the cobbles outside the window.

'I don't think you could say, gentlemen,' Kitchingham said proudly, 'that Mr Williams showed himself lacking in duty to a wife that was never a well person. The day after that bath was delivered, he was with her at Dr French's. Epileptic seizures, she having had a bad one the day before, with him there to see it.'

'Forgive me,' said Holmes quietly, 'the inquest report contains no evidence that this lady had bitten her tongue or showed any sign of having had such a fit.'

'Which was remarked, Mr Holmes, but which isn't invariable, it seems.'

'That, at least, is true,' I said reluctantly.

Constable Kitchingham took courage from my approval.

'Dr French thought it advisable to administer a mild

sedative of potassium bromide, which would do no harm in any case.'

'Nor much good,' I said. Kitchingham looked at me with the reproach of a man betrayed. Then he resumed.

'However that may be, Mr Holmes, the doctor was fetched two nights later at 1.30 a.m., when the lady had had another seizure. He found her flushed and clammy. Heart and pulse were normal, but she complained of a headache.'

'The files of the *Herne Bay Press*, which I had the pleasure of consulting in the public library yesterday afternoon, tell us that,' Holmes said dryly. 'On another page the paper also records the July temperature for that week as varying between 78 and 82 degrees and remarks on the humidity of the season. I should imagine the entire population of Herne Bay might have been flushed and clammy on such a night. Nor do I see how Dr French could say much about an epileptic seizure which must have been over before he got there. Unless she had bitten her tongue or something of the sort, which once again was not the case.'

Kitchingham shrugged. His tone now assumed a melodramatic self-importance, with which he had no doubt told the story to a good many people before us.

'Two days later, according to Mr Williams, they rose as the town hall clock sounded the half-hour at 7.30. He went out to buy some fish. He didn't fill the bath, so his wife must have done it herself. On his return, about a half hour later, he called out to her, received no reply, and then went into the bathroom. She was lying on her back in the bath, which was three-quarters filled. Her head was under water, her trunk on the bottom, legs sloping up, feet just clear of the surface. He pulled her up, so that she lay against the slope of the bath, her head clear of the water. Then he sent a message to Dr French. "Can you come at once? I am afraid my wife is dead."'

'What does French have to say about it?'

'He came about fifteen minutes later and found her on her back, her head having slipped beneath the water again. There was no pulse, but neither body nor water was cold. She was clutching a piece of Castille Soap in her right hand. They lifted her out and laid her on the floor. Dr French removed her false teeth and tried artificial respiration for ten minutes, while Mr Williams assisted by holding his wife's tongue. But she'd gone. Clean gone, sir.'

'That I do not doubt. When did you first see her body?'

'About two hours later, as coroner's officer sent to take their statements.'

'Where was it?'

'Lying on the boards of the bathroom floor. Being quite a small room it was behind the door as you opened it.'

'What was it covered with?'

'It wasn't, Mr Holmes.'

'Do you mean to tell me that this man left his dead wife naked on the floor behind the door for two hours, while policemen and coroner's officers, landlord and undertakers, the world and his wife, tramped in and out?'

'If you put it like that.'

'If you can think of another way of putting the matter, Mr Kitchingham, I should be obliged to hear of it. Now, the report in the paper says nothing of evidence at the inquest as to the height of the lady and dimensions of the bath.'

Kitchingham gave a fatuous and self-satisfied snigger.

'There was none of that sort of thing given, sir. Where there's no call for it, we don't go in for your kind of clever arithmetic down here, Mr Holmes.'

'Indeed not,' said Holmes with an icy fury that suggested Mr Kitchingham had now caught a tiger by the tail. 'What you go in for, down here, appears to verge upon criminal negligence. When did Williams leave the premises?'

'Almost at once,' said Kitchingham, whose face had reddened gratifyingly. 'Mrs Williams died on Saturday, the inquest was on Monday . . .'

'Before her relatives could hear of it, let alone attend it, I daresay!'

'Couldn't say, sir. Then she was buried on Tuesday, next day.'

'Large funeral was it? Something elaborate?'

'Very small, in the circumstances. Decent but not expensive, as Mr Williams said. Common grave. Still, what could that matter to her, as he remarked?'

'What, indeed?'

'Never saw a man so struck down,' said Kitchingham, warm in justification of the widower. 'Before the burial he saw the agents' clerk, Miss Rapley. Ended his tenancy. Sobbing his heart out on her desk, poor gentleman. Only once he brightened and said, "Wasn't it a jolly good thing I got her to make a will?" Fair play, it was. You don't want grief aggravated by intestacy at a time like that.'

We freed ourselves from the morbid enthusiasms of Constable Kitchingham and strolled back to the Royal Hotel.

'Some mute inglorious Borgia here may rest!' Holmes gestured furiously at the sea-front of Herne Bay. 'For all that the local constabulary know or care!'

'They cannot work without evidence . . .'

'Evidence!' His cry was loud enough to cause an elderly couple ahead of us to turn and stare in some alarm. 'Does no one observe the psychopathic delight of a man in exposing his dead wife to strangers, naked on the boards of the bathroom floor for more than two hours? Does it mean nothing when he asks on the day of her burial in a common grave whether it wasn't a jolly good thing that he got her to make a will? Constable Kitchingham takes it as mere proof of what a splendid fellow he was!'

'Holmes,' I said gently, 'much as you may deplore the inquest, the verdict was never in doubt on the evidence. Bessie Mundy died in an epileptic seizure, which caused her to fall back with her head beneath the water, so that she drowned. The jurors made the only reasonable finding, death by misadventure.'

'I have as little faith in coroners' officers and inquest juries as I have in policemen, Watson. I know only that Miss Constance Maxse is in mortal peril, God knows where. Policemen and jurors will do nothing for her. Truth and facts will save her. Great is truth and shall prevail. Even in Herne Bay.'

In our sitting-room after dinner, at the end of our first day, he stared morosely beyond the lace curtains, where a late sun glimmered warmly on the placid waters of the North Sea and on the rusty sails of barges steering for the Essex shore. Then, without a word, he took from his pocket a telegram and handed it to me. It was a simple reply from Inspector Lestrade concerning the death of that other Mrs Smith, Alice Burnham, lost at Blackpool. THE POLICE HAVE NO SUSPICION OF FOUL PLAY.

The case against George Joseph Smith as anything more than a bigamist and trickster, depended solely on the fate of Bessie Mundy at the hands of her devoted and hygienic husband.

## VI

In such unpromising circumstances, I never knew by what means Sherlock Holmes was able to command the attendance next morning of Mr Rutley Mowll, the East Kent Coroner, Mr Alfred Hogbin, undertaker, Dr Frank Austin French, Miss Lily O'Sullivan of the Herne Bay Aquatic Belles, and the unfortunate Constable Kitchingham. The venue was the bathroom of 80 High Street, which was in one of its periods of vacancy. Whether the unseen hand of Lestrade, or of Mycroft Holmes, had contrived this ensemble I have no idea. One thing, however, was certain. Holmes was in the mood of a sergeant-major addressing a defaulters' parade.

An exception to his displeasure was the prettily costumed Miss O'Sullivan, whose swimming dress of frilly blue pantaloons and bodice would have graced the most sophisticated lido. For the rest, Holmes was in a mood to brook no contradictions or evasions and I had never seen any group of people look so thoroughly petrified in his presence.

'We will, if you please, begin with filling the bath!' The words rapped out in that bare, hard room with the grey light of the High Street filtering through its mean windows. 'Constable Kitchingham! Take the two gallon bucket to the kitchen downstairs. Fill it from the copper, which is now brimming. Carry it up here and pour it into the bath. Continue until the bath is half full, then three quarters full, as both you and Dr French found it. Do not interrupt us otherwise.'

He was plainly enjoying his revenge upon them all for what he still called their 'criminal negligence'. He pointed to the cast-iron enamelled bath with its four lions' feet. It stood with its head just under the street-window, as it had done at the death of Bessie Mundy. Then his finger stabbed at the lugubrious black-clad figure of Mr Hogbin, the undertaker of High Street, Herne Bay.

'Now, sir! Take that useful implement of your trade, the tape-measure! Read off the length of the bath!'

Mr Hogbin nervously did as he was told.

'The upper length is just five feet, Mr Holmes. The length at the base is three feet eight inches.'

'And since it is too narrow for her to move much to either side, it is the length which is crucial. You also measured her for her coffin?'

'I did, sir.' He stood with the tape round his neck and shoulders drooping, like a mournful carrion crow.

'How tall was Mrs Williams?'

'Five feet nine inches, sir. Tall for a lady.'

'Such a pity the inquest did not hear that,' said Holmes savagely. 'Nine inches longer than the bath at the top! More than two feet longer than the bath at the bottom!'

'She was found lying flat along it, Mr Holmes,' said Coroner Mowll quickly, 'flat along the bottom but with legs sloping upwards and feet out of the water.'

'I am aware of how she was found, sir! My interest is in how she got where she was found!'

'If you have read the report of the inquest, you will know that it was the result of an epileptic seizure, which caused her to fall backwards under the water.'

'I am informed, Mr Mowll, that you hold your position as East Kent Coroner by virtue of being a solicitor. I wonder if you have the slightest knowledge of the sequence of events in an epileptic seizure.'

'I believe I have some little experience in the matter.'

'Who heard the scream?'

'The scream?'

'An epileptic seizure, unlike *petit mal,* is almost always preceded by a scream of such intensity that those who hear it seldom forget it. There is a street not more than a dozen feet below these windows, which are open in summer no doubt. There are rooms on either side of these flimsy lath and plaster walls. Curiously, when Mr Williams claimed to recite the symptoms of his wife's first fits, several days before, he also made no mention of such a scream.'

'No one heard a scream.'

There was a pause while Constable Kitchingham carried a laden bucket across the bare floorboards of the room and splashed it into the bath.

'A primary characteristic of such a seizure is rigidity,' said Holmes with great deliberation. 'The woman's feet would be jammed against the far end of the bath and her trunk bolt upright. It would be as nearly impossible for her to get her head under water in a bath sixteen inches deep as one can imagine.'

Mr Mowll's eagerness to protect the reputation of Herne Bay led him to ingratiate with Holmes, as one who should pat a hungry lion.

'She was on her back, sir, with her legs sloping up and feet out of the water.'

'Which a single pair of strong hands would accomplish in a moment.'

'Mr Holmes,' said the coroner firmly, 'your reputation goes before you. You are known for your skill in the most difficult cases. However, no man can be expert in every field . . .'

'I trust you may be able to produce authority for that insinuation!' my friend snapped back at him.

'I merely point out, Mr Holmes, that you are plainly not *au fait* with events as they occurred. Nor is your expertise in medicine sufficient to tilt the scales in doubtful questions, where medical men themselves take varying views . . .'

'Forgive me, Mr Mowll, but I decline to undertake responsibility for the vacillations and mutual hostilities of the medical profession.'

That brought silence for a moment until Mr Mowll tried again.

'There is no case of murder by drowning known to English jurisprudence, Mr Holmes, in which a victim who is conscious has not offered the most desperate and violent resistance, sufficient to cause bruising and abrasions to both assailant and assailed. Neither husband nor wife in this case displayed a single bruise or scratch. Nor did Dr French find a drop of water spilt on the floor from a bath three quarters full.'

'As to the last observation,' said Holmes coolly, 'absorption by untreated wood and evaporation on a summer day with the temperature in the eighties would in any case reduce the time that water would be visible on the floor. However, we shall now put the entire question to the proof, with your permission. The bath is only half full, but that is enough for my purposes.'

'If you wish,' Coroner Mowll stood back wearily, with folded arms.

'Miss O'Sullivan, if you please,' said Holmes courteously.

Our bathing belle in her water-costume skipped forward, as if making her bow at a pierrot show.

'One moment,' murmured Holmes, 'allow Constable Kitchingham to add this last bucket of water.'

The final bucket was emptied into the bath with a sound like a gently breaking wave. Miss O'Sullivan raised a dainty foot and stepped into water that came half way to her knees. She adjusted the laces of her cap and lowered herself gently into the wider end of the bath. She gave us all a quick smile and a flutter of her lashes.

'Now, my dear young lady,' said Holmes, more affably than he had said anything to anyone that morning, 'I apologize for the coolness of the water but happily you are accustomed to that in your profession. This will not take long. Let us suppose that you are sitting upright in the bath. Sponging your arms, shall we say. You have no idea that anything is amiss. Of course you have in reality, but let us pretend. You have not a care in the world.'

She sat there, wiping her arms with her wet hands in dumb-show as Holmes removed his jacket and rolled up his sleeves. She smiled at him, a little nervously as I thought. Holmes gave her a quick smile and approached. We were watching to see him place his hand upon her head. He stooped a little at the bath, slipped his left forearm under her knees, his right arm round her shoulders, for all the world like a loving groom about to lift his bride and carry her to bed. It was so naturally done that she began to put her left arm about his shoulders to complete the embrace.

Then, without a word of warning, his left arm that was under her knees lifted them high. The right arm was withdrawn and Miss O' Sullivan went down on her back with her legs drawn high. The shelving depth of the bath was so narrow where she lay that her arms seemed imprisoned, though she managed several futile swimming motions with them. Her neck and shoulders jerked spasmodically and in vain to get her face above the water.

'If seeing is believing,' Holmes said grimly to the rest of us, 'you now know how Mrs Bessie Williams, *née* Bessie Mundy, met her death.'

I thought that no one who saw this dreadful experiment being carried out could have the least doubt of that.

'Mr Holmes!' Coroner Mowll's cry was one of shrill alarm.

'As little as thirty seconds might suffice!' Miss O' Sullivan's struggles seemed feebler as Holmes muttered these words. 'As long as two minutes and more might be necessary!'

'Holmes! For God's sake!'

The girl's face was horribly evident under the slight turbulence of the water as her arms went limp. Her eyes were staring up at us, her cheeks bulging, and a thin stream of bubbles reached the surface. He seemed not to hear me.

'Holmes!'

It is not too much to say that I threw myself upon him from behind. For a second or two longer I could not break his grip. Then the brawny Mr Hogbin joined me and between us we drew him off. Miss O' Sullivan floated to the surface. Her eyes, which had been wide open, fluttered and closed. Letting go of my friend, I drew from my pocket the silver medicinal flask, which my father had given me when I left to join my regiment in India. I unscrewed it and touched it to her lips. The warming whisky made her retch a little and then brought her round.

'So much for epileptic seizures,' said Holmes imperiously to the onlookers.

They stared at him, shocked and terrified, for they could all have sworn he meant to drown the girl as a demonstration. Holmes was completely unperturbed.

'And then there is the matter of the piece of soap, said to be clutched in the right hand. It is also said by Dr French in his evidence that the hand was limp.'

'And so it was,' said French nervously.

'A limp hand cannot clutch a piece of soap or anything else. Perhaps I may refer you to the work of Dr Alfred Swaine Taylor on the matter. Only a quarter of those who drown die of asphyxia. When they do so, the hand would be limp. Had there been death in an epileptic seizure, which there was not, you would have had to prize the hand open. According to your evidence, the hand opened of its own accord and the soap fell out.'

Though Holmes had rattled their self-confidence, he had not changed the mind of the coroner. Mr Mowll was angry now, as well as frightened.

'All that you have done, sir, is to tell us what we knew already. There are two possible explanations in this case for almost every aspect of it. The jury at the inquest heard them all and found its verdict of misadventure. You have stated the alternative hypotheses but you will not change that verdict.'

Holmes looked at him with a mixture of simulated surprise and undisguised contempt.

'I do not deal in hypotheses, sir, but in facts. This man was a brute in his dealings with women and a thief in respect of their money.'

'He was known here only for his loving affection to his wife.'

Holmes took from his pocket several papers.

'With the assistance of the records office, I have spent my leisure hours in town before coming to Herne Bay by following up one or two of the bigamous wives, for there have been several beside the ones so far mentioned. You may have their statements. Miss Pegler of Bristol. "*The power was in his eyes. They were little eyes that seemed to rob you of your will.*" Here is another, cited in her divorce petition ten years ago by one of those whom he flogged into silence when he could be secure in no other way. "*Often he used to brag to me about his numerous women acquaintances. Once I met one of his victims and warned her to her face about him. She was greatly shocked. That night he came home and thrashed me till I was nearly dead."* There, sir, is the true character of the man whom your jury acquitted of all blame.'

'It does not prove the present case!'

Holmes seemed to look through Mr Mowll to a world beyond.

'In the past three-quarters of an hour, in this room, the case against Henry Williams, *alias* George Joseph Smith, has been established beyond the least doubt.'

'You have not done so!'

'Perhaps, sir, I have not. But Constable Kitchingham certainly has.'

They stared back at him and Holmes continued.

'To fill the bath three-quarters full, which Dr French and others observed to be the level, has taken Constable Kitchingham fifty minutes. It is unlikely that Bessie Mundy could do it faster – and her husband swore that he did not do it at all. Suppose Williams, *alias* Smith, has told the truth in his statement to the inquest. Then the couple rose at 7.30. The water was warm when Dr French tested it, therefore the bath could not have been filled earlier or it would have been stone cold. Let us allow that the husband went out, as he said, and returned at eight. We know it was not later, for at eight he sent his message to Dr French that he feared his wife was dead, and that Dr French received the message a little before 8.30.'

'Oh, God!' said Coroner Mowll suddenly.

'Precisely. The filling of the bath would have taken from 7.30 to 8.20 or thereabouts. Let us be generous to the husband and say it was only half filled. I have observed Constable Kitchingham and may tell you that it took him thirty-five minutes to reach the half-way point. If that is the case, even so the filling could not have been completed – let alone Mrs Williams undressed and in the bath – until five minutes after the message to Dr French saying she was dead. Not only was she was still alive when George Joseph Smith returned from the fishmonger, she had probably not even got into the bath when he sent for Dr French, saying that he feared she was dead!'

As so often, the chilling logic of Sherlock Holmes left his audience speechless.

'Smith, *alias* Williams, is not a mere lady-killer,' said Holmes quietly, 'but one of the most cold-blooded assassins that ever walked the face of this earth. You have much to answer for Mr Mowll.'

'I have nothing . . .'

'Indeed you have. Miss Alice Burnham . . .'

'I have heard of that, thanks to you, sir. There is a vast difference between a domestic tragedy and a swimming or bathing accident upon a public beach, as her father describes it.'

'You may yet find them identical. Far worse, at the moment this bigamist, embezzler, and murderer is in possession of a young woman, Constance Maxse, who knows nothing of her danger . . .'

'I did not swear it was epilepsy,' Dr French interrupted hastily, as Herne Bay began to break ranks, 'only that I could not swear otherwise. There was only what I was told by the man and the woman. I had qualified only two years.'

'His demeanour after his wife's death,' said Mr Hogbin,

'his treatment of the poor dead body. Upon reflection it was callous and hateful in the extreme.'

'I shall return to my office,' said Mr Mowll, 'and seek advice.'

'When you get there,' said Holmes equably, 'you will find Inspector Lestrade of Scotland Yard, waiting to give you a good deal of it.'

Before we left, I gave my professional counsel to Miss Lily O' Sullivan.

'My dear young lady, if I may advise you, we must take you home at once by cab or carriage. It is essential that you should sustain no further exertion and that you should rest, preferably in bed, for the next day or two.'

She gave the shortest laugh I had ever heard.

'Ha! Much chance of that! I should miss two performances tonight.'

'But to take part in them is unthinkable, in your present state of distress.'

Her eyes sparkled.

'Oh,' she said, as if understanding at last. 'You mean this?'

I saw again the gargoyle of the drowning maiden, the dreadful bulging eyes, the swelling cheeks, the blood stagnating in her face.

'You never knew? Mr Holmes never told you?' She grinned at me, but it was not a smile. 'That's part of my act, that is. I can stay under for two minutes or more, if I have to. Only Mr Holmes thought it might look better the way he and I did it. Pleased to meet you. Ta-ta.'

'I was so overcome, as she flounced off to change

her dripping costume, that I almost said "Ta-ta" in return. I managed my half-bow only just in time.'

We remained in the Royal Hotel to see what Lestrade might accomplish. By 4p.m. a warrant had been issued, in respect of bigamy, larceny, and murder, for the arrest of George Joseph Smith, *alias* George Baker, *alias* George Oliver Love, *alias* Henry Williams, *alias* Charles Oliver James, *alias* John Lloyd, described as a gymnasium instructor and general dealer. Lestrade had discovered from the criminal records that the wanted man served two years in the Northamptonshire Regiment, teaching gymnastics. Small wonder that poor Bessie Mundy was no match for those powerful hands.

That evening after dinner we looked out from our room across the darkening sea and waited in the hope that Lestrade might have time to pay us a visit before his return to town on the late train.

'He can only be tried for one murder at a time,' I said thoughtfully. 'The evidence in the case of Bessie Mundy is strong but not conclusive. There is almost nothing, except perhaps the filling of the bath, that might not be overturned. Even there, to hang a man because he has the time wrong by twenty minutes . . . It is a cruel thing to say of the poor girl, but if only Alice Burnham had died at home, rather than swimming . . .'

He shook his head in despair.

'Watson! Watson! Of course she died at home, not on the high seas! It is one of my greatest blunders that I did not go to her father at once. However, he could not even bring himself to attend the funeral of that one person in the world whom he loved. So I had hoped, knowing that he could not bear to hear of the tragedy nor to speak of it since it was first reported to him, that I could spare him in this investigation. It was not to be.'

He spread out on the table by the window two telegram forms, one the copy of a message he had sent to Mr Maxse, and one which he had received in reply that afternoon.

> TELEGRAPH AT ONCE TEXT OF NOTIFICATION TO YOUR FRIEND CHARLES BURNHAM BY HIS SON-IN-LAW OF THE DEATH OF ALICE BURNHAM STOP. REPLY PAID TO HOLMES, ROYAL HOTEL, HERNE BAY.

How had the scoundrel broken to the father the news of his beloved daughter's death?

> ALICE DIED YESTERDAY BATHING NORTH SHORE STOP. SMITH CONNAUGHT STREET BLACKPOOL.

Reduced to the form of a telegraph message there was also the report of the inquest cut from a few lines at the foot of a column in the local press.

> NORTH SHORE TRAGEDY: INQUEST VERDICT: A VERDICT OF ACCIDENTAL DEATH WAS RETURNED AT THE INQUEST ON ALICE BURNHAM (25) OF CONNAUGHT STREET, NORTH SHORE, WHO WAS DROWNED LAST TUESDAY WHILE BATHING.

'Unfortunately, the word "bathing" has two meanings and two pronunciations,' said Holmes quietly. 'Such was the deceit practised on the unhappy father. The head of the inquest report was snipped out and the rest withheld, so that Smith might persuade him his daughter had died in a swimming accident, when the truth was he had drowned her in her bath. Remember, the murder of Bessie Mundy was already to his credit by then. Therefore, the fewer questions the better.'

'Those telegrams will do no good,' I said, 'if he can only be tried for one murder and the jury know nothing of the other wives.'

Holmes sat down and lit his pipe.

'From my brief and hardly satisfactory experience of student law, Watson, I recall something known as system. It is true that a man may only be tried for one murder. However, where he is charged with others but not tried for them, they may be brought into the case to show evidence of "system".'

'System?'

'Yes. The other cases may not be used to suggest that he committed the murder for which he is tried. But they may be used to show that, if he did commit it, he did not do so accidentally.'

'To stop a verdict of manslaughter?'

He chuckled in a manner that would chill the blood of the greatest optimist.

'In this case, Watson, to ensure that the jury knows every abomination in the career of this reptile. Leave those telegrams on the table a moment. The boards outside our door creak in a manner that betrays a constabulary boot. Come in, my dear Lestrade! We have something here that may interest you.'

As the world knows, George Joseph Smith was tried at the Old Bailey in the first summer of the Great War for the murder of Bessie Mundy. By a choice irony, our friend Sir Edward Marshall Hall was briefed for this hopeless defence. Despite Sir Edward's best efforts and arguments, evidence of system was admitted. With that, his client was doomed. The jurors listened with visible horror to the stories of young women, living and dead, three of them at least drowned as 'Brides in the Bath'.

On a warm August morning, in an early stillness when the rumble of guns on the Western Front could be heard dimly in Hyde Park, George Joseph Smith was led to the execution shed in the yard of Chelmsford Gaol, attended by the chaplain, governor, warders, and the two silent figures of Pierpoint and Ellis. So faltering was his progress that the drop was two minutes late in falling open under him.

That evening, as he took his old-fashioned chair in Baker Street, rum and water in his glass, Holmes sighed and said, 'We have saved Miss Maxse from an early death, Watson, though not, I fear, from a fate worse than death. Be so good as to pass me the *Morning Post*. There is a curious series of incidents in which live rats and rabbits have been deliberately introduced into the plumbing of some of the most elegant addresses in Mayfair and St James's. Such a diversion is, I suspect, the tactic of a master-criminal bent on the greatest robbery of the age. As such, it deserves our attention.'

# The Case of the Talking Corpse

## I

Of all the problems submitted to Sherlock Holmes in the years of our friendship, there were few indeed where I was the means of introducing the case to his notice. There was certainly no other experience of mine to compare with a series of grotesque murders which afflicted Lambeth and the shabby areas of the Waterloo Road in the final decade of the last century.

Holmes was wont to argue that the eccentricity or singularity of a criminal is always a clue. Conversely, 'The more featureless and commonplace a crime is, the more difficult it is to bring it home.' There was no lack of eccentricity or singularity in the present investigation. The apparent lunacy of the murderer led him to correspond cheerfully with Scotland Yard, offering to solve the mysteries for money, if the police themselves could not do so.

Our antagonist also appeared to possess a gang of assistants, all as mad as he – and women were among his accomplices. It even seemed we might be wrong in supposing the actual killer and tormentor of the fair sex to be a man! May not a woman have a grudge against the poor creatures of the street? With so much singularity, if Holmes was right in his hypothesis, such maniacs should have been easy enough to catch. Unfortunately, a long passage of time was to prove otherwise.

Let me begin at the beginning. One fateful Saturday evening, I had arrived at Waterloo Station after an informal reunion of several old friends. We had served together in the 5th Northumberland Fusiliers, during the Afghan campaign a dozen years before. Fowler, Osborne, Scott, and I had been subalterns in the draught that was sent up from the depot at Peshawur to the forward encampment of Khandahar. My own military career was short and inglorious. I was detached to the Berkshire regiment for the coming battle of Maiwand, where a Jezail bullet shattered the bone of my shoulder and grazed the subclavial artery. Nor was that the worst. At the base hospital of Peshawur, I was first a convalescent from my wound and then, more dangerously, a victim of enteric fever. How I came home an invalid and made my first acquaintance with Sherlock Holmes is described in my account of the Brixton Road murder, made public under the somewhat sensational title of *A Study in Scarlet*.

More than ten years later, in the mess at Aldershot, the four of us talked much of these things. As I returned from that convivial luncheon, it was as if the gullies and bare mountain ridges of Afghanistan rather than the tenements and warehouses of Nine Elms and the Waterloo Road rose before my eyes. The sound of the well-lit trains thundering into the great terminus under fiery pillars of steam might have been distant salvoes of our artillery covering the withdrawal to Jellalabad.

I walked out of the great railway terminus into a drizzling October evening, the gaslights of the busy street flickering and shining on the wet cobbles. It was a scene of market-stalls and flower-sellers, beggars and ragged children. Thinking of the welcoming fire in our Baker Street rooms, I turned towards the rank of two-wheeled hansom cabs and four-wheeled growlers.

Then I heard a scream, as sharp as any Jezail's knife at Maiwand.

'Help me! Oh, God, help me!'

I cannot do justice to the intensity of it. How common and plain her words appear set down in print! Sometimes I hear that shriek again, in the quiet of the night. The terror of it, in a shabby thoroughfare of market-stalls and four-ale bars, returns as shrill as ever. It was a cry of agony, but more of panic. A physician who has witnessed the worst deaths might recognize it as heralding the cruellest ending of a life. Nothing in the butchery of men and beasts in battle lives with me as clearly as that sound.

The street from Waterloo Bridge to St George's Circus was so crowded at that hour on a Saturday night that, at first, I could not make out where the cry had come from. It was somewhere on the further side of the busy thoroughfare, not far from the double bar-room doors of the York Hotel. The pavement was lit through the windows by chandelier-light, clouded with tobacco smoke. I thought I heard a softer following cry. That was soon lost in the rumble and crash of barrels on a tarpaulined dray, turning out from the railway goods yard.

Then there came only the bursts of laughter and a snatch of music from the hotel's public bar, as the doors swung open and closed again. But that scream was not the cry of a young woman playing the fool. Crossing between the cabs and twopenny buses, I paused as I saw an unkempt girl staggering against the wall of the hotel, her arms clamped across her midriff. She was twisting and lurching as a drunkard might. Her voice was quieter now but with a terrible and sober appeal.

'Help me! Oh, someone, help me!'

Before I could reach her, she had slithered down the wall and was sitting on the stained wet paving, a plump young woman with a frizzy mane of fair hair gathered roughly in a tail and worn down her back. I cannot say that she began to vomit, rather that she strove to do so without effect. By the time I reached her, the screams had stopped. She lay curled on the paving, still groaning more in fear than in pain.

In such a place and with such an appearance as hers, her profession was not in doubt. The street was crowded at that time of night and, even before I had reached her, several people were standing by and looking down at the poor creature. I pushed my way through.

'Let me come to her. I am a doctor.'

This produced a murmur of interest among the spectators, as if the spectacle might be better worth watching. The poor girl's face was ghost-white with pain and her hair was plastered on her forehead by a sweat of agony. I tried to question her as gently as I could but she seemed not to hear me. Her eyes were motionless, staring in an uncomprehending horror. Then, through clenched teeth, there issued a series of shorter, rising hisses as the spasm came again. Her face was set hard in a rictus of convulsive frenzy. It was like that terrible death mask which is sometimes called the 'Hippocrates Smile'. I could get nothing from her. It was as if she could not hear me. Having guessed her way of life and her occupation, I supposed that she was in a last stage of delirium tremens.

Kneeling down, I felt a pulse that was rapid and fluttering, which confirmed my supposition. The torment of alcoholism that she endured had brought on an acute cardiac distress. Her breath was still uneven and she was glistening with perspiration. I asked her what she had been eating or drinking, though the sweet spirituous odour of gin was strong upon her and on her clothes. Her reply was incoherent at first but then I made out that she had been drinking in the York Hotel with a man called Fred. She had drunk gin with 'something white' in it.

'Fred Linnell,' said one of the women in the crowd. 'She's one of his girls. Lor' look at her! She's had her whack all right!'

The dying girl shook her head, struggling to deny the words. There was another scream, feebler this time. Her head went back and her knees came up abruptly into her stomach, as the shrillness fell to an inhuman grunting and jabbering. It was the first of several tetanic convulsions that I was to witness and I knew she would die on the pavement unless treatment was given at once.

Just then a market trader in cap and apron pushed though the crowd carrying a board from a trestle table. Two of his assistants were with him.

'Get her home on this,' he said to them, ignoring me. 'Number eight, Duke Street, off of Westminster Bridge

Road. She's Nellie Donworth. Lodges with old Mrs Avens.'

I nodded to his two assistants, for the girl could not be left where she was. I also took out my card and handed it to Jimmy Styles, as the stall-holder's name proved to be, first writing on it 'delirium tremens', 'syncope', and '8 Duke Street'.

'Go as fast as you can to St Thomas's Hospital. Give this to Dr Kelloch, the house physician, or whichever assistant may be on duty. I shall need help at Duke Street. Ask them to send a four-wheeler, to get her to hospital. She lodges close, so we shall have her home before they arrive.'

I had written 'syncope' to emphasize the urgency of the message, for it was now apparent that the poor heart must fail very soon under the distress of such extreme convulsions as were seizing her with greater frequency.

Styles went at a run between the traffic, past the railway terminus, towards the embankment of the dark river, where the hospital stood. His two men took up the board with the girl lying upon it, her body alternately limp and then drawn into a spasm. By the wine vaults on the corner, we turned into Duke Street, a squalid ill-lit alley behind the coal wharves. She was carried to her room on the first floor of a tenement and laid gently on an old brass bedstead covered by linen that was worn to rags.

There was little that I could do until Kelloch or his assistant came. I noticed a dark bottle on the stained wash-stand, labelled as bromide of potassium. Though it is a standard prescription for alcoholism, I dared not give it to her until I knew how much gin she had drunk, for fear I should do more harm than good. Instead, I sent down to the landlady for carbonate of sodium as a palliative.

I had hardly expected that Dr Kelloch would be able to come in person but fifteen minutes later a four-wheeler turned the corner and rattled into Duke Street, bringing his assistant, Mr Johnson of the South London Medical Institute. We had a hasty and murmured consultation outside the bedroom door, the purport of which, on my part, was that the unfortunate young woman should be conveyed to hospital without delay. Though Mr Johnson agreed, I could see that it was already too late.

So passed this young woman of the town, she who had depended for her bread upon prostitution in the streets of a great and cruel city, one of that legion of the lost whom we see about us every day. Like so many of her kind, she had sought oblivion in drink from her brutal way of life and from the squalid lodging houses that were the only home she knew. Like so many victims of drink's false comfort, she had paid the last terrible penalty that the body exacts for such brutish indulgence.

With these sombre thoughts, so different to the memories of military comradeship that had been woken earlier that day, I walked back to Waterloo and called a cab to Baker Street. The case now belonged to Dr Kelloch and Mr Johnson. I had no reason to suppose that I should ever hear of it again, except perhaps as a matter of courtesy. The bottle on the wash-stand, with its familiar 'Bromide of Potassium' label, was evidence that Ellen Donworth was already 'under the doctor' for alcoholism. The coroner seldom sees any reason for calling an inquest, when the cause of death is so plain.

I mentioned the young street-walker's tragedy to Holmes, as an explanation for my late return. However, he seemed disinclined to interest himself in the fate of this 'unfortunate'. Somewhen during that night, in the darkest hours when the city had fallen silent, I woke with the memory of that terrible scream rising from the recesses of my mind. Unnerved by this, I vowed that I must put poor Nellie Donworth from my thoughts.

On the following morning, the bells of Marylebone Church pealed through a thin autumn sunlight. The streets and squares rustled with fallen leaves. Just before noon I received a wire from Dr Kelloch. He thanked me for my attention to the unfortunate girl but regretted to inform me that Ellen Donworth had suffered a final delirium tremens in the cab. In consequence of this, her heart had failed and she was dead upon arrival at St Thomas's Hospital. So, it seemed, a too-familiar Waterloo Road tragedy had come to its conclusion.

I did not mention her death to Holmes just then. What purpose would that have served?

## II

Sherlock Holmes was the most precise and meticulous of men in word and thought, but the most careless and untidy being who ever plagued a fellow lodger. The tray which held his abandoned supper would lie casually on his work-table among piles of papers, or next to some unsavoury chemical experiment, designed to raise fingerprints upon a glass or to separate the contents of a poison-bottle into their constituents. An important clue in a case of homicide or adultery was apt to lie concealed, for safety, in the butter dish.

So it was with some surprise, while the October light turned to dusk under plum-coloured rain-clouds, that I returned from a consultation at the fever ward of the military hospital to discover Holmes putting our Baker Street sitting-room into unaccustomed order. A full three days had passed since the tragedy of Nellie Donworth and I had heard nothing further from Dr Kelloch or Mr Johnson.

As I entered the room, I noticed that the work-table was unusually regimented. Indeed, Holmes had so far forgotten himself as to arrange the cushions in the arm-chairs. A window had been opened at the top to air the fumes of black tobacco. He glanced up as I came in.

'Be so good as to turn the settee to the fire a little. Look lively, my dear fellow! We are to have a visitor.'

'Oh, indeed,' I had heard nothing of a visitor that morning. 'And cannot Mrs Hudson . . .'

'If you will recall, Watson, the week has reached Wednesday afternoon. On that feast of Woden, Mrs Hudson is accustomed to take tea with her married sister in Clapham. Be so kind as to pass me that other antimacassar.'

'What visitor? And why so suddenly?'

'A wire from Lady Russell,' he said firmly, adjusting the angle of a chair to the hearth. 'She comes suddenly because the matter is urgent. Why else?'

My consultation at the military hospital had been

long and difficult. I was not best pleased to find a quiet evening disturbed in this manner.

'A good many of the English aristocracy bear the name of Russell,' I said rather shortly. 'Which is this? The law lord's baroness? Surely not the prime minister's widow?'

He looked up at me, as he carried a laden wastepaper basket to conceal it quickly in a far corner of the room.

'Neither of them. Our visitor is Mabel Edith, Countess Russell. I daresay that even you must have heard of her.'

'I wish I had not. She is one young lady with whom our practice could well dispense.'

'Balderdash,' he said, brushing his hands together smartly, to indicate that his domestic chores were complete.

'You may call it balderdash, Holmes. I am told, on the best authority, that her mother Lady Scott was divorced by Sir Claude for reasons one does not usually discuss. Reardon, at the club, assures me that her ladyship's sister works to this day as a masseuse in Cranbourn Street. Walk past and you will see the building at the corner. The ground floor is occupied by that rogue Arthur Carrez, selling certain French books and Malthusian devices, which have several times drawn the attention of the Metropolitan Police upon him.'

Holmes straightened up and looked round him, as if he had not heard a word that I had spoken. He seemed satisfied that the room was fit to receive his young visitor. Then he said, 'It is neither her mother, nor her aunt, who seeks our help, Watson. This young woman herself is in trouble. She asks our advice.'

'That does not surprise me in the least. Advice about what, may I inquire?'

He shrugged in his off-hand manner.

'Oh, a little blackmail. Money demanded with menaces. And murder, of course. We could hardly do without that could we? We have been too idle of late. I confess that even the most insignificant problem would have been welcome in these stagnant autumn days. This one may prove far from insignificant.'

I still feared the worst. The newspaper public had lately been treated to stories of the scandal attending this young woman and her husband, Earl Russell. Frank Russell, as he preferred to be known, was in his early twenties. He had been brought up by his grandfather, the great prime minister, after the death of his parents. His career at Oxford had been brief. He was dismissed in a few months by the master of his college for what was politely described as 'disgusting conduct'. Then, while his brother Bertrand absorbed symbolic logic at Cambridge, Frank Russell threw himself into the pleasures of a certain type of London society.

In no time, that notorious harpy Lady Selina Scott had her claws into this weak young man. Rumour insisted that, at twice his age, she wanted him for herself! The idea was so preposterous that she thought it better to have the young fool enticed into marriage by her daughter, Mabel Edith. Within the year, a splendid wedding in Eaton Place was followed by unedifying court action. The young bride alleged depraved conduct by her lord. She demanded, and got, her separation with a handsome settlement. Since then, she had kept a prudent distance from respectable society, occupying a suite at the Savoy Hotel.

I was still pondering this half an hour later when Holmes crossed to the window.

'Holloa! Holloa! Here we are, Watson!'

From the street below came a familiar stamping of hooves and the long grind of a cab wheel as its metal rim rasped against the kerb. The door bell sounded and the housemaid, whom Mrs Hudson had lately taken into her service, burst in upon us, twittering with excitement like a beribboned sparrow.

Presently, there came a frou-frou of a woman's skirts on the stairs. Then, in the full glare of the light, a slim, dark-haired figure stood before us, a veil over her face, a mantle drawn round her chin. Her breath came quickly, as if the stairs had been an exertion. Every inch of her lithe figure seemed to quiver with strong emotion. When she put up the veil, her young face was clear-cut with a straight nose, dark brows, glittering eyes, and a thin mouth that seemed as if it might form a dangerous smile. The neatness of her face and the skill with which it was painted gave her the air of an expensive doll.

My friend crossed the room to greet her.

'Mr Holmes?' she inquired, her voice low yet richly modulated, 'Mr Sherlock Holmes?'

'Ma'am,' said Holmes punctiliously. He did not bow to this daughter of the aristocracy, for that would have bruised his Bohemian soul, but there was a slight inclination of the dark head and aquiline profile.

Her lips parted in a promise of hopeful innocence, as she took his hand. Still holding the hand, she looked long and directly into his eyes. Holmes stared at her, as if mesmerized. Then he said, as if in an afterthought, 'This is my associate, Dr Watson, before whom you may speak as freely as before myself.'

As I took that cool, delicate hand and looked into the frank blue eyes of our client, I thought that she was the type of young woman who would make you all the world to her for that moment, and dispense with you the next.

'Pray be seated, ma'am,' Holmes said gently, 'and tell us how we may be of service.' He allowed her to choose her place on the settee, watched her sit down, then took his own place in a chair diagonally across the carpet.

'Mr Holmes,' she said quickly, as she arranged her skirts, 'I will come straight to the point. You will know that I have been separated from my husband for some months. There is no communication between us, except through our lawyers. However, I am told that there is evidence in the hands of a certain person which would convict him of murder. Of two murders, indeed.'

'Lord Russell?'

She nodded, stood up again, crossed to the small occasional table where she had left her reticule and took a miniature silver box from it. She lit a cigarette and chose a fresh arm-chair, for all the world like a modern matinée heroine at Her Majesty's Theatre or the Haymarket.

'I believe my husband capable of many moral crimes, Mr Holmes, but scarcely of the murders of young women who are strangers to him.'

The slim fingers of one hand curled tightly over the

end of the chair-arm, her gaze cool and direct. I saw why Holmes had responded to her appeal for help. A series of young women murdered? Lord Russell? The grandson of England's greatest prime minister in the past fifty years? If there were a word of truth, it was surely the sensation of the century.

'I cannot say whether the charge of murder is true or false, Mr Holmes. I mean to know, however, for a threat of blackmail is made to me.'

Holmes nodded, as if he approved of her determination.

'Whom is it said that he murdered?'

Only the denting of the white cigarette by her fine nails betrayed her anxiety.

'Two names are mentioned in a letter, from Mr Bayne, a barrister. He claims that since our separation Lord Russell has frequented houses in Lambeth and Southwark. The allegation is that Lord Russell derives his pleasure by making poor fallen creatures swallow noxious draughts to cause them torment. A fortnight ago, by accident or intent, he caused the deaths of two young women.'

Holmes looked askance.

'Lady Russell,' he said presently, 'such pathological pleasures are happily rare. They were indulged by certain Byzantine emperors and Renaissance princes, to be sure, and by the Comte de Sade at Marseille in 1772. In my own practice I have met not a single example. May I see the letter?'

She blushed very slightly, unfolding the sheet of paper and giving it to him. Holmes read it, looked at me and raised his eyebrows.

Without asking her leave, he handed me the paper to read.

*To the Countess Russell,*
*Savoy Hotel,*
*London*

*Madam,*

*I am writing to inform you that, since your parting, your husband Lord Francis, Earl Russell, has been a regular patron of many houses of ill-fame in Lambeth and Southwark. He has killed several girls. A week or two ago he gave enough strychnine to Matilda Clover and Lou Harvey to kill a horse. Only it killed them. Two letters incriminating him were found among the effects of Clover after her death. Think of the shame and disgrace it will bring upon you and your family if Lord Russell is arrested and put in prison for this crime.*

*My object in writing this letter to you is to ask if you will retain me at once as your counsellor and legal adviser for a fee of two thousand pounds. If you employ me at once to act for you in this matter, I will save you from all exposure and shame. If you wait until your husband is arrested, then I cannot act for you, as no lawyer can save you after the authorities get hold of Clover's papers. If you wish to retain me, just put an advertisement in the personal column of the* Morning Post, *saying* Lady R. wishes to see Mr Bayne the Barrister *and I will drop in and have a private interview with you.*

*I can save you and your husband if you retain me in time, but not otherwise.*

*Yours truly,*

*H. Bayne, Barrister*

As I put the letter down, I confess that my heart had quickened with relief. Whoever Matilda Clover and Lou Harvey might be, they were neither of them the young woman whom I had found dying on Saturday evening.

'How was the letter delivered?' Holmes asked quietly.

'By mail this morning, sent by yesterday's post, the final collection last night.'

Holmes nodded.

'Tell me, who is your solicitor?'

'Sir George Lewis, of Lewis and Lewis.'

He nodded again and brought the matter to an end, as it seemed.

'Then you have no need of my services, Lady Russell. There is no better man than Sir George. Take the letter to him. Request him to bring it to the notice of the Commissioner of the Metropolitan Police. That will put a stop to blackmail. The police may ask you to insert the notice in the *Morning Post*, as a trap to catch the criminal. I doubt if you will hear from your blackmailer again. There is spite in this letter, rather than blackmail. However, if Mr Bayne, or whatever his name may be, attempts to contact you, the police will have him. They will do as much for you as I could.'

Her eyes showed a glimmer of petulance.

'And the young women my husband is said to have murdered a fortnight ago?'

Holmes smiled at her.

'Lady Russell, one murder – let alone two – would have been reported, however briefly, in the press. I assure you there has been no such report. Scotland Yard, in the person of Inspector Lestrade, is also kind enough to take me into its counsels. I believe I can say that neither I nor Mr Lestrade has so much as heard of Matilda Clover or Lou Harvey. Either they do not exist, which is most likely, or they are names of girls alive and well, put there for spite against them.'

'Perhaps the murders have not been discovered?'

'In that case,' Holmes said gently, 'if the murders were secret, there would be no point to the blackmail. Would there?'

She did not answer. I could swear she was almost disappointed to find there was no evidence against her husband. Her fingertips rattled on the chair-arm.

'I will also speak to Sir George Lewis,' Holmes continued, as if trying to mollify her. 'If there is any way in which I may assist you further, he need only say so.'

'Speak to whom you please!' She was standing up now and so were we. 'You may hang Lord Russell at Newgate a dozen times for the murder of Matilda Clover or Lou Harvey before I will pay a farthing to Mr Bayne!'

'Admirable,' Holmes said with every appearance of sincerity.

Lady Russell took her leave with a further assurance that Holmes would be at her beck and call, if Sir George said the word. Then my friend sat down with his legs out straight, the tips of the fingers touched together, his eyes closed.

'Let Sir George Lewis puzzle out the letter,' I said cheerfully, trying to console him. 'That is the end of the matter so far as we are concerned.'

He spoke without opening his eyes.

'My dear Watson, the significance of this case eludes you. What blackmailer would propose a scheme that is bound to put the handcuffs on him as soon as he approaches his victim? You saw, did you not, the script? Sharp and yet curiously florid in its decoration of open letters. The initial B of Bayne and the R of Russell were obvious examples. Such a hand is strongly indicative of inherent mania. I think, my dear fellow, that this is not the end of anything at all. I fancy, however, that it may be a most promising beginning.'

Two hours later the street-door bell emitted a single vigorous clang.

Holmes glanced at me, uneasily as I thought. The housemaid's steps rattled up the stairs and she burst in upon us, ribbons fluttering.

'Mr Fred Smith!' she gasped. 'Most urgent Mr Smith is, to see Mr Holmes!'

Holmes looked at me with an ironical despair.

'Then let Mr Fred Smith be shown up,' he said languidly. 'I should not like to think, Watson, that our evening was to be entirely without further diversion.'

## III

A sense of farce, as if one actor crossed the stage in pursuit of another, now began to threaten a case which was to prove one of the grimmest. While the maid went downstairs, I stole a glimpse of the windy street from behind the curtains. There stood a dark carriage, its coachman dressed in black, with a crape hat-band and arm-band, a black crape bow on his whip. At this hour on a stormy night, he seemed like a messenger of death come to bear Don Juan down to hell.

A moment later his master was before us in a fur-collared coat, the length of a black silk weeper trailing from the hat he handed to the maid. Now that 'Fred' Smith stood before us, we recognized a man of great influence in England's political and commercial life. His face had lately graced the weekly magazines as the son and heir of a famous bookseller and Leader of the House of Commons, the Right Honourable W. H. Smith, who had died a fortnight since. With his square-set face and quick eyes, the Honourable Frederick Smith, himself a Member of Parliament, appeared as a paragon of action and integrity.

Holmes crossed the room, his hand extended.

'You need not introduce yourself, sir, for Dr Watson and I had the pleasure of meeting you last summer. It was at the Stationers Company, the occasion of a most informative address by Mr Walter de Grey Birch of the British Museum. The chemical effects produced upon logwood ink by the introduction of wood pulp in paper milling.'

Mr Smith faltered.

'You are quite right, Mr Holmes. I had overlooked that.'

'And now,' said Holmes in a graver tone and with a slight inclination of the head, 'permit me to offer you my condolences upon the death of your father.'

Frederick Smith looked as if he hardly knew how to go on. Then he said quickly, 'It is in that connection that I have come to you, Mr Holmes, rather than to the police. I fear that my family's grief is to be compounded by a painful scandal.'

Holmes looked at him a little more keenly.

'I should be sorry for that, Mr Smith. Pray be seated.'

Our visitor sat down, though first he handed my friend an envelope.

'This letter and enclosure came this morning. It is preposterous, of course, and cruel in its persecution of a bereaved family. I hope I may look to you to ensure that we are not taunted in this way. I cannot believe I am obliged to take this nonsense to the police. I should rather trust you to keep a watching brief. You know already, I daresay, of the murders in Lambeth. The death of an unfortunate young woman, Ellen Donworth . . .'

The sound of that name was as if a prize-fighter's fist had knocked the wind from my solar plexus. Holmes gave me a quick look which counselled silence but Mr Smith must have seen something for he repeated carefully, 'Ellen Donworth, and . . .'

'Matilda Clover?' Holmes suggested brightly.

Frederick Smith shook his head.

'Louisa Harvey – or Lou Harvey as he calls her.'

Holmes caught my eye again and looked quickly away.

'Indeed? May I read this curious letter?'

'By all means.'

Holmes glanced at the paper and began to read out loud for my benefit.

*'To Mr Frederick Smith, 186 Strand. On Saturday night, Ellen Donworth, sometimes calling herself*

*Ellen Linnell, 8 Duke Street, Westminster Bridge Road, was poisoned with strychnine. Among her effects were found two letters also incriminating you in the murder of Lou Harvey. If they ever become public property they will surely convict you of both crimes. I enclose a copy of a letter Miss Donworth received the day she died.'*

Holmes glanced at the second letter but then continued to read the first.

*'Judge for yourself what hope you have of escape if the law officers ever get hold of those letters . . .'*

My friend skimmed down the page a little, humming to himself.

*'My object in writing to you is to ask if you will retain me at once as your counsellor and legal adviser. If you employ me to act for you in this matter, I will save you from all exposure and shame. If you wait till you are arrested before retaining me, I cannot act for you. No lawyer can save you after the authorities get hold of those two letters.'*

He sat for a moment with his brows drawn down, staring at the sheet of paper.

'Read the end of it,' Mr Smith said curtly.

*'If you wish to retain me, just write a few lines on paper, saying, "Mr Fred Smith wishes to see Mr Bayne, the barrister, at once." Paste this on one of your windows at 186 Strand next Tuesday morning. I will drop in and have a private interview with you. I can save you if you retain me in time,*

*but not otherwise. Yours truly, H. M. Bayne, Barrister.'*

Holmes looked up from the paper again and there was a moment of silence, save for the wind from the street rattling the windows.

'It may comfort you to know, Mr Smith, that you are not the only person to be persecuted by the malicious letters of this madman. It is, I assure you, malice rather than blackmail. As a criminal expert, it is my habit to keep track of such murders as may occur in this city. Indeed, I am fortunate enough to be admitted every day or two to the counsels of Inspector Lestrade of Scotland Yard. I may tell you that, to my certain knowledge, no young person by the name of Lou or Louisa Harvey has been found murdered or reported murdered. As to Miss Ellen Donworth - or Linnell - it seems that she was taken ill with a terminal attack of delirium tremens on Saturday evening and that she died on the way to St Thomas's Hospital. My colleague Dr Watson was in the Waterloo Road at the time and was able to render some comfort to the poor soul until the arrival of the hospital assistant. I think you may confidently put aside all thought of accusation or scandal. I recognize your correspondent only too well.'

Frederick Smith sat upright in his chair.

'You know his name?'

Holmes shook his head.

'At present, I merely recognize his type. One of my student textbooks, long since, was Henry Maudsley's *On Criminal Responsibility*. Your antagonist is the hardest type of the criminally insane to deal with. Such a personality is moved by impulses and attracted to beliefs at which you and I could scarcely guess. Worse still he is, like Iago, a man who will smile and smile, and be a villain. May we turn to the second letter which is said to have been found among the unfortunate Miss Donworth's possessions?'

He scowled at it and began to read.

*'Miss Ellen Linnell, I wrote and warned you once before that Frederick Smith of W. H. Smith & Son was going to poison you. If you take any of the medicine he gave you, you will die. I saw Fred Smith prepare the medicine he gave you, and I saw him put enough strychnine in it to kill a horse. Signed H.M.B.'*

Frederick Smith leant forward in his chair.

'There is no H. M. Bayne in the lists of the Inns of Court. That has been checked. I infer that the medicine he describes was a preparation to procure an abortion.'

'Put blackmail from your mind, sir.'

Holmes handed me the letters. Their copper-plate was a script taught to every child at school. It seemed as impersonal as scraps cut from a newspaper.

'You are entirely right, Mr Holmes,' Frederick Smith said simply. 'Of course it is quite mad. Whoever heard of a blackmailer demanding that his victim should employ him as an attorney? He would be arrested the minute he showed himself. I shall burn this poisonous nonsense and forget the matter.'

Sherlock Holmes looked truly alarmed.

'On no account can you do that, Mr Smith. This villain must be caught. You will greatly oblige me by putting the message in your window as he commands. Meantime, I beg you to take these letters at once to

Inspector Lestrade at Scotland Yard. The blackmail threats are too absurd to be carried out and our man must know that. What then is his true object? Perhaps to divert suspicion from some crime of his own that he intends. He shows all the characteristics of a psychopath, and he is at large. There is no time to be lost in the matter. As for his absurd and malicious accusations, I may promise you that no publicity will attend them.'

I should like to say that Frederick Smith looked reassured but that was not so. He stood up and, with a look of reluctance, prepared to make his way to Scotland Yard. As our guest took his hat, Holmes called him back.

'One moment, Mr Smith. A question had best be asked now, since it will be asked sooner or later. Where were you on Saturday evening when this unfortunate girl, Ellen Donworth, died?'

A brief resentment glimmered in the eyes of our visitor but it was soon gone.

'You are quite right, Mr Holmes. That question must be asked and answered. From seven o'clock until half-past ten, I was with the platform party at the Christian Guild meeting in Exeter Hall. I dined at home before that. The Bishop of London was my guest. If you want from me what I suppose you would call an alibi, I was in company from four in the afternoon until a little after eleven.'

'I think we may say that disposes of the matter,' Holmes said smoothly.

'Does it? Am I not accused of preparing a mixture for this poor woman which might destroy her whenever she took it, days or weeks later?'

I was happy to intervene and put his mind at rest. 'You need not concern yourself with that, sir. Miss Donworth showed the classic symptoms of alcoholic poisoning while I was with her. Indeed, there was bromide of potassium on her wash-stand which had evidently been prescribed by a physician to treat this condition.'

After Frederick Smith had gone, we sat for more than an hour with our glasses of warm whisky and lemon. Holmes was unaccountably silent.

'I should rather like to be a fly on the wall of Scotland Yard,' I said, as if to cheer him up. 'I imagine that Sir George Lewis would despatch Lady Russell's letter to Lestrade at once. Just as the poor devil is packing up for the day. Then, no sooner will he have read it and written his report than he will have two more letters brought by Mr Frederick Smith. It would be worth a sovereign to see his face!'

Holmes looked at the door.

'I believe it would be a wasted journey, my dear fellow. Unless I am greatly mistaken, when Lestrade has read those letters, you will see his face here soon enough.'

I suppose it was a little after nine o'clock when the door-bell sounded below us.

# IV

It was no secret that Sherlock Holmes regarded Inspector Lestrade privately as what he called 'the pick of a bad lot' among the senior detective police of Scotland Yard. However, the inspector's defects of reasoning and intuition were redeemed by a gruff tenacity, when once he got his teeth into a case. Moreover, his habit of looking in upon us of an evening kept us in touch with all that was happening at police headquarters.

Mrs Hudson had returned from her sister in time to take our visitor's waterproof before she showed him up to our quarters. He appeared in the doorway, a small wiry bulldog of a man, his pea-jacket and cravat giving him a decidedly nautical appearance. With a short greeting, he put down the attaché case he had been carrying, seated himself, and lit the cigar that Holmes had given him. Soon he was relaxed before the fire, warming his left hand round a glass of warm toddy. The tone of his visit to us was less amiable than usual. He had the look of a man who has triumphed and is bursting to show it.

'I hear, gentlemen, you have had visitors this evening. Out of the top drawer, as you might say. Lady Russell and the Honourable Mr Frederick Smith.'

'Quite,' said Holmes punctiliously, leaning forward with the poker and stirring the fire to new life.

Lestrade shot a fierce look at my companion.

'Well, we shall have a word about those folk presently, Mr Holmes. In the matter of Ellen Donworth, however, I think you will find that I have been a little in front of you this time!'

The mention of the girl's name knocked the wind from me again. Holmes laid down the poker and looked up.

'Really, Lestrade? You don't say?'

'But I do say, Mr Holmes! I fear that I must have given Mr Frederick Smith something of a knock.'

'I see.'

'I don't think you do, sir! I don't think you do at all. There were you and the good doctor, promising him that the poor young creature had died of alcoholic poisoning. And there was I, sitting across my desk from Mr Smith, with a post-mortem note on Home Office stationery in my hand. From Dr Stevenson this afternoon. Alcoholic poisoning? Ellen Donworth had enough strychnine in her to kill half of Lambeth! What about that, Mr Holmes? Eh?'

Again, I felt the dull blow of dismay. Holmes gazed into the fire.

'Were you a medical man, Lestrade, you would know that tetanic convulsions, accompanied by violent vomiting, are symptomatic both of delirium tremens and of acute poisoning by certain vegetable alkaloids. Dr Watson was present and merely rendered what immediate assistance he could. He is not a walking laboratory. I suppose that it took a Home Office autopsy before the combined intelligences of Scotland Yard so much as thought of poison.'

I tried to recall any evidence of poison on that Saturday evening. There was none that could have been obtained, short of laboratory samples from the victim. That Ellen Donworth was under treatment for alcoholism had further compounded the difficulty.

'She said that she had been given a glass of gin by a man called Fred,' I ventured, 'a glass that had something white in it.'

Lestrade swung round in his chair with a look of pure satisfaction.

'So one of the other witnesses heard her say. Jimmy Styles, the market-trader. Quite took the colour out of the Honourable Mr Smith, though, when I told him the man we wanted was called Fred, the same as him.'

Holmes yawned, the inspector's triumph becoming insufferable to him. But there was no quenching the light of satisfaction in Lestrade's dark eyes. His tongue was moving humorously behind his teeth.

'One word to you,' said Holmes, 'Mr Smith was in company from six until eleven on Saturday evening. I advise you to tread lightly in these matters.'

The inspector grinned.

'I know that, Mr Holmes. But you should have seen him all the same.' He fell silent, puffing at his cigar, then added, 'Mr Smith had no part in this, nor Lord Russell. Whoever the brute was, we deduce he was in the shadows of the Waterloo Road, gloating over his handiwork as she lay there.'

'Forgive me,' Holmes said quietly, 'that assumption has the sound of a fine theory and a questionable fact.'

Lestrade shook his head firmly.

'Oh, no, sir. When Dr Stevenson performed his post-mortem this morning, he found the strychnine had been mixed with morphia. Now why should a man do that, if he only meant to kill her, as he knew strychnine must? The only reason, Dr Stevenson says, was to make sure the poor soul should not die too quickly. Without morphia, it would have been over in a few minutes perhaps. This devil wanted to see and hear her lying there, as Mr Styles did, trying to press her stomach on the pavement to ease the agony, pleading with them not to lift her.'

Holmes took a glowing cinder with the tongs and lit his cherrywood pipe. For a moment he said nothing, then he leant back in his chair.

'Perhaps you should arrest Mr Styles. Or Dr Watson. Or anyone who happened to be outside the York Hotel.' He paused and drew at his pipe. 'Forgive me, pray continue with your narrative.'

'The matter of these letters,' the inspector said shortly, 'I don't know what we shall make of them. The one accusing Mr Smith of murdering Nellie Donworth was written a full day before the poison was found in her by Dr Stevenson. Who could know the truth but the murderer himself?'

Holmes waved his pipe.

'True. Or very nearly so.'

'But the letter enclosed with it, and the one to Lady Russell! No one by the name of Matilda Clover or Louisa Harvey is dead, so far as we know, let alone murdered. Wires have gone out to every police district in London and the cities throughout the country. All with the same result. Nothing known for either name.'

'Will you not include the names of Clover and Harvey in your investigation?'

Lestrade looked at him, as if my friend should have known better.

'And a pretty dance our man might lead us! Every time he gives us a name we must send men on a murder hunt! He might give us a new name by every post!'

'And that is the best advice you can offer?'

'No,' said the inspector, 'by no means. There is another side to this, though it won't disturb you here in the quiet of Baker Street. Since this morning, rumours have been flying about as to how Ellen Donworth died. We think they came from an attendant at Westminster mortuary, after the post-mortem. You don't need me to tell you that the mention of strychnine has caused a panic among certain classes in Lambeth. So nothing is to be said about Harvey and Clover. It won't do to have the public mind agitated further by rumours of young women murdered who never have been. You know as well as I, gentlemen, that tragedies of this kind are too often an opportunity for sick minds to vent their frustrations.'

'Indeed,' said Holmes languidly. 'In this case, however, you tell me that the date of posting proves conclusively that this sick mind knew of the strychnine when the rest of the world still called it alcoholic poisoning.'

'Which is just what I thought you would say, Mr Holmes. So, as to Clover and Harvey, I left orders that Sergeant Macintyre is to visit Somerset House tomorrow morning and go through the registers of deaths for Clovers and Harveys, from all causes, for two years past. If our man tries us with any other names, we shall do exactly the same. You'll see we can manage these things quite well enough for ourselves, when we have to, Mr Sherlock Holmes.'

## V

Somewhat to my surprise, I came down to breakfast on the following morning to find that Sherlock Holmes had already finished his meal. He was sitting in the large old-fashioned chair, eyes gleaming from a haggard face. Beside him on the floor lay the dismembered relics of the morning papers. He looked like a man who has not been to bed all night, rather than one who has risen early.

'Make the best of it, Watson,' he said, gesturing at the remaining place laid for me, 'I fancy we shall have another visitor before long.'

'Not Mr Bayne the Barrister, I trust!'

'Lestrade, my dear fellow. I have frequently observed that his boast of being able to manage well enough on his own is usually followed by a request that I should supply the deficiencies of the detective police.'

'I doubt that we shall see him, Holmes. After his mood last night, I doubt it very much.'

I had scarcely finished my last slice of toast when the doorbell rang. Presently the familiar wiry bulldog figure appeared, as Holmes had predicted. The inspector seemed a little subdued this morning but by no means defeated.

'Do sit down,' said Holmes, as genially as if the two men had not met for several months, 'and tell us more news of the Lambeth murders.'

Lestrade looked a little uneasy as he said, 'There is only one, Mr Holmes. Ellen Donworth, that is all. Sergeant Macintyre reported to Somerset House at eight this morning and went through the entries for two years past. It was a simple enough matter. There is no entry of the death of Matilda Clover, nor of Lou or Louisa Harvey.'

'Good,' said Holmes, pouring coffee for the inspector. 'Let us be glad of that at least. However, your investigation has plainly run into difficulties or you would not be here. Will you not tell us what they are?'

Lestrade sipped his coffee and stared at Holmes over the rim of the cup.

'We are not in difficulties, Mr Holmes. Indeed, we have more evidence.'

'Oh?' said Holmes sceptically. 'Then let us be glad of that too.'

'A further letter was received this morning by Mr Wyatt, the Surrey coroner. As a matter of courtesy, I thought you should be informed.'

'Ah!' said Holmes triumphantly. 'Our man has set a puzzle of some kind for you?'

Lestrade handed him a single sheet of paper and my friend read it out for my benefit.

*'Sir,*
*I am writing to say that if you and your satellites fail to bring the murderer of Ellen Donworth,* alias *Ellen Linnell, late of 8 Duke Street, Westminster Bridge Road, to justice, then I am willing to give you such assistance, as will bring the murderer to justice provided your Government is willing to pay me £300,000 for my services. No pay if not successful.*
*A O'Brien, Detective.'*

Lestrade looked at us and asked quietly,

'Well, gentlemen. What do you make of that?'

'I think you might throw it in the fire,' I said at once. 'I know, of course, you cannot do that but at least commit it to your files. There is nothing here but a wild goose-chase. Follow the evidence in the case.'

Holmes shrugged.

'Three hundred thousand pounds! I do not think I should ever be able to command a fee so large. If Mr

O'Brien can obtain three hundred thousand pounds for a single case, he is a far better man than I. Perhaps, Lestrade, you should accept his offer.'

'I call it an outrage,' I persisted, irritated by such facetiousness, 'that the members of a bereaved family like Mr Smith's should be made sport of in this manner and the police put to such trouble by one criminal lunatic!'

'Or two,' Holmes said quietly.

'Or two?' Lestrade was half out of his chair.

'Of course there are two.' Holmes contrived to look astonished and alarmed that the inspector should have missed this. 'I feel sure, Lestrade, that you have not come without the letters to Lady Russell, to Mr Smith from Bayne the Barrister, and the enclosure to Ellen Donworth from H.M.B. Kindly look at them and tell me what you see!'

Self-consciously, Lestrade took the three sheets of paper from his case and made a pretence of reading them. Holmes poured ample salt upon the poor fellow's tail.

'Great heavens, man! Did you truly not see the difference? Come, of course you did! You are merely teasing us! The letter to Frederick Smith and that purporting to be written to Ellen Donworth are in quite different hands. Copperplate can never quite disguise those slight temperamental flourishes!'

'I see nothing,' Lestrade said uneasily.

Holmes sighed.

'Very well. I daresay you do not. To the trained eye, however, it is evident that the epistle to Mr Smith was written by a right-handed scribe, the enclosure by one who is naturally left-handed. No right-handed man could compose that second epistle with such assurance while using his left hand. The acute angle of the backward slope has the character of one who is uniquely left-handed.'

The unfortunate inspector began to struggle a little. 'Then why did you keep silent last night, Mr Holmes?'

Holmes shrugged.

'I suspected that we should soon hear from our correspondent again, as has proved to be the case this morning. It is not in the nature of such compulsives to keep silent. I daresay I would have said something last night. Indeed I was about to do so when you informed me that you would be quite able to sift the problem for yourself.'

An uncomfortable silence followed this piece of temperament on my friend's part. Presently Holmes said, 'I wonder why there are four?'

'Why should there not be four letters as well as any other number?' I asked.

He shook his head.

'No, Watson, you misunderstand. Why should the four letters have been written by four different people? The common experience of the criminal expert is that poisoning, whether for pleasure or expediency, proves to be a solitary occupation. At the most there is one accomplice. Here we have four people. Four letter-writers. Two of them must be known to one another, since their communications came in the same envelope. Indeed, all four appear to be united in a common enterprise.'

Lestrade's unease had grown to consternation but Sherlock Holmes was prepared to salt him a little more.

'Very well, Lestrade. We find that the four letters are in different hands, despite an attempt at similarity of style. However, you may not have had leisure to examine this morning's epistle closely enough to see that it comes from a woman.'

'A woman!' Lestrade's dark eyes suddenly appeared the size of marbles.

'Oh, yes,' said Holmes, surprised that the inspector and I could have missed anything so obvious. 'The script appears to be a woman's and, though this is sometimes simulated, I believe in this case it is genuine. A man who was imitating female script might copy well enough the usual rotundity of individual letters, even of complete words. Here however, even with my magnifying glass, I can detect none of those necessary breaks in a word or a letter which always occur sooner or later when another scribe merely imitates an unfamiliar hand. No, my dear fellow, this is too flowing – too much of a piece – to be anything but a female hand.'

'You cannot say that!' Lestrade snapped.

'I can and I do,' Holmes remarked jauntily. 'I also say that while I was reading out the contents of the note just now, for Watson's benefit, I was able to make a close inspection of the watermark. It is Mayfair Superfine, much favoured by ladies for casual correspondence. That in itself is nothing, of course. A man might use it for disguise. However, as I held the paper I was conscious of the faintest air of white jessamine, imparted by the writer's wrist or sleeve. As I have remarked before, there are seventy-five perfumes which it is very necessary that the criminal expert should be able to distinguish from each other, of which this is one. I do not believe you will find that any man who murdered Miss Donworth would affect such a perfume as white jessamine upon his sleeve.'

'Then we have a criminal gang of three men and a woman?' I exclaimed. 'A gang of blackmailers? A gang of poisoners?'

'Out of the question!' Lestrade said abruptly. 'In the findings of Dr Stevenson, we have evidence of a single criminal degenerate. Crimes of this sort are committed by a maniac working alone. He knows, if he is caught, he will be hanged. He would not dare trust his neck to others, even by using them as his scribes. What you say, Mr Holmes, suggests strongly to me that the letters are from a group of mischief-makers. They are not the murderers but are merely exploiting a lust-murder committed by someone utterly unknown to them.'

Holmes shrugged and sighed.

'Then you must explain to me, Lestrade, why two of the letters, in different hands, claim that Ellen Donworth was the victim of strychnine. Except for an unbelievable degree of coincidence, that fact could have been known only to her murderer at the time the letters were posted.'

'Very well,' said the inspector desperately, 'let us take it as a coincidence. I would remind you, Mr Holmes, how often you have said that when all the impossible explanations are discarded, whatever is left, however improbable, must be the answer.'

'I think not,' said Holmes quietly. 'When stated correctly, that is a principle known as Occam's Razor. However, I do not believe that old William of Occam would have thanked you for shaving with it in such a manner.'

This produced silence until Holmes spoke more gently, for the inspector's benefit.

'Perhaps it would be better, Lestrade, if you were to recall how often in the past I have remarked that it is a capital error in our profession to reason in defiance of the facts, however little one may care for them.'

This quiet reprimand induced a silence that no one seemed inclined to break.

## VI

With that, the case was at an end – or so it seemed. In the following weeks, the tenuous thread that had connected Inspector Lestrade with the ghostly murderers was to grow more slender, until it seemed to vanish altogether. No more letters were received from murderers or blackmailers. No further clues were gleaned from those which had already arrived. The criminal gang appeared to have shut up shop, as Holmes remarked with a rare absence of concern.

Somerset House was visited by a more senior officer and its records more meticulously checked. No one with the name of Matilda Clover was found in the register of deaths for twenty years past. No entry existed for Lou or Louisa Harvey. The Lambeth murder ceased to be of interest to the press. Even Sherlock Holmes appeared to turn his attention elsewhere.

Once, the inspector thought he had his man in the person of Mr Slater of Wych Street, Holborn. Slater's ways were odd to say the least. He was wont to cross Waterloo Bridge from lodgings near the Strand and make a nuisance of himself in Lambeth, urging repellent suggestions on street-women there. Two of them resented him more than most. Eliza Masters and Elizabeth May swore that this man who molested them was the very person they had seen with Ellen Donworth, not an hour before I had found her dying outside the York Hotel.

Holmes and I were invited to attend the identification parade at Bow Street police station, an event which promised to end the Lambeth mystery once and for all. The two young women walked down the line of men drawn up in the corridor. Each picked out the shabby figure of Mr Slater, a little too easily as it seemed to me. They were thanked and sent on their way.

Lestrade cautioned Slater that he would now be questioned in the matter of the death of Ellen Donworth. He did not look in the least apprehensive, merely surprised. He shrugged his shoulders and said, 'All right then, if you like.'

When asked to account for himself on that fateful Saturday evening in October, Slater reminded Lestrade that he had been detained by a police officer that morning on a complaint by a respectable young woman in Lower Marsh, twelve hours before Miss Donworth's death. Lestrade had been told nothing of this by the Lambeth division and so suspected a trick. However, Slater coölly recalled that there was no magistrates court to deal with him on a Saturday, so that he had been detained in a Lambeth police cell until Monday morning, then bound over to keep the peace. It was quite impossible that he could have had any connection with the young woman's death. This, as Holmes privately observed, was a fact which Lestrade and 'A' Division of the Metropolitan Police at Scotland Yard could have established to begin with, had they cared to communicate with 'L' Division, a few hundred yards away on the other side of Westminster Bridge.

Holmes was both furious and yet triumphant in the face of such official incompetence. For several days, he referred bitterly to 'A' Division as 'Lestrade's Gendarmerie', giving the words a comic opera pronunciation. Then he turned his attention again to other things, declining as he said to supply the deficiencies of Scotland Yard.

It seemed that we faced, as Samuel Johnson once said, a conclusion in which nothing was concluded, until the events of a fine cold morning a month or two later. It was, I suppose, a little before noon when the bell rang below us. I glanced down from the window and saw the uniform cap of a Post Office boy with a telegram. A moment later, Mrs Hudson was before us with the blue envelope on her salver. Holmes opened it, read it, and handed it to me.

HOLMES, 221B BAKER STREET, W.
PREPARE TO COME AT ONCE STOP.
LAMBETH MURDERER THREATENS MASS POISON
STOP.
POLICE OFFICER ON WAY TO FETCH YOU STOP.
LESTRADE, SCOTLAND YARD.

'You may tell the boy there is no reply,' Holmes said smoothly to our anxious housekeeper.

By the time we were at the door, a cab was drawing into the pavement with a helmeted constable inside. A few moments later we were bowling down Baker

Street towards Regent Street and Trafalgar Square. The matter was plainly of great secrecy. We did not speak to the constable, nor he to us.

From Trafalgar Square we turned at great speed into Northumberland Avenue, past the imperial fronts of grand hotels or offices, and under chestnut boughs. Our hansom rattled towards the glitter of the Thames, almost as far as the rear entrance of Scotland Yard. But then the constable tapped sharply on the roof of the cab and it drew up outside the fine entrance and marble steps of the Metropole Hotel. Why we had been brought to such a place as this, I had not the least idea.

'What are we doing here?' I asked, a little put out.

Before our escort could reply, Lestrade opened the door of the cab and we stepped out into a scene of confusion, like the rout of a great army. The broad pavement of the avenue outside the hotel was stacked with portmanteaus, cabin trunks, hat-boxes, luggage of every description. We could scarcely have reached the back entrance of Scotland Yard for hansoms and growlers ahead of us, each loaded with the possessions of those scrimmaging to escape. There was such shouting of directions, such arguments and questions bawled out, that the place was perfect bedlam. Inside the grand foyer I saw luggage strewn round the gilt-columned mirrors, and across the thick carpets, while porters and page-boys endeavoured to make order out of chaos.

'And which of all these very expensive people is our Lambeth murderer going to slaughter?' Holmes inquired amiably of Lestrade. 'Surely not all of them?'

The inspector was bristling with indignation.

'Each one of them, Mr Holmes, each and every one of them has received one of these.'

For a moment I expected him to produce a phial of strychnine but it was a plain printed card. I had never seen such insanity in my life as in what I read just then.

*ELLEN DONWORTH'S DEATH*

*To the Guests of the Metropole Hotel*

Ladies and Gentlemen,

I hereby notify you that the person who poisoned Ellen Donworth on the 13th last October is to-day in the employ of the kitchens of the Metropole Hotel and that your lives are in danger as long as you remain in this hotel.

Yours respectfully,

W. H. Murray

Sherlock Holmes was not a man much given to outbursts of laughter. They began deep in his throat, as a rising growl. Then, if the occasion warranted, he threw back his head and shouted aloud at the richness of the humour. To Lestrade's dismay, he did so now. His Olympian merriment echoed through the panic and over the luggage on the pavement, across the lavishly decorated foyer, where the hotel manager in his frock coat and striped trousers stood wringing his hands at the centre of the tumult.

Holmes laughed so long that, in the end, he was obliged to wipe his eyes before he could turn to the scowling inspector, 'Well, my dear Lestrade, I can certainly tell you one thing. You may be sure that our man did this in order that he should be here to see the fun. I swear he is here now. Which do you suppose it can be? That horsy fellow over there in the tweed suit, the neat moustache and the barbered eyebrows? The little old lady in black velvet with her ivory-knobbed stick? That tall colonial with the brick-red face who looks as if he might be scanning new horizons in Australia or Brazil? Any of them or all of them!'

Lestrade's colour rose at the thought that the murderer might be within a few yards of him and that there was nothing he could do. He looked about him furiously.

'Since you are always so much to the forward, Mr Sherlock Holmes, perhaps *you* would like to choose which of them it shall be!'

Holmes laughed again, more gently.

'You had far better give it up, old fellow. Mr Bayne the Barrister, Mr O'Brien the Detective, Mr Murray from the hotel – whether they be three or one – may be stood next to you this moment, or in the foyer, and you would not know.'

I had never seen Lestrade's face so thunderous. The Lambeth poisoning had vanished from the papers but now it would be back, a story of how the hunted man had made fools of Scotland Yard. At the manager's request, Lestrade had summoned Holmes by telegram to investigate the hotel kitchens but the inspector was now so furious that he could not bring himself to ask the favour.

When we came home that afternoon, Holmes was still chuckling at the discomfiture of Lestrade, the Metropole Hotel, and its luckless guests.

'You believe the man who sent that note was there this morning?' I asked, as we took off our overcoats and rang for tea.

'I was never more sure of anything in my life.'

I do not know why I said it, but the next moment I blurted out.

'It was you! It was you, Holmes! By God, you sent that circular! No wonder you were so sure that the man was there! It was you!'

He looked quickly at me with bewildered innocence. Not quickly enough, as I thought.

'What purpose would that serve, Watson? What purpose in the world?'

'To start the case moving again. To flush the criminal or criminals from cover,' I said doggedly, but he would discuss the accusation no further.

## VII

The evening newspapers got wind of the 'Metropole Sensation', and so it was blown about all over London. Though he would not admit it, I swore this was a subversive attempt by Holmes to 'start the ball rolling' again by means of a clandestinely-printed circular. If the murderer of Ellen Donworth resembled the egomaniac of our fancy, he would be unable to resist a riposte. However, I never expected the ball to roll with such sudden speed or in the direction that it did. Holmes spent a day or two, lounging as languidly and jadedly as ever. A good deal of his time was passed in the old-fashioned chair, a musical score before him, easing his tedium by the mellow tone of his faithful violin.

After lunch two or three days later, he was drawing a mournful beauty from the slow movement of the Violin Concerto of Ludwig van Beethoven. His bow moved effortlessly, his eyes were mere slits, and he seemed almost to sleep. I sat in an opposite chair, listening but letting my thoughts drift over other matters.

The music stopped abruptly, in mid-phrase. The bow and fiddle rattled down on the table as he seized the score that lay open on its stand.

'By God!' he cried. 'What fools we have been! What blind, unutterable fools!'

He was not looking at me but at the score of the concerto, dismayed as if he had seen a ghost there. Then he glared at it and threw it down. I wondered whether the strain of the investigation was leading to some cerebral episode.

'Do you not see?' he cried. 'We have been looking for Matilda Clover . . .'

'I daresay,' I said, rousing myself.

' . . . when all the time we should have been looking for Matilda Clover!'

If I thought his reason tottered the moment before, I was even more inclined to believe it now. He looked at the score again and said, 'Let us pray that dear old Beethoven has succeeded where Lestrade and his minions have failed.'

Then he began bustling about for his ulster, his cap, his gloves, and his stick.

'I must go,' he said sharply, 'I shall not be more than an hour or two.'

'Shall I not come with you?'

'No!' he said severely. 'I can manage this perfectly well on my own. If I am wrong, which I entirely doubt, I shall bear the blame of error alone.'

Then he was gone, to call a cab off the rank. Holmes

was often secretive and vexing, but I had never known him behave quite so outlandishly. I picked up the score. It was from Augener's in Great Marlborough Street, a German 'Edition Peters' published at Leipzig. I saw only what I would expect to see, in gothic type upon the cover, 'L. van Beethoven, Konzert Opus 61 D dur'.

How this could have anything to do with the Lambeth mystery was beyond me. I sat and waited for his return, so perplexed that I could neither read nor attend to any other business. More than two hours passed before I heard the cabman's voice and my friend's key in the lock of our Baker Street door. I knew that he bore success and not failure by the way his long legs measured the stairs two at a time – and by the way he came in, flung down his ulster and looked at me.

'Matilda Clover, Watson, died in October of delirium tremens, in Lambeth.'

I could only stare and ask, 'How the devil did you find that?'

'By looking in the very place where Lestrade and his incompetents have been looking for a month past. Somerset House. The registers of deaths.'

'How did you find it, when Lestrade could not?'

He picked up the musical score.

'What a fool I have been! Look, my dear fellow! Konzert – not Concerto! How many times have I seen that word these past weeks and not recognized the truth! Of what use is a consulting detective who never considered that Klover – rather than Clover – is a not uncommon patronymic of Westphalia and Upper

Saxony! Such a possibility would never, of course, have crossed the mind of Lestrade.'

'She was German?'

'I very much doubt that,' he said impatiently, putting away the violin in its case. 'Her father or grandfather may have been a sailor who came ashore at the docks. Or perhaps one of the German medical students at the hospital made out her death certificate and gave her the wrong initial letter. Who can say? But at last we have her, Watson, and she brings us very interesting news.'

'How can that be?'

He sat down and looked at me with a mad laughter in his eyes.

'Matilda Clover, as we will continue to pronounce her, died on 20 October.'

'Impossible!'

'In other words, Watson, when Lady Russell came to us complaining that her husband was accused of murdering Matilda Clover - Matilda Clover was still alive. Allow that the note took two or three days to reach Lady Russell, then the death of Matilda Clover was foretold by at least a week.'

A man who writes that his head began to spin is usually guilty of exaggeration. In my own case, at this moment, I swear that the Lambeth case spun my brain like a child's top. I could not see that even Sherlock Holmes would make sense of it. When I looked up at him, he was chuckling like a schoolboy.

'We must inform Lestrade at once!' I said sternly.

He shook his head, still chuckling.

'Oh no, Watson. Miss Clover is to be ours alone for the next day or two. Finders keepers, as the saying is.'

## VIII

Despite my misgivings, perhaps it was as well for our investigation that we gave ourselves a few days of grace. On the following afternoon, Holmes had gone to examine a skull, to be purchased in his pursuit of criminal phrenology. It was said to be that of the famous highwayman and informer, Jonathan Wild, hanged at Tyburn in 1725. A little before three o'clock there was a scampering on the stairs, a hurried knock at our door, and the entry of Master Billy. There was generally a 'Master Billy', employed by Mrs Hudson as what she liked to call a 'page boy' but whose duties were merely to fetch and carry. They were all known as 'Billy' and the present holder of the office had proved himself a useful source of information on two or three occasions.

'Medical gentleman to see you, Dr Watson, sir,' he gasped, catching his breath, 'most immediate.'

The young imp handed out a card on his salver. I took it and read 'Dr Thomas Neill, M.B., B.Ch., Faculty of Medicine, Macgill University.' I did not know the name but, naturally enough, I assumed that this was a matter concerning one of my own consultations. I told Billy to show the gentleman up. As he did so, I turned the card over and saw two words pencilled on the back: MATILDA CLOVER.

It seemed indeed that my heart missed a beat. At that moment the door of the room opened to admit a pale, rather scholarly figure, wearing a cape and holding a silk hat in his hand. He had the myopic look of an earnest student and wore a pair of pince-nez with strong lenses.

'Dr Watson?' he said, in a voice that was low and deferential. 'It is a pleasure to meet you, sir, and so good on your part to receive me without an engagement.'

I shook his hand, which had a lean and sinewy grip, then ushered him to a chair.

'If you wish to discuss the matter of Matilda Clover,' I said hastily, 'it is my colleague Sherlock Holmes whom you should see.'

He looked up at me with a nervous smile.

'To meet Mr Holmes would be a great privilege,' he said earnestly, 'and one that I greatly look forward to. However, to speak frankly, I am not sorry to have an opportunity to speak first as one medical man to another. For some reason I cannot pretend to understand, I seem to be the victim of a plot – or hoax – involving the death of a young woman whose name you may already know but I do not. It is rumoured among members of the Christian Guild that Mr Frederick Smith himself was similarly insulted and that he came to you for advice. Indeed, his name is now linked with scandal in the very streets and lodging houses round the hospital. Hence my concern for my own reputation. If you were able to assist Mr Smith, perhaps you can advise me.'

'You are pursuing your studies at St Thomas's?'

He inclined his head.

'I have that honour, sir. However, I am mostly in the country, reading and taking notes. I have rooms near Lambeth Palace, when I am in town.'

Without further ado, he handed me a letter in an

envelope. The postmark was two days old. Though I read it with some dismay, its contents now saved us the trouble of searching for the last dwelling-place of Matilda Clover.

*Dr Thomas Neill*

*Sir,*

*Miss Clover, who until a short time ago lived at 27 Lambeth Road, S.E., died at the above address on the 20th October through being poisoned by strychnine. After her death a search of her effects was made, and evidence was found which showed that you not only gave her the medicine which caused her death but that you had been hired for the purpose of poisoning her. This evidence is in the hands of one of our detectives, who will give the papers either to you or to the police authorities for the sum of £1,000.*

*Now, sir, if you want all the evidence for £1,000 just put a personal in the* Daily Chronicle, *saying you will pay Malone £1,000 for his services, and I will send a party to settle this matter. If you do not want the evidence, of course, it will be turned over to the police and published, and your ruin will surely follow. Think well before you decide on this matter. It is just this – £1,000 sterling on the one hand, and ruin, shame, and disgrace on the other. Answer by personal on the first page of the* Daily Chronicle *any time next week. I am not humbugging you, I have evidence enough to ruin you forever.*

*M. Malone*

Regardless of the different handwriting, this effusion surely came from the minds of 'Mr Bayne the Barrister', 'A. O' Brien, Detective' and the rest of the incognitos. Beside me, Dr Neill's face was a study in quiet despair.

'Tell me, Dr Watson,' the poor scholar asked plaintively, 'what am I to do? I have never heard of Miss Clover. I have only twice in my life been in England and I was not here on 20 October!'

'You should take this beastly letter to the police,' I said firmly, wondering as I spoke why the malicious devils had picked on this other-worldly soul.

'Then to the police I suppose I must go.' There was no doubting the sincerity of his thanks. 'I dread doing so, however.'

'I do not see why you should.'

'Because, sir,' said the mild-mannered American, 'though there is not a word of truth in the accusations, I fear a public inquiry might be ruinous to a medical man. This scoundrel already thinks that he can frighten me into paying him because I know the damage that mere rumour and innuendo can do in our profession. The world, here and in my own country, will say that there is no smoke without fire.'

'I believe you may rely upon the discretion of the English authorities in such matters.'

'I am glad to hear you say so.' There was no mistaking the poor fellow's eagerness to believe me. 'There is, however, something else I should like to share with you.'

'Pray do.'

He looked more wretched than ever.

'My practice has been in Ontario and Chicago. I am

here for study leave, a week or two more, to pursue my research into the treatment of nervous disorders. Very few people in England know me. I am not Mr Frederick Smith nor Mr Sherlock Holmes, after all! This fact drives me most reluctantly to the conclusion that my blackmailer – if he be such – my persecutor anyway, is someone to whom I am personally known and who is known to me. Someone very close. Can it be otherwise?'

How often had I seen the keen eyes of Sherlock Holmes narrow as he probed such a confession further! I could only ask lamely, 'Do you have any suspicion who it might be?'

He shook his head, then paused.

'I hope – I believe – it could not be one or two men whose names have crossed my mind. Your advice that I should take this letter to the police is good and right, Dr Watson. My fear is that they would ask me the question you have put. That I might be persuaded to give them the name of a young man who might very likely prove innocent. That would not lie easily on my conscience, sir.'

If the blackmailer – or blackmailers – should be close to Dr Neill and known by him, we were surely very close to the answer of the Lambeth mystery. As cautiously as if I was on tiptoe behind an escaped cage-bird, I said, 'Will you tell such a name to me?'

He hesitated.

'Can you trust me in this matter, Dr Watson?'

I could scarcely say I would not trust him! I nodded.

'Very well. I had hoped this afternoon to hear you say that you knew all about this business and had tracked the criminal down – or very nearly so. Well, that cannot be. Very good. Then allow me a little space to pursue my own inquiry. If my suspicions are correct, I will do all that you say. If they are not – then the police may have the letter for what good it will do. I confess I would rather be mistaken in my suspicions and return to America the week after next with matters as they stand. I will be guided by the event – and by you.'

There was little more to the interview than this. I had hoped Sherlock Holmes might return before its conclusion. However, my visitor stood up to take his leave. At the door, he turned and asked the question I had been dreading.

'Tell me, Dr Watson, is it true that the crime of murder was perpetrated against this unfortunate young woman?'

As yet, only Holmes and I knew that she had lived and died. I did not relish sharing the information with any third person in the absence of my friend. My reply was true but less than candid.

'The police know nothing of any such crime or any such person.'

There was no mistaking the relief on his face.

'Then you persuade me that this is not blackmail, sir, but a jealous hoax! I have half a mind to tear up this foul letter and forget the matter.'

I stood there like a fool, not knowing how much to say.

'Perhaps you should preserve the letter, Dr Neill, until the truth of the matter is known and in case you may receive another of these wicked communications.'

But that was as far as I could go.

# IX

Holmes returned half an hour later, glowering. He pronounced the so-called skull of Jonathan Wild a fake. Taking up Dr Neill's card, he glanced at the writing on the back, and remarked sardonically that at least the American scholar had not written any of the blackmail letters himself. But at the mention of an address for Matilda Clover, he summoned Billy at once to whistle a hansom to our door.

Before the sun set that afternoon, the cab bore us across Westminster Bridge, the river so crowded by coal-barges at high water that you might almost have walked from bank to bank. On Holmes's instructions, we turned into the Lambeth Road, where the Waterloo trains shook a low plate-iron bridge overhead and the blue sky was veiled by sulphurous vapour from the engine-stacks. We drew up at the corner of Hercules Road, by a grim mock-Venetian tenement of Orient Buildings. The character of the area was spoken for by the manner in which several shabbily-dressed but feather-boa'd young creatures paraded outside its entrance.

Ahead of us, on the Lambeth Road, stood a row of plain-fronted terraced houses, crusted and blackened by railway soot, with the Masons Arms public house beyond them. Holmes led the way to a door, with the number '27' painted upon it, and rapped the tarnished knocker. As he did so, I noticed that his ulster was unbuttoned at the neck. Either his own collar was oddly disarranged or he now wore the clerical collar of a clergyman. The effect was the same, either way.

The door was opened by a woman of about sixty, wearing a white apron with shoulder-straps over a plain beige dress. Her ginger hair, grown thin from constant colouring and artificial curling, was fluffed out so that one saw a ghostly vision of her pale head through it. She looked at us, attempted a smile, then seemed to think better of it.

'Good morning, madam,' said Holmes punctiliously, though the fastidious nostrils flared just perceptibly. 'My name is William Holmes of the South London Mission. This is my colleague, Dr Watson.'

I had never heard him use his other baptismal name as a *nom-de-guerre* before.

'I believe,' he said to the grim-faced housewife, 'that Miss Matilda Clover lived here at the time of her death?'

'Perhaps she did,' said the woman suspiciously.

Holmes became uncharacteristically deferential.

'May I take it that you are the lady of the house, Mrs . . .?'

'Phillips. Mrs Emma Phillips.' She still looked less than pleased by his missionary appeal.

Undeterred by her surliness, Holmes drew out a small black notebook and smiled at her.

'Mrs Phillips. Quite so. Miss Clover was under our care, so far as we were able to help her. She came from a respectable family in Kent, much afflicted by her way of life and the manner of her death.'

'I never knew!' said Mrs Phillips, plainly astonished.

'You may take it from me that it was so. Her people are most anxious that those, like your good self, who were friends to her in her last days should not be left out of pocket in respect of any little debts or contractual obligations incurred by Miss Clover . . .'

Until he began to talk of money, the woman's expression had generally remained that of a feral creature defending its burrow. Now her face and voice softened.

'Is it insurance, then? Friendly society?'

Holmes appeared to consult a notebook, whose pages I could see were blank.

'One might say that it comes to the same thing. Tell me, it was in this house that Miss Clover died on 20 October last?'

'Oh, yes! Definitely this house.' I could almost hear in her voice a fear that perhaps she might be disqualified from whatever good things were about to be offered. 'She died here all right! In the top bedroom that she rented a few weeks before. Back in October. To be precise, very early on 21 October. DTs and heart failure. Drunk an entire bottle of brandy the night before, not to say what else. Took very bad about three in the morning, died just after eight. And if you'd known her, you'd only be surprised it hadn't happened before!'

'Indeed!'

'The doctor's assistant was here most of the time. Foreign-sounding young gentleman but quite agreeable. You could ask him. He made a report to Dr Macarthy and they gave her a certificate. Would it be much, the money? See, she had two rooms at the top of the house, in the attic, and there's still rent not paid for her last five weeks, let alone the time since, for which notice was never given.'

'I shall certainly make a note of that,' Holmes said

enthusiastically, pencilling something on the blank page of the notebook.

'And the clearing up of the room! Not very nice, at all! Sick? I should say she was sick! By the bucketful! This money, would it be cash? See, unless it was in cash, you'd have to pay me as Mrs Emma Vowles – not Phillips.'

Holmes repeated the name and wrote 'Emma Vowles' and 'not Phillips' in the little book.

'Five weeks' rent, you say?'

'Just that, except there being no notice given, of course. And the room not fit to use.'

'Shall we say six weeks? I see no reason why we should not advance cash today. I wonder if there are any other outstanding liabilities that her friends might know of. Did she have a particular friend who might have helped her out?'

Emma Vowles, *soi-disante* Phillips, pulled a face. Then she shook her head.

'One, p'raps, lodging in this house as well. You can see her now, if you like. She moved into the attic rooms herself, after Mattie Clover was gone.'

'If you would not mind,' Holmes said courteously.

We followed the woman up the stairs with their smell of damp plaster and rotting carpet until we came to a door in the low-ceilinged attic level. Mrs Vowles tapped on it and went in without waiting. We heard her say,

'There's two missionary gentlemen, anxious to see all poor Mattie's debts are settled. I suppose you'd know.'

We heard a murmur from the occupant of the room.

Mrs Vowles stepped back, opened the door wider for us, let us pass and said, 'Here you are then . . .'

'Lucy Rose,' said the girl's voice. She stood up from the trestle bed on which she had been sitting, a faded Pre-Raphaelite dove, the face plain and scrubbed, the hair in two braids, a look of weariness in her eyes, as if our presence made no difference to her one way or the other. The last fading of a bruise might just be seen on her right cheekbone. The room itself was all too familiar, its frayed carpet, plain washstand with jug and basin, a single chest of drawers, low windows cobwebbed and stuck fast by old paint.

The Reverend William Holmes took her hand gently. 'Lucy Rose? You were a friend to poor Mattie Clover.'

'We were friends,' she said guardedly, drawing her hand away, 'not close, though.'

'Well,' said Holmes, smiling at her, 'I hope we are all her friends. There is a little money put by which her family would like her friends to have.'

He counted three sovereigns from one hand to another and then gave them to her. She took them without a word of thanks or comment. Holmes looked about him.

'How long have you lived like this?'

'Three years,' she said with a shrug. 'I'm a distressed milliner, ain't I?'

'I see. And how old are you, my child,' inquired Holmes the Missioner.

'Twenty.'

He nodded, as if he believed her. Then he said, as though struck by a pleasant thought, 'And when is your birthday?'

'My birthday? What do you want to know that for?'

He smiled again, as if at her foolishness, 'You were kind and good to Mattie. I believe her mother would like to be kind to you. Next year, Lucy, will be your twenty-first birthday, a very special one. How nice it would be for her mother if she could send you something to commemorate it. If it does not offend you, that is.'

'It doesn't offend me,' she said, staring up at him, 'I just can't see why anyone'd want to do that.'

'Because they are good and kind Christian folk,' said Holmes.

She shrugged.

'Well, fourth day of April it is, if that matters.'

'Tell me,' Holmes said with an air of quiet concern, 'what happened on the night that she died? Were you with her?'

I feared the girl might refuse to discuss this but Holmes had pitched the question with great skill, suggesting that he only wanted the information to comfort someone else.

'She came back with a man,' said Lucy Rose indifferently. 'She was always bringing men back. I saw him in the hall, so did Mrs Phillips and her sister, but they turn a blind eye to that sort of thing in a place like this.'

'What did the man look like?'

'Well, he had his back to the light but he was quite stout-built with a brown moustache. A bit red-faced like a navvy. He was wearing a top-coat and bowler hat. They went up to the room, then she comes down and goes out for some beer. I went to bed, but I heard them go down about an hour later. She opened the door, he said "Good night," and she said "Good night, dear." That's all.'

'I see,' said Holmes, in the tone of a disappointed man returning a bribe to his pocket.

'Until about three in the morning,' she said hastily, 'then I woke up and heard screaming. She'd wedged herself over the end of the bed, pressing her stomach down to get ease from the pain. First thing she said was someone must have poisoned her with some pills she took, not wanting to get in the family way.'

'Do you think she was poisoned?'

'Course not!' said Lucy Rose scornfully. 'Unless she poisoned herself with drink. The doctors didn't think she'd been poisoned, did they? Old Mattie used to booze enough for a couple of draymen together. How she screamed, though. Then she'd go into fits and twitch all over. Her eyes rolled about something terrible. It's only drink does that. The DTs.'

'Did she say anything else?'

'She said she was going to die. Well, she was right about that, wasn't she?'

The notion that this hard-faced little dollymop would be a friend to anyone was quite beyond me. However, Holmes played his part and slipped her two more sovereigns. She grinned at him.

'You?' she said scornfully. 'You're not a missioner! No more than I am.'

'I assure you . . .'

'You paid twice! Missioners is too bloody mean to pay twice! What you are . . .'

It pained me to see Holmes worsted by this little slattern.

'What you are,' said Lucy Rose triumphantly, 'is a

newspaper man! A reporter! Ain't that it? They're the ones that pays for what they want to hear. Five sovs? Well, I hope it was worth it to you! What d'you want to know about it for?'

'Dear me, young woman,' said Holmes amiably, 'you have the makings of a true detective.'

'You bet,' said Lucy Rose.

As we returned in the cab to Baker Street, I remarked that we should get nowhere in the face of such impertinence.

Holmes spoke quietly, looking out at the evening crowds who pressed homewards across Regent Circus.

'Then how fortunate it was to have a medical man present. We might otherwise have been in danger of confusing an impertinent little minx with a vexed and frightened child. Might we not?'

I looked at him sharply. However, I got nothing more, except his comment that we must give a little help to our friend Lestrade, who seemed to have lost heart over the case.

## X

My American visitor, Dr Neill, need not have worried. He was only one among several medical men to get a copy of the mad blackmailer's letter, which he had shown me. By the next morning's post I heard from Dr William Broadbent of Seymour Street, once a fellow student at Barts and now a successful oculist. Broadbent had received a similar communication. In this case, Mr Malone and his operatives had demanded £2,500 for suppressing their 'evidence'. It was quite mad, of course. How should an oculist be in a position to administer strychnine? It was plain to me that whoever was behind this campaign of blackmail had very little knowledge of medicine.

Holmes seemed weary of the letters and more intent on pursuing the case of Matilda Clover. As for Dr Neill and Dr Broadbent, he referred to them with a certain heavy facetiousness as 'your clients' or 'these clients of yours', as if he was washing his hands of any responsibility for their complaints.

After three days, he was prepared to share his recent discoveries with Inspector Lestrade. But when we saw the Scotland Yard man again, it was under circumstances of such horror as I shall never forget. Two nights after our visit to the Lambeth Road, I felt that I had scarcely fallen asleep when I was awakened by a tugging at my shoulder. It was Holmes, standing over me fully dressed. I opened my eyes rather painfully against the light of the candle in his hand. The flame shone upon his eager stooping face and his expression left me in no doubt that something was badly wrong.

'Get up, Watson! Lestrade is in the sitting-room and we must go with him at once. Bring your medical bag, you will certainly have need of it.'

I felt no sense of adventure, only a cold and certain dread. His words must mean Mr Bayne and his friends had taken another life. In my career, I had grown used to nocturnal alarms but had never answered one with such sick foreboding at what awaited me. I pulled on my clothes, picked up my bag, and went into the sitting-room. Holmes was already buttoned into his ulster with a cravat about his throat, fastening his travelling-cap with its ear-flaps, for this was a bitter night.

'Stamford Street,' Lestrade said, as soon as I entered the sitting-room, 'I doubt if much can be done for them but . . .'

'Them?' I was aghast that there should be more than one.

'Yes, sir. There are two young persons this time, doctor, both of the unfortunate class. We shall have to make haste before they are too far gone to tell us what has happened.'

The streets were clear and Lestrade's cab went full pelt through the lamplit city to the Strand, Waterloo Bridge, and Lambeth. Stamford Street ran behind riverside wharves and warehouses, from Waterloo Road to Blackfriars. Its broken and discoloured slum-terraces, whose doors opened on the pavement, were another Duke Street.

The narrow road ran for a considerable distance. Long before we came to the house with '118' painted roughly in white on its door, we saw a little crowd outside. A uniformed constable in a tall helmet and carrying a bulls-eye lantern stood guard at the door. There was a four-wheeler waiting, ready to set off for the hospital, but with no sign of a doctor or an assistant. Small wonder that Lestrade had wanted my company, I thought. From the sounds of disorder that reached us you might have thought a mad party was going on in the house. A man was shouting and women were screaming but the shrillness was of pain rather than merriment.

As we got down from the hansom and went into the narrow house, two policemen with their helmets off appeared to be struggling with a pair of disorderly harpies, as if to get them into the waiting four-wheeler.

But the sight of the pair suggested figures in some landscape of the damned, their faces plastered with the sweat of agony and their hair in disarray. Alice Marsh, as I later knew her to be, was covered by her night-clothes, kneeling on all fours over a chair in the hallway, clinging tighter at every attempt to move her. In the front room, Emma Shrivell lay prone on the sofa, where the second uniformed constable had just administered an emetic of warm water and salt, which now caused her to vomit spasmodically. Like her companion, she was wearing her night-clothes, as if she had woken suddenly from sleep.

Though it was hard to question the two policemen in the shrillness and shouting, I heard the first man, Cumley, say to Lestrade that he and Eversfield had been trying for the past ten minutes to get the two girls to the four-wheeler for St Thomas's Hospital. They had brought them with difficulty to the foot of the stairs, where both victims had resisted being moved further as they clutched the chair and sofa to themselves with the strength of pure terror.

If ever there was a vision of hell, it was in that house on that night. Alice Marsh seemed not even to understand what was said to her. Emma Shrivell, perhaps as a result of the emetic, was able to answer a little. For several minutes, until the rising cramp of another spasm robbed her of normal speech, she muttered her answers to my questions. She had eaten tinned salmon and drunk bottled beer with Alice Marsh and a man they had brought back to the house. He had offered them each a long slim capsule, promising that these would heighten their pleasure in the perversities that he proposed for the three of them.

Later he had gone away. Soon afterwards the first plucking of their final agony began.

Alice Marsh was too far gone to identify her assailant. Emma Shrivell could only describe a man with dark hair and a moustache. Eversfield had first thought that the girls might be suffering ptomaine poisoning as a result of contamination in the tinned salmon. Believe that who may!

How little prepared is a retired army doctor to confront such a crisis in civil life! To stand in that cramped house, deafened by the noise and sickened by such sights, was a horror in itself for any humane person. Far worse, was the situation of a medical man. If this were another strychnine poisoning, nothing would save them. I could have given them morphia, but that would ease their agony very little and would prolong it for several hours. Indeed, as it later appeared, whoever had chosen these victims had once again mixed morphia with the poison. Strychnine alone would have killed them by now. To wish the two poor creatures out of this world so speedily will seem inhuman only to those who did not see their terrified grimaces or hear the sounds that filled the slum terrace on a winter's night. Was the devil who had devised this drama now haunting the shadows of the alleys and streets outside, listening with a mad delight to the result?

There was nothing more I could do. I insisted to Lestrade that the two young women must by any means be got to hospital where their final hours might be made more comfortable. By taking them to the four-wheeler one at a time, the two constables and I managed to get first Alice March and then Emma Shrivell into the cab. They struggled and shuddered, shouting uncomprehended protests in our ears.

There is little more to add. I went with them as the four-wheeler rattled into the Waterloo Road, turned into Westminster Bridge Road and drew up at the hospital. Just as we came in sight of the river, Alice Marsh uttered a rising cry and fell into a fit. The next moment, the breath came from her in a long groan that emptied her lungs as she fell back against the cushions and died. Emma Shrivell was carried into the hospital entrance on a stretcher. I later heard that she had lived until eight o'clock that morning without adding another word to the evidence she had already given.

In all the investigations which Sherlock Holmes and I had undertaken, I confess I had never felt so badly shaken as by this double homicide. There had been murders enough but none as malicious and brutal as these two. Many criminals of our acquaintance had killed out of passion or for gain, sometimes for jealousy or avarice, but never with such hideous and cruel triumph.

Holmes, when he looked back on the events of this case, was more intrigued than repelled by the criminal mind behind them. He would quote the Renaissance tyrants or 'Philippe the Poisoner' as the Regent of France for Louis XV had been called. These men had poisoned their victims to clear the way to the seats of power. The Comte de Sade's depravities of this sort at Marseille had been mere aphrodisiac experiments. Other young sparks of the *ancien régime* had been content to persuade the Marquise Gacé that she had drunk an incurable poison which they had concealed in her glass. For several hours, they relished her terrors and despair until she realized that it was a mere trick. This time, however, we confronted what Holmes laconically described as 'a great original'.

'I regret, Watson, that the demands on my time do not permit of a little monograph upon the subject of "The Poisoner as Artist". I think, however, I shall write a few lines to the good Professor Krafft-Ebing. I must put him on the trail of that rare mental type whose pleasure lies in obtaining by poison a complete possession of the victim's body and all its functions, controlling every nuance of thought and feeling. It is a significant lacuna in the great professor's otherwise admirable systematization of psychopathology.'

We were at breakfast several days after the deaths of the two poor girls when Holmes delivered himself of this deplorable observation. I drew open my copy of *The Times* newspaper as a refuge from such conversation and merely said, 'It is quite enough, Holmes, that we must deal with such a scoundrel. You had far better leave it there.'

He sighed, as if I should be his despair.

'I have thought for some time, Watson, that you have no appreciation of this case. Without it, you will never arrive at the truth. Among poisoners, I am bound to say that even the great Dr William Palmer of Rugeley or the curious Catherine Wilson, whose last moments I witnessed at a time when executions were still a public spectacle, came woefully short of our present antagonist.'

To me, this was utterly heartless. I was about to say, in no uncertain terms, that I had done my best for two dying girls, while Holmes had airily discussed the finer points of the crime with Lestrade. To talk of the degenerate beast who had killed them – as an artist! – was beyond endurance. Perhaps it was well that we were interrupted by Mrs Hudson with Lestrade at her heels. Before our housekeeper could say a word, the inspector was in the room and holding a sheet of paper towards us.

'As you'll both be witnesses at the inquest on the two young women, Mr Holmes, you'd both of you best see this first. It came for Mr Wyatt, the Southwark coroner, through the post first thing this morning. It's our man, or one of them, from first to last. Perhaps this time he's gone too far. Perhaps there might be something in it that will give him away.'

I hardly knew whether to feel hope or despair at the sight of it. Holmes read the letter. He looked up, raised his eyebrows, and handed it to me, saying, 'If there is a word of truth in this, Watson, perhaps one of those clients of yours might prove a useful source of information.'

*'Dear Sir,*

*I beg to inform you that one of my operators has positive proof that a certain medical student of St Thomas's Hospital is responsible for the deaths of Alice Marsh and Emma Shrivell, he having poisoned those girls with strychnine. The proof you can have on paying my bill for services to George Clarke, detective, 20 Cockspur Street, Charing Cross, to whom I will give the proof on his paying my bill.*

*Yours respectfully,*
*WM. H. Murray*

I noticed that 'Murray' had been copied from the Metropole Hotel circular.

'Tell me, Lestrade,' said Holmes thoughtfully, as I handed the letter back, 'you and I remember something of George Clarke, do we not?'

Lestrade's face tightened.

'What I remember is Clarke left the Metropolitan Police under a cloud, fifteen years ago, as a senior man. Went to be landlord of a public house in Westminster. Still, we can be sure he has nothing to do with this Murray.'

'May we? And why is that, pray?'

There was no mistaking the satisfaction on the inspector's face.

'George Clarke, Mr Holmes, was gathered to his fathers three months ago. Dead. Gone to his long, last home, wherever that may be.'

Unworthy though it might be, I confess I was glad to hear the intellectual fog of Professor Ebing and poisoners as artists dispelled by the cold radiance of fact.

## XI

Even before the Stamford Street inquest began, the death certificate of Matilda Clover had been examined and her place of burial was established as Lambeth Municipal Cemetery. Though it took its title from Lambeth, the burial ground was out at Tooting, under the new public health measures introduced by the Burial Act of 1852. On a raw morning, as the frost was dissolving into dew, Miss Clover's mortal remains were to be exhumed upon the orders of the Home Secretary. Holmes and I travelled by the South-West Railway from Victoria to Tooting, where Lestrade would be waiting to take us the short distance to the cemetery gates.

It had scarcely been necessary for the inspector to insist to the recipients of the blackmail threats that no public reference should be made to the anonymous letters. Lady Russell or Mr Frederick Smith, MP were the last people to wish their names tarnished even by innocent association with such crimes. The notes to the coroner might be shown to the jurors, if that seemed necessary, but no reference was to be made to them in the hearing of the press.

As our train pulled out of Victoria station, Holmes with his sharp eager face framed in his ear-flapped travelling-cap, opened the *Morning Post* and finished his reading of the day's agony column. The early hour of our start had deprived him of a leisurely survey of the day's press. At length he folded the paper, thrust it under his seat, and offered me his cigar-case as we passed through the damp leafless suburbs.

'It is reassuring, Watson, is it not, to find so much continuity in this case?'

I wondered what he had in mind.

'Continuity? I have seldom known a case more plagued by chaos, rumour, and inconsistency.'

He thought for a moment and said at length, 'Take the letters, however. The composition of those sent to the coroner is plainly the work of the same author as the letter to Dr Broadbent. Yet the handwriting is not the same. However, the copperplate of the latest epistle is in an identical hand to that written to Mr Frederick Smith. The threads of this correspondence cross and cross again, do they not? It shows what I would call continuity.'

'It only goes to prove,' I replied abruptly, 'that these blackmailers are known to one another. They must be.'

'Must they? Are they all known to one another – or is there one master to whom each individual servant is separately known?'

'They share the same knowledge and the same style, as well as an identical method of extorting money.'

'You are entirely right about that,' he said at once, 'I could not have put it better.'

The answer seemed too plain to be held back.

'We shall never progress, Holmes, until we accept that the letters are quite distinct from the murders. A maniac is poisoning these poor girls. A gang of blackmailers is exploiting the crimes. They know their victims did not kill any of the young women. Yet they know by experience that innocent people may be weak or foolish enough to pay for their good names. Most will not pay but what does that matter? One or two successes will make the attempts worthwhile.'

'Your friend and client Dr Broadbent will pay, perhaps, or Dr Neill?'

I had expected this.

'Both know they are innocent. Yet if, for example, it is rumoured that Broadbent went to court over such matters, the world would say there is no smoke without fire. In his position, reputation is everything. A scandal might destroy him, innocent or guilty. Being a figure of honour and principle that will not deter him. The extortionists picked the wrong man, of course, but they may be luckier next time.'

Holmes lay back in his corner seat.

'And the fact that they accused Lord Russell of murdering Miss Clover almost a fortnight before she died? That, I suppose, was just a happy chance for them.'

'No,' I had a good part of the answer now, 'she was known to be dying of drink, but not dead. But if a man will pay to have his good name preserved, it scarcely mattered if she was alive or dead. How could he tell? He would implicate himself as much by asking questions. Indeed, why should Miss Clover not have been part of the conspiracy? Prostitution is a trade that runs easily to blackmail!'

Holmes drew the pipe from his mouth.

'And when they told Mr Smith that Ellen Donworth had been poisoned, while the world still thought she died of drink, was that a happy chance for them?'

'Anyone who was outside the York Hotel heard her say that she had been given gin with some white stuff in it by Fred. A rumour of poison would run round a neighbourhood like that. Blackmailers are not dealers in fact. They intimidate those who will pay and who ask few questions. They are not murderers.'

'Well,' he said thoughtfully, 'if they are not, someone else certainly is.'

'I believe,' I said boldly, 'that I may have your blackmailers before long. At least their ringleader. Dr Neill may be a rich American but he is naturally known to only a handful of people in England. He believes the threat comes from someone close to him. It must be so. Let that be our way forward.'

'My dear fellow!' he said in gentle admiration. 'You will have this case concluded before we know where we are.'

But now I could face him on his own ground.

'The last letter, addressed to the inquest on Marsh and Shrivell, says that the two girls in Stamford Street were murdered by a medical student.'

'Very well.'

'You agree that it was written by our blackmailers?'

'As it would seem.'

'In the hope of it being read out at the inquest so that rumours may begin?'

'Quite possibly.'

'Then I will make a wager with you. After the inquest, there will be another letter. It will be sent either to a wealthy medical student, or perhaps to his family. It will accuse him of the murders, for which the writer has proof, and demand a large sum of money for his safety. Will you believe me then?'

He stared at me as if something had distressed him.

'My dear friend, I should never disbelieve you. To disagree is another matter. However, after your success with your clients, I daresay you are closer to the truth of this terrible business than anyone could imagine.'

'They are not my clients,' I said shortly. 'They are our clients.'

He laughed and shook his head.

'Oh no, Watson! I have never met them! How can they be my clients? It is only right that you should have clients of your own. You have long experience and ability. You deserve them, if I may say so, as much as they deserve you.'

A few minutes later, with a grinding of steel on iron, the train rounded a curve and drew into Tooting station. Lestrade, in formal black, was waiting with a cab. The cemetery, behind its plain railings adjoined a main road. Within the gates were the private family plots with crosses and obelisks, weeping Niobes and marble angels. Further off lay the burial ground of the poor, the common graves whose occupants were dug up after twelve years and their scant relics burnt on cemetery fires at night. Green canvas screens had been erected on the frosted grass round one of these graves. The diggers were already at work. As we entered the gates, a crowd of happy urchins ran beside the cab and saluted us with cries of 'Body-snatchers! Burke-and-Hare! Burke-and-Hare! . . .'

'Encouraging, is it not,' Holmes remarked, 'to see how ignorance and illiteracy may be redeemed by a knowledge of the criminal heroes of our past?'

Such was the jumbled burying of the poor that a number of coffins were raised and opened before that of Matilda Clover was found. Holmes and Lestrade watched the gravediggers from a distance as the damp morning turned to a cold drizzle and the piles of yellow London clay grew taller at each new excavation. The railings along the edge of the cemetery were now lined by idle children and their elders. Lestrade glowered at them, then turned to Holmes.

'And what is to be done about Louisa Harvey, Mr Holmes? Whom no one could find, dead or alive?'

'I really do not know,' said Holmes indifferently. He gestured across the expanse of the cemetery. 'I daresay I could find her, if I was obliged to.'

There was no mistaking that this gesture irritated Lestrade.

'One thing we are quite sure of, Mr Sherlock Holmes, is that she is not here. That has been investigated through and through, since Miss Clover was run to earth.'

'Oh, she is here,' said Holmes in a far-away wistful tone, 'I have no doubt of that. She is certainly here.'

'In this cemetery?'

'Where else?'

'I don't see how you can say that, Mr Holmes!'

'I can, Lestrade. I begin to think, you see, that Louisa Harvey and I are quite old friends.'

'Old enough for her to be in the cemetery!' Lestrade said angrily. He stamped off to take a pull at his flask against the raw cold and to shout at a pair of his subordinates who were idling by the canvas screens.

I tried to recall the heroines of our past adventures and could not match a single one to the mysterious Louisa Harvey. I endeavoured to press Holmes about his assertions but it was useless. He watched patiently in the growing mist until a call and a signal from the diggers marked the discovery of Miss Clover.

The body was removed to a shed near the chapel, which became an improvised mortuary. Here Dr Stevenson, on behalf of the Home Office, waited for it with an enthusiasm bordering on the unseemly. The coffin was opened and the well-preserved body of a prematurely-aged young woman was revealed to us.

Until the afternoon, Stevenson was busy in the shed with scalpel, saw, and specimen jars. For all my medical experience, I can never quite accommodate myself to the post-mortem sounds, the cutting of flesh that imitates a rending of tent canvas and the sawing of skull or bones that is crude carpentry. When it was over, Dr Stevenson had filled an array of jars labelled

'Brain of Matilda Clover', 'Intestines of Matilda Clover' and 'Stomach of Matilda Clover'.

Sherlock Holmes, as might be expected, witnessed all this with the curiosity and relish of a true investigator. At the end, he looked at Stevenson who caught his glance, shook his head, and said, 'No doubt of it.'

He took a glass slide, touched a rod to it, and held it out to Holmes.

'Taste that!'

Holmes extended a forefinger. I could not watch, but turned my head away. When I looked again, the lips of Sherlock Holmes were moving like a man savouring the rarest nectar. He stopped and stared at Dr Stevenson.

'Strychnine!' he said, like a happy child.

## XII

For all the good it did, we might as well not have found Matilda Clover. So far as I could see, the discovery of strychnine offered not a single clue as to the identity of her murderer. Lucy Rose's description of the thickset visitor with a moustache and a bowler hat might fit a hundred thousand men in London.

Holmes lapsed into another of those irritating moods that enveloped him during certain investigations. He took to his violin and the Beethoven concerto again. He smoked, massively. He attempted to goad me repeatedly by referring to the Lambeth murders facetiously as 'This investigation of yours . . .' or 'This case, which you have so nearly brought to a successful conclusion . . .' and to our visitors as 'These clients of yours . . .' He had surely washed his hands of the whole business. Such work as he did was at his chemical table, where he continued his experiments into base coinage. His attempts at electro-plating gave our sitting-room the sour and acid smell of a battery-charger.

'Do you,' I had asked abruptly next evening, 'still maintain that Louisa Harvey is in Lambeth Cemetery?'

'No,' he said quietly, not looking up from his weighing of tiny metal.

'So, yesterday . . .'

'*Varium et mutabile semper femina*, Watson. The adorable change and variety of womankind.'

'You mean she has dug herself out and walked off?'

'Something of the sort,' he said, touching the scales gently with his little finger.

There was no point in discussing the matter further. I became silent and more morose. I could not conceal my chagrin when we received a report next morning that twice the lethal dose of strychnine had been found in Matilda Clover's body. I still wanted to hold to my belief that we faced two distinct sets of criminals. Yet how could the blackmailers know a fortnight in advance that Matilda Clover would die of strychnine poisoning, unless they murdered her?

The alternative, which Sherlock Holmes apparently embraced, seemed to me equally absurd. We must believe that a gang of men and women, the authors of the various blackmail notes, had perpetrated these four murders and others beside. According to their threats, there was at least one other body, though Louisa Harvey was not to be found in the register of deaths at Somerset House under any spelling of her name.

Under what sobriquet, then, had she been buried in Lambeth cemetery?

For three days this state of affairs persisted. Then, on the third evening, we heard the measured tread of Lestrade's boots upon the stairs and the familiar bull-dog figure in the pea-jacket and cravat appeared in our doorway.

'Lestrade!' said Holmes, in gentle admiration. 'Do come in and take a chair, my dear fellow. We have missed your visits of late, have we not, Watson? I dare-say that the matter of Matilda Clover and Louisa Harvey is keeping you busy just now.'

The inspector sat down scowling and ignored the offer of the cigar case.

'I don't come to talk about those persons, Mr Holmes. We have another letter and I think we may have our blackmailer.'

'Dear me,' said Holmes softly, 'you have quite stolen a march upon us all this time. Pray, do explain.'

'Read this!' Lestrade said sharply. Each in turn we read the curious letter, addressed to Dr Joseph Harper of Barnstaple.

*Dear Sir,*

*I am writing to inform you that one of my operators has indisputable evidence that your son, W. J. Harper, a medical student at St Thomas's Hospital, poisoned two girls named Alice Marsh and Emma Shrivell on the 12th inst., and that I am willing to give you the said evidence (so that you can suppress it) for the sum of £1,500 sterling, or sell it to the police for the same amount . . .*

Even before I read the rest I knew that there would be

the threat to 'ruin you and your family forever', and a command in this case to answer the letter through the columns of the *Daily Chronicle*, with the message '*W. H. M. - Will pay you for your services. - Dr H.*' The conclusion of the letter revealed a familiar name, the blackmailer of Dr Neill and the Metropole Hotel.

*If you do not answer at once, I am going to give the evidence to the Coroner.*
*Yours respectfully,*
*W.H. Murray*

Holmes offered the cigar case again. This time, the inspector helped himself to a corona.

'You say you have your blackmailer, Lestrade? Under lock and key?'

The colour rose a little in our visitor's cheek.

'Not as such, Mr Holmes. I believe we know who he is, though. An arrest at this moment might be imprudent.'

'Ah,' said Holmes, as if this explained it all, 'and who might it be?'

Lestrade looked like a man on the verge of some grand pronouncement.

'The son of the man to whom this letter is addressed, gentlemen. Mr Walter Harper, the medical student.'

Holmes affected simple bewilderment.

'Then young Walter Harper accuses himself of the murder of these two girls?'

'Only to his father, Mr Holmes. We can't see he is the murderer. He may be or he may be not. However, we believe he knew both girls and that he got one of them into trouble, or nearly so, while she was at Mutton's down in Brighton.'

'But why accuse himself?'

'Because he believed that his father, knowing something of the rumours about his son, would never take this letter to the police. He would pay, rather than see his son disgraced by scandal and his career ended before it had begun. Our information is that young Harper never wanted to be a medical student but was compelled by his father's wishes. If the young rogue is half what we think, his allowance was spent long ago. He is in debt to the money-lenders, and he must have seen one way to clear himself. By blackmailing the only person that would never give him away, having first tried to blackmail a good many others.'

'And the murders?' asked Holmes hopefully.

'As to that, Mr Holmes, how was it the blackmailer and his gang knew so soon that Ellen Donworth had been poisoned? How did they know Matilda Clover would be poisoned before it happened? Take all that together with the accusations in this letter and Mr Walter Harper may have to face something stronger than blackmail before he's finished.'

When the time came for the inspector to leave, Holmes stood up and shook his hand.

'Well, my dear Lestrade, I congratulate you. You have proved yourself the best man in this case and the best man has won. I can only apologize if my own humble efforts, such as they have been, have in any way interfered with your investigations.'

Lestrade glowed a little with satisfaction.

'Very noble of you to take it like that, Mr Holmes. Very generous, I'm sure.'

'One thing, if I may ask. How tall is Mr Harper?'

Lestrade stared at him.

'Tall?'

'High, if you prefer.'

'What has that . . .'

'Believe me it has.'

'Very well, then. About five feet and nine inches, I should guess.'

'Build?'

'He played scrum-half for the hospital rugby, I'm told.'

'Clean shaven? How barbered?'

'Medium brown hair. Short military moustache.'

'Does he wear a bowler hat?'

'He was indoors!' Lestrade said impatiently. 'What might all this amount to?'

'A portrait of your murderer,' Holmes said amiably. 'Mere idle curiosity on my part.'

Idle curiosity or not, I could not help feeling that the inspector was a good deal more uneasy when he left us than when he had arrived.

As soon as the door was closed, I said to Holmes *sotto voce*, 'Did you not see the address of young Harper's lodgings in the letter?'

'Of course I saw it! It is the house where your client Dr Neill lodges on his visits to London.'

'No wonder that Neill thought the blackmailer was someone close to him.'

'No wonder at all,' he said.

'And was not the scrum-half with the brown hair and moustache the man that Mrs Phillips saw at the door with Matilda Clover the night she died?'

'To be sure.'

He leant forward and stirred the dying fire with the poker.

'Then Lestrade has got his man!' I exclaimed.

He looked up at me.

'I never doubted that, my dear fellow. He has got his man. Have we got ours?'

He was back to his old mood again. I gave him a few minutes of brooding over the embers, then asked casually, 'I suppose, Holmes, that you may find it convenient in the next day or two to pay me the money you owe.'

He looked startled.

'Money? What money?'

'The wager,' I said quietly. 'On our way to Lambeth Cemetery the other day, I wagered you that after the letter to the coroner, accusing an unnamed medical student of the Stamford Street murders, the next letter would be an attempt to blackmail a wealthy student or his family. So it has proved to be.'

'By Jove!' he said softly. 'So you did – and so it has. However, just help me with one thing first, there's a good fellow.'

'What sort of thing?'

'With your assistance, Watson, I should like to see the inside of Walter Harper's rooms. I do not much mind whether he is acquitted or hanged but I think it desirable that one or other of these events should take place before much longer. Then we will settle the wager.'

## XIII

Two days later, poison in Lambeth threatened the entire borough. Maisie, maid-of-all-work to Mrs Emily

Sleaper, answered the knocker in Lambeth Palace Road. The door stood in a respectable set of houses. The day was Monday, the time 9.30 a.m. The wide length of the road lay empty, the trees down either pavement were bare in the approach of spring. On Mrs Sleaper's doorstep stood a stout man of medium height in a bowler hat and moustache, a watch-chain looped ponderously across the waistcoat of his well-worn suit.

'Jeavons,' he said with the least tilt of the bowler, 'Area Inspector, South London Gas Company. Mrs Sleaper home?'

'No, sir,' said Maisie, blushing a little under her white mob-cap.

'Who might be in charge, then?'

In deference to his air of authority, Maisie almost performed a half-curtsey.

'There's only me, sir.'

He glanced at her and his mouth tightened.

'Any smell of gas in the house?'

'No, sir. Don't think so, sir.'

'Don't think so, sir? Meaning what, precisely?'

'Meaning I haven't been through every room yet,' she said petulantly, 'and Mrs Sleaper's gentlemen are all gone out this time of day, so I can't ask them.'

'Any naked lights or flame?'

'Kitchen fire, I suppose.'

'Put it out immediately.'

'I can't do that! She'd skin me!'

His brows tightened.

'Young woman, you have heard of the Lambeth poisoner, I daresay.'

'Oh, yes.' There was a slight but delicious shiver. 'I heard of him, all right.'

'What you haven't heard of is his letter to the gas company yesterday, promising to poison all occupants of houses in this area with household gas, by over-pressurizing the main. In other words, even with taps turned off, the gas leaks at loose pipe-joints, too soft for you to hear. Day or night. You don't smell it and you get drowsy. You fall deeper into your last long sleep. All done in ten minutes.'

'Oh, God!'

'Act sensible,' Inspector Jeavons advised, 'Mr Crabbe, my mechanic, will be here any minute, working his way down the road. Your joints need tightening, miss, that's all. If you smell anything peculiar meantime, come straight out.'

He closed the door, leaving the terrified maid to douse the kitchen fire. In the stillness of the road, a baker's barrow passed, pulled by the roundsman between its shafts. A milk-cart stopped. The man called 'Milk down below!' and whipped up his horse. Then the front door of Mrs Sleaper's house flew open and Maisie almost tumbled down the steps.

'Gas! Gas! Mr Jeavons! There's gas in the house!'

His self-assurance calmed her a little, as he shouted to his mechanic.

'Mr Crabbe, attend to these joints next, if you please.'

Mr Crabbe resembled a turtle more closely than his marine namesake. A large man with fine chest and paunch, bandy-legged from weight, rheumy eyes behind thick glasses, a hopelessly drooping black moustache, and a tattered cap. He had the stoop of one whose life since boyhood has been spent down manholes and in conduits. His tools hung in a greasy satchel over the shoulder of his overalls. His voice had the slight but chronic hoarseness of the inveterate whisky drinker.

'Have the goodness to show me, dear,' he said to Maisie, who scowled at his familiarity. 'Just point out the whereabouts of the pipes.'

She led the way to the front door, taking care to enter only a few feet.

'Don't strike a light, and you'll be all right,' he said roguishly, making to pull loose one of the ribbons behind her apron, as she twisted away from him. He undid his satchel and selected an adjustable wrench, humming to himself, 'I can't get away to marry you today . . . My wife won't let me.'

'Don't you smell it?' she insisted.

'I smell it, my sweetheart. Just wait here.'

A black rubber mask from his satchel covered his nose and mouth, making him a grotesque and frightening clown from Venetian carnival. He went round the ground floor rooms and she heard the grip of the wrench on the piping.

Now he was on the stairs, climbing lightly. Two rooms opened off each upper level, the tenant identified by a printed *carte de visite* slotted into a small brass holder on each door. These apartments were duplicated indefinitely in this neighbourhood of the great hospitals. Entering the first, after a respectful tap on the door, Mr Crabbe found it unoccupied. A well-worn carpet lay before a black-leaded grate, gas-mantels at either side. A mirror hung over the greater width of the mantelpiece. The furniture was spartan and black-varnished.

A wardrobe stood in the adjoining bedroom and two tiers of desk-drawers in the sitting-room. Mr Crabbe drew open the desk-drawers one by one. With a hoarse cough and a sniff he unmasked and rummaged. Then, whistling to himself, 'Here's the very note . . . and this is what he wrote . . .' he drew out a pad of ivory-cream writing paper. Holding it firmly, he tore off the top sheet and burst into full-throated chorus, 'There was I, waiting at the church . . .' He stopped and listened. A black marble Parthenon clock on the mantel ticked away the silence. He sang a little more, as he checked the other rooms. The spanner was heard tightening joints, then he came cantering down the stairs.

'Safe enough now, miss,' he said cheerfully. The pinch that he aimed was rather half-hearted, giving her ample time to turn her back to the wall.

'You sure it's safe?'

'Tight as Noah's Ark. He can turn up the pressure as much as he likes. The joints in this house won't give, gas won't leak in here. Sound as a pound.'

But what if this man was the Lambeth murderer and had loosened the joints instead? She dodged him once more.

'You're not a gentleman!' she shouted after him angrily, 'I've a good mind . . .'

Mr Crabbe swung rakishly down the road. His voice carried back to her.

'You be thankful, my girl, that you ain't a-singing "Too-ra-li-too-ra-li-too-ra-lay-ay!" with the 'eavenly choir!'

He turned into Lambeth Road and paused in the dark under a low bridge, its iron ringing at the thunder of Waterloo trains. With no one in sight, he opened his satchel and slipped his cap in. Unhitching the shoulder-bands of his overalls, he stepped out, folded them small and added them to the cap. Glasses and moustache followed. At the Waterloo cab rank, Mr Jeavons was waiting, his foot on the running-board to detain a hansom.

'Though I say it myself, Watson,' the Gas Man chuckled, 'that was one of the neatest and quite the jolliest of all my impersonations to date. You have the bag of peeled garlic and tar that I lodged within the kitchen door?'

I assured him I had. As for what he might have found in Walter Harper's rooms, he would only insist that I must wait and see what I would see on our arrival in Baker Street.

Holmes took the blank sheet of cream paper straight to his work-table. With infinite care, a delicate sprinkling of graphite revealed the indentations of a message written on the sheet above. Rather, it revealed some of them.

*I am writing to inform . . . operators . . . indisputable evidence . . . son, W. J. Harp . . . St Thomas's Hospital . . .*

'The young devil!' I exclaimed. 'Then he *was* trying to extort money from his own father!'

Holmes stared at the paper and stroked his chin.

'So it would seem.'

'But he dared not use his own writing, which his father would recognize. So there are at least two of them in this. Surely this is our blackmail gang!'

He drew from his pocket an envelope, addressed to 'Dr Thomas Neill, 103 Lambeth Palace Road SE.' I stared at it.

'Holmes! You have searched my client's room! You have removed his papers!'

He leant back and laughed.

'I have emptied his waste-paper basket left outside his door, my dear fellow, as the maid would have done in any case. It is as well I did, for the writing on this is identical to the letter received by Frederick Smith. My life upon it, Watson!'

'That woman who wrote to Mr Smith also wrote a blackmail letter to Dr Neill? Why did Neill not mention it when he showed me the other?'

'With that very question in mind, I searched the drawers of his desk. The reason he did not mention this envelope to you is that the woman did not write him a blackmail letter. The letter which matches this envelope, and which I took the precaution to scribble down, is a love letter.'

At that point I lost the thread completely. In Holmes's scrawl I could make out that the letter began 'My dearest', referred to the provisions made for the lady in Dr Neill's will, and ended, 'Your loving Laura.' The sender's address was merely 'Chapel Street'. Perhaps the postmark on the envelope, if there was one, would reveal the rest. After this revelation, however, there could only be one answer to the Lambeth riddle.

'Walter Harper and Laura, whoever she may be, must be in this together,' I said, 'They are the blackmailers, perhaps with several others. The man blackmails Dr Neill, the woman seduces him into leaving everything to her in his will, and tries to blackmail Frederick Smith into the bargain! One way or another, they would strip Dr Neill as they mean to strip Dr Harper of Barnstable!'

'Well,' said Holmes thoughtfully, 'Dr Neill is your client.'

'Our client!'

'Your client, if you please. I have never set eyes upon him.'

'Then I must tell him everything.'

'You can scarcely do that without accusing me of housebreaking.'

'That is true. Then what are we to do?'

Holmes chose a pipe from the rack and made a great show of lighting it.

'To speak frankly,' he said at length, 'I should like another corpse.'

'I should have thought there had been enough corpses in this case!'

'I have in mind a special kind of corpse, however. One that will answer when I speak to it. What I need, my dear fellow, is a talking corpse. I believe I could find one, if I had to.'

I gave it up. Next morning, the papers carried stern condemnations of a prank by medical students who had terrified respectable householders into believing that the Lambeth poisoner was about to kill half the neighbourhood with household gas. 'Such humour in our physicians of the future,' wrote *The Times*, 'is highly to be deprecated.'

## XIV

All too soon, I was to learn why Holmes insisted upon the distinction between those clients who were mine and those which were his, and why he had referred facetiously to the Lambeth mystery as 'this case of yours, which you stumbled upon one night in the

Waterloo Road'. I woke on the second morning after our incognito excursion to read in the paper of the arrest of a suspect in Berkhamstead, on suspicion of extortion. Holmes himself had not yet risen. Indeed his place at the breakfast table remained undisturbed for a further half-hour. Nor was there any sign of him when the telegram arrived.

To wake Sherlock Holmes, when he was determined upon sleep, was next to a physical impossibility. Having been informed by Billy that an immediate acknowledgement of the wire was demanded, I tore open the blue envelope.

> HOLMES WATSON BAKER STREET STOP. YOUR
> ENVELOPE AND TRANSCRIPTION RECEIVED STOP.
> ESSENTIAL YOU ATTEND HERE IMMEDIATELY TO
> SUBSTANTIATE EVIDENCE STOP. CONFIRM BY
> RETURN STOP. LESTRADE SCOTLAND YARD.

I had not known that Holmes had already forwarded to Lestrade the purloined envelope and the scribbled copy of the letter to Dr Neill. However, I now answered the message in two words. PROCEEDING FORTHWITH.

Though this was less than accurate, it spurred Holmes into a more rapid consumption of breakfast and a foregoing of the newspapers. By eleven o'clock, our cab turned from the Embankment, where the trees were just coming into bud, and through the gateway of Scotland Yard. I confess that I looked forward with a certain vindictiveness to confronting the blackmailer of my client.

Those who have passed along the Embankment by the headquarters of the Metropolitan Police will know something of that curious structure, its towers and turrets of red brick banded with white, like a storybook castle of legend. Lestrade's quarters, though plainly furnished, had the size and spaciousness of a drawing-room, with a bay window overlooking the river.

He greeted us a little more gruffly than usual, as he bade us take our chairs before his desk.

'We are indebted to you, Mr Holmes, for the envelope and the transcription. How you came by these is not a matter for my consideration at this moment.'

'The carelessness with which dustbins are emptied in certain quarters of London leads to many such scraps of paper blowing in the wind.' Holmes spoke with sufficient insouciance to indicate that he did not care twopence for Lestrade's 'consideration' of his methods.

The inspector favoured him with a glance.

'Very well, sir. Let us just say that it is thanks to your quickness of thought and action that the woman, Miss Laura Sabbatini, is in custody and that Mr Harper is watched by one of our officers.'

Holmes sighed and sat back in his chair with something of a small-boy's sulkiness.

'I wish, Lestrade, that you had made better use of my poor offerings.'

Our host was mystified by this.

'Play fair, Holmes,' I said, 'Lestrade has compared and identified the hand on the envelope as being that of Mr Smith's blackmailer and the other paper as having come from Harper's own stationery. He has ensured that Harper cannot escape us. If Harper and Miss Sabbatini are not the entire gang, they are at least two of its leading members.'

'What is more,' said the inspector indignantly, 'I have complied with your request, Mr Holmes, that nothing concerning the letter or the envelope should be made public. I have done so against my better judgment.'

Holmes had been listening with eyes closed and fingertips pressed together.

'I should find it hard to conceive of a more certain way of making those items public than by detaining a suspect within hours of receiving them.'

Again I came to Lestrade's defence.

'Dash it all, Holmes, anything less than arrest or surveillance and the birds might have flown. The woman first and her friends in short order. It was the best move on Lestrade's part to bag one of them and keep another in his sights.'

He only seemed to sink further into gloom.

'The bird or birds, as you so felicitously term them, have either flown already or are even now testing their wings. My dear Lestrade, I daresay you will recall my second request – that I should be allowed to put certain questions to your suspect before she was invited to make a statement or was charged?'

'And that undertaking is now to be honoured, Mr Holmes.'

My friend nodded. When he looked up, his eyes were brighter but he scarcely appeared like a man who has lost a penny and found a shilling.

'Then, if you please, we will have the lady brought in so that I may speak to her.'

Lestrade stepped outside and I heard him giving orders to one of his officers. There was a pause of some minutes and presently he came back, following a demure young woman of warm complexion, raven hair, and slim figure. She was modestly but finely dressed in a pale grey walking-gown, a matching hat and a light veil which she now put up. Lestrade brought a chair for her and she sat down. Holmes looked at her for a moment, then said, 'Miss Sabbatini, my name is Sherlock Holmes. It is possible that you may have heard of me.'

'Oh, yes!' she said eagerly, as if his was the first friendly voice that had spoken to her since her ordeal began. 'Yes I have.'

'Very well. I am not employed by the police. In any case, you are under no obligation to answer my questions or theirs. However, if you are willing to tell me what I want to know, it is possible that I may be able to save you a good deal of trouble.'

'Yes,' she said again, though her hands gripped the arms of her chair until her knuckles whitened, 'by all means, Mr Holmes.'

'In that case, Mr Lestrade, may we have the letter written to Mr Frederick Smith MP and the envelope addressed to Dr Neill?'

He stood up and these were handed to him. He held the blackmail letter to Mr Smith before her.

'Did you write this letter, Miss Sabbatini?'

It took only a glance before she said eagerly, 'Yes. Oh, yes. I wrote that.'

'A letter blackmailing Mr Smith . . .'

'Yes, but I did not mean to . . .'

'We will leave that for a moment, if you please. Is this also your writing on the envelope addressed to Dr Neill at 103 Lambeth Palace Road?'

'Of course. It is the same. It is how I always write.'

'And you are, I believe, sole beneficiary under the will of Dr Neill?'

This startled her, for she did not see how Sherlock Holmes could know such a thing. Nor did Lestrade.

'You have evidently discovered a good deal about us, Mr Holmes. However, you are correct. I am the sole beneficiary under his will. Why should I not be? We are engaged to be married!'

It was now the turn of Sherlock Holmes to look surprised but he quickly composed himself. Such engagements, after all, are easily made and easily broken on the part of the lady.

'How long have you known Dr Neill?'

'A year or so. We met in America when I was there with my parents.'

I confess that this demure figure, answering his questions so frankly, was not at all how I had imagined the blackmailer of my client. However, the bomb that had been ticking quietly under us all was now about to be detonated.

'You admit that you wrote the letter to Mr Frederick Smith. Why?'

'Why should I not? I wrote it because Dr Neill was too busy.'

'Too busy? Busy with what?'

Now she turned away from Holmes and looked at Lestrade.

'It is possible that you know something of this, Mr Lestrade, being a policeman. Dr Neill has a great reputation as a pathologist. He was retained some months ago on the advice of the Commissioner himself, Sir Melville MacNaghten, to advise the police about the poisonings in Lambeth.'

Lestrade looked as thunderstruck as any of us had been.

'Pray continue, Miss Sabbatini,' he said, now trying to look as if he had known about the Commissioner's recommendation all along.

'Dr Neill was extremely hard-pressed to discharge all these commitments, in addition to his work at the hospital. Documents came to him from the police and were then passed on by him to the coroner's office. It was essential that he should make copies of them for reference. There was a very great number. We were in Hertfordshire together, you understand, and they were to be posted to London as a matter of urgency. To help him, I copied out several in my own hand. The letter to Mr Smith was one of them.'

'You have told me what I suspected from the first, Miss Sabbatini,' said Holmes gently. 'We will leave it there for the moment, if you please. I shall confer with Inspector Lestrade upon your answers to my questions. However, I should be very surprised if your troubles are not at an end by this evening.'

Lestrade got up and escorted Miss Sabbatini to the door. As it closed, Holmes turned to me.

'Your client, Watson! By now Dr Neill is probably on his way back to America, where he will no doubt find safety!'

Lestrade stood with his back to the door.

'Safety from what, though, Mr Holmes?'

Holmes swung round on him.

'Blackmail! Blackmail at least. Very possibly murder, though we do not yet know that he resembles the suspect or that he could have been in the place where any murder was committed. Who ever heard of such a gang of blackmailers? Was it not obvious from the first that this was a single-handed criminal? What had he to do but persuade other men and women to copy documents for him? To do so on the pretext that he was a medical consultant to Scotland Yard is, I confess, a nicer stroke than I should have thought him capable of.'

'Not so fast,' Lestrade interrupted, 'Miss Sabbatini might do it for love. How could he depend on the others?'

Holmes looked at him in despair.

'Do you still not see it? Give me pen and paper, send me out into Lambeth, or Bermondsey, or the docks. There are communities from all over Europe and Asia who scarcely speak English, let alone write it. There are scribes who take down their letters for them but to whom English is almost or completely a foreign tongue. A man of moderate resource and intelligence could have any document copied for him by such a person, who would not understand more than a word or two of what it contained. I could bring you back confessions of my guilt in the Lambeth poisonings by this evening in a dozen different hands. Would you believe me then?'

Lestrade shifted uncomfortably in his chair. Holmes continued imperturbably.

'If I were Dr Neill and I wanted to incriminate a man for my offences, I should choose such a one as Walter Harper. Unless he is much maligned, that young gentleman has used his father's money to live high upon the hog, as they say. I should wait my chance, enter his room, and purloin his notepaper for a few hours. I would take it to one of my dupes who would indite a blackmail demand to the young man's father. I should hope that the current rumours of Walter Harper's involvement in the deaths of two young women would lead the police to search his rooms. There they would find the same undoubted evidence of his complicity in blackmail as I have done. You see? Who better placed than Dr Neill to accomplish this? He knew Harper well, could follow his movements, and had access to his rooms.'

'Very well, Mr Holmes. Then Dr Neill and he alone is our blackmail gang. Perhaps he is also our murderer.'

Holmes pulled a face.

'As to that, my friend, the evidence in your hands points rather away from Dr Watson's client than towards him. I daresay, however, that we may congratulate ourselves on the prospect of seeing him go to prison for the next fourteen years on charges of attempted extortion.'

Lestrade looked brighter than at any time since our arrival. But Holmes had not done with him.

'May I remind you, however, that such a prospect diminishes with every minute that you sit here? Should Dr Neill evade us, it would not look well in the annals of Scotland Yard, when 103 Lambeth Palace Road is scarcely twenty minutes' walk away.'

## XV

The behaviour of Sherlock Holmes on that spring day continued to veer between the unpredictable and the erratic. Had I not known him so well, I might have detected a taste of sour grapes as he wished me well with my case, and washed his hands of it. If proof of this were needed, it was surely provided by his positive refusal to accompany Lestrade and myself with half a dozen uniformed officers, in our descent upon Lambeth Palace Road.

'My dear fellow,' he said humorously, 'you will manage it well enough between you. And if you cannot, then I am sure my presence would make no difference. I shall return to Baker Street, to Mrs Hudson's admirable tea and cakes.'

'Holmes! We must catch this fellow before it is too late.'

'So you must, Watson. For me, however, the call of tea and cakes was ever irresistible.'

With that, he waved down a cab on the Embankment and was driven away. Lestrade looked after him in blank astonishment. So it was that I alone followed the inspector with his search warrant into the solid suburban terrace, while the uniformed men stood at the front and back to prevent an escape. There was not the least difficulty in entering Dr Neill's rooms for such apartments within a house are seldom locked when men live *en famille*. Of the fugitive, there was no sign. His possessions appeared to be in place, though Mrs Sleaper could not lay hands upon a Gladstone bag that was usually in the wardrobe. She had thought nothing of it when her 'charming Dr Neill' had gone out that morning and she had heard him hail a cab for Charing Cross.

'Which can only mean the boat-train for France, I suppose' said Lestrade gloomily, drawing out his watch. 'I daresay he'd be there by now. They won't send him back neither, they never do. Sailing out of their ports, he could be anywhere tomorrow. And, of course, we can't stop their ships. Act of war.'

The search did little credit to Dr Neill, revealing as it did some disgusting photographs of young women, but neither did it produce evidence against him. There was a salesman's sample-case of medicines of the most ordinary kind. One drawer yielded several unfilled gelatine capsules, far more commonly used in America than in England for administering evil-tasting medicines. As for blackmail or murder, there was nothing.

'We'll go through it with a toothcomb,' Lestrade said wearily, 'carpets and boards up, furniture apart. Still, it looks to me as if we've lost him.'

As the search continued, I was apprehensive that the maid-of-all-work, Maisie, might recognize me as the gas company inspector of the other day. The one stroke of fortune in all this was that it proved to be her afternoon off, during which this good girl invariably walked with her 'young man' in Battersea Park.

An hour and a half had passed in a fruitless ransacking of Dr Neill's rooms. I was about to follow Holmes to Baker Street, when I heard a commotion in the street. I went to the sitting-room window and saw that a cab had drawn up. Two unspeakable ruffians, who looked as if they had never in their lives until now ridden in a hansom, got out and slouched off. Then through its open doorway, very slowly, emerged the frock-coated and silk-hatted figure of Dr Neill. Behind him came Sherlock Holmes, holding at his side what looked very like my service revolver. So much for tea and cakes!

Dr Neill saw before him two uniformed police officers. With an inspiration born of terror, he turned and took Holmes by surprise, knocking him flat and diving back into the cab. From my vantage point, I saw Neill burst out of the far door and race across the road towards an alley between the opposite houses.

'He won't get far down there,' Lestrade said confidently. A few minutes later, a dishevelled figure reappeared between two uniformed men, the handcuffs on his wrists.

I truly thought 'this case of mine' was at an end. How mistaken I proved to be!

For the moment, Sherlock Holmes was as smug as the cat who has had the cream.

'I quite anticipated, Watson, the capital error of which you and Lestrade would be guilty. Great heavens, man! Since the papers appeared this morning, Dr Neill has known that Miss Sabbatini was arrested yesterday. Chapel Street, Berkhamstead. What more need he be told? He guessed that she would, however innocently, speak his name to the police and reveal his part in the letters. Did you suppose he would still be waiting for you in his lodgings at three in the afternoon? He fled, it would appear, almost empty-handed, which suggests a fine state of panic, does it not?'

'Where else were we to start our search? And where did you find him?'

'My dear fellow, the criminal investigator must hold in his mind certain data. He cannot, to be sure, carry the timetable for the entire railway system of Great Britain. At a minimum, however, he must have in his head such items as the departure-time of the boat-train from Euston to connect with the Transatlantic sailings of the White Star Line from Liverpool. You tell me that

Dr Neill hails from Chicago. That would be his quickest route home, would it not? I grant that you might send wires for the arrest of Dr Neill – but I shall eat my hat with pleasure if that proves to be more than a *nom-de-plume*.'

Lestrade gave a start at this and Holmes continued.

'I was already present at the great terminus of the North-Western Railway when Dr Neill's cab arrived in good time for the five o'clock train. Two friends of mine, whom you saw decamp from the cab just now, and whom, in deference to their own desire for anonymity, we will call "Cats-Meat" and "The Groundsman", made a rendezvous with me there at the cab-rank. Dr Neill could not arrive too early, of course, for that increased the risk of his being spotted at such an obvious location. Once we saw him draw up, it was a simple matter. My two friends and your handy little revolver persuaded him to step back into his cab rather than out of it. Charing Cross? To be sure, he would take pains to let Mrs Sleaper hear him shout "Charing Cross" to the cabbie this morning, the better to put us off his trail.'

In the sequel to this, Dr Neill was taken to Bow Street police-station, whither Holmes, Lestrade and I accompanied him. He was brought before the desk-sergeant and charged with demanding money with menaces, contrary to the Larceny Act 1861. He seemed not the least concerned.

'You have got the wrong man, of course,' he said genially, 'but fire away. What I asked Miss Sabbatini to assist me with was all done for Mr Walter Harper, for some work of his. He it was who claimed to be devilling for his tutor who, in turn, was a police surgeon of some sort. Of the other letters I know nothing. There you have it, gentlemen. If he will murder girls in Stamford Street, he will hardly stop at blackmail. I was a fool, I suppose, not to twig him from the first.'

After that, he declined to say another word.

'At the worst,' said Lestrade doubtfully, 'I must release him as an innocent dupe.'

'At the worst,' Holmes muttered, 'he is the Lambeth poisoner.'

The evidence of that seemed to fade by the hour. Lestrade tried him by asking how it was that the blackmail demands relating to Ellen Donworth and Matilda Clover could have been written other than by the murderer, a day before anyone knew the first girl had been poisoned and almost a fortnight before the second one had died.

'I guess,' said Dr Neill good-naturedly, 'you would have to ask the man who gave me the letters to have copied. Walter Harper.'

That young man could no longer be left out of it. During the evening, Lestrade gave orders to what Holmes called his 'minions' to bring Walter Harper to Bow Street.

'For it amounts to this,' the inspector said grimly, 'we may never convict Dr Neill of blackmail unless we first convict him of murder.'

So it was that on the following morning Dr Neill took his place in a line of men who stood the length of a wall in Bow Street yard. He was among twenty or thirty men, all dressed in suits and hats, the tallest at the centre of the line and the others falling away to either end, as if it had been a group photograph. Three witnesses attended. There had been time enough to bring Mrs Phillips from the house where Matilda Clover lodged. Lestrade's men had also found Sally Martin and Jenny Frere, two of those who 'hunted in the same pack' with Matilda Clover. Unlike her friend Lucy Rose, they had been out with her every night for a week or two before she died and had seen the man she was with on the last night of all.

Sherlock Holmes still had an air of patient endurance, the courteous man who considers his time is being wasted but who is too well-bred to speak of it. He stood with Lestrade and two uniformed officers in a far corner of the sunlit yard. Mrs Phillips, like a galleon under sail, made her stately way down the line. She scarcely looked at Dr Neill but passed on and touched the shoulder of a shorter man almost at the end of the line. Sally Martin and Jenny Frere followed her. One by one they passed by Dr Neill, though Sally Martin paused and looked quickly at his boots. Then they walked on and touched the shoulder of another man. When they had gone Holmes favoured Lestrade with a look of worldly wisdom. For all three women had walked past Dr Neill and touched the shoulder of Walter Harper.

When we were alone together, while Lestrade left his office to give instructions for Harper's continued detention, Holmes turned from the window and said quietly, 'You know, my dear fellow, that I would not for the world offend you?'

'I daresay you would not intend to do so.' It was the best that I could manage.

'All the same, I wonder if you would permit me to lend you a little assistance in this case of yours. You have managed it admirably to this point in many respects. Now, however, I cannot help observing that the threads of your evidence appear remarkably tangled. You would not sleep easily, I know, if you were instrumental in assisting Lestrade's blockheads to get an innocent man hanged.'

'Once and for all,' I said irritably, 'it is not my case – it is our case. And you may do what the devil you like with it!'

'Capital,' he said with a smile. 'Then we will return, if you please, to this matter of the talking corpse.'

## XVI

For the whole of the next spring day we followed the arteries of pleasure lying just south of the river, a warren of streets and alleys where the mild sky was dulled by smoke and the tin thunder of trains echoed from every bridge and tall archway. Holmes began at Westminster Bridge, where the entrance canopy of Astley's Amphitheatre and Circus extends over the pavement. We followed the walls of the Canterbury Music Hall and Gatti's Palace of Varieties, whose blue and red placards boasted Head Balancers and Acrobats, Minstrels, and Performing Horses. We searched streets of brick terraces, darkened by soot and decay, upper floors painted with advertisements for cigars, confectionery, embrocation, and Old England Snuff. In the little windows of tobacconists' shops, the covers of the week's *Tit-Bits* and the *Police Budget* had yet to placard the news of Dr Neill.

It was early evening when we paid for our entrance to the Canterbury, whose interior was a domed oriental palace with gold-painted stucco adorning the boxes and galleries. Its speciality was the 'Fish Ballet' performed by ladies in silver fleshings behind a thin gauze curtain drawn across the arch of the stage.

On his rare visits to the music hall, Holmes showed little interest in the performance. Life for him was at the rear, along the promenade bar, which looked on to the stage in front but whose windows at the back surveyed the streets below. The chatter and laughter, the clatter of glasses, the oysters served with brown bread and butter were all the entertainment he required.

It would be foolish to pretend that the majority of strollers in the Canterbury's Long Bar were other than counting-house clerks masquerading as top-hatted swells and discreetly-painted street-girls in cloaks and bonnets. Holmes and I sat with our plates of oysters and glasses of hock at a round marble-topped table while we watched the passing show. Hour followed hour and I was suddenly aware that we were sitting through the stage performance for a second – or perhaps third – time. Then he stood up, smiled, and to my dismay accosted one of the girls. To me, she looked indistinguishable from the rest.

'Happy birthday, my dear!' he said jovially. 'Happy birthday, Lucy Rose!'

'Beg your pardon?' She swung round upon him, not best pleased, but Holmes continued to smile in sheer amiability.

'We are a week early but our wishes are no less sincere! Happy birthday, Lucy Rose! Or perhaps I should say, happy birthday, Louisa Harvey!'

This brought me to my feet, which was just as well

for the girl swung round and then was about to run. Finding me in her way she stopped and Holmes took her by the arm.

'Have no fear, Louisa! We mean you no harm.'

'What the devil is this?' I said to him with some little spirit, 'You swore she was in Lambeth Cemetery!'

'And so she was, were you not, my dear? Standing with the idlers by the railings, watching in dread as poor Mattie Clover's body was brought up.'

The keenness of his eye, in picking out a face from a crowd, was legendary but my astonishment must have been all too visible.

'Watson, Watson!' he said softly. 'How much the world owes to Somerset House and its register of deaths, which we have all been searching! But how much more to its register of births, where I alone have spent my leisure hours. 4 April is the young lady's birthday, if you recall. Now, there is no Lucy Rose born on that day, if the records are to be believed. But seventeen years ago, Louisa Jane Harvey uttered the first notes of a career which has brought her to where we find her now.'

He held her so gently by one arm but she might as well have struggled against a steel trap.

'What d'you want with me?'

'The truth,' he said a little more sternly. 'The truth you have kept to yourself too long. The truth you owe to Matilda Clover. The truth about Dr Neill.'

There was no more resistance in her now. She sat down at the little marble table as suddenly as if her legs might not have supported her. She said nothing. Holmes snapped his fingers at the waiter for three glasses of sherbet.

'Come,' he said, sitting opposite her, 'tell the truth and he will never more be free to harm you. Keep it hidden and he will be set at liberty to find you.'

She breathed deeply for a moment, then said, 'I was so frightened!'

'You were with Matilda Clover when the two of you met him, of course.'

Louisa Harvey, as I must now call her, nodded.

'As I supposed,' Holmes said. 'This man thought he had murdered both of you. But Matilda was alive two weeks later. And you escaped him. How?'

'It was the Alhambra in Leicester Square,' she whispered, 'the long bar, like this one. He asked my name and said he came from America and was working at the hospital. I was to spend the night with him off Oxford Street, a hotel in Berwick Street. Later we went to the Northumberland public house near the Embankment and Mattie was there. He wanted us both. He said he had special stuff that made it more frisky. Something he got through being a medical man. He gave us each two long pills. I pretended to take mine but switched them to the other hand and then threw them behind me. He made me open my hand to show I'd swallowed them. But I was rid of them by then. Mattie slipped hers in her pocket. He promised to meet us later at the hotel, saying he'd got an appointment at the hospital first. I waited but he never came.'

Holmes gave a long sigh.

'He is, I daresay, certifiably insane. It will not help him, of course, for the law has its own very peculiar definition of insanity. I do not doubt, however, that the great Dr Maudsley would find his brain most instructive, when our prisoner has no further use for it himself.'

'I was so frightened!' the girl exclaimed, not listening to him. 'I kept to the house and never went out. Then I walked out one night, and in Stamford Street I saw him again. He didn't see me, I think, being too far away. Later I heard that two girls died there and I was so scared he might find me at Ma Phillips's. I ran off to Brighton and worked at the bar in Mutton's. I'd been there ever since, until yesterday. Yesterday I came back, thinking perhaps he might be gone to America by now. When I heard your voice behind me, saying my real name like that, I nearly died of fright, thinking it might be him.'

'Let us hope,' said Holmes reassuringly, 'you will not need to die of anything at all for many years to come. It is plain to me that your poor friend Matilda kept the two pills he had given her and later, perhaps for a lark after she had drunk that half-bottle of whisky, she took them. But her murderer could not know that she had kept them so long or that you had never taken them at all. So he accused one of his dupes of killing you both, when you were still both alive.'

He turned to me and I was surprised to see his face relax in a smile.

'Tell me, Watson, does not our young friend make a very charming corpse?' The girl gave a start at this but he went on, 'Louisa is the talking corpse whom I promised would sooner or later provide the solution to our case.'

I was about to ask how long he had known all this and kept it from me. But I was so relieved to hear him refer to 'our case' at last that I let the matter drop.

At Bow Street, after we had relinquished charge of Louisa Harvey to a police matron, Lestrade was waiting for us. He was not quite pacing up and down but his difficulty in avoiding such exercise was plain.

'Another letter!' he said furiously. 'Postmarked in Holborn last night at 10 p.m. and therefore sent at least four hours after Dr Neill was taken into custody!'

Holmes read the sheet of paper, chuckled, and then handed it to me.

'Very good!' he said merrily. 'Very good indeed! Is it not, Watson?'

*Dear Sir,*

*The man you have in your power is as innocent as you are. I gave the girls those pills to cure them of their earthly miseries. Others might follow Lou Harvey out of this world of care and woe. Lord Russell had a hand in the poisoning of Clover. If I were you, I would release Dr T. Neill or you might get into trouble.*

*Yours respectfully Juan Pollen, alias, Jack the Ripper.*

*BEWARE ALL! I WARN BUT ONCE!*

'I fail to see, Mr Holmes, what is good about an event of this kind.'

'Only, Lestrade, that there are so many explanations of the message that it hardly merits thought. Oh, very well. If nothing else will do, Mr Slater hears a rumour of the arrest and the crime, then enjoys a little revenge on the Lambeth constabulary. A dozen malcontents might do it. Set it aside, my dear fellow.'

So, next morning, Louisa Harvey looked from a window into the Bow Street yard where the men were drawn up again. Unlike the previous witnesses she confessed herself too terrified to confront her would-be murderer face to face.

She picked out Dr Neill at a glance.

'And is there no other man in that line whom you have ever seen before?' Holmes asked gently.

She shook her head. He directed her attention to young Walter Harper.

'Not that one?'

Again she shook her head.

'No. He is quite like a boy that goes with the girls here in London, and down at Muttons in Brighton. All the same, he ain't the one.'

'Then you identify only Dr Neill?'

'Dr Neill? Oh, no! I don't see any Dr Neill.'

Lestrade uttered a gasp of dismay, audible to everyone in the room.

'Just now, you picked out one of those men as Dr Neill, miss!'

A third time she shook her head, more emphatically.

'Not as Dr Neill.'

In that instant my spirits also sank, as our carefully-wrought solution to the Lambeth murders seemed to disintegrate. Then a miracle occurred.

'You never asked,' said Louisa Harvey reproachfully. 'You only asked if I'd know his face. That's him. But that's not his name. 'Least not the one he told me. He's Dr Cream. Funny sort of name, Cream, the sort you'd remember. He showed me a letter he'd had from America. Addressed to him at Anderton's Hotel in Fleet Street. It had Dr Cream on it. No doubt of that.'

Holmes turned slowly and accusingly to Lestrade.

'He arrived at Euston the other day with no luggage.

Whatever he took with him must have been deposited and was waiting there. I take it your men have by now searched the cloakroom at Euston for any article belonging to Dr Neill?'

The inspector's face was, to coin a phrase, an arena of conflicting emotions.

'A Gladstone bag was missing from his rooms, according to Mrs Sleaper. That has been sought for in the cloakroom and the lost-property office . . .'

'And not found,' said Holmes patiently, 'Perhaps they would be better employed searching for a Gladstone bag whose ticket-holder is Dr Cream.'

A little after nine o'clock that evening, Scotland Yard became possessed of a Gladstone, containing the passport and personal effects of Dr Thomas Neill Cream. Long before the first police dossiers crossed the ocean, the bound notebooks of Sherlock Holmes yielded several entries from the Chicago press, recording suspicious deaths among Dr Cream's female patients and a prison sentence imposed for the death by poison of a male patient, Daniel Stott, of Grand Prairie, Illinois.

## XVII

Such was the conclusion of the Lambeth poisonings, thanks to Sherlock Holmes and his 'talking corpse', who had survived such a villainous design against her life. Holmes himself seemed little surprised that there were such degenerates as would put their victims to an agonizing death as a matter of entertainment. He would shrug and talk again of Roman emperors, Renaissance princes, the Marquise de Brinvilliers at the court of Louis XIV, as if they were the most common thing in the world. However, he spared me the observation that when a doctor went wrong, he was the worst of criminals.

Yet, after all, this was not quite the conclusion. Once the name of Dr Cream was revealed, a good deal else followed. He was not American by birth but Scottish. So far as he had a medical speciality it was in the trade of abortion. His dealings were with women of the streets in Chicago and from one of these he had contracted a disease which affected his body and mind alike.

As soon as Holmes heard this, he needed no other explanation. Dr Neill, or Dr Cream, or Dr Neill Cream as he was now generally known, was a man with the fury of an avenger, the inspiration of a demon, and the skill of a torturing fiend. All the murder and all the blackmail had come from that one perverted genius, which lay disguised behind the shallow geniality of his mild manner. There are men who commit crimes as terrible as his, to the astonishment of those who know them. How can a man so amiable and self-effacing be the murderer of half a dozen young women? In his case, however, once the truth about him was known, it fitted a pattern that had been half-visible all the time.

Sherlock Holmes, though he seemed to wash his hands of the investigation, had not taken his eyes from it for one moment. It exhibited to him a degree of human depravity which Professor Moriarty or Colonel Moran, or even Charles Augustus Milverton the arch-blackmailer, could scarcely have matched. Dr Neill Cream, as I now call him, was mad as well as bad, to an extent which these other villains had never been.

A man in his middle years, however evil his course of life may have been, will generally show some development of character. The Lambeth murderer offered not the least sign of remorse, never a murmur of repentance during his weeks in the death-cell of Newgate gaol. We were assured by Lestrade that the poor wretch sang and danced and capered like a music-hall clown to while away his last hours. When he conversed, it was merely to boast of his amorous conquests and to claim the murder of still more victims. It was as if his mind had been driven into one narrow and terrible track by the very exposure of his guilt. He no longer made any attempt at geniality or gentility, nor did he show the least fear at the prospect which he faced.

Sherlock Holmes was of the opinion that Dr Neill Cream should have been reprieved, in order that this specimen of morbid psychology might be investigated by the alienists. He was mad, of course, by the standards of psychopathology. However, the English law takes its definition of insanity from a period fifty years before when either a man must have been unable to know what he was doing or, if he did know, he did not know it to be wrong. The cold-blooded destruction of the victims in this case made nonsense of such a plea.

In those days, of course, there was no Court of Criminal Appeal. A prisoner's only hope was a recommendation by the Home Secretary for a reprieve from the gallows to life imprisonment.

A week or two went by. I woke one November morning to find that a thick yellow fog had settled upon London. It was scarcely possible from our windows in

Baker Street to see the outline of the opposite houses. A greasy, heavy brown swirl of vapour drifted past us and condensed in oily drops upon the glass. Sherlock Holmes pushed back his chair from the breakfast table and gazed at the weather which promised to keep him immured for several days to come. Then he glanced at his watch and his mood lightened.

'I had almost forgotten, my dear fellow.'

I put down the paper.

'Forgotten what, Holmes?'

'That client of yours, Watson. They hanged him at Newgate a full two hours ago. I cannot claim that I have always given full satisfaction to those clients who have been good enough to consult me, but I do not think that I have ever contrived to get one of them hanged.'

# Notes

## The Two 'Failures' of Sherlock Holmes

i. Marshall Hall's view of the Crippen case is given in Edward Marjoribanks, *The Life of Sir Edward Marshall Hall*, Victor Gollancz, 1929, pp.277–84. Marshall Hall believed that, had the defence been entrusted to him, 'Crippen would have been convicted of manslaughter or of administering a noxious poison so as to endanger human life.' Such a course, however, might have imperilled Ethel Le Neve's defence. 'Crippen loved Miss Le Neve so tenderly and wholeheartedly that he wished her to escape *all* the legal consequences of his association with her. He had, indeed, brought the tragedy upon her, but to ensure her complete scathelessness he was willing to die for her.' Marshall Hall's great rival, F. E. Smith, Lord Birkenhead, wrote of Crippen, 'He was, at least, a brave man, and a true lover.'

ii. Both George Lewis and Oscar Wilde's friend Robert Ross considered that a prosecution of Lord Queensberry for a criminal libel on the playwright was ill-advised. Lewis's view was that Wilde should tear up the insulting card and forget about it. However, goaded by Lord Alfred Douglas and encouraged by his solicitor Charles Humphreys, Wilde swore out a warrant for Queensberry's arrest on 1 March 1895. Cf. Richard Ellmann, *Oscar Wilde*, Hamish Hamilton, 1987, pp.411–13

Wilde's purloining of other men's epigrams is described in G. M. Young, *Victorian England: Portrait of an Age*, Oxford University Press, 1960, p.163n.

## The Case of the Racing Certainty

The career of Harry Benson and William Kurr as international swindlers is combined with the exposure of corruption at Scotland Yard in George Dilnot (ed.), *The Trial of the Detectives*, Geoffrey Bles, [1930]. The book contains a transcript of the 1877 trial. Following this scandal, the Detective Police of Scotland Yard was restructured as the Criminal Investigation Department, or C.I.D. A Special Branch was also created, principally to counter the threat from Sinn Fein, as well as an independent power of prosecution in the office of Director of Public Prosecutions.

## The Case of the Naked Bicyclists

A full account of the case appears in F. Tennyson Jesse (ed.), *The Trial of Samuel Herbert Dougal*, William

Hodge, 1928. In her finely intuitive introduction, Fryn Tennyson Jesse remarks of the nude bicycling that Dougal liked 'a touch of an orgy' in his activities. 'What a picture in that clayey, lumpy field, the clayey lumpy girls, naked astride that unromantic object, a bicycle, and Dougal, gross and vital, cheering on these bucolic improprieties.'

## The Case of the Sporting Major

Though the case against Alfred John Monson was found 'not proven' under Scottish Law, Edward Scott, *alias* Sweeney, was never brought to trial. When he did not appear to answer the charges of murder and attempted murder in 1897, he was outlawed by the High Court of Justiciary in Edinburgh. The year after Major Monson's trial, Scott was discovered to be appearing as assistant to a music-hall magician. Curiously, no proceedings were taken against him and the decree of outlawry was eventually rescinded.

## The Case of the Hygienic Husband

George Joseph Smith (1872–1915) served three prison sentences, totalling three and a half years, for larceny and receiving. Between 1898 and 1915, he also contracted eight marriages, seven of them bigamous. Three of these wives, Bessie Mundy, Alice Burnham, and Margaret Lofty, were drowned by him in their baths. Smith was an amateur musician and, having left Margaret Lofty dead in the depths of her bath, he took advantage of a domestic harmonium in the next room to give a farewell rendering of *Nearer, My God, To Thee.* His principal motive in the drownings was mercenary but he had no conscientious objection to murder. He was tried only for the killing of Bessie Mundy, for which he was hanged. A transcript of the trial is included in Eric R. Watson (ed.), *The Trial of George Joseph Smith*, William Hodge, 1922. The editor remarks on the familiar truth that psychopaths of Smith's type find it easiest to attract victims from the educated and articulate middle class, 'be it governess or lady's companion, or young lady in business'. In this view, Smith the ex-regimental gymnastic instructor and petty thief, had a knack of detecting 'fires of repressed passion' in outwardly-conventional young women of the professsional class.

## The Case of the Talking Corpse

On the gallows trap, Dr Neill Cream is said to have made a last-second confession, 'I am Jack—' Billington pulled the lever before the name was completed. According to the records, Cream was a prisoner in Joliet Penetentiary, Illinois, until 1891 for having poisoned Daniel Stott. Could he have committed the Whitechapel murders in 1888? In *The Times* on 12 March 1985, Donald Bell, a Canadian journalist, offered evidence that anonymous letters from Jack the Ripper and others known to be by Neill Cream were in the same hand. Though Cream should have been in Joliet in 1888, it was alleged that in nineteenth-century

America a convict with money could pay another man to serve part of his sentence for him.

A further curiosity is that Marshall Hall went into court during Neill Cream's trial and recognized him as one half of an ingenious double-act. Two men, whose appearance was near-identical, had worked a system by which they gave one another alibis. One of them had been Marshall Hall's client in a case of bigamy and the lawyer recognized him as the man now in the dock under the name of Thomas Neill Cream. On the other hand, Marshall Hall considered Neill Cream's claim to be Jack the Ripper as no more than the characteristic vanity of the professional criminal. Cf. Edward Marjoribanks, *The Life of Sir Edward Marshall Hall*, pp.47–8.

www.ingramcontent.com/pod-product-compliance
Ingram Content Group UK Ltd.
Pitfield, Milton Keynes, MK11 3LW, UK
UKHW022320280225
455674UK00004B/389

9 781471 904547